I AM THINKING
OF MY DARLING

Mrs. Mil. Long! Lord, have I not made violent haste; I have asked every living thing I met for you; I have inquired after you, as after a new fashion.

I AM THINKING
OF MY DARLING

VINCENT McHUGH

Introduction by

MARK SINGER

YARROW PRESS

NEW YORK 1991

The publishers wish to thank Patricia McHugh for her gracious assistance
in the republishing of this book.

Copyright renewal 1970 by Vincent McHugh

Introduction copyright © 1991 by Mark Singer

Yarrow Press Edition copyright © 1991

I Am Thinking of My Darling was first published in 1943 by Simon & Schuster.

Library of Congress Cataloging-in-Publication Data

McHugh, Vincent.
I am thinking of my darling/by Vincent McHugh: with an
introduction by Mark Singer.
p.   cm.
ISBN 1-878274-05-8: $9.95
I. Title
PS3525.A2457I15   1991
813'.52—dc20   90-25933
                                                              CIP

Printed in the United States of America

Cover design by Richard Eckersley

Yarrow Press
225 Lafayette Street
New York, New York 10012

For

Private Johnny Armstrong
Ensign Val Davies, U.S.C.G.R.
Lieutenant Phil Haberman, Jr., U.S.A.A.F.
Private Ed McHugh
Private Jerry Mayer
Corporal Mac McKinnon
Private Earl Murphy
Private Ken Rew
Private Hecky Rome
Lieutenant Dave Ruhe, U.S.P.H.S.
Private First Class Norm Smith
Captain Gael Sullivan
Private Don Thompson

and

The Other Guys

This Long Letter

From

The Old Folks' Home

. . . puella nam mei, quae meo
sinu fugit,
amata tantum quantum amabitur
nulla . . .

INTRODUCTION

AMONG the visionary accomplishments that entitle Vincent McHugh to our grateful appreciation—that contemporary readers, unable to locate his books, have been denied the chance to appreciate him at all underlies the reissuing of this lyrical novel—is his grasp of the imaginative potential in the conjunction of sexual fantasy and urban planning. Hart Crane had a passion for the Brooklyn Bridge; what was there not to love? More daringly, McHugh fell head-over-heels for the entire New York City five-borough hurly-burly, of which there was plenty not to love but not enough to dampen his rapture. In 1943, when he published *I Am Thinking of My Darling* (which subsequently he always referred to as *Darling*), "infrastructure" was decades away from entering common parlance. Nevertheless, McHugh clearly was enthralled by the whole business: tunnels, bridges, subways, public utilities, emergency services, harbor management, health care delivery—also sex.

Nothing about McHugh's rendering of the *mise en scène* suggests that he had seen too much or that he had become jaded. He had the self-taught eye of an architecture critic and the natural ear of a poet. His narrator and reluctant hero, Jim Rowan, the Acting Commissioner of the Department of City Planning, cannot enter a room without cataloguing its finer appointments. In a typical digression, Rowan appraises the Board of Estimate room in City Hall: "A half dome above, decorated with a course of laurel leaves and a fretted cornice. Nice clean Ionic columns and a crystal chandelier with globes on it and a lacy white cornice dome over the main window behind the chairman's seat. A gathered valance, brocade, and the modest gilt eagle topping it. A little thronish, maybe, but easy and clean and comfortable and urbanely balanced. Damned good, in fact."

When he focused his descriptive powers on bipeds, McHugh could generalize in vivid ways. The Society for the Preservation of Happiness holds a revival meeting in Madison Square Garden: "A little of everybody. A few tailcoats. Broadway sharpies and the Village look. Men and women and kids from Amsterdam Avenue and East Broadway and Lenox Avenue and Rockaway and Roosevelt Avenue and Kingsbridge Road. Hoping for something, and trying to get together on it. It scared me for a minute. This could turn into anything. What the hell was happiness?"

Throughout, McHugh imbued *Darling* with a Whitmanesque flavor of democratic possibility. Also like Whitman, he knew how to inject meaning into the invocation of a place name. These rigorously marshaled and precise details notwithstanding, however, the comic adventure plot that frames *Darling* doesn't bother much with verisimilitude. Time skews out of whack, conflated only slightly less than the story of Creation. The narrative spans seven days, during which New York City teems with a freshly loosed tropical virus that causes anyone infected to abandon inhibition. Not the least tantalizing symptom of "the fever," as it is called, is guilt-free concupiscence. As the virus spreads, hundreds of thousands of people leave their mates or quit their unsatisfying jobs, the mayor resigns to devote time to his toy train collection, the city is cordoned by a quarantine, the entire emergency services bureaucracy is restructured and its workforce redeployed, a huge fire erupts on the Brooklyn waterfront, six hundred thousand surgical masks are manufactured and distributed free and adopted by the citizenry as a fashion statement, researchers in a lab in a municipal hospital make heroic strides toward the discovery of a vaccine and a cure for the virus.

Against this backdrop, Jim Rowan orchestrates the city's antivirus assault and simultaneously manages to get infected himself, searches all over town for his fever-stricken runaway wife, sleeps with several beautiful women only because they've got the fever and how could he stop them, sings the blues in a Harlem jazz club, persuades the federal government to approve a vast housing project on the lower East Side of Manhattan, forges rewarding friendships with a taxi driver and a livery driver who actually speak English and know their way around town, and buries one of his closest friends. Along the way, as if dictating memos from his stream-of-consciousness, he expatiates knowledgeably about interior design, couture, cuisine, meteorology, physics, microbiology, pharmacology, epidemiology, and psychiatry. He also throws in thumbnail genealogies of a few dozen marginal characters. All this is presented in a winningly deadpan *faux*-wiseguy style.

Like most of New York City's ardent literary explorers, McHugh was from out of town. He was born in Rhode Island in 1904, arrived in Manhattan in the twenties, and spent the next quarter century or so examining the city with constantly refreshed wonder, in the familiar manner of those of us who emigrate from someplace completely different and then have the chutzpah to try to pin Gotham down on the page. *Darling* was the most commercially successful of his five published novels; his *oeuvre* also included a collection of stories, two volumes of poetry, a book of criticism, and three translations of Mandarin poetry. Usually omitted from his bibliography is the remarkable work he did as a writer, editor, and administrator in New York City for the Federal Writers' Project, the New Deal bratty brainchild. No sooner had he gone to work on the Project, in late 1936, than he was given responsibility for the *New York City Guide*, which at that point totaled an amorphous eight million words. By 1939 he had shaped the manuscript into two publishable volumes and had contributed an introductory essay to one of them. When Clifton Fadiman included McHugh's essay, "Metropolis and Her Children," in his classic anthology, *Reading I've Liked*, he stated forthrightly, "Mr. McHugh writes brilliantly." He added, "I do not know anyone who has written more truly about New York in as little space."

What came through in that essay (and was, of course, later reflected in *Darling*) was McHugh's highly specific familiarity with the city—its waterways and the vessels that traveled them, its neighborhoods and their occupants, its buildings and their underpinnings. New York was "a state fair grown to magnificence, a Main Street translated into the imperial splendor of Fifth Avenue. . . . the place which is not wilderness, the place of light and warmth and the envelopment of the human swarm, the place in which everyone is awake and laughing at three in the morning. These things are not altogether true, of course—but magic does not need to be true."

So McHugh was a romantic; but he was also a reporter. And, as it happened, he was also a jazz enthusiast whose love of that then-subterranean culture extended literally to the city's entire subterrain, a subject he set out to celebrate, circa 1941, with a nonfiction book whose working title was *Under New York City*. According to Jim McGraw, a fellow stalwart from the Federal Writers' Project, the prospective publisher of *Under New York City*, overly eager to avoid a clash with the wartime censors, killed the book on the odd premise that the Nazis or the Japanese might have exploited it for sabotage. Or, as McGraw explained, "They were afraid the enemy would figure out how to bomb New York from the sewer up." For whatever reason, no other publisher stepped into the breach. Though temporarily crushed, McHugh eventually salvaged much of his research when he hatched the idea for *Darling*. His technological fluency translated nicely from one literary form to the next; in its embryonic stage, the novel lacked only sex (plus the characters to engage in it).

"No one should come to New York to live unless he is willing to be lucky," E. B. White wrote in "Here is New York," the famous essay that appeared ten years after "Metropolis and Her Children." By the time *Darling* was published, McHugh had become a colleague of White's at *The New Yorker*, where he spent almost five years on the staff, contributing short fiction, light verse, "Talk of the Town" pieces, and book reviews. During the Second World War, he was a writer–director of film documentaries for the Office of War Information. His fifth, and in his opinion finest, novel, *The Victory*, was based on his experiences in the South Pacific aboard a merchant marine ship. The immediate postwar years found him back in New York, working on *The Victory*, teaching at New York University, and contributing occasionally to *The New Yorker*. When he left the city once again, in the late forties—temporarily, he assumed, to go to Hollywood to write screenplays—it turned out he was leaving for good and was about to get *un*lucky in a way that constitutes a weirdly ironic coda to *Darling*.

It did not take McHugh long to get fed up with the movie business, and after a few months he decided to repatriate to the East Coast. En route, he stopped in Reno, where he met a woman from Texas who was in town for a quickie divorce. Before long, McHugh had become her husband-on-the-rebound and had settled with her in Texas—in a small town that resembled neither Providence nor Manhattan. When the gravity of this miscalculation became apparent to him, he decamped for San Francisco. From that point on, his career decelerated. Across the years, there were periods when he regularly wrote travel pieces for *Holiday* and other magazines, there was a time when he supported himself as a street photographer on Fisherman's Wharf, and there was a long stretch when he gave English lessons to the employees of a bank in Chinatown. Habitually nocturnal, he became a late-night/early-morning fixture at the City Lights Bookstore—City Lights was his mail drop—where his friends included Ferlinghetti and Ginsberg and that crowd. Unlike the others, he wore Brooks Brothers clothes. A compatriot from those days has described him as "a classic twenties liberal, middle-class bohemian."

He married at least twice more, happily at last in 1965, to a woman who turned around his nutrition—a food neurotic, for most of his adult life he had subsisted mainly on strained soup, tea, and milkshakes—and with whom he resettled in Sacramento. He died there in 1983, about the time a mysterious and malignant virus, the absolute opposite of the one he had concocted more than forty years earlier inside his brain, began to ravage thousands of lives in New York and San Francisco and beyond. In "Metropolis and Her

Children," McHugh wrote hopefully of New York "emerg[ing] in greatness from the paradox of its confusion." In *Darling*, one of his characters says direly, "This is a mass epidemic of good feeling. Joy. Happiness. Whatever you like. Potentially it's as dangerous as a riot or panic or any other disturbance." Today, in the world outside fiction, beyond the dark edge of sexual fantasy, we would weep tears of thanksgiving for peril so benign.

—*Mark Singer*

I AM THINKING
OF MY DARLING

ONE

1 I HAD dinner with Jerry at the Mayflower and took a cab to the station. The night was drizzly and warm. I'd had a week of it and I wanted to get back. The town was all lighted up, whirling with cars, and from Lafayette Square the White House looked clean as calcimine in the floodlights. Clean and lonely behind the February elms. The Old Man was working late again.

I mentioned the weather to the driver and he said he didn't like it. The jacket hung in pleats from his shoulder blades. He came from Vermont—most of them were Southerners—and up there they had a saying that green winters make fat churchyards.

'Been this way all up and down the coast for a week now.'

'We'll get a blizzard to top it off,' I said.

Some of the rest of the week is blurred, but I remember everything about that night. Everything before I found Niobe's note and everything afterwards. It had to be a note. The theatrical touch. I felt that later in the whole city, New York, running wild like an idiot girl with some dream of lilacs in her little canine skull. Not quite, of course. For me, it was more like being the sober host at a terrific party where everyone else has a fine glittering edge. That is, until I got it too.

God yes. Big me. I had to stick my finger in the dike and hold it there until it damn near dropped off. And what did I get for it? Well, they elected John Kane Mayor that fall. I was glad for John. Why not? I was doing what I wanted to do and I'd found out that it isn't every man who can say that. But sometimes after-wards in the winter dusk the traffic lights down Lexington Avenue from the sixties were the open block signals for an express that would never end. I could tell myself that I'd done a little to keep her from being flagged down.

I got out at the Union Station with the light whipcord coat over my arm. Something made me look around in the portico and there he was. The Senator. A tall awkwardly boned man in a baggy dark-blue suit, yellow shoes, a black string tie, and a huge pearl-gray Stetson with a narrow black band. Incredible. He walked slowly and self-consciously—stalked, really—his level pale-blue eyes swivel-ing left and right with a solemn country slyness. A real boy. I knew him by sight—Senator Glenn B. Rowley of Arkansas—and almost choked as I remembered that I'd asked Niobe before I left what she'd like me to bring her.

'A Senator,' she said.

'Any Senator?'

'A big one.'

He was big enough, God knows, and I thought of tapping him on the shoulder and saying: 'Do you mind, Senator? My wife is very anxious to see you.'

I might have saved myself some trouble if I had. But I got my bag at the checkroom, picked up a *Washington Post*, and that was the first I heard of it: a box on page one, something about an out-break of fever in New York. Niobe would get it, of course. She got everything, fashionable or not, had a short violent struggle with it—very sexual in character—and got up panting but victori-ous. This one was rather mild apparently. Even so, Dick Wirth would have his job cut out for him. It might be a little gift from the tropics. They didn't seem to know.

The colonnade depressed me—those half-lighted stone figures glooming over the huge vaulted room—and I wandered out to the loggia, thinking about Daniel Burnham, looking across at the twinkle of the plaza fountain near Louisiana Avenue and the far-off imperial shine of the Capitol dome.

2

Burnham was dead now, but God knows he had his monuments. This Union Station, for one. Damned good too, if you liked the style and could carry that much weight on the top of your head. The rumor was that he'd got to be a mere showman later on, that his partner Root had done most of the work. I didn't know. He'd been in on a lot of stuff: the Columbian Exposition, the Flatiron Building, and the McMillan Commission's plan for the reconstruction of Washington.

It was a style all right, a compound period style. American Roman. Tombs for the giants. Big immovable tombs. I didn't like it. What I did like was that when Burnham and his boys put up the Flatiron Building, they'd had sense enough to hang each floor on a cantilever out from the steel wall grid. We'd gone on from that and other things, step by step, to the terrific lifting flank of the RCA Building, all one piece and light enough to fly.

The train was made up. I went in and found my seat. On top, when I opened the bag, were the two bottles of Viña Santa Rita. A present to Niobe from Gonzáles O'Leary at the Chilean Embassy. Everyone called him Mike, of course. The O'Learys were one of the old colonial Irish families in Santiago. She'd be pleased. The note said: 'Love from Mike and best wishes to *Wild Goose Chase.*' Her new play.

The train jerked softly and glided free for a moment, gathering way. Seeing Mike and the others again, as I seldom had time to do, made the early years in Washington come back. They seemed a long time ago now. The shifting from agency to board to commission, the kind of outraged social feeling deep in most of us, the finagling and grinning at insults. Other things too. More naked opportunism, climbing on people's backs, careerism, and throat-cutting than you could shake a stick at. The trouble was that nobody *did* shake a stick at it.

We lived in an endless buzz of communal fever. When we had a night off, which wasn't often, we'd go down to hear Jelly Roll Morton at the little joint where he was master of ceremonies, bouncer, sweeper-upper, and professor of the blues. Stomach ulcer was the occupational disease. I'd ended up in the National Resources Committee, before Herman Grierson took me back to New York with him.

I sat a moment in the running train, in the funeral-parlor hush of the car, thinking of Niobe: a devil in a black Russeks suit trimmed softly with mink. The mink gave her cheeks the childish flush of sweet peas. I got papers out of the bag and worked on the zoning material, trying to calculate what could be done against what needed to be done. Bill Cornbill, the administrator, had sent me a memo for the Wednesday hearing. I went over that too.

When I looked up the train had stopped. A station platform, a light in the window of a shabby house, a red neon sign BEER on a long street going off into darkness. Wilmington. As the car began to glide forward again a girl sat up in the chair ahead on the right. A dish. Taffy-colored hair brushed straight up and under a dinky black hat, the little clean tendrils curly at the nape of the neck, and a soft wool dress. She felt it (women have eyes all around their heads for that), turned and gave me a good slow look. Thank you, Taffy Top. Some other time. Tonight I'm going home to mamma.

I went back to the diner. It was almost empty. In the little pantry at the end the chef and the waiters were clowning quietly, opening their mouths and raising their eyebrows, or bending over to laugh silently. The only other passenger in the car, a thickset young man in a tobacco-brown suit, was smiling at them.

I stayed on to watch, ordering ice cream and angel cake. They were ribbing a little light-brown Negro with a big mouth. He scowled. He grinned easily at them. He said: 'Yeah! Yeah!' satirically and softly, nodding his head, and almost shook it off in denial. He pulled at their sleeves. The chef waggled a beautifully knuckled long black index finger at him.

The only thing I caught was the little Negro's vehement whisper: 'You think I'm jivin' you? You wait we get back to New York. You see.'

The young man watched them with a relaxed and happy look.

4

I must have been sitting in the men's lounge for ten minutes, smoking and staring at the imitation-walnut paneling, when he came in.

He sighed. 'Wonderful people.'

I said I thought so too. The car was hot and it might have been that, but his face looked warm and his eyes were glowing. I told him I'd been in Washington for a week and he asked what I did.

'I work for the city planning office in New York.'

He nodded eagerly. 'That's a job I'd like. What do you do there?'

'Well, at the moment my title is Acting Commissioner of the Department of City Planning'—I reeled it off satirically—'which makes me Acting Chairman of the City Planning Commission. Double or nothing.' I smiled. 'The commission sets 'em up and the department does the dirty work, more or less. My boss died last month. Commissioner Grierson.'

'He wrote that book on highway planning.'

'That's right. How do you know that?'

'I'm a highway engineer. Work for the state. My name's Holloway.'

'Mine's Rowan,' I said.

We shook hands.

He grinned at me. 'How're things going? You people haven't been down there long, have you?'

He must have been just under thirty, but he talked like a kid. His brown eyes gleamed at me through the glasses and his forehead was shiny and red.

'Only since the new charter,' I said. 'The appropriation is a little better now—it was pretty bad at first—but we did have the advantage of starting fresh. A pretty tough advantage—getting things organized, I mean. Grierson was wonderful at it. He could look at a problem and pick the bones out of it like a market man fileting a flounder.'

Holloway shook his head. 'I'll stick to my grades and shoulders. You probably have to know a little of everything for that job.'

5

'Just about,' I said. 'Somebody has to, anyhow. It isn't just civil engineering or traffic control or zoning. It's architecture and meteorology and sanitation and biometrics and human geography and politics and divination by signs. Oh, and a little high finance. We make up the capital budget too. All great sport.'

'Not for me,' Holloway said and smiled, a little too brightly. 'I like a nice cement job with a deadline on it. How do you make sense out of all that?'

'We try,' I said. 'Ever hear of Patrick Geddes? Well, it's human ecology—trying to figure out the smoothest interaction between the way people act and the place they live in. That's the theory. Actually we spend most of our time settling rows over garage sites in Queens.' I shook my head. 'We've inherited three hundred years of the God-damnedest confusion man ever made.'

He looked as if he hadn't been listening. No wonder. Me on me.

He hesitated. 'When you said confusion I thought—— Look, Mr. Rowan. You say you left New York a week ago?'

I nodded.

'Well, I came from there yesterday. I—I don't know how to tell you. But I think you're going to have a tough time when you get back. Things're happening.'

'What things?'

He shook his head. 'They don't make sense to me. The newspapers print them all right—some of them—but it sounds as if a lot of crackpots are doing them. They're not.' He looked at me. 'Everybody's doing them.'

Everybody's doing it doing it doing it. I said: 'What?' patiently.

'They say it's the fever. I—I saw a Fifth Avenue bus, a No. 9— it wasn't a special—going out Henry Hudson Parkway to Westchester. People blowing tin horns on the top deck. Like a coaching party.'

'It must have been a special.'

'Nobody's going to work. The current's dim all up the West Side, where I live. And you can't get into the free movies.'

'What free movies?'

6

'All the movies are free.'

His face was rosy and there was a gentle excitement in all his movements. He'd certainly made sense up to now, he didn't have a breath, and his pupils seemed normal. He saw me looking at him and got up.

'Okeh, Mr. Rowan,' he said. 'I—I guess you don't—— Well, good luck.'

When I came out, the lights of Philadelphia were flowing past the window.

2

WE GOT in at Penn Station and even downstairs you could hear the whoops of the crowd echoing in the vaults. Then Holloway passed me with Miss Taffy Top on his arm, raising his hat gallantly, and a train announcer was bawling: 'Express leaving for Mayaguana, Mozambique, Ambrizette, Mossamedes, and Sebastian Viscaine Bay. Track 9. All abooord.'

I stood there becalmed and gaping in a pouring rush of people, all singing and shouting. A crowd bigger than the outgoing mob on Labor Day week end, loaded with everything from skis to outrigger canoes. This was three o'clock in the morning and for a minute they all looked like Holloway.

The porter got me started out and in a corner of the station a young man and a girl were sitting on the floor kissing hard. What the hell, I thought. They probably like each other. We passed three more couples doing the same thing, or a little more so if anything, and when we got out to the cabstand the porter refused a tip.

I was shaken.

'Why not, for God's sake?'

'Man, we don't need it any more. See what you want you just stoop and pick it up.'

He opened the cab door.

Just the way the driver put his clutch in and went pouring down the ramp made me feel that I was home. I looked at his hackie's card: the big number and the *Dominic J. Paravecchio* and the heavy-set face, about fifty. A father of children.

We rolled into the long neon shine of the uptown avenue. The air was moist and warm as rain water and I almost expected to see crocuses springing up in the sidewalk grilles. He opened the slide and leaned back.

'No hurry? Yeah. Fine night. I like to take a little run in the park sometime. Okeh? My treat. Nice to get back, eh?'

'You bet,' I said, wondering what the hell I was talking about.

We drove gently through a red light. The cop on point duty waved—he was out there genial at three in the morning—and Paravecchio waved back. He pulled through Thirty-Eighth Street, stopped and opened the glass hatch. The moist air came in and the stars were quiet and soft in the opening. Then he climbed back and we rolled casually up Fifth Avenue.

People were out and singing, and except that more windows were lighted up, it looked just about as I remembered it on the morning of January 1, 1929, when a man in tails bowed to me, bowed to the girl I was with, and asked her if she would accept his hand in marriage. She said thank you very much, but I have already accepted this gentleman's hand, indicating me, though it happened to be true only in an extralegal sense. Indeed, said Tails. Shall we compound a felony and make it double? So he took her other arm and we walked up the avenue together. He turned out to be a broker who knew somebody, I forget who.

Paravecchio leaned back. 'You know I come home early my wife say: "You knocking off no money?" When I come home late she say: "I don' know where you are all this time." I don' know. Maybe I don' go home no more.'

'You sound pretty happy,' I said.

He nodded at me. 'I couldn' be no more happy if I was just

born. I feel free. You know? I *see* everything. I *hear* good. I like to smell the park. Like when I was a kid.'

In the shimmering windows at Bonwit Teller, gotten up to look like some Marie Laurencin fantasy of a set of Paris interiors in the 1850's, the live models were prinking for a party. One handsome black-haired girl in wine silk and shoulder-length black gloves had the ruffles pulled up over her knee while she fixed her garter. As we rolled past I could see the back of another girl in a pale-lemon corset, doing her hair in a room lined with quilted violet satin. The things you learned being married to an actress.

I'm not sure I didn't imagine the waltz music. It was all very pretty and it gave me a cold turn. My mind went galloping over all the things people take for granted, all the things that could go wrong: lights, water, subways, food supply, elevators, sanitation, fire control. Anything could happen. I smiled and settled back.

We made a circuit through the park. In the bleaching glow of the lights the willows were budding and a forsythia near the Mall was obviously in bloom. Dominic whistled *The Sidewalks of New York* with neat, corny little trills. I laughed. I was beginning to feel good too. We came out of the park at the Seventy-Second Street exit and drove to my apartment in East Sixty-Eighth Street.

'Wait for me,' I said.

'Lucky you got here in time, Mr. Rowan,' the elevator boy said. 'I'm going up to the Uptown House. Got a little party on.'

'Don't you work all night?'

'Supposed to. But I get sick of it.'

'Oh. What'll the superintendent say?'

'He's coming too.'

I opened the door and put the lights on. The white walls, the cranberry-colored chair, the books and records. The big Scott combination and the Kirman-Lavehr rug with its fine soft colors. Nice and shabby.

Niobe gone to bed? I looked. No, probably at Ada's. Whistling, I took the wine out of my bag and set it on the mantelpiece.

Then I saw the note: 'Dear Brain (that was her family name for me—*The Brain*): I feel perfectly humming and I haven't had anything. Not a drop. So I'm going right out to do all the other things I've always wanted to do, and God knows when I'll be back. I've got loads and loads of money. Elizabeth and Rachel will be in as usual. The ice cream is in the oven. Niobe.'

'The ice cream is in the oven,' I said aloud. 'Why that Goddamned, impertinent, high-breasted idiot. What does she——'

It was in the oven too. I sat down in the plum chair. Not really worried. She'd be back all right. My first reaction was purely marital and male. I was mad because my routine had been broken up, because the traveler got no welcome home, because I couldn't grouse gently about getting the run-around from Eli and listen to her troubles with Mallett, the producer, and a director who couldn't make up his mind what he wanted. All this, perhaps, while we had a sandwich and a glass of milk together and got ready for bed. That too. No bed. No Niobe smelling warm as the August Wabash meadows we'd both come from, but with the perfume that made the difference between then and now.

She had money and she probably wouldn't get into any serious trouble. If she did, God pity the trouble—with her talkfast wit and the way she got people to do things for her. It wouldn't be a man—I was pretty sure of that—though it might be half a dozen. There'd been a period in her life when she gobbled little boys of forty or under like Schrafft's Indians.

It couldn't be anything but the fever, whatever that was. All right, I thought, getting up. I know her and I'm paid to know the town. Here we go again.

3 Nick was dozing at the wheel. 'I had a dream,' he said. 'I was a big bunny like. My ears was floppin'. Where you want to go, Commissioner?'

So he'd been talking to the night doorman. We stopped for newspapers at a red stand. I felt the way you feel in New York late on a spring night, when everything is soft and quiet and the very stone relents. The air is moving a little like soft water on your face—that same southeast breeze I'd noticed in Washington—and you remember all the girls you were willing to be in love with once. The spring dances, and the canoe where the water came down in a wide angle at the pillars of the bridge. Stan Shaw was on the radio, turned low.

We went to a place I liked, Herman's place, a little red-and-white-fronted bar, bistro style, off Madison Avenue. The light came sedately through the bottles on the shelves, into the faces of the men along the bar. They turned and looked as we came in and Herman nodded. He picked up the bottle of Library rye and set it down with a glass of water. He stocked it for me. I'd never been able to get up any heart for the dank and dreary liquid my Highland ancestors called whisky.

'Mrs. Rowan been in, Herman?'

He shook his head. 'Not since yesterday. She came in about five in the afternoon. Miss Booth was with her.'

The compact radio was made of marbled plastic. Like the big agates we had when we were kids. Stan Shaw was talking. 'Ah me, these wires are getting screwier and screwier. Listen to this one: "Dear Stan: Please play house. You be the daddy and I'll be the mamma." Signed: "Agnes." ' He sighed. 'Can't do it, Agnes. Not with things the way they are. Much obliged. And here's one that says: "Dear Stan: Nobody else is working. Why should you?" Signed: "Jukebox Benny." Ah me, Jukebox Benny. I fear you've got the fever. Yessir. I'm a holdout. If I keep on working long enough I might get to be Mayor. Here's a new tune by Duke Ellington.'

I ticked off the papers for news of the fever. There wasn't much and what there was seemed guarded. The *Herald Tribune* and the *Times* had a handout from Dick Wirth, the Commissioner of Health. He predicted that the epidemic—he didn't call it that, of course—would be over in a few days. I grinned. Dick must be having pups. Some of the other items were startling: the power failure in Astoria, and the number of cars going out of town (biggest day since the George Washington Bridge was opened). A girl wearing what appeared to be a Greek tunic had been reported on Swinburne Island in the Lower Bay, combing her long blond hair and beckoning to passing mariners.

Herman leaned over and said business was all right, but slow. 'Must be the weather. Lot of people come in and order one drink. Look like they been smokin' moohahs.' He nodded. 'I hope I don't get it.'

That was exactly how Nick looked, sitting over his beer. I ordered another for him and got a handful of nickels. Hell of a time to be calling people. The dial wouldn't work but the operator answered. I tried the easy ones first—Ada Booth, Niobe's agent, and three or four of her other women friends. Ada had seen her in the afternoon, had dinner with her. Niobe had mentioned being a little feverish.

I put in another nickel, gave the number, and the operator said: 'Hope you find her. You got a nice voice. Gee, I'm tired. It's so warm in here.'

It took me a second to realize that this was one of the company's girls and another to convince myself that she wasn't swacked.

'Take it easy,' I said. 'They'll fire you for that.'

'What's the difference? I can eat free at the Automat and my landlady's in love. Nobody else around here. Gone bye-bye. Wanna know how I feel? Coral beaches and soft guitars. That's right. Coral beaches and soft guitars. The old Mullarkey,' she said reflectively. 'What's your name?'

I told her.

'Well. Commissioner Rowan. The handsome Commissioner. No kidding?'

'From the heart,' I said. We ribbed Al Elias for saying that. 'What time do you get off?'

arrow Press books are distinguished by their style and quality in both content and production.

To receive a catalogue of our full list of books, please complete and return this card. We will also be happy to add your name to our mailing list.

Title of book: _____

How you learned of this book:

_____

Purchased at: _____

Gift: _____

_____
Name

_____
Street   *Apt. No.*

_____
City

_____
State   *Zip*

YARROW PRESS
225 Lafayette Street, No. 312
New York, New York 10012

'In about half an hour my relief is due. *If* she comes. *If* Mr. Birnfeldt lets her go.'

'Okeh,' I said. 'I want two more numbers. I'll pick you up in half an hour. Buy you a drink or something.'

Her name was Marguerite and she told me where the exchange was. I got Eunice Flattery, my secretary. She had an apartment with two other girls off Broadway in the nineties.

'Why, Mister Commissioner,' she said bitterly. 'I've been trying to get you since yesterday morning.'

'Never mind that now. Listen,' I said. 'I got home tonight and found a note from Niobe. She's skipped. I'm afraid she has that damn fever. God knows what she'll do. Get on the phone in the morning. Call her beauty shop, her bank, her agent, Equity—any place she has an account. Try the Algonquin. Tell them if she comes in—oh, tell them it's her birthday. I want to surprise her. Tell them to call me and hold onto her until I get there. Never mind the theater. I'll talk to Mallett. And look. If the phones are out, make the rounds in a cab.'

Eunice sounded serious. 'Okeh, Jim. Don't you need me tonight?'

'What?' I said. 'Get some sleep. Get down to the office as early as you can and hold on till we get there. You can reach me at Bill's. I'm on my way there now. Starry dreams and everything.'

'Oh, you!' She hung up.

I tried Dick Wirth's house and his wife gave me a number to call. 'What the hell is it?' I said.

He sounded as if he were wringing his hands. 'We don't know, Jim. We don't know. Nothing we've ever seen before. It looks like some of the fevers caused by tropical organisms. Every bacteriologist in town is on it. We have cultures, but we can't isolate it properly.'

'How many cases?'

He whispered: 'Jim, we've had nearly seven hundred thousand reported.'

Almost ten per cent. 'What about deaths?'

'Every one we've traced is something else, aggravated by the fever.'

'We've got to move fast,' I said. 'The phone exchanges are going out. People just get up and wander off. What do the symptoms look like?'

'Fever, of course. It seems to be a kind of euphoria. A little like three or four drinks, or even GP—but the orientation isn't affected. Improved, if anything. Great sense of well-being. Personality harmony. But it seems to—— Wait a minute.'

I could hear him talking to three or four people at once.

'Yes. It seems to block the conscious controls. No will. No moral sense. No sense of responsibility. People just do what they damn please.' He sounded tired. 'Autonomic reflexes. Doesn't seem to be any violence, though. Everybody's good as gold. If we can only keep things moving till we find——'

'Niobe's got it,' I said. 'She's wandered off somewhere. I'm hunting her now.'

He told me how sorry he was. I was sweating as I came out of the booth. Nick sat hunched over his fourth beer. The bartender's white coat shone dimly and there were five or six men along the bar, talking in low tones with the radio going.

As I sat down, all the lights in the place went out. Two or three more words came out of the radio before it cooled off. The street lights were out too. Nick's red tail lamp shone quietly in the darkness. Over toward Rockefeller Center a patrol-car siren rose and wavered and fell again.

'The joint is pinched,' Herman said softly.

4 Nick drove with care down the black chute of Madison Avenue. It reminded me of Norway, going up the Sogne Fiord to Aardal one night on a small steamer, with the rocky cliffs bending

over us on either side. But the look of the shop fronts and people walking, as the car lights picked them up, was more like the scenes I remembered in *The Informer*. It wasn't sinister. You felt a sort of screwy relief, like being let out of school early when you were young.

'My old woman will kill me,' Nick said. 'Always c'plainin' about bein' sick and old. She's thirty-four. I tell her when she's ninety I trade her in for three thirty-year-olds. She think I been out gettin' lushed. You know I ain' been drinkin', Commissioner. I feel good. It don' affect me none.'

I answered him, but I was thinking that Consolidated Edison's big Waterside Plant at Thirty-Eighth Street must have gone out. The street lights glowed weakly for an instant, then went dead again. Somebody was trying. Men with flashlights, grunting under big Stillsons, working to keep the dynamos serviced, the oil flushing into the boiler feedlines, the fires leaping like a terrible fountain of molten glass. The boys who stuck to their jobs when there wasn't anything in it for them. The wonderful lugs all over town who knew what they were doing and did it, and how are you?

'Here,' I said, and Nick took a left turn with no traffic lights in sight. I told him I'd promised to pick up a girl at the telephone exchange.

'What you going to do with her, Commissioner?' Nick asked.

'Talk. She's got the fever. I want to see how she reacts.'

As I said it, I knew it would probably be useless. I didn't know what she'd been like in the first place.

Marguerite was waiting on the steps of the dark exchange. She got in and lay back gently, looking up through the hatch at the misty stars. What I could see before Nick shut the door was brown-haired and good-looking.

She said like a child: 'Where are we going?'

'To Bill Cornbill's place on Forty-Fourth Street. The Beaux Arts. He'll give us a drink. How do you feel?'

'Lovely,' she sighed. 'Like down in Delaware when I was a kid. Have you ever been there?'

I said I'd only stopped over a few times. Her family had moved up North a little later. She'd finished high school in Brooklyn. Erasmus Hall.

She took my arm. 'We had an old brick house near Little Creek, about three miles from Dover. Below Bombay Hook. When we were kids we just lived in the marsh. Sometimes a bunch of us would go along the shore all the way to Port Mahon.

'My father was a muskrat trapper before he was married. He worked for old Mrs. Fox, the Muskrat Queen.'

'The Muskrat Queen?' I said.

She nodded her cheek against mine. 'Uh-hm. I used to go out on the oyster schooners in summer. When they were seeding. It was wonderful. You know something?' she said gently. 'I haven't felt like this since I left.'

'How *do* you feel?'

'Did you go swimming when you were a kid?'

'Yep. In the Wabash, in Indiana. We had a farm between Merom and Oaktown.'

Her voice was drowsy. 'Well, afterwards you come out and lie in the sun. You know. You feel nice and tired. Sweet and warm and —and good. That's how I feel.'

'We didn't. When we dried out we had to dust the clay off. Didn't the boys ever try to make love to you?'

'Uh-hm. Lots of times. We didn't let them. That's funny. Why didn't we?' she said sleepily and earnestly, as if she were asking me. 'I can't remember. We just didn't.'

'Did you afterwards?'

'Nope,' she said, her mouth small and round. 'Not even with Palmer, my boy friend. He went to Mexico to work on the Pan American Highway.'

The lights of another car came into our faces. Nick was listening. She sighed and touched my cheek gently.

'Don't you like me?'

'Sweet. You know I do.'

'Yes,' she said sleepily, twining and sidling like a child. Her

16

knees were in my lap and her mouth against my cheek. I almost groaned, thinking of Niobe.

A cop put his light in the window.

'I'm sorry,' he said. 'I'm sorry indeed.'

And he offered us penny candy, Tootsie Rolls out of a paper bag. Each of us took a piece, and Nick and the cop smiled at each other like nursemaids bending over their sleepy children.

We all groped upstairs to Bill Cornbill's seventh-floor apartment. Even in the checked robe, with the flashlight in his hand, he looked like a Middlesex farmer being roused by Paul Revere.

'Hello, Jim,' he said in his quiet deep voice. He looked at Marguerite and sighed. 'Beautiful.'

I said: 'Marguerite and Nick want a drink, Bill. I hope you'll do your duty. Marguerite and Nick, this is Bill Cornbill.'

'Is his name *really* Bill Cornbill?' Marguerite said in her sleepy voice. 'How cunning.'

The light in Bill's hand wavered up at her. She reached up and kissed him, gently but decisively.

'Well, well,' Bill said, as calm as ever. 'Marguerite, do you suppose you could do that again and——'

'Wait a minute,' I said softly.

Marguerite took his arm. 'I love you, Bill.' She pointed at me. 'But I love him too. How am I ever going to——'

'Lady! Lady!' Nick cried.

Bill put the light on him. He was pointing to himself vigorously with both hands, his eyebrows up.

Marguerite kissed him neatly while we howled.

TWO

1 THE sun in my face woke me next morning. Warm south-east breeze, pale April tremor of the sky, strange room, no Niobe. I felt as I used to feel when I'd come to New York fifteen or sixteen years before, nice and green from a Gibson County farm and Indiana University. It was a good feeling too, egged on by Owney Madden's gin and the girls and the other feeling that you could knock over anything you tried. It might take a long time but you could do it. Go ahead, the city said. What's stopping you?

I thought of one of the things I'd wanted to do then. I'd wanted to play hot clarinet a little better than anybody else—better than Rappolo or Benny or Pee Wee or Sidney Bechet or Tesch. I did some gigging, as we said, and made a few records with pickup bands in the old Perfect Studio.

The Wolverines came East for a record date in the early fall of 1925 and I made two sides with them for English Brunswick. Clarinet and vocal on *Miss You* and *Do You Ever Think of Me?* Moody little pop tunes that had our period feeling about them. When I played the record now the clarinet still sounded fairly fresh but the voice came out dark and blurred, nothing much left but the rhythmic accents and the recollection of that early October morning beginning to be hot in the studio with our jackets off and the two-inch cowhide belts we wore then and Brunis clowning with the long horn.

I got up and looked around. Everybody gone. Bill had slept with

19

me, Nick on the couch and Marguerite in Bill's bed. All very correct. Odd, Bill not being more clubby with Marguerite. She'd probably been telling him about her boy friend. That made for detachment. Too, as a fairly conservative husband I might have a rather enlarged idea of what the boys on the loose got done.

Bill didn't have a wife. Four or five years ago he'd inadvertently married a woman who was out to save the world. This caused him a good deal of inconvenience. Bill said her nipples erected at headlines. Uncanny. He'd disengaged himself quietly and firmly, with not too much alimony, and gone on doing his job. It was a good worthy job, and well done.

I tried his electric razor. It worked—they'd got the current back on—and I set about mowing what Niobe called my Early American face: the long homely bones of the Scot modified by the Midwest, a complexion like a market fisherman's after two days ashore, gray-blue eyes, and a big mouth. Anyhow, it was a face. I was grateful for small favors.

No coffee at the drugstore on Second Avenue. Deliveries stopped, the clerk said. I had stewed apricots and toast and tried to get Christopher Mallett, Niobe's producer, on the phone. No dial tone, no busy signal, no operator. I took a cab to his office in West Forty-Fourth Street. The elevator got stuck at the third floor but we made it to the seventh. I chatted a minute with Henrietta Abend, his middle-aged secretary, in the bare outer office with framed playbills on the walls. Niobe was fond of her.

'What a shame!' Henrietta said. 'I've been calling all over town.'

'Good girl, Henrietta. Nothing?'

She shook her head. 'Unless—— I just thought of a couple more.' She whispered that Mallett had gone broody on her.

Mallett came round the big dark carved oak desk slowly and shook hands with me.

'Hello, Jim.'

A fine place to be broody in: Venetian blinds down, dark plain rug, heavy Florentine pieces, and a tremendous sailfish mounted on an oval of golden oak.

He raised his arms a little and let them fall as he sat down. A big man—a good inch over me, and I was six one. Recessive brown hair, rather prominent brown eyes, about fifty.

'Unbelievable,' he said in a melancholy voice. 'We post bonds, sign agreements, draw up contracts, lease theaters, deposit funds. Everything is arranged, we've thought of everything.'

I thought of all the little things that might be waiting for me. 'When did you see her last, Chris?'

He didn't answer. He picked up a large card behind the desk, the kind used for lobby display, set it down in front of me, and there she was. At the top of the card, above the play announcement, a color blowup of the first-act curtain in *Wild Goose Chase*.

Niobe standing at the door, her gloves in her hand, very tall in the dicty, softly fitted black moire peplum jacket and black thin wool skirt. A tall girl for a clotheshorse every time. The fine modeling of the calves and flanks, the good bones in hands and face and shoulders, the delicately sedate but impressive breasts.

All very fine. Very fine indeed. And the red hair, a good deal nearer to red black than what was called red gold—though not quite black either—brushed up under the small black glazed hat. A short veil, perhaps. I don't remember. Oh, and the fine gray eyes, organ of sensibility. The nice clean color of a herring gull's wings. Very fine. Very dashing. But the woman was a witch. Old French witch from Vincennes, Indiana. Alice of Old Vincennes witch.

It was the scene in which she waits for an answer from Bentley Evans, who sits writing. She gets none and goes out. He looks up as the door closes. Pure tension. She doesn't say a word. I don't remember what the question was. I do remember kidding her about it as she read it to me. The script wasn't bad. It was good, really, subtly done. It didn't depend on the usual incompatibilities or perversities or inexperience or egotisms or outside agents.

But the woman herself was making a characteristically imprecise female demand for happiness, I said. Everybody had a surplus of desire over satisfaction. That was what made the world go round. Most people could define the ends they were after, though they

21

might be a little vague about the means. This frilly in the script didn't know what she wanted, or how.

Niobe had looked at me over the steel-rimmed glasses she wore for reading, the glasses that prompted me to refer to our little tête-à-têtes as Evenings with Grandma. That's true, in a way, she said. But it's completely in character. You believe that she feels that way, don't you? Yes, I believed it. Does everybody that's unhappy know why—or even that he is unhappy? Do you suppose you can't get so desperate that you'll do something without knowing what you're doing, or why?

Not me, I said grinning, thinking of John Kane's story about the man who cried: I'm not crazy. See? I got my discharge from the insane asylum. Not you maybe, my pet, Niobe went on. But other people. Thousands and thousands of them. How many people do you suppose are really satisfied with the way they're living? You wait. This play will move them. It will touch something in them, something they didn't know about themselves.

I could hear her saying it now, with her own peculiar soft vehemence, as Mallett told me that he'd talked to her the night before on the phone. She seemed in very good spirits, very gay, he said mournfully. He'd never seen her so gay, though she'd been a little under par at rehearsal the day before. I was still thinking about it as I picked up my coat and listened to his bundle of woe about the date registered, the theater engaged, all the expenses ticking on and on, with the star and cast and author vamoosed. He'd taken the fatherly attitude and he was very hurt at Niobe's defection. I gathered that he felt the whole thing had been arranged expressly to ruin him.

Thinking about it a little more as I said good-by to Henrietta and walked toward the subway, I tried to remember exactly what the note had said. Something about: '. . . all the other things I've always wanted to do . . .' The other things? What other things? Suppose she'd understood the woman in the play because she shared her feeling? Even if it were possible, Niobe wouldn't be naïve enough to transpose her personality into the actual part. But suppose it meant that whatever she had with me wasn't enough? Well, didn't it?

When I caught up with her I intended to make it enough, or up the ante. Meantime I could hardly believe that she'd been deeply discontented. As it turned out, she hadn't. She hadn't even abandoned her charming profession, as Mallett thought. I found that out in an hour or so.

The city had the feel of an April day, soft and palely bright, a day of small white clouds and disconnected reveries. Something else in the air too: good time coming, everybody out, like the morning of circus day in a small town. The city's deep-breasted tides and ebbs and cycles, the great migration routes, were beginning to be confused now, in crossrips.

I seem to remember flowers. A cart trotting up Sixth Avenue loaded with begonias and heliotrope in pots, and when I turned into Times Square a man with a market basket, a man who looked like Johnny Appleseed, giving away ragged sailors, sweet peas, and fat fresh gardenias. The strange thing was that people took them without suspicion. A little half-pint girl picked out a fine gardenia, curtsied to me, and reached up laughing to put it into my lapel. Then she kissed me. I began to see how things were going.

At the IRT entrance a man strolled past wearing a sandwich board that read: THE WORLD IS YOURS FOR THE ASKING. The front page of the *Times* was riddled with typos, and as I started down the music came pouring up out of all the entrances and corridors of the subway, reverberating and clashing on itself. An astonishing music. Dixieland. *That Da Da Strain*. The two horns led it, the jostling timbres, pushing each other hard, the nervous-trigger phrasing of the cornet and the powerful thrusting, upward blurt of the trombone. Muggsy and George Brunis. The clarinet leaped high out of the melee, wriggling and flashing. A pure and balanced nimbleness. Fazola.

I got on the New Lots express behind them. People were crowding in from the other cars and the guard had a tough time getting the doors closed. The musicians formed up in the middle of the car, the bass, Earl Murphy, with his back to the seat end. Muggsy took his horn down and grinned, his face moving in concentric wrinkles, then set the mouthpiece in his lip muscle again. Brunis played at me with the hook of the trombone, prancing. It was Riverboat Shuffle now and the boys were breaking it up.

I walked up the dead escalator at Park Place and cut over between City Hall and the City Court Building. Past the gray-green mottled bark of the sycamores that reminded me of my own country. Their leaves made a lacy light on the still, hot mornings in summer.

An old newspaperwoman, her canvas apron belted with sisal cord, was feeding the pigeons. Four or five people stood around, and then there were a dozen, and the pigeons kept coming too. I liked the pale milk-chocolaty ones with the dark iridescent rippling ruffs. A sparrow hopped in and caught a peanut under the bills of the pigeons and I heard the old woman's high cackling laugh.

The streaked bronze solidity of Bonnard's Greeley. Not a bad man to keep an eye on City Hall. I waited a full minute for the traffic in Centre Street and just as I started across the thing hit me. The laughter was an old woman's all right, perfectly imitated, but the voice was Niobe's. I brushed past the cop on point duty and got back there fast but she was gone, the little crowd broken up, the pigeons strutting round and round among the peanut shells, cooing querulously.

2

WINDY as ever under the big colonnade of the Municipal Building. Now why was she doing that, for God's sake? She couldn't have known I'd take the West Side subway downtown. I got off the main building elevator and said good morning to Pop Mancini in the tower elevator. When I asked him how he was he grunted.

'The town's goin' to hell.'

I opened the door. Carlotta Breyer, the receptionist, jumped up behind the office-green metal counter and put her hand on my arm. 'Don't move, Mr. Rowan. Stay right there. They ast me to hold ya.'

'What's the——'

She started for the inner offices, waving me back and calling over her shoulder: 'Just a minute, Mr. Rowan. They got it all fixed.'

I stood there like a fool, looking at the place again. You didn't see it at all unless you'd been away. The odd air of impermanence about American government offices in our time. The look of having been knocked together hastily by amateur carpenters and loaded up with secondhand furniture. Everything loose, ready to be given a number and moved out again.

The black-and-metal INFORMATION sign on its triangular wood base. The big fan. The slotted map case. The mahogany cabinet and mirror over the washbasin, lighted by a single bulb. The row of smaller offices, fake grained mahogany, and glass rolled in a sheaf design. The Westclox on the wall jumped to a new minute.

They were coming out now, standing in front of me. Engineers and stenographers and draftsmen in shirt sleeves. I could see Bill standing behind them. All smiling. The girls shook their heads at my raised eyebrows. Watson Cartwright, the economist who headed the Division of Capital and Assessable Improvements, pushed his way through to the front. A good man but a pretty glum article. Wife trouble. Must be something serious in this if he was heading it. I didn't tumble at all. Why were they smiling?

'Mr. Rowan,' he said gruffly, looking at the floor, 'the staff wanted to welcome you home again. Of course we realize you've only been gone a week.'

Laughter.

'But we felt we—we'd like to memorialize the occasion with a little gift. Something appropriate at the present time. If you'll accept this token of——'

One of the girls passed him something. He brought it out and handed it to me and they were all clapping and laughing. A gas mask. They'd sent a messenger down to Governors Island to borrow it.

I tried it on and took it off again. More laughter.

'Thanks. I'll wear it to the Commissioners' lunch.' An office joke. 'Maybe I won't be able to taste the food.'

They drifted back to work and Eunice met me at the door of her little office that led into mine, a batch of papers in her hand. A tallish girl, brown-blonde, looking handsome in a gray print dress. She was smiling too.

'Fun, huh?' I said.

She and Bill must have cooked it up.

'Jim, here's a——'

'Give me five minutes.'

I went into my own office and shut the door. Good big maps on the wall. Reference books on top of the filing case: Henry Wright's *Re-Housing Urban America*, Behrendt's *Modern Building*, and four or five others. Two chairs. A desk. A telephone. Two wire baskets, in and out. The chair turned until I could look out over the dark Gothic bridge and the classic American slums of the lower East Side. A reminder we couldn't miss. My mind wasn't working that way at the moment. So she's playing an old woman? What about it? Where does that—— I swung around in the chair as I remembered.

One night coming home from a party at Mason Emery's. Niobe leaned her head back in the cab. Two or three drinks over, but handling herself beautifully except for a slight oral slowness, a tendency toward overemphasis. Some day I'm going to—— Never mind, she said. I said: Never mind what?

She said slowly and carefully: Some day I'm going to play some *real* roles. Not in a theater. Ohhh no. I'm going to play *people* right out with other people. In the streets and places. Wall Street office girls and old women and—and attendants at the Mu—seum of Natural History—and housewives in—in Woodhaven, she finished triumphantly.

26

What for? I said. If you're good enough nobody'll know. She slapped my knee. That's it, brother, she said vaingloriously. That's the—the greatness of it. Get the theater out of grease paint and into the streets, she declaimed with gestures. I laughed. Do you mind if I tell you that you're skivvied, my pretty? I said. No, she said solemnly. No. Because I am. Then she was asleep.

I pressed the buzzer and told Eunice.

'Good,' she conceded slowly. 'All right. But doesn't it sound like something she might just toss off when she'd had a few? Maybe it wouldn't signify, huh?'

'Can't tell,' I said. 'Probably it *was* just a spur-of-the-moment idea. But it's good this way. Niobe *is* nuts about the theater. It's the right *kind* of idea—the kind that would be likely to hit her when she got the fever. And if it's right, it gives us a predictable pattern. Worth a play. What've you got?'

She gave me the list of Niobe's contacts. Nothing stirring.

'Good. Do this every morning. Okeh? And give me a swindle sheet, will you?'

'Don't worry.'

'Wait a minute. The Missing Persons Bureau. We'd better give it to them. Captain Ellison. He knows me. Dark-red hair. Gray eyes. Height five ten. Weight about one thirty-five. Age thirty-four. Third finger on the left hand looks a little crooked. She had it broken once. The ring finger.'

Niobe had been the kind of little girl who plays ball with the boys.

'Last seen wearing——'

'I don't know. But it doesn't matter. She'd get rid of it. And you might ask Mallett to send down some pictures.'

A memo from John Hickey, Sanitation Commissioner, to remind me of the usual Thursday Commissioners' lunch at his office. The Mayor was coming. That meant fireworks.

A sheaf of forms, petitions for zoning changes that would come up at the regular hearing that afternoon. Some of them I'd seen on the train. I riffled through them and stacked them.

'We've got to call it off.'

Eunice looked at me doubtfully. 'It's never been done. Isn't the law——'

'Unanimous consent,' I said, and reached for the phone.

I got an outside wire and the operator said sweetly: 'Sorry. We cannot connect you with that number.'

'Why not?'

'The exchange is out of order.'

I managed to get Ed Collins, the Commission Secretary. He said he'd notify the petitioners. 'How many are there?'

I counted. 'Thirty-one. You have the list?'

I got one more commission member, Eunice called Western Union messengers for the rest, and Alberta on the main building switchboard said: 'Mr. Emery is waiting to talk to you.'

Mason Emery, Commissioner of the Department of Housing and Buildings, and Chairman of the New York City Housing Authority. Connecticut family, money from a cotton-webbing process his father had developed, Harvard '26, international expert on housing, done a standard technical book on the subject. Taller than average, a bit Abercrombie & Fitch as to clothes (the dog!), noticeably large ears, slight stoop, gray eyes, brown hair beginning to thin in front. Our good friend.

I said: 'Yes, Em,' and he said: 'Terribly sorry about Niobe. Any news?'

'One little break. And a hunch. Tell you about it downstairs. How are things?'

'Molting. We're being swept out to sea. Ollie is contemplating his navel and the boys are howling for a showdown.' The Mayor, Oliver Bodine. 'What luck in the nation's capital?'

I'd gone down there to talk to Jerome Cobb, United States Housing Authority Administrator, about a project we had planned. Jerry had refused to okeh the lower East Side site we wanted. Our argument, the standard one, was that it would replace bad housing with good and at the same time keep up Manhattan tax values.

Jerry wanted to buy cheaper land in a run-down industrial section near the Brooklyn water front. He'd make a better showing on his appropriation that way, get more spread over the whole country, but you couldn't call it slum clearance. I was against it because it would break up a feeder highway I was trying to put through behind the water front.

'What luck? Not good,' I said. 'Jerry said he couldn't see it. I tried to get hold of Eli. He fluffed me off for five days and went to Virginia for the week end. The greatest Secretary of the Interior since Caleb Blood Smith.'

I could hear him chuckle.

'I did get to Puckett on the Senate Housing Committee. He promised to see what he could do, and with that in my poke I went back to Jerry. Had dinner with him just before I left. He says there's something out West. They may not be able to raise their part of the appropriation. If they don't, he'll assign the funds to us. Let us know in a week.'

'Sounds as if we have a chance. Good work, Jim. See you at lunch.'

Eunice had some other papers. They could wait. I was thinking about a plan that had occurred to me that morning.

'Oh,' Eunice said. 'A man named Paravecchio phoned. A cab driver. Says he's waiting for you down the street.'

I said: 'Okeh,' and grinned. Bill passed her on his way in, like somebody in a bad play, and sat down. Twenty-one people missing out of sixty-odd in the office, mostly from the Division of Capital Improvements.

'How are the map-makers?'

'One gone.'

'That all? Good. We may need them. What about this fever, anyhow? What's been done?'

'Practically nothing,' Bill said. 'I mean virtually nothing. Wirth's people have been digging like hell to find out what it is. No luck yet. The Board of Transportation sent down a couple of its own men to help run the trains. Former motormen. The cops are dropping away like the leaves of autumn.' His voice rose and fell gently.

Eunice brought in some wires from the other City Planning Commissioners. All of them agreed to the postponement. The one from Ferry said: 'I have it and it's delicious. Transcendent. I'm painting like mad.' Water colors, he meant. He'd always wanted to do water colors, turned sick with envy at a Marin. We grinned at each other. If the rest of them had only taken to painting water colors.

Bill sat smoking calmly. The phone rang and I recognized Marguerite's voice. 'I wanted to thank you for being so nice to me.'

'Bill's here,' I said. 'Thank him.'

Bill's face relaxed slowly.

'No, you,' she said. Me? 'Have you got to work?'

'Why?'

'I want to go to Staten Island. Clove Lakes Park. It's the nicest place.'

'Aren't you going to work?"

'Nope. Not any more. I'm tired of it.'

Something the New York Telephone Company hadn't thought of. Bill took the phone. The nice even sleepy voice: 'Listen, honey pie. You're our mascot.'

We might need one before we were through. Bill arranged to meet her for dinner. When he put the phone down I looked at him a moment, thinking.

'Suppose this thing gets worse?'

'It will.'

'All right. I don't know exactly what's happening yet, but if it does we may be licked. Really licked. Our factor of safety will go up the pipe. We get to thinking of the city as institutional. It isn't —not basically, anyhow. It's people. You know that. A city is just a lot of people who've agreed to live together in a certain general way. But if enough people—especially the key ones—decide they can't be bothered, the whole thing stops running.'

'Maybe. Maybe we've got more margin than that,' Bill said slowly. 'Just the momentum, the regular ways of doing things, might keep us going for a while. Don't forget we've got some fast improvisers in this town too.'

'That's right,' I said, nodding. 'The Cornbill momentum theory. Fire, earthquake, hurricane. We could depend on people to hop to the spot where they were needed like—like leucocytes. This may be different, though. This is people changing their habits. The toughest social force there is, probably. How the hell can we run a fire department when we can't be sure the men will be there—or even that they'll get an alarm when it's turned in? That goes for the other service departments too: police, health, markets, hospitals, water supply, transportation. All the rest.'

'So what do we do?' Bill said. 'Keep replacing them with reserves and volunteers?'

'We might, in some departments. It wouldn't work for most of them. Not enough trained men. What it comes down to—if it gets any worse, I mean—is that we can't keep up the organization. It'll get too damn thin. Not enough people to man all the fire trucks or keep all the precinct stations going. Too scattered. We'll have to shorten our lines.'

'How do you mean?'

'I don't know exactly yet. I don't know whether it would work. I thought of general control stations. Consolidate everything. Put everything into one center in each neighborhood. Police, fire, ambulance service. Light and power, gas—steam in Manhattan—and water-supply repair crews. Police emergency crews. Everything we need. We might have to borrow some people from the private companies, of course.'

'Let's see,' Bill said. 'What do you get then? Full crews. Enough reserves to fill in when people get the happies. Enough for relief too. Fine. Why not just pull in all the services separately—the way they're organized now? Just abandon two or three firehouses in each neighborhood?'

'Might be better in some ways,' I said, 'if we could do it. Always better to try to use what you've got. Probably wouldn't work,

31

though. Chances are the fire station or police station wouldn't be centrally placed in the bigger district. That might be pretty important with the longer hauls they'd have to make. We might pick a fire station or precinct station wherever it's possible. A city building, anyhow. Throw the other services into it. We could have everybody sleep in. Eat in too. You'd get a certain amount of segregation that way.

'The main thing, though, is keeping in touch. The telephone company's in a jam already and the police- and fire-signal systems are beginning to crack. No good. We've got to have something fairly positive.'

Bill nodded slowly. 'Radio?'

'Yep. Not the broadcast band. It might scare hell out of people, having that stuff coming over all day. Tough to manage in other ways too. Contracts, red tape. We need the regular radio for morale. But what about short wave? What about the police and fire short-wave stations? We could put a couple of short-wave sets into each control station and we'd have something fairly workable.'

'You mean use the radio station as a clearance point? Feed all the telephone alarms, fire and police signals into it? Wouldn't you get a choke point right there?'

'Sure to. But just as soon as we got it set up we'd begin to decentralize, if we found we needed to. We've got four police transmitters and one fire, besides the radio hams we could call on. Decentralize by boroughs or types of service—fire calls, ambulance, riot, whatever. By boroughs would be better, of course. We wouldn't need duplicate receivers for each station.'

I got up and went to the big health-stations map.

'I don't know. This might be the nearest to what we want. Better than voting precincts. How about it? Can you get the boys to rough out a map? Thirty or thirty-five districts. Each district limited by the range of the service that's likely to get the hardest workout. Use a good street map. Try to pick the right kind of building for headquarters in each district.'

'How about overlap?'

'Oh, say a block all round. The dispatcher can assign calls in the overlap. All he'll need to do is pick the station that has equipment free. Don't bother with borough boundaries. If we have to decentralize we can assign a certain number of districts arbitrarily to each transmitter. Just a mockup. We can correct it later. How about it?'

'When?'

'Can you get it down to me in Hickey's office about one-thirty?'

Bill whistled. 'I think so,' he said gently, and wandered out. I knew we'd get it. Great power was hidden under that glistening hood.

On the way out I told Eunice I was going to Hickey's lunch. Call her back later.

'Are you coming back?'

'I don't know.'

Young Joralemon came past as I was washing up at the little office stand. A nice kid.

'Will you get a messenger and send him downstairs for me? There's a cab driver named Paravecchio, thickset man, Parmalee cab, waiting down the street. Centre Street. Tell him I won't need him till about two o'clock.'

3

I COULD hear them—the steady, not loud interplay of voices: my confreres in session over the fruit cup—as I went through John Carey's outer office downstairs. John's secretary smiled at me and the other girls stopped typing a moment to listen.

'How's the baby, Ellen?'

'Oh God! Teething.'

I opened the door. Hands raised a little. Two or three nods. Murmurs of 'Hello, Jim.' Henry Feuerman, the Commissioner of Markets, called: 'Just in time for the barbecue,' and Adam Hanauer, the Fire Commissioner, leaned his big round head back as I passed behind the chairs.

'The Mayor will be here with the soup,' he muttered.

'Or in it.'

He gasped, shaking, and leaned to tell his neighbor. Not very good. Political jokes didn't have to be good. Lodge stuff. Abracadabra to the general. I sat down beside Mason Emery near the foot of the long coffin-shaped table—an old subject for jokes. I was a pretty small frog in this pond. A probationary frog too. *Acting* Commissioner.

Thirty or so Commissioners and department heads around the long table, besides the Borough Presidents, the Comptroller, and the President of the City Council, John Kane. The waiter brought oxtail soup, but the Mayor didn't come with it. He came with the coffee, much later. Em murmured that the boys were getting up a head of steam.

I watched them for a minute over the soup, the city's informal cabinet, meeting every Thursday in this long walnut-paneled room. Venetian blinds. The national and city colors on standards to either side of the main door. Flanking them, tall bronze lamp stands topped with acanthus-leaved Corinthian urns for indirect lighting. Good comfortable black leather armchairs.

The meeting was coming to a boil all right. People agreeing with each other in chorus. Arnold Genovese, the little sandy-haired hard-bodied Borough President of the Bronx, seemed to be the hottest. John Kane was baiting him jovially.

He called down the table: 'What'll you do if he doesn't come, Arnie?'

The others laughed, watching Arnie.

'Listen, John,' Arnie yelled, shaking his hand at Kane. 'For your information——'

I didn't catch the rest of it because Em had asked me about Niobe. The waiter put coffee down beside my plate. Em listened, his big homespun shoulders hunched over the table a little, his gray eyes amused and sympathetic, while I told him what had happened the night before.

'No sign of her?'

'Nothing,' I said, 'until this morning. I actually saw her. An old newspaperwoman in City Hall Park. Feeding the pigeons. I heard her laugh and——'

I could see his eyes changing, getting grave, looking not at me but at my face, suspecting that I had it too, and suddenly I realized that I was the only one in the room still talking.

The Mayor had come in with Charley Porter, his No. 1 secretary, a small plump baldish man who looked fussy but knew his way around blindfold. He seemed pretty grim and we found out afterwards that he'd spent the morning in the Mayor's office, trying to get him to change his mind. A bad day for Charley. There were people who said that Ollie Bodine wouldn't have been Mayor if Charley hadn't managed his campaign, but that was too strong. It was easy to underestimate Ollie.

At first glance he looked as impressively cadaverous as ever in the pin-striped brown hard-worsted suit. The bones of his face and skull seemed thin, faintly invalid. Flat brownish hair, sallow skin with a welted look under the cheekbones, a rather full mouth. Harvard '12. Old Huguenot New York family—or Brooklyn, rather. Banking connections. They'd made money early in the two-way cotton-shipping trade of the 1820's: up to New York from the South and across to Liverpool by packet. A pretty strait-laced crowd. Their names had been mixed up in city affairs for more than a century.

Ollie had some of that. The integrity, anyhow. Bred to be responsible, to take hold and hang on. That was what made the thing so shocking. He was intelligent enough, too. You could say that he just didn't have the horsepower for the job or that he was a very complex animal who had never quite jelled. But we'd backed him to a man, moved beyond the mere need for co-operation by that curious talent of his, the half-feminine way he had of getting people to do things for him; and when he gave it to us, we felt personally betrayed. Silly, of course, in the circumstances. He couldn't help it. But it was a public failure too, God knows, and we were in on it. We were his men.

35

John Kane offered him a chair but he shook his head and stood with his yellowish hands on the back of John's chair, Charley just behind him, looking down the long table. His eyes were shining and there was a faint unbelievable tint of pink in his cheekbones. I could see hands along the table absently laying down the jagged snowcaps of napkins, and a waiter brushing off the cloth sounded loud in the big room.

'I came over today,' the Mayor said, 'to tell you that I understand how serious things are.'

I could see John Kane turned round in the chair, gazing up at him, the cigar motionless in his hand. Two or three of us glanced at each other. It sounded hopeful.

'We've let things go too long, Ollie,' Genovese said in a mild conversational tone. He didn't look up. He was making a ticktacktoe box in the tablecloth with his fingernail. 'Another day and we'll have the whole works on our necks.'

No fight, Arnie's tone meant. He was willing to take part of the blame himself, take it for us too. Wirth and McKeogh and some of the others looked relieved. They were anxious to let it go that way. That was the effect Ollie had on us.

He had a deep slow voice. 'Yes, I know, Arnie. I came to you as soon as I'd made my decision because I knew it would take a little time to find someone else who—who could attack the problem.'

We sat there like the dead. Ollie looked down, looked up again.

'I find I'm not equal to the task. I—I have lost interest. I realize the gravity of the situation but I do not feel that I personally can——'

Wirth said in a choked voice: 'Now wait a minute, Ollie.'

Two or three of the others protested. John Kane got halfway out of the chair and waved them down. 'Wait. Let him speak his piece.'

'As you know,' the Mayor said, 'I didn't want the position when I was asked to run. I agreed to serve. But I find that I—I am not equal to it. This epidemic is an additional burden.'

He paused. When he began to speak again I could see the others trying to follow him.

'The annual exhibition of the New York Society of Model Engineers is only a few weeks away,' Ollie said. 'You may not know that most of my spare time in the last year has been spent building a Chicago & Northwestern E-3 Pacific-type locomotive. Four-six-two model. A lovely thing. Runs on O-gauge track. Seven-pole armature motor. AC relay reversing, sprung driving wheels and oil-less self-aligning bearings.'

His eyes lighted softly and he seemed to relax a little.

'Now,' he said, 'I find that I've got to pull it all down and put in a new fifteen-to-one gear ratio. This will give it a scale speed of eighty miles an hour. With rheostats for sequence reverses and——'

John Hickey's downright Irish voice said: 'What are you going to do, Ollie?'

The Mayor looked down at the table. 'Resign,' he said.

'Resign now?' Al Elias shouted.

'Yes. I'm going down to my place in East Hampton. I must leave the situation in your hands.'

'But why, Ollie? Why?' Henry Feuerman pounded once on the table.

They were all shouting together but Arnie Genovese pushed the chair out of his way slowly as if it were someone trying to hold him back and got up. He held up his hand.

'Wait a minute,' he called, and paused until we were quiet. 'Mr. Mayor,' he said. His face was red and he didn't look at Ollie. 'When I was seventeen years old I worked in a machine shop in the Bronx. The stairways were falling down. Somebody mighta broken his neck. The contractor was too busy. He couldn't be bothered. So I took a day off and went downtown on the el to see the Commissioner.'

He looked at Ollie for the first time, his lips turned in, and nodded fiercely around at us.

'His old man.' He jerked his head at Ollie. 'I was a young punk.

He'd never seen me before. Do you know what he told me? "I'll have them fix it or I'll shut them up. They can take their choice." The contractor had an in down at the Hall and it took the Commissioner two years to do it. *Two years.*'

Arnie slapped the table softly with the flat of his hand.

' "I'll have them fix it or I'll shut them up. They can take their choice." '

He sat down.

The Mayor looked down at the table and we sat there a moment without speaking. Hickey whispered something to George Romanelli, the Docks Commissioner. Onderdonck, the Commissioner of Hospitals, was ruling deep lines on a scratch pad.

'This is final, is it?' he asked quietly, as if he were taking notes on a case.

I saw the Vandyke tighten around his mouth as the Mayor nodded and turned to go. Charley Porter looked sick. He hadn't said a word. When they were halfway to the door Arnie called despairingly: 'Ollie, you can't——'

The Mayor turned and smiled at us. I never saw a happier man. Then the door shut and the room was buzzing, everybody talking at once. Wirth and Onderdonck had their heads together and Wirth raised his hand.

He said: 'We can't be sure, of course, without an examination, but Onderdonck agrees with me that the Mayor probably has the fever. It seems obvious.'

Onderdonck snorted. 'Toy trains!'

'What's next?' Hickey said cheerfully.

Charley Regan, the Borough President of Queens, motioned ironically at John Kane.

'Our next Mayor, gentlemen,' he said.

They called: 'That's right.' 'Take the chair, John.' 'You're elected.' 'Lucky you didn't have to go to the voters again.'

I tried to remember how the succession went. It didn't make much difference. John was it all right. Gordon Lummis, the Deputy Mayor, was in Argentina on a trade relations tour with municipal officials from other cities. Anyhow, his powers were pretty strictly limited.

John got up slowly at the head of the table. A tall big-shouldered graying Irishman from Manhattanville. Second generation. About fifty. Pure politician, and all granite, with that odd core of ethical ruggedness some of them had, but without the puritanism. A great reader. Heavy stuff: Scotus, Spinoza, Locke, Dewey, even queer fish like Kierkegaard. He didn't talk about it. A teller of neighborhood stories and a horse-player. An ex-Councilman. He'd put his name up on the Coalition ticket when a New York Irishman wasn't doing that for fun, or even expediency. John was right.

'Whoa. Whoa,' he called, knocking the bottom of a tumbler gently on the table. 'Just a minute.' We quieted immediately under his experienced hand and all the heads turned to face him. 'Let's read the bible first.'

Hickey called Ellen. She came in, glancing at the rows of faces. No, they didn't have a copy of the charter. But it was in the Tanzer book.

Hickey read it out in a strong voice:

10. a. The president of the council shall act as mayor
(1) whenever there shall be a vacancy in the office of mayor, or
(2) while the mayor shall be prevented from attending to the duties of his office by reason of sickness, absence from the city, or suspension from office.

There was a lot more to it, qualifications of powers. Nothing specific about the Mayor resigning. Kane asked Harold Brownell, the Corporation Counsel, for a ruling on it. Then Blaine, the Welfare Commissioner, suggested that we bring in a stenographer to take down the proceedings, and they moved a table and chair in for Ellen. Poor Ellen. She held on until the people from the secretary's bureau of the Board of Estimate took over. The record made twelve printed volumes.

Kane rapped again. 'Quiet, everybody. Quiet, now,' he said

slowly. 'The charter sounds as if I'm stuck with this. All right. But I've got a little package for you too and here it is. You know I've got no business sitting here. We've got a job on our hands—the toughest pickle this town ever got into. What do I know about it? I'm a politician. I get things through the Council. I know how *that's* done. I don't know how Justin runs his police or Maurice handles his markets.'

Dave Klingerman, the little Parks Commissioner, slapped his forehead and called in a high voice: 'Ey-yi! A politician who admits he don't know something. Samson should pull the temple down on his own head already.'

There were tense grins up and down the table. John grinned too. 'That's right, Dave,' he said. 'I don't know. What can *I* do in a spot like this?'

We called out to him but he grimaced and waved us down. 'Listen, boys. I'll front for you. I'm not going to rat on this. But to do the job you've got to have a man who knows something about the whole show. Not a specialist. It doesn't look to me as if we could spare a Commissioner from the service departments. Come on. Nominations?'

'You want a job, Arnie?' Dave Klingerman said to Genovese in a tone of the softest buttery insinuation, and we laughed again.

Roswell Young, the Comptroller, looked down at Dick Wirth. 'Isn't this something for a medical man? What do they call 'em? An epidemiologist?'

Dick Wirth smiled at him. He looked tired. 'Hugh Onderdonck and I have too much to do already. Epidemiology is only a lick and a promise yet. No. This is too big for a medical man. That's only part of it.'

Arnie Genovese slapped the table suddenly. 'Wait a minute. What's the matter with Rowan?'

The heads were turning my way now.

'What did I ever do to you, Arnie?' I said.

He was excited. 'Never mind. I'll see you later about that.' He ticked things off on his fingers, bending them back. 'His department can spare him. He's the only man that's got to know about the whole business. He's got to plan for it. Who makes up the capital budget? Who else has to know every dinky schoolhouse and bridge and pipe line in the whole setup? He makes the maps. He figures out how everything fits into everything else.' He looked at me tenderly. 'I used to wonder what the hell we kept him for. Now I know.' He threw a kiss at me. 'He's the over-all guy.'

I tried to interrupt him. 'No. No,' he said. 'Wait a minute. I kept the best one for the last.' He paused, leaned across the table. 'He's a professor. How can we go wrong with a professor?'

They were smiling at me now. 'What about Rich Jones?' I said quietly. Richmond P. Jones, Chief Engineer of the Board of Estimate. Everybody knew Rich wasn't the man to start things. He kept them rolling.

'I'll back you, Jim,' he said quietly, and meant it. I could almost feel that settle it, but I wanted to be sure they wanted me. I was going to need all the support I could get.

'I'm a carpetbagger,' I said. 'A Hoosier hayseed. Where's your local spirit?'

'That's okeh,' Hanauer said generously, and they laughed and agreed. Like the other laughs that day, it had an edge of strain to it. We could feel the city outside, falling apart while we talked.

'All right. I've never even been elected dogcatcher.'

Hickey nodded blandly. 'We'll take a chance on that.'

'But is he honest?' Romanelli asked, looking around naïvely. They laughed again.

'I've copped more melons and pears and gooseberries——'

'Listen,' Arnie said, jerking a thumb at me. 'Listen to him. He means off bushes. Not off the Greek.'

'Cut it,' Justin McKeogh said grimly. 'Put him up and we'll hang him.'

John rapped again. 'All right. We'll have to work out the legal angle later. Nominations for the post of executive assistant to the Acting Mayor. At no salary.'

They laughed again. Dick Wirth made the nomination, Justin seconded, and I was elected with three dissenting votes.

Em squeezed my shoulder. Hickey called: 'It's your baby, Jim,' and they clapped smartly as I went round to the head of the table beside John.

4

STANDING there, I had the feeling that we could do it and I wanted to make them feel it too.

'Mind if I talk a little, John?'

He waved grandly. 'Go right ahead. It's your show, Jim. You'll have lots of time for talking. You won't be busy.'

I said: 'Thanks to you,' sat down, and got out a scratch pad. I wrote the date at the top and looked up. I could feel Ellen watching me.

'Thanks for the job,' I said quietly, 'and the applause. I hope I can live up to it. Anyhow, it looks as if the Mayor picked the wrong time to walk out on us.'

They stared.

'I mean he's going to miss the fun. Pretty rough fun—but fun. No kick like doing a job that looks just a little too big for you.'

I could feel them relaxing a little, and Hickey said gently: 'That's right, Jim.'

'One more point before we go to work. You know whose necks are out. It may not be our fault, but we're off to a bad start. And you know what town this is. We're going to do this job in the newspapers. The eyes of Texas are upon you, gentlemen.'

They clapped ironically.

'John,' I said, 'do you think we should try to figure out how to split this job between us first?'

He considered. 'I'll have to move into City Hall. I can use Charley Porter and the other secretaries. We'll take care of any routine stuff I have authority for.'

'What about publicity, John?' Em called, leaning in on the table. 'We'll get into a mess if we don't watch out. I mean the every-man-for-himself system may be all right for Washington, but —I don't want to make myself unpopular'—he glanced up and down blandly—'but why can't we turn all our reports over to John's office and let him work them up?'

Somebody said, 'How do you mean? *Doctor* them?' and John laughed.

'No,' Em said earnestly. 'People have a right to know what's going on. Even now. Ollie didn't do enough talking. But it has to be done all in one piece, with—with tact, and timing. I should think so.' He looked around. 'We don't want to panic people, and they won't panic if we give them the facts in—in proportion. Just so one thing, one part of it, doesn't look too big. John can do that.'

People nodded, and nobody objected, though I could see nascent objection, or hope dying, in two or three faces.

I said: 'Want to leave it that way?' and it was clear that they did. 'It's yours, John.'

John hadn't missed anything. 'We'll handle it,' he said quietly. 'Might save you fellows some steps.' He knew how to sweeten the pill. 'I'll get radio time and put some of you boys on for talks. We can do the contact work over there too, and take care of Albany. Anything else?'

Nobody seemed to be able to think of anything else.

John waved. 'All right, Jim. It's settled. I'll do the talking. You do the job.'

'Not alone,' I said. 'If you gentlemen think I'm going to take this rap alone you're kidding yourselves. How about making this a committee? Call it, say, the Committee for the City or Committee for the Public. Any ideas?'

Plenty of ideas. Young, the Comptroller, and Robert Porter, the Director of the Budget, felt that John and I ought to have all the authority and hand out jobs to the others. Regan of Queens and Lester J. Long, the Treasurer, sided with them. Arnie Genovese, Dick Wirth, and Penforth Reger of the Department of Investigation wanted a full committee to vote measures. In about a minute more we had the old row about whether democracy is workable in a crisis blowing up in our laps.

I knew what I thought. I thought that two heads were better than one and a dozen were better than two, if you only knew how to use them. I was damn well convinced that Wirth knew more about Health and Feuerman more about Markets than I did. Why couldn't I just consult with them? Because that way the import of their knowledge might be distorted by my authority or my personality.

I couldn't trust myself to be totally fair or totally just. No one could. All of us together couldn't, for that matter. But if we all put our knowledge on the table and formed opinions on that basis, they could vote and I could carry out their decision, knowing that each man's opinion had been given its full weight and that I could expect their support. It wasn't perfect, but it was better than the alternatives, and I liked it.

So did most of the others, of course. Young and Porter and Long, being financial men, had a natural bent for authority. Some of us suspected that Reger must be pretty close to the CP's, which spelled authority of another kind. When a CP began to yell about the vote, you could be pretty sure he must be fresh from a party caucus with orders in one pocket and a squeeze play in the other.

It was pretty clear that most of them were for a committee.

Arnie got an arm up. 'Wait a minute,' he called. 'Let's get Jim's idea. What did you have in mind, Jim?'

They quieted a little.

'A nonpartisan committee,' I said. 'Or call it nonpartisan. All the city officers. The City Sheriff and the City Register. The opposition boys from the Council. Two or three names to represent the public.'

Maurice Satin, the Public Works Commissioner, was shaking his head at me.

'What is it, Maurice?'

He looked sad and disappointed. 'You know it won't work, Jim,' he said. 'You won't get anything done with a mob of people like that. A dogfight.' He gestured.

'I'm sorry, Maurice,' I said. 'I didn't mean an executive committee. I was thinking of a policy-making body. Something like an enlarged Board of Estimate.' They began to nod at that. 'It might work like this. John, or I, or any of you could submit major proposals to the whole committee. We'd explain them and discuss them. Then——'

Maurice nodded. 'Then we could vote them down or put them through. If we approve them, you carry them out as executive.'

'That's it,' I said. 'Once they go through I decide how to carry them out and call on you for what help I need.'

Maurice looked around. 'What's the matter with that?'

'That's all right,' John said.

Porter said: 'An enlarged Board of Estimate? What's the advantage there?'

'This is executive, Bob,' Arnie said patiently. 'We tell Jim what to do. Then he tells us how to do it. Right, Jim?'

He looked at me with his eyebrows up. He was proud of me. I was his protégé and I was doing well.

'That's right, Arnie,' I said smiling. 'Then I report back to you.'

Everybody looked pleased at the tit-for-tat clarity of this explanation.

'It'll work all right,' John said gruffly. 'Take a vote, Jim.'

His way of telling me when to strike. We took the vote and it passed easily, with about seven nays. We picked the citizens' representatives and John promised to notify them and the others.

I suggested that I'd like to take the rest of the day to look the situation over. Make some recommendations at the next meeting. Why not get together here every day for lunch?

That was approved too, and I raised my eyebrows at the way things were going.

'Don't worry.' Al Elias flapped his hand at me. 'This is the honeymoon. Wait'll you try to get some work out of them.'

They laughed at his comic bitterness. Young Joralemon came in

45

hesitantly with Bill's map, a little scared of our importance, and I thanked him. Some people, Bill. I decided to hold the map until tomorrow.

'The next thing,' I said, 'is that I don't know what's going on. I've been in Washington. How did this business get started?'

'You know as much as most of us, Jim,' Adam Hanauer said.

Three or four of them nodded.

'I'm trying to catch up on what's going on in my own department,' Hickey muttered.

They looked at each other and Justin McKeogh said: 'I'll start it. My department had the first contact.'

'Didn't Dick Wirth get the——' Arnie said.

Dave Klingerman shook his head. 'No, a cop picked them up, Arnie.'

Arnie said: 'Oh,' nodding, and subsided.

I watched Justin as he talked. I knew him fairly well. A grimly practical man. Third-generation New York Irish, and a career cop. Not many temperamental faults, except a tendency to stay mad about small things, which he'd learned to control. He didn't care whether he was liked or not. All iron as an executive. That was the puritan peasant moralist in him, though he'd managed to temper that too a little. Thin man, a little over average height. Sharp face, striking black brows, dark-blue eyes. The story was that his wife hounded him. He humored her patiently, never talked about it. Two grown children, the girl at New Rochelle College for Women, the boy at Georgetown.

He talked in the dead and dogged toneless voice you hear on the police radio. 'The United Fruit liner Roncador, inbound from a trip to Central America and the West Indies, docked at one-thirty P.M. Sunday at the foot of Morris Street, Manhattan. She carried seventy-eight passengers and a crew of ninety-seven men and five women. The passengers were all off the boat by four P.M. and the lighters came alongside to discharge the green fruit.'

He passed his hand over his face and looked down at the table-cloth.

46

'At one-fifteen A.M. Monday, almost exactly twelve hours after the ship docked, a radio car from the 17th Precinct responded to Signal 32 and went to——'

'Hold on a minute, Justin,' Hickey said. 'I haven't been arrested recently and I'm a little weak on the terms. What's Signal 32?'

Justin looked at him for a moment as if he neither saw nor heard him. He was one of those people who can concentrate themselves right out of the room.

'Investigate a disturbance at——' He gestured slightly. 'The two patrolmen went to the Savoy-Plaza Hotel at Fifty-Ninth Street. An assistant manager was waiting for them. He was all upset. He told them that five people, three women and two men, were walking on the cornice just below the mansard roof at the twenty-ninth floor of the building.

'They had engaged a suite earlier in the evening, he said, and had been discovered on the roof by a maid working on the floor below. The bellboy reported that they had ordered only two rounds of drinks. One of the patrolmen put in a call for the Emergency Squad and then both of them went with the assistant manager to a small balcony outside a room on the twenty-sixth floor.'

No one spoke. Justin lighted a cigarette slowly and went on. 'The first patrolman, Cahill, reported that as he flashed his light and looked up he involuntarily averted his eyes. An instant later he realized that the light might cause them to lose their balance and turned it away. He also put his finger to his mouth and shook his head at Nunes, the second patrolman, and the assistant manager. The five people were walking in single file along the cornice just over his head, balancing with their arms like boys walking a railroad track. The young man in the lead was whistling softly in his teeth. The patrolman heard the girl behind the first man say: "No fair touching!" in a conversational tone and the other girls giggled. The man who was last in line said: "Tell Hanse I've got my eyes shut." '

Justin's voice had the faintest grim undertone of humor now but nobody laughed.

'Cahill said he realized by this time that they were playing the children's game called follow-the-leader. They appeared to have a remarkable sense of balance and seemed normal in other respects. Then he noticed that a series of mansard windows came out flush to the edge of the cornice all along the roof. As the first young man began to climb around one of these windows Cahill said he averted his gaze again, went inside, and beckoned the others in. He believed at this time that it might be possible to save at least three lives if they acted quickly.

'The two patrolmen and the assistant manager ran to the twenty-ninth floor and scattered to the nearest windows. Nunes opened the door of a lighted room. He observed that the window was open and a man's voice outside said: "All in." Nunes remained in the doorway because he was afraid that he might startle them. A man slid in, said: "Drafty out there," and began to dust off his trousers. "Drafty!" a girl's voice said behind him. "My skirts were up around my neck." The girl behind her said: "It wouldn't be the first time, darling." Nunes, who had recently been married, waited until they were all inside before he came forward, and as he did so the one who seemed to be the odd girl threw her arms around his neck, kissed him, and said: "I knew I'd get the prize." He immediately placed them under arrest for disorderly conduct.'

Some of the boys were chuckling now. Justin shrugged slightly and continued. The newly married Nunes, a dull type, had evidently gone righteous and persuaded the assistant manager to make a complaint. This was good persuading. Dicty hotels don't like to have it known that their guests walk the cornices like banshees after midnight. So the five promenaders were taken to the 17th Precinct station on Fifty-First Street.

The desk sergeant questioned them. The five people—two young married couples and a girl—all had upper East Side addresses. They'd come back from a cruise on the *Roncador* and left the ship soon after she docked. None of them had bothered to go home, apparently. They'd been all over midtown: bars, restaurants, a newsreel theater, one act of a musical, three night clubs, and the

48

Savoy-Plaza. The sergeant's report made it clear that they weren't drunk, but otherwise he was baffled. They were courteous enough. They just didn't seem to care.

The sergeant later informed his superiors that the married couples, legally sorted, had made love—"all the way," as he put it—in the cell block. (The lone girl was off in another cell, practicing her samba steps.) All perfectly proper, except for the sergeant, who must have been peeking. After that they sang *Lazy Mary*:

> *What will you give me if I get up,*
> *If I get up, if I get up?*

The answer was a slice of bread and a cup of tea, or a little maroon canoe for two, or a ride on my big velocipede, or a nice young man with rosy cheeks. Each time they came to the nice young man they got up and danced. This went on for five hours, until the sergeant got tired of the whole thing and sent them to Bellevue for observation.

That was where the break came. A sharp young intern got hold of them and tried everything he could think of. By Tuesday afternoon he'd about decided that this was something new and different. He went to the hospital superintendent.

'From there on out it's Dick Wirth's story,' Justin said. We clapped him and he looked up half sheepishly, his face a little red.

Dick took it from there. I was fond of Dick. He was one of the people you could get hot defending. Niobe and I had had dinner back and forth two or three times with the Wirths. West End Avenue. Good hock and guinea hen once, I remember. Emma was sweet, fussing about him—and about me too. The great gift in a woman: she could make a man feel so valuable. All mother, but no fool. They didn't have any kids, though they'd tried all the hormone things. Hard on Emma.

Dick's family was old New York Jewish. German-Jewish. Not too much money. More arts-and-sciences and social service. His brother was head of the Cass Foundation for Medical Research

49

and his mother had been a famous concert pianist. A little past fifty, and normally a thinnish, medium-sized man, Dick had put on a little nervous fat in the last few weeks. Lost his usual high color. Black hair, thick glasses, very light-brown eyes. Quick-moving. He'd sit silent for long periods with his lips pressed together. When he talked, he talked fast. An administrator who seemed to be a little flustered but was always right on the ball.

'Well, it's as much Hugh Onderdonck's story as mine,' Dick said quickly. 'Hugh checked on what young Galves had found. The intern. All five people showed about the same reaction. No sign of drugs or anything else. Orientation excellent. Better than normal, if anything. Reflexes very good, exceptionally quick and well co-ordinated, like an athlete's at the top of his form. Apparently nothing neuropathic. Unusual brightness of the eyes, some skin color. Temperature up about one degree. Pronounced euphoria. Great sense of well-being. Personality harmony. And no more morals than a tomcat. No responsibility. But no rough stuff either. Very well behaved. Gentle. Too happy to want to hurt anybody. Very nice, in fact. Likable people. Refreshing just to talk to them.'

He took off his glasses and wiped them thoroughly, looking around with his dim brown eyes.

'Is that where you came in, Dick?' Al Elias asked.

'Yes.' Dick nodded. 'Hugh called me when they began to show up in batches of a dozen at the hospitals that same day. Tuesday. The police were picking them up. Minor infractions. Talking to girls on the street. Things like that. We took some blood samples, couldn't find anything bacteriological. But later we did manage to separate something out. Probably a virus. We got it fixed so that it showed a uniform reaction in mice. The human symptoms. Very happy, skittering around, making love and so forth.'

He gestured. I could see all the little white mice running around making love. Fun.

'That's about all we've got so far in the laboratory,' Dick said. 'At the same time we checked what seemed to be the point of entry. The quarantine station at Rosebank had given the Roncador clearance by radio. Free pratique, it's called. Regular thing since 1937. The ship applies for clearance the day before she gets in. The ship's physician must be on the Public Health Service approved list. Healy on the *Roncador* was. He goes over the passengers and crew. If the ship is clean he reports it by radio and she goes right in to her dock.'

'Didn't Healy slip up?' Regan asked.

Hugh Onderdonck shook his head. 'Anyone might have missed it.'

Dick nodded. 'I talked to him later. He felt pretty bad. These people were steady drinkers. The kind of people who like to have a slight edge on all the time. He'd even had a few drinks with them. He said he noticed some change but thought they'd just picked up a little color at sea. No, Healy's a good man. Too bad this had to happen to him.

'We got the *Roncador*'s passenger list. Crew too. Sent district nurses to check them at home. Covered the hotels for out-of-town passengers. Had the police watching the railroad stations, bus terminals, the airport. Some of the people had already left town. We found hundreds of cases, all but two in Manhattan, the others in Auburndale. Only twelve of the passengers and crew we caught had failed to develop it.

'Even if nothing else had happened, those first five people would have done for us. When they went through midtown it was already too late. Like—like trying to catch snow while it's falling. Most people seem to have very little resistance. Never been exposed before, in all probability. Like Eskimos with the common cold. One reason it runs through a crowd so fast. No way of estimating the probable degree of resistance. Titer, we call it.'

He shook his head. 'We investigated the people who'd come back on other ships from Central and South America. The West Indies. The few cases we got seemed to be infections picked up here. We went over the *Roncador* with traps. Caught a few rats, mice, three tarantulas, all kinds of creepies and crawlies. Looking for vectors. Disease transmitters. The Typhoid Marys of the sub-

51

human world. None of them showed any signs of it. But we managed to infect them. Oh yes. Easily. Just about all of them. Interesting sight—the tarantulas in love.' He smiled, tired. 'Two males and a female. Poor girl.'

'Lucky girl,' John said, and we laughed. He looked suddenly at Ellen behind him and put his hand over his mouth. But she was bent demurely over her pad.

'I suppose so.' Dick smiled. His face was drawn. 'Not so lucky for us though. You see what it means? Every rat, mouse, spider, and God knows what else in the city is a potential vector. Besides the human carriers. We've issued a list of health rules. Don't cough or breathe in other people's faces and see that they don't do it to you. Keep warm and dry. Stay at home unless your work requires you to go out. Don't congregate in public places. Drink eight or ten glasses of water a day. The usual things.'

He sighed. Hugh Onderdonck said quietly: 'And you'll find two or three of those—the water and the staying at home—in Defoe's book about the London plague. Two centuries ago. Crookshank said it in 1919, during the influenza epidemic. We can give no more warning of an epidemic now, he said, than a Weather Bureau that couldn't tell it was raining until people began opening umbrellas. That's how far we've got.'

'Isn't it customary to close the schools and colleges? Forbid all public assembly?' Roswell Young asked.

Dick shrugged. 'My understanding is that the schools and colleges are about empty now. Isn't that true, Leslie?'

Wahler, the President of the Board of Education, nodded. 'Substantially. We had about eight per cent pupil attendance yesterday up to senior high.' He took off his glasses slowly.

Brownell felt we ought to close the schools officially and John asked Wirth what he thought.

'It can't do any harm,' Dick said. He glanced at Onderdonck. 'Our point—and I think Hugh will agree—is that we're not going to check it by such methods. We've been using the roughest sort of sampling to get a case-load estimate. The influenza epidemic in 1918—it ran into the next year—showed about 130,000 cases reported. Our estimate this morning was about 900,000.'

Arnie whistled in his teeth. The faces looked shocked.

'I may sound as if I'm treading on somebody else's toes here,' Dick continued. 'I'm really asking for advice. I may be wrong. I'm in favor of closing the schools down now. But where do the kids go then? What about the theaters and concert halls and bowling alleys and the rest? Close them too? What do we gain by closing them if people go to work every day massed in subways and busses? Or just ride around visiting? Do you want to stop the subways too?'

He paused and looked down. 'Here's the real point. Isn't this a problem of public order? This is a mass epidemic of good feeling. Joy. Happiness. Whatever you like. Potentially it's as dangerous as a riot or panic or any other disturbance. We can't keep people at home. They won't stay there, feeling as they do. They feel sociable. And we can't force them. Not unless we ask for troops. That's even more dangerous.' He smiled wanly. 'The troops might get it too.'

'But if we close the theaters and the other places, where will people go? Pack Times Square as they do on New Year's Eve? Crowd into the shopping districts for free merchandise? We can't close all the stores. That's the problem—whether we're going to gain more than we lose by shutting things up.'

He looked around. No one spoke. John said: 'Whew!' softly to himself.

'What about closing the schools, as Dick suggests,' I said, 'and postponing action on the other things?'

We discussed it and it was voted and carried that way.

'One more point,' Wirth said. 'The Health Department laboratory has found out something else about the fever agent. It may be important. The virus can be inactivated by chilling it at thirty-two degrees Fahrenheit or less.'

'The cold kills it?' Arnie said.

'Well—no,' Dick told him. 'It's pretty hard to kill some kinds of viruses. Harder to make them stay killed. Intermittent heat is one method. Tyndallization, it's called. Usually if diseases die out when the weather turns cold—poliomyelitis, for example—it may mean that the vector, the common housefly or whatever, has died off for the winter. This one seems to be something else. The agent itself is sensitive to cold. I won't say that it lacks the power to transmit the disease when it's chilled. We don't know yet. But so far we haven't been able to pass it along at those temperatures. Makes the idea of tropical or semitropical origin a little more likely too, perhaps.'

'So if the weather changes, we've got it licked?' Arnie said. 'It's the warm spell that's doing it?'

'You could say that,' Dick told him. 'It's safer to say that a cold snap would make things a lot more difficult for the bugs.'

John Hickey stirred his massive intellect. 'Why don't we get Justin to round up all these people and pack them into the cold boxes at the morgue?'

He laughed softly to himself.

'What's the matter with meat safes?' Arnie called down to him.

'Isn't that what I said?' Hickey cried.

It was agreed that John should try to make as little as possible of my job publicly, so that I wouldn't be interfered with.

I also asked for a daily summary of the situation from each department. John promised to collect the first batch for me that afternoon and we broke up. I remembered to take Bill's map. On the east flagstaff in front of City Hall, I could see the blue-white-and-orange flag of the city of New York whipping out in the southeast wind.

We jammed up at the door and Ellen squeezed my hand.

'You'll do all right, Mr. Rowan.' She nodded firmly at me.

'Thanks, Ellen. I hope your baby sleeps all night.'

54

5

Onderdonck took my arm as we were moving out and told me that he'd had to transfer the first five cases, the Savoy-Plaza ones, to Kip's Bay Medical Center, a voluntary hospital.

'Some of their people made a row. The old middle-class idea about city hospitals. We chop 'em up for mincemeat.' He sighed. 'Jenkins was mighty glad to get them for that new virus research project of his.'

'Pete Jenkins? I know Pete. Went to school with him. Haven't seen him for a year or so.'

Hickey's outer office was crowded with a solid battalion of reporters, all sober and in their right minds, calling quietly: 'Anything for me, Commissioner?' 'Can you give us a statement, Mr. Hanauer?' 'Any change, Dr. Wirth?' Quiet and a little tense: the voices of bookies and bettors as the horses go to the wire. We moved through them slowly, the other voices replying: 'No comment.' 'Sorry, boys.' 'Hello, Walter. Nope. Nothing.' 'See John Kane.' 'John's the talker.' And the reporters settling around John, his big voice going as he promised to give them a full statement in an hour or so.

I got past without a question—who cared about a City Planning Commissioner?—and found Paravecchio down the street. He was slouched down with the radio going softly, reading *Field and Stream*.

'Hello, Nick. Whitehall Building. What're you doing with that?' I pointed at the magazine.

He shook his head as he pulled out on the light. 'Would you believe I'm nuts about fishin'? All the time. Can't get enough. My old woman she says I spend all my time fishin' instead of in bed.'

He laughed. 'Every day I get off I go out to Seepshead Bay. Maybe Montauk. Maybe Jersey. Over the wrecks. One time I got seventeen flounders.'

I listened with half an ear as we rolled down Broadway. I was looking at Bill's map. Good. An amazing job. Areas of the districts about right—most of them. Good selection of buildings for control stations. We could take a trip with Nick and look them over that night.

The Battery seemed almost crowded with lookers-out-to-sea. I took one of the big old elevators to the thirty-second floor in the tower of the Whitehall Building that faced across the park to the Upper Bay.

The Weather Bureau. Rather like the offices of an old-line shipping firm in the 1890's. Heavy oak furniture. Slant-top chest-high mercantile desks, long tables, and leisurely men in shirt sleeves and gray alpaca jackets. Dull brass instruments. A big glass wall map of the United States, chalked with thin blue whorls, red pointers, and a broad blue saw-toothed band.

The woman at the small ancient switchboard directed me to a quiet sandy-haired man about my own age. Blue oxford shirt and rawhide suspenders. Howard Carson. I told him my name and what I wanted. I worked for the city.

'Do you want to know what the chances are in the next few days, or about how these winter lows work generally? That's what it is. A low.'

Middle Western accent. Kansas, probably.

'Well, both,' I said smiling.

'I think I have just about——'

He reached far up the wall, pulled a sheaf of maps out of one of the long slots in the case, looked at them, and spread them on the table.

He talked steadily and evenly. 'Here we are. I worked these up myself. A winter low in February, 1936. Know anything about it? No. Well, a low is a low-pressure area. Pressure is an expression of weight. Air is denser in a high. Has more weight. High barometer. Less dense, less weight in a low.'

He went on talking. Winds counterclockwise in a low. Having them that way now. About southeast to south-southeast. Both lows and highs usually move from west to east. Go out over the

Atlantic. Both usually move faster in winter than in summer. Sometimes they stick. The one we were having was sticking.

I said I didn't like that and he gave me the tolerant and curious glance technicians reserve for people who intrude with something irrelevantly human.

'See. Here,' he said. The maps looked like heavy parchment. Each day's map had a legend pasted in the lower right-hand corner. The red lines were barometer lines. The pointers indicated wind direction. He showed me the 1936 low, how it centered in the eastern Mississippi Valley, around Chicago. Strong Bermuda high over the ocean. Usually the highs mean clear weather and the lows unsettled.

'You look for high pressure moving in from the West. Here she is. The first sign.' The whorl of a high moving down from the Arctic. The northwest states getting colder. A clockwise wind over the prairies of Montana. It began to creep down across the open center of the continent, patched here and there with a front of snow.

He kept looking up at my face to see if I got it. His pencil sweeping wide arcs above the map. It didn't seem possible that it could be as simple as that. It wasn't, of course. The cold lapping eastward about four hundred miles a day. Fairly slow. As the maps turned I could see it coming, catch the temperature fall in New York, the low bassoons of the wind, the clouds, the sweep of the snow.

He saw me lighting up and was pleased. He didn't know I had even more of a stake in it than he had. I looked out the high windows, under the overhang of the bow roof, while he told me that the situation now didn't promise much change. Nothing stirring. Pretty sure to be two or three days before a new high began to move down.

There was no land in sight under us. Like the view from a clipper's main truck. Governors Island in its eighteenth-century neatness of a fortified place, the Brooklyn shore, the hump of Staten Island in the blue. A quarter of a mile off the Battery, a middle-sized liner was being pushed in circles by three merry tugs, her siren going like a wounded bull.

I told Carson we'd like to bother him for reports a little ahead of time, say twice a day. He said sure, go ahead. As I began to explain, a tall old man in a green eyeshade behind us got up, yawned, muttered: 'I'm sick and tired of this,' and put on his top-coat. His cheeks were pink and he waved behind him as he went out the door, calling something about a boat for Maracaibo.

That seemed to shock the place. Carson murmured that he was the station senior. Forty-one years. They'd given him a dinner last year. Out only three days in the last ten years. He listened earnestly as I told him what the laboratory people had found out about the virus and how the weather might help.

'We'll do what we can for you,' he said. 'Is it going to be bad?'

'Thanks. Pretty bad—Kansas.'

He nodded and smiled. 'That's right. Let's see. Little Egypt country maybe?'

'Pretty close. Southern Indiana,' I said. We shook hands.

Going down in the elevator I thought of how Niobe studied each role with the care of a great criminal lawyer working up a case. Killed herself with detail.

I phoned Eunice. 'Eunice. Look. Call the newspaper circulation departments. Ask them if they've got a new dealer in the last few days. An old woman. In the City Hall Park district. Try the Department of Licenses too. Get the name and address. Yes. Niobe. I'll call you back.'

'Wait. Jim. Congratulations.'

'Oh. That. They elected me clay pigeon. But thanks, woman.'

I went out to Nick and we cruised slowly through the East Side streets just behind City Hall—Frankfort, Spruce, Beekman, Rose—asking the kids in each block if an old woman had moved into the neighborhood lately. Not as many kids around as usual.

We edged into a softball game and they draped themselves all over the cab.

58

A fourteen-year-old looked at me. 'A cop?'

'Do I look like a cop?'

'How do I know what a cop looks like?'

Finally another gang of kids in Vandewater Street, just north of the bridge, remembered an old woman in their block. They argued about it. 'Yeah. Yeah. That's right. A schnorrer. She wouldn' pay my old man the extra cent for a loafa bread. Yeah. When it went up. Whataya wanta see huh for?'

'She's my wife.'

The kids stood in a ragged half-circle, studying me.

'He's crazy,' the leader said calmly, spitting hard.

I grinned and flipped them a quarter. They went diving for it in the street, then came with me to show me the house.

A woman on the first floor said: 'Are you from the police?'

'No.'

Two or three other women came and stood behind her. I couldn't see very well in the hallway. She said: 'There was a woman like that here. She come home this morning and moved out. We thought she got in trouble.'

'Moved where?'

She shrugged. None of them knew. The old woman was carrying a queer kind of hat. What kind? Something like a fireman's hat. What was it made of? Canvas, another woman said. She'd seen them in the movies. A tropical helmet, I thought.

I thanked them and called Eunice from a cigar store. She'd picked up information at three of the papers. Old woman named Amelia Santanini. Address on Vandewater Street. I said never mind and told her what I'd found out. Things were getting worse, Eunice said. Most of the bus lines in the city out. People ranked on Whitestone Bridge, fishing with mile-long lines. Something for Nick. Everybody crowding up into the Empire State tower, where, as natives, they'd always felt it a little improper to go. But it was free now. Wirth had called a conference of public-health people at his office. Three o'clock. I promised to be there.

6 WE HAD twenty minutes. I bought all the afternoon papers, Nick pulled the cab in behind the big Corinthian pile of the Supreme Court Building, and I went through the papers, making notes. They were all pretty scrambled typographically, but the *World-Telegram* looked as if somebody had tried to make duck soup out of the galleys.

The Mayor's resignation all over the front pages. Nothing about the model trains. They hadn't got John's statement yet. Fifth Avenue busses running one to the hour. Mobs of gleeful kids raiding the stores. That was why I hadn't seen them around. Queues of women from the lower East Side and Greenpoint and Hell's Kitchen and San Juan Hill staggering home under Himalayan burdens of free food and liquor. The old joke about the improvident woman: steaks and chops, and not a drop of gin in the house.

People moving to the country in trainloads, of course, and more men leaving their wives than had ever left their wives before in the whole history of marriage. Vice versa too. *The New Yorker*, lone defender of temperance, opened the forms that week, I remember, to get in an editorial intimating that polygyny (or polyandry) might be a little cloying if you weren't used to it, which was true, and a cartoon by Alan Dunn showing a man sitting glumly at dinner with his wife. The legend was: 'I'm sure some people will stay together, Wilfred.'

Gary Cooper, coming in at LaGuardia Field with his wife, had been buried under a pile of what the *Sun* called 'absolutely shameless cooing women.' His wife was right in there, silently trying to haul them off by an arm or a leg. The reporters got a statement out of him. 'They twisted my ankle,' he said. One of the women, who 'appeared reluctant to talk,' said they'd only been trying to hold him down. 'If he hadn't struggled he wouldn't have been hurt,' she said.

Nick drove me over to the white neoclassic Department of

Health Building that faced the little park on Worth Street. Neoclassic without fuss. An effect of vertical fenestration. Getting to be a popular style. I was a little early and found Dick in his office. They were holding the meeting upstairs in the auditorium. He gave me a mimeographed slip: the agenda. A general Advisory Committee for the Department of Health. The usual thing. They'd had one in the polio epidemic of 1916. A tentative list of names—epidemiologists, psychiatrists, psychobiologists, bacteriologists—from Presbyterian-Columbia, New York-Cornell, Kip's Bay, Harvard, Johns Hopkins, and so on. People from the Health Department. Wirth himself, the members of the Board of Health, the two Deputy Commissioners, the Sanitary Engineer, the directors of the Bureau of Laboratories (Dr. William H. Park's old job), District Health Administration, Nursing and Preventable Diseases. There were a half dozen more items on the list.

Dick was anxious. He asked me what I thought. It looked good. Made a clear, well-co-ordinated division of effort. Would they put it through? Yes, he was sure they would. Substantially. Might be a row between the psychiatric crowd and the bacteriologists. I ran into that later in the little set-to between Pete Jenkins and Hutchinson. But nothing serious, Dick thought.

I told him a little about my unit-control-stations plan. Tentative, of course. I wanted to check the reports from departments and take a look around before I proposed it. Bill had picked out three or four of the neighborhood health-center buildings for control stations. They'd make perfect quarters. Would Dick consider turning some of them over to us?

Yes, he said immediately. But not the child-health centers. Bill had marked two of them. Dick was sharp about it. They were his passion. Almost religious. Partly the no-children-of-his-own thing. I said flatly that I wouldn't have asked for any of them and he looked at me with sudden soft gratefulness. We talked about the problem of getting physicians and ambulance units for the stations. He penciled that in on the agenda.

Looking out the window, he said: 'Do you realize we've had no recoveries yet, Jim? Anything can happen. Deaths on a mass scale. We know nothing about it. Aftereffects. People crippled. Mental derangement.'

He turned to me.

'My God! I hadn't thought of it that way.' It sounded naïve. He put his hand on my shoulder. 'Think about it, Jim,' he said. Gentle. The old hurt care for humanity in his eyes.

We went up to the auditorium together and I sat down in the rear. Most of them were already there. About two hundred people. A few women. I recognized only a dozen or so: people from the Health Department and the Department of Hospitals, Pete Jenkins from Kip's Bay, Iago Galdston of the New York Academy of Medicine, Dochez of Presbyterian (the common-cold research man), Libman of Mount Sinai, and Dick's brother Walter from the Cass Foundation.

Pete Jenkins told me about some of the others later. People from the Academy of Medicine, Rockefeller Foundation, Memorial Hospital, the Red Cross, the U. S. Public Health Service office in the Subtreasury Building, New York Hospital-Cornell, Columbia-Presbyterian, New York University College of Medicine, the N. Y. State Health Department and Department of Mental Hygiene, the five county medical societies, and a lot more. Research people and actuaries from the insurance companies.

Things seemed to be rumbling along all right up on the platform, with Dick Wirth as temporary chairman. They voted the Advisory Committee, and then there was a short, crisp exchange over the candidates for the chairmanship of the Committee. But fairly sedate, on the whole. Pete explained later that you couldn't expect fireworks from a lot of public-health people, bacteriologists, and such. Only the GU men managed to keep up a moderate reputation as the playboys of the medical world. The things you learn.

It was rather like watching a ball game when you didn't know who was playing. They elected a thickset brown-haired man in a blue worsted suit. The man next to me, who might have been

Hugh Young for all I knew, told me that the new chairman was a well-known psychobiologist from Cornell. Dr. Alexander Leeson.

Then they began to pick names for the commission. Most of Dick's slate went through. The local people. People from out of town. Gordon, the epidemiologist from Harvard. Hyde, the laboratory specialist in viruses, from Johns Hopkins. Strecker, a psychiatrist who had done some work in crowd psychology, from the University of Pennsylvania. A little window dressing too, but not much. The commission would investigate and make general recommendations.

I was more interested in the real working group, the Co-ordinating Committee. Four subcommittees: on laboratory research, psychiatry, organization of physicians and nurses, and etiology and statistics. Etiology, I found out later, referred to the investigation of causes. Nice words the boys had, though hardly as bad as some of our social-science jawbreakers.

It was a good setup and it passed all standing. The Public Health Service people took over most of the etiology and statistics job. They promised to bring in more workers for it. The Academy of Medicine crowd, with some help from the county societies and the Red Cross, would staff the subcommittee on physicians and nurses. When they got a chairman, Dick talked to him and sent a note down to me promising co-operation with the control stations, if we decided on that.

They settled down to picking members for the various committees. When I saw things were pretty well fixed, I went up and touched Pete Jenkins on the shoulder. His head turned slowly, his gray eyes opened a little wider, and he smiled at me. I nodded toward the door and we tiptoed out.

7

WE SHOOK hands outside.

'What are you doing in there?' Pete asked quietly.

'This is confidential,' I said. 'I'm really running the show.'
We both laughed. We were walking toward the elevators.
'What show?'
'The whole show,' I said. We laughed again and I told him about it. He nodded. I could see he was pleased.

'Always said you'd never amount to anything,' he told me as we got into the elevator. The elevator boy took a quick look at me.

We got off at Dick's floor and I introduced Pete to Hannah Miegs, Wirth's handsome middle-aged secretary.

She took off her glasses. 'Oh, I know Dr. Jenkins. I've had my eye on him for a long time.'

Pete colored faintly. 'We must have been l-looking right at each other, Mrs. Miegs,' Pete said softly. He stuttered a little when he was flustered.

She laughed and made a face at me. 'He's nice, isn't he?' She looked at us in turn. 'Now what do you want?'

I wanted the conference transcript sent to my apartment and we both wanted a look at the district nurses' reports on the fever cases. She got them for us.

They were good. There was an accountant up in Throg's Neck who spent his time tabulating clouds, puppies, sparrows, and babies with one of those clicker things they use to count traffic. For fun. He had it broken down too. He could tell you within a possible error of four per cent how many twin perambulators would pass the corner of East Tremont Avenue and East 177th Street on a sunny afternoon. 17.04.

A glazier in Maspeth, Queens, had been arrested and fined for cutting holes in the windows of women's specialty shops. He was a collector of those little foot-high manikins in tiny girdles and brassières. Cute. The investigator said he showed her into a room lined with nearly four hundred manikins on shelves. He didn't seem to be a fetishist. His wife laughed about it. 'Oh, so long as he's happy,' she said. The nurse was rather sniffy about his taste. She said it appeared to be conventionally masculine. He favored the dolls in black lace lastex panties.

Pete and I smiled at each other. It was funny all right but a little melancholy too. For the first time in God knows how many thousand years, people had the golden apples of the Hesperides in their hands and this was the best they could do. Happiness was a bug that invaded the normal unhappy tissues, and Pete and I, two social-minded animals if you ever saw one, were doing our best to kill it off.

Mrs. Miegs gave us copies of the report breakdown. We looked at them as we went out. Several hundred cases. People who liked their jobs stuck with them. People who didn't cut loose. The proportion was about twenty-eighty. Bad sign for us. Out of two hundred and eight adult males checked, both married and unmarried, one hundred and twenty-four had left home. About two-thirds as many women, most of them married and between the ages of thirty-five and forty-five, had vamoosed. Nearly three hundred people had registered for educational courses or taken up new studies, mainly the arts and aviation.

The job turnover was deceptive. The people who had had no jobs were finding a few now. About a quarter of the people who left their jobs had taken new ones. An architect became an insurance man, a florist opened a gymnasium, and so on. Hope there for us. But everybody seemed to shy away from a good many of the essential jobs.

I introduced Pete to Nick as we got into the cab.

'Glad to meet you, Doc,' Nick said. He opened the panel and twisted his hand over his shoulder. 'Say, Doc, I got a kind of ache right here. All the time.'

Pete shook his head. 'I'm not that kind of doctor, Nick,' he said quietly. 'I'm a crazy people's doctor. You feel all right up here?' He tapped his forehead.

Nick laughed uneasily. 'Me? Oh sure. Sure.' He slid back behind the wheel. In a moment he caught me grinning in the rear-view mirror. 'You're kidding,' he said without turning round.

We smiled at him and he shook his head at himself. I asked him to drive us up the West Side Highway.

'Wait a minute,' Pete murmured. 'I'm due back at the hospital. I thought you might like to come up and see how we do things, Commissioner.'

'We'll get you back, Doctor,' I said. 'I'd like very much to see how you do things. I want to pump you a little first.'

'Another free consultation.' He sighed and lay back as Nick went over to Sixth Avenue. A truck cut him at Canal Street, straight across the light, and Pete and I slid gently down off the polished tan cushion.

We crawled back, looking at the pale windy blue sky through the hatch. Sky of crocuses, of anemones, of marble games and girls in new dresses. Incredibly warm for February. All of seventy degrees.

Then we were pouring along the elevated highway uptown, the shapes of the city revolving past us on the right in close-order drill against the tender sky: the near ones wheeling back, the far ones advancing. The North River showed deep ultramarine in the flurries and the smoke blew low over the dark towns along the cut of the Palisades. For a moment it was the Wabash, full in spring between the sycamores, and a young red-haired girl on the bluff with her dresses blowing. I didn't want to play any more. I wanted her back.

Pete lay relaxed with his eyes closed and the wind from the open hatch on his face. Just about the most relaxed man I'd ever known. But a little indrawn too, with the puritan tension of making himself toe the line. He seemed smaller than he was. An inch under six feet, and one hundred and sixty pounds. A general effect of quiet paleness: the very clean white skin, straight rather coarse light-brown hair neatly clipped, and light-gray eyes.

Not a formidable man, you'd say, and it would be true so far as ill will went and probably not true about the rest. He could tumble like a bear cub, he was the poor man's Davy Crockett with a small-bore rifle, and at one time he had licked me regularly and disgracefully at badminton, tennis, pingpong, and chess. Muscle and mind.

That was at Harvard, between 1929, sainted year, and 1931. Pete

66

was a couple of years younger than I was, just entering medical school. His name wasn't really Pete. It was Seneca B. (for Bowman) Jenkins and he came from Cattaraugus County, New York, by way of Colgate.

I'd gone to Cambridge for my doctor's degree in sociology. At Indiana University I'd started out by wanting to be a writer (when I wasn't playing clarinet), but Professor John R. Commons' sociology tradition was still powerful at Bloomington in the early twenties and I'd got religion in my senior year.

Before that I'd been perfectly willing to let the world go to hell in its own way. Willing, even, to hop aboard for the first lap. Might be sport, as we phrased it then. I remember an instructor who was young enough to understand us deploring the fact that we didn't take seriousness seriously. I don't know about that. I know I wanted some means of looking at human society that would make sense to me (a small order), and the new sociological techniques seemed to promise the lenses I needed. In any case, they were almost sure to finish off the old idea of sociology as a set of speculative notions intended to confirm the vested interests of the current ethics. I didn't want any part of the current ethics. We were out for a whole new deck.

At the end of my sabbatical year in jazz, the feeling was still strong enough to send me on to the University of Chicago, where I took an M.S. under Harry A. Millis, Commons' former pupil. I didn't give up the clarinet. My old Selmer put me through school, in fact, though my father helped when he could. Club dates around Boston and the North Shore. College dates. The Cape one summer. A few solid weeks now and again with a pickup band. Jimmy Rowan and His Famous Five.

Pete opened his eyes. 'What did you want to pump me about?'

I said: 'I wanted your professional opinion about our prospects. All of it.'

He straightened up and looked at me. 'All of it? I think our prospects are beautiful. We've spent a lot of time training for a job like this and now we have it dumped right in our laps. My part isn't official. But I've got the chance to work on it. The equipment too. Is that what you wanted to know?'

'Go on.'

He leaned back again, closed his eyes, and murmured: 'Don't get your back up. I'm not going romantic. But—I feel like—like one of the Elizabethan navigators. We've got ships and money and crews. Each time we make a voyage we raise new lands, new islands. When we get back we talk to the others. They've found new lands too. We see it. We see it beginning to piece together. It isn't just that we're finding things either. The things we find are making a new kind of people out of us. Very few people know about it yet. Other people don't understand it. In a year, two years, a dozen years, someone will sail all the way around the world.'

His voice didn't change. It was quiet and matter-of-fact. He'd never talked that way even in school. A queer sort of bacteriologist: the extensive imagination as well as the intensive.

'Not romantic?'

'No,' he said easily. 'Not romantic. The things that are happening in experimental science—— They may be more important than anything we've had since Leeuwenhoek and the great vintage years of discovery in the 1840's.'

We'd come out on the broad river esplanade of the Henry Hudson Parkway. The roadways looked very white in the sun. People were walking. The apartments built up into an artificial cliff and the bridge ahead looked like a soft aluminum cutout.

'This is what's happening,' Pete said. 'The physicists have new energy sources. Uranium. They put manganese or sodium into a cyclotron, kick it with a few million volts, and part of it comes out radioactive. They hand this over to the physicians. In lots of places it can be used instead of radium or X rays. They've taken a field of negative electric particles, shunted it through a magnetic channel, and found that it makes a much better microscope than glass or quartz. The electron microscope. I'll show it to you.'

He looked at me.

68

'An industrial chemist working with proteins, a plant virus man, a geneticist fiddling with his genes——'

We grinned at each other.

'—a hormones-and-enzymes man, an investigator studying vitamins, a biochemist experimenting with amino acids, a cancer research man, an atomic physicist—all these boys are beginning to meet each other coming around the same corner. A psychobiologist horns in and picks up some ideas about enzymes he can use. A pediatrician finds that certain vitamins help to make little boys behave. A public-health official—— See what all this adds up to?'

I thought I did. 'You mean it's getting to be more than just random swapping? The experimental sciences are really beginning to mingle, to run together? A virus and a protein and an enzyme and—oh, a synthetic chemical, I suppose—may all be the same thing. All right. So it's just a difference in terminology and approach?'

Pete shook his head. 'Uh-uh. More than that. For one thing, if we can bring a dozen techniques to bear on a single problem, we've got that much more chance to figure it out and lick it, haven't we? And if we can once mark off, oh, a fixed working relationship between all these techniques, so that they'll reinforce each other without getting in each other's way, we may have something new. When you change the relationships of things, you change them. The least we'll get is a choice of weapons. The best, probably, might be what amounts to a master science in this particular field.'

'Yes, and when you've got it all centralized you'll find it's too big to be workable. You'll have to break it down again into smaller units. Maybe a new kind of unit. Ever notice that law of organization?'

Pete nodded. I could see the tips of his clean well-shaped ears over the turned-up collar of the navy topcoat. He worked his glove off and shook a cigarette loose for me.

'But hell,' he said gently, bending close to my match in the wind, 'the point for us is that we haven't got much of that yet.

The tools, yes. But not the organization. We're just beginning to put things together. This—this little goon you've handed us makes a beautiful test case.'

'Now you're getting hot, Doctor. Pray proceed.'

'You know what they gave me over there? Two isolation pavilions and all the equipment on one of the main laboratory floors. They even fenced it in for me. My God, I'm walking in clover. Dick Wirth's brother got the Cass people to put up half the money. One of the Board of Governors of the hospital chipped in with the rest. Three years of it, if we're careful. Officially it's called the Cass-Jordan Laboratory for the Investigation of Virus Diseases. We've been open for business two months now and I can hardly believe it yet. I didn't do anything to rate the job. They——'

'Your modesty ill becomes you, Jenkins,' I said. 'Talk.'

He laughed. 'We were feeling our way into two or three things —equine encephalitis was one—but we hadn't found what we wanted. Then this thing came along and we decided to do a full-dress job on it. We've had cases since the second day, long before Onderdonck sent his mountain climbers over to us. Nice of him.'

'Wasn't it?'

'Yes. A fine barrel of monkeys. I've been thinking of keeping the nurses locked up. The earlier cases were something too. You know we took quite a lot of blood for tests and when the assistant came round the third time one of the boys, a truck driver from over around St. Gabriel's Park, said: "Listen, chief. Uh, don't these regular blood donors get paid?" '

I laughed. 'How did you begin on the thing? Where did you start?'

'Simple. Needle in the haystack. We test every straw to make sure it isn't the needle. Finally we know the needle *is* a needle because we've made sure that all the other things are straw.'

'Because it ain't hay?'

'Yep. Because it ain't hay.'

We were passing under the George Washington Bridge approaches. Girls in shorts playing tennis along the river, and the

rigging of the bridge overhead like the stays and shrouds and hal-
yards of some inconceivable ship. Nick looked around but I nodded to him to keep going.

'What did you try for first?'

'Oh, we had lots of possibilities. Do you want to hear all this?
The thing looked brand-new but of course we know such things
aren't—very often. All kinds of choices. The probable tropical or
semitropical origin made it even broader. Drugs. Stimulants. Vitamin deficiency or perhaps even too big a dose of some vitamin.
Mass psychoneurosis. Protozoa or bacteria. Viruses. Some new
strain, or a variant strain, or a combination. Perhaps one of the
encephalitides. The Economo type or the St. Louis or the Russian
forest-spring strain. Or some synergetic action.'

'Dick Wirth told me they went through the drugs.'

'We did too,' Pete said. 'We were lucky enough to get Myers.
Good drug man. Trained under Vaughan at the University of
Michigan. He tried for all the usual things first. Opium derivatives.
Ether. Caffeine. Marijuana. Benzedrine. Nyopo.'

'Wups. Never heard of it.'

'Something the South American Indians take. It's a powerful
mental and muscular excitant. Made from acacia pods.'

'No soap?'

'Not a sign of it. Then amphetamine sulfate. We use it in the
treatment of narcolepsy. Pervitin is pretty close to it. Staves off
fatigue, keeps the energy level up. Alles at the California Institute
of Technology developed it. Then demerol. Synthetic drug. It's
actually an anesthetic, but it gives you a wonderful feeling even if
you take it without the pain factor. We tried peyotl too. That's
interesting.'

'The stuff the Indians take?'

'Well, not all. Mostly the Plains Indians. It's very old. Used in
Mexico for several hundred years. A cactus button. They eat it, or
drink an infusion. Peyotl soup, as it were. It's a sort of religious
cult. Father Peyotl. Had me guessing for a while. The personality
effect seems to be almost the same as what we're getting in the

fever. Nine separate alkaloids in it. Some act like strychnine. You get exhilaration first and later a feeling of dreamy well-being. No desire to sleep. That's damned close to the fever. I was startled by one account. A man who'd taken it experimentally said he had a feeling of universal brotherhood. Said he felt as if the millennium had come. Some of the higher types who get the fever talk just like that.'

We looked at each other.

'Suppose those people on the Roncador did bring back a supply of it?'

'No. We thought of that,' Pete said, 'but Myers found the joker. Two or three jokers. And didn't find the drug. One joker is that alcohol and peyotl are like cats and dogs. Just won't work together. But those Roncador people and some of the others were three-bottle men. Peyotl dulls the orientation and these fever people are sharp as tacks. Another thing is that peyotl isn't for amateurs. You'd almost have to go in training before you could tolerate it.'

We were coming up to Dyckman Street. 'Are you trying to abduct me, Commissioner?' he said. 'Let's get back to the hospital. I'll show you around.'

I laughed and spoke to Nick. He cut east around the shoulder of Fort Tryon Park, made a U turn, and we started downtown again.

'See how obliging we are?' I said. 'But I'm still pumping you. Go on.'

'Well, vitamin deficiency in drinkers. You know about that. Not enough of the right foods. Perhaps a lowered vitamin intake in the population generally. New York in February. Or some new method of food processing that might be taking an essential substance out of the diet. But most of the people seemed to be in pretty good shape. A tremendous overdose of thiamin might just possibly act like the fever. We saw no signs of that. My friend Rowland Hutchinson—he's assistant to the head of the psychiatry department—is trying like hell to make out it's mass psychoneurosis.

'Meanwhile, of course, we'd been making routine laboratory

tests. Urine. Feces. Sputum. Blood. Stomach juices. Slides. Metabolism. Most of this seemed pretty close to normal, except where the histories indicated previous irregularities. Hutchinson, by the way, found some psychoneurotic indications in about twenty per cent of the cases and a few more in the family histories. Actually that may not be much higher than the incidence in the general population. He's still trying.

'So there we were. Unless we'd missed something, we were down to one good possibility. A virus.'

'Yep,' I said. 'Dick Wirth has one too.'

'I'll bet,' Pete said grimly. 'We'll have to hump just to stay even with him. That Department of Health laboratory is full of beans.'

I hesitated. 'Professional courtesy?' I said smiling.

He glanced at me, punched me lightly in the ribs. 'Wait a minute, mister.'

I had him rattled.

Pete said: 'Wirth is a b-bacteriologist himself. You know that. He's a damn good organizer too. I've gone and looked at what he's doing. S-some of the things he's pulled off down there are just as important as old William Hallock Park's work and he's had—what? —less than eight years of it.

'Park was an international figure. People like Ehrlich, Wassermann, Koch used to go down to Park's old place on East Sixteenth Street and trudge around just listening. Now everything's taken for granted. We're bastards if we can't shut off an epidemic in three days. It's our f-fault anyhow, isn't it? Will you believe me if I tell you that the child-health job Wirth is doing can't be *touched* anywhere else? It's a whole new departure in preventive medicine. We know it, even if the public doesn't.'

'All right. Make like I didn't say anything. I have a rough idea how good Dick is.' I laughed. 'How is it you boys never say an unkind word about another member of the order?'

Pete smiled slowly. 'Want us to gossip?'

We looked up as a car came off the Drive above and started down across the grass. A woman pushing a baby carriage reared back. A small boy, alert, jumped behind an elm and stood holding it as if it were a basketball. The car grazed an empty bench and jounced across a path. It was coming straight at us. Nick stamped on the throttle and as we drilled ahead the car hit the cement roadway turning on two wheels, righted, and came up fast behind us. We could hear Nick mumbling as it passed. The driver smiled. He looked very happy.

'How's his orientation, Doctor?'

'He must have complications,' Pete said.

8

I CALLED Eunice again on the way to the hospital. 'Eunice, my darling.'

'Who's—oh. I'm not your darling.' She sounded almost sad. 'For a hundred and seventy dollars a month I should be your darling too?'

'Okeh. Get me Bill then. Wait. Did the Mayor's office send those department reports over? Will you bring them uptown to me tonight? Good. Thank you.'

Bill said: 'We've got a corrected map just about finished. Better spotting for about a dozen stations.'

'You're amazing,' I said. 'And you did it without even asking Daddy. I just thought we ought to check the buildings. Yes. This afternoon. We can take a look around ourselves tonight. Might make out a list of about ten points. Type of buildings. Water and toilets. Elevators, or not too high up without them. Room for a hundred beds or so. Aerials. Good garage or parking lot near by. We might close off a side street for parking if the rest is okeh. Oh. Any alternative buildings you can find.'

'I'll do that,' Bill said.

'How about people? Say five or six. From the research division. Hollander. O'Boyle. Larsen? And Clutes. Who? Yes. Good. Will you try to get the reports before you come uptown? They'll have to hop. My fault. I should have thought of it earlier.'

'It shall be done, master.'

'Master, hell. Oh. I got a tentative promise at the doctors' meeting that they'd co-operate. Yep. Worked out all right. I'm on my way to Kip's Bay with Pete Jenkins. Call you later.'

I went out singing: 'I'm on my way to Kip's Bay, master,' very softly, but Pete blocked the cab opening with his foot.

'Are you sure you haven't got it?'

'Yes, master.'

Nick went through a cross street, pulled into First Avenue, and the vast fan of Kip's Bay Medical Center opened out a block to the north. A site along the river about two blocks square, some of it made land, skirted by the East River Drive. I'd never had a good look at it. It stopped me dead, not because it was bluntly powerful, but because it was so good.

It composed. You got the whole thing in one look. As if you could go all around it and watch it fall into proportion at every angle like a good statue.

Some of the things I noticed myself. Mason Emery had taught me what to look for. Pete explained some of the other things.

Tough problem for an architect. A hospital that big was really a specialized city. From the air, Kip's Bay would look like the head of an aster flower chopped in half. Eight petals, the pavilion wings, rayed out to the east, south, and west. Lots of space between them. In the New York area, that was the best disposal for taking advantage of the sun and the prevailing southwest breeze in summer.

The cut half of the flower disk, rather elongated, was the central building. Reception rooms, elevator banks, administrative and service units. Facing north, it blocked off the winter winds from all but the two end pavilions. That saved fuel. The powerhouse and incinerators were down on the riverbank, beyond the drive, where the west winds could carry off the smoke. Practical enough, though it begged the question architecturally.

We cruised slowly up to it with our heads up through the hatch.

75

Exciting, the movement of the wheeling wings. They'd take the southerly winds like the blades of a turbine. They seemed to fold into each other.

The whole building was twenty stories. It looked much higher. The ends of the wings rounded off in stacks of sunrooms instead of angle piers and the broad health-glass windows along the sides made one vertical sweep upward to the rather narrow plain well-proportioned cement roof course. No breaks but the silvery metal window frames set out a little from the wall.

What you got was a *whole* effect. You saw it mainly in the solution of the old problem: how much window to wall? A lot, here. The piers between windows, about a fourth as wide, caught just the right note of graceful strength without making the place look like a lithographing plant. The piers were faced with glazed brick in a light clear soft green, the color of water in a swimming pool. Pete said they'd found this color had a soothing effect. Standard practice in operating rooms. The architects had decided to try it outside, set off by light, dull but warm burnt-orange Venetian blinds.

I blocked off part of the building with my hand. The vertical effect on any one pier, seen alone, struck you as being a little too much. But the whole thing, with the form repeated in series and the main flange to back it, had a kind of vertical-horizontal tension, like the stresses in a bridge, that pulled everything together.

I shook my head. 'I'll see what I can do about getting a city to match it.'

Pete smiled suddenly. 'That's what you do feel, isn't it? But this is a pretty good city too.'

'This is a pretty good city,' I said.

Nick swooped down the ramp and dropped us at a side entrance. From there on it was Pete's party. I put the questions and did what I could to keep up.

He led me through a corridor lined with glass brick. The floor was like glare ice. We got off the elevator at the sixth floor in the main building and I noticed a big red star set in underfoot.

'Subversive?'

'No, east,' Pete explained. 'Red and blue stars east. Yellow and green west. Like Daniel Boone's blazes.'

He showed me how the whole east end had been partitioned off for his project, leaving a corridor to I-6 and J-6 pavilions. Some of the regular laboratories. Then he unlocked a green steel door and we were in his office. White walls hung with neatly framed pen-and-wash medical drawings. Slices of tissue, a lovely—as they said—sarcoma, wandering cells, bacteria in fission. Each neatly signed *H. Detrand* and the date. Usually literal stuff, a simplified makeshift for color photography. This was different. This artist was a little master of line and Felicien Rops color. I knew damn well I wasn't being precious. Often a layman couldn't tell, really. All medical drawings were disconcerting. But I felt something there, as if Detrand were trying to reveal an equal and delicate terror in all the visible forms of the world.

'My God, they're wonderful. You're a man of taste, Jenkins.'

Pete sat down at a bare glass-top desk with a row of filing cases behind him. He looked pleased. 'I thought you'd like them. Henri is good, isn't he? I know him. A little neurasthenic. It shows.'

'Yes. I felt something like that.'

He got up and brought a chair over for me, then sat down again.

'I want to give you some background on this virus business before we look around. What did you get from Dick Wirth?'

'Well, nothing much, except that they'd looked for drugs or bacteria and found a virus.' I told him how it was affected by low temperatures.

'That's interesting,' he said and made a note. 'Anything else?'

'Oh. In Dick's office, before we went up to the meeting. He got very serious. Said we'd had no recoveries yet and anything could happen. People crippled or going off their heads. Even mass deaths.'

Pete sat looking straight ahead. 'That's good, Jim. The same idea we have. That's why we're trying so hard. You know this thing may well be one of the encephalitis mutations. We can't keep track of them. Again, if the hypothalamus—— Well, we'll get to that later.'

'It might be serious, Pete?'

He said evenly: 'It might be—a disaster.'

I sat there feeling suddenly sick, thinking of Niobe.

'Well, let's try to give you an orientation first,' he said. 'I'll talk fast. If there's anything you can't quite fathom, sing out.

'When I told you we had only one good bet left, I didn't mean there weren't still other possibilities. It might be etiologically tropical or semitropical. It looked like something new. It affected large groups of people, and the behavior patterns it induced had serious effects on—what?—social organization. Or rather, they were just plain socially disorganizing.'

I could feel, rather than hear, dull humming sounds, motors probably, beyond the partition. The walls were acoustically soft, planned to deaden sound. Something Aalto had pioneered in the big hospital at Helsinki.

'So we had a variety of approaches,' Pete said. 'Tropical etiology. Epidemiology. Bacteriology. Social psychology. Half a dozen other things. Some people have tried to set the term *romantic diseases* for the tropical diseases, though God knows most of them aren't what that sounds like.'

'It might fit this one.'

'We'll see,' Pete said grimly. 'But I can give you some idea of the complications if I tell you that tropical medicine alone involves, oh, helminthology—parasitic worms—entomology, protozoology— many of the tropical agents are Protozoa or Metazoa, single- or many-celled organisms—pathology, mycology, pharmacology, bacteriology, and a few others. Besides the psychology and epidemiology in a case like this.'

Someone phoned him and he said: 'Yes. About twenty minutes.'

He got up and walked around in front of the desk.

'Our main approach here, of course, is bacteriological. But we have to take all the other things into account. I was lucky enough to be able to round up a pretty good part-time staff—from the hospital and outside. Our tropical man is from the Rockefeller Foundation. Then Hutchinson for psychiatry. A psychobiologist—psychosomatologist. I've never really been able to figure out the difference. A pathologist. A brain specialist. A toxicologist—his job is pretty well done now. A pharmacologist. An immunologist. He's on our regular staff. A physicist, who also works full-time for us, and his assistant. They handle the machines. An endocrinologist. Biochemists, of course. A stereochemist—one of the boys who figure out how atoms and molecules hook up in space. A histologist. That's a cell-and-tissue man. Let's see. That's about all, except for the regular staff. Are you getting all this?'

'Following right along, Doctor.'

'Okeh.' He was doodling on a scratch pad. 'This is emergency stuff. We're trying to carry on all these experiments more or less simultaneously, and at the same time apply what we get to the patients under treatment. Actually, we're set up as a research laboratory but operating as a clinical research laboratory. Know the difference?'

'Well, a clinical laboratory, I suppose, is trying to get results directly for the patients, and the research thing works on——'

'Problems. Set problems. That's about it.' He was beginning to warm up. 'A combination like that is almost standard in the better hospitals and medical schools, though it generally works the other way round. Clinical and research. Perhaps some teaching too. Barker at Hopkins, for example, was one of the pioneers in that kind of laboratory organization.

'When we set up shop we were smart enough to put in a bid for two pavilions, K-6 and L-6, with twenty-four beds each. Actually I wanted to test out a fairly new routine here—or new in this form. I wanted to get a group of patients under control conditions and work all the way around the circle: from patient to clinical to research and back to the patient. That is, if we found something, some immune serum or chemical substance that might work. Or somebody else found it. In that case, we could take it at any stage

79

of research and carry it through. Of course that wouldn't be very practicable in the whole field of bacteriology now. But if we picked out one thing at a time—St. Louis encephalitis, say, or the Australian X disease—in such a relatively unexplored corner as the viruses——'

'Yes. That's what you meant by being lucky. But wait. How did you know it'd turn out to be a virus?'

Pete shrugged. 'We didn't know. We made preliminary tests for bacteria and nothing showed. It was a good prospect.'

'Oh. And about the patients you've got. Isn't that what the layman calls experimenting with patients?'

He grinned. 'Ask me that again when you've seen our laboratory animals. No, the routine is the same as in ordinary research. More direct, that's all. Oh, I mentioned control conditions. This is all an isolation unit—laboratory, pavilions, everything. There's another door over there that leads to a general delivery room—not for babies—and the nutritional service pantry. The boys leave all supplies there. Food comes up on electrically heated trucks and the nurses bring it in. No outsiders get into the laboratory or pavilions. The staff eats inside in the nurses' conference room. That reminds me.'

He dialed the phone, said: 'Will you ask Miss Felton to come in in about ten minutes? Yes.'

He sat back again. 'So you can see my job is mainly organization. Most of the specialists have one or two or more people working under them. Subprojects. I keep these subprojects from stepping on each other's toes and try to crossbreed them. Keep the histologist's boys up to date on what the physicist has found out about cell charges. Meantime I work through assistants on the main bacteriological investigation—and take care of the patients, of course.'

'I knew you'd never amount to anything,' I said.

He grinned. 'Now we'll get down to cases. A little something on the virus before we take a look. I might as well tell you that what we know about viruses and related subjects at the moment is one hell of a mess. And it's coming in so fast, with the new laboratory methods, that we have to up the ante with a fresh hypothesis every day or so just to keep up. I'm not complaining. I love it.'

He rubbed the back of his head. 'Even when we'd excluded the bacteria and found a virus—or what we thought was a virus—that looked like the villain, we still had a long way to go. First, we attacked it empirically. As if we didn't give a hoot *what* it was so long as we could identify it as the causative agent and find something to fight it. We're still doing that, of course. But it was important for us to find out what it is, too. It might be a variant strain of something we knew about. Some special clinical treatment might be indicated. It might be the sort of thing that yielded to metal-salt therapy or the hydrocupreine derivatives.

'So, after the bacteria, we went on a still hunt through the rickettsial diseases. Named for Howard Taylor Ricketts, who managed to transmit Rocky Mountain spotted fever. About 1906 or '07. We haven't got a good definition of the rickettsials even yet. The agents are called Rickettsiae. Very small micro-organisms. Grain negative. Rather like bacteria in some ways. There's the typhus group, and the spotted fevers, and the tsutsugamushi diseases. Tsutsugamushi is passed along by mites, so we could pretty well rule that out. The others were only faint possibilities too. But they were all originally classed as viruses, mainly because they could be grown only in living cells.

'So—we had the viruses.'

'What *is* a virus?' I said. 'You haven't told me that yet.'

He smiled slowly. 'Now you've got me. We don't know.'

I raised my eyebrows. 'Don't know, Doctor?'

He shook his head. 'Not what you'd call knowing. Of course we have theories. Dozens. Hundreds of them. Some very ingenious too. One of the most ingenious is that a virus is a very seedy organism that's gone down in the world, so far down that it's had to pawn not only its watch and overcoat but practically everything —skin, bones, liver, lights, respiration, even the ability to reproduce itself.'

81

'Touching.'

'Not this little goon,' Pete said sternly. 'Like a worm with nothing left but his teeth. He's got to find an apple—a living cell, in other words. Not just any apple. Not a Baldwin, or a Delicious——'

'Or a Rome Beauty,' I said, grinning. We were both farm boys. 'Or a Winesap, or a greening——'

'Well, he has a cousin who likes greenings,' Pete said. 'Used to myself. Nice and pearish. But this fellow can't use anything but a—a McIntosh Red. So he finds a McIntosh Red, chaws his way inside, and something very funny happens. He eats away and after a while he seems to get his faculties back. He's almost a whole worm again. He can even reproduce himself. And does. Very freely. But the apple begins to rot.'

'That's a hell of a story,' I said with false admiration. 'Why don't you write a play about it?'

Pete looked at his wrist watch. It had a sweep second hand.

'Your education is going to be very rapid, Commissioner,' he said. 'Sit tight. Viruses used to be called filterable viruses because, oddly enough, they weren't filterable. Couldn't be strained out. They ran right through the smallest pores in the filters we had. The Berkefeld W candles. Made from diatomaceous earth. The Mandler candles. The Chamberland-Pasteur candles. Kaolin-quartz. Fine white porcelain clay.

'So the first notion we got was one of size. Smaller than just about everything we'd tried to handle before that. Real peewees. Measured in millimicrons. A millionth of a millimeter.'

He took some round photographs out of a desk drawer and shoved them over to me. Barnard's early ultraviolet-light photographs of viruses. The one that showed foot-and-mouth virus looked like tiny nodules of rather coarse pepper sprinkled on something that appeared to be spaghetti in a fog. Magnification x 3200. Quartz lenses. The ones taken with a dark field looked like odd corners of the Milky Way. Then Pete slipped a few bigger ones off the bottom, and the viruses were relatively huge. His physicist had taken these. Electron-microscope photography. Magnification x 100,000. He held one out, looked closely at it, and passed it to me.

'There's your villain.'

'The fever?'

He nodded. I studied it. Nothing there about power plants going out, people leaving their jobs, and Niobe on the loose. The pattern reminded me of something. A photograph I'd seen once of buckshot a couple of hundred feet from the gun, beginning to splay out a little. Faintly silvery here and there. I was disappointed.

'Wonderful photograph.'

'Yes. The man's good. So there's one main point about viruses. Size. Though of course some bacteria are larger than some viruses. The next point is that they can operate only in living cells. Symbiosis. Antipathetic symbiosis, it's called. They don't just eat up the cells, as most bacteria do. They move right in like the worm in the apple and huddle up inside, causing certain distinctive intracellular changes.

'Those things we're fairly sure of: the size and the guest that eats you out of house and home. They still don't give us a good basic definition. I mentioned one, the idea that a virus may be an organism so degenerate that it has nothing left but an appetite. It's true that most viruses don't seem to be able to breathe or reproduce alone. People have suggested that the bacteriophage may be a virus that gets chummy with bacteria. In a deadly way. Or that the virus may be an autocatalytic protein or nucleoprotein.

'Stanley calls it a conjugated protein—meaning *fused*. Or it may be a sort of maverick gene. Sometimes a virus causes cells to multiply instead of breaking them down. So it does act as a toxin or a stimulant. It may even be something that comes out of the chromosomes in the cell nucleus, with a little priming from the virus itself. Had enough?'

'I'm reeling, Doctor.'

'Just a few more. Gordon, up at Harvard, suggests that we call them "obligate intracellular parasites." That's pretty good. Rivers, one of the best early investigators, seems to think they may be not one but a number of things. The very small ones may be inanimate "incitants of disease," as he says. We'll come back to that later. The middle-sized ones, such as the yellow-fever agent, may be primitive life forms. The larger ones—vaccinia, for example—may be full-blown micromicrobes. Autonomous organisms, like bacteria. Large calls the viruses molecrobes. There's an old biological word that might do too. Commensals.'

'I think I like your word goon best.'

'I do myself,' Pete said. 'Now one more point. These goons attack plant cells too. There's a kind of virus called tobacco mosaic. Makes cloudy patterns on tobacco leaves, usually. Two Americans, Vinson and Petrie, found that they could make this behave more or less like a chemical. That was pretty odd in itself.

'Then a worker named Stanley, over at Rockefeller Institute in Princeton, decided to have a crack at it. About 1935. He used mostly the standard biochemical tricks for salting out enzymes. Ground infected tobacco leaves in a mortar, then leached the liquid through diatomaceous earth. He got something that looked like Coca-Cola without the bubbles. Then he changed the pH— pH is an expression of acidity. Or alkalinity. He increased acidity in this case. The liquid turned cloudy and got nice and shimmery on top, like saffron on Swedish soup. The shimmer was the virus.

'Then he treated it with ammonium sulphate, did a few other things to it, and got a pure heavy protein crystal. Not quite, though. What we call a paracrystal. Like tiny slivers of broken glass instead of a cube.'

'Was that wonderful?' I said. It sounded like a good trick, but too complicated to have much audience appeal.

'Marvelous,' Pete said. 'The first time what appeared to be living material had been turned into what looked like a pure chemical. Oh. Miss Felton.'

I got up slowly for the smiling neat brown-haired nurse in the fluted muslin cap. Fortyish, cheerful, and bright.

'This is Mr. Rowan,' Pete said. 'Miss Felton. One of our n-nicest people. Miss Felton, can you spare a few minutes to help us get scrubbed up? I'd like to show Mr. Rowan what we're doing.'

'Yes, of course,' Miss Felton said. 'The prairie dogs too, Dr. Jenkins?'

They laughed.

'That's an office joke,' Pete said. 'Some of the other animals like to run around and show off. Especially show off. They have other interests. But with the prairie dogs it's love and love alone, as the Calypsos used to sing it. Leave your clothes here. You won't need to take off your shirt. Just roll up the sleeves.'

Miss Felton led us to a small room lined with half a dozen washbasins. The taps had spatula-shaped stainless-steel handles, to be worked with the elbows.

She ran hot water for us, said: 'Hold out your hands' to me, and laughed at the face I made as she poured them half full of cornmeal.

I looked at Pete. 'I thought you said Miss Felton was a nice girl?'

'She is,' Pete said calmly. He was getting it too. 'First we'll wash with cornmeal, soap, and hot water for one minute. This isn't going to be quite as bad as what a surgeon does when he scrubs up for an operation. But we have to be pretty careful. We're an isolation section in here. Then too, when you're fooling with viruses, you've got to watch out for cross-infections. We have the devil's own time getting them pure in the first place and we don't like to complicate things.'

I splashed right along with him, and rinsed and shook, rinsed and shook. Miss Felton handed us orange sticks and while we were working on that she ran fresh hot water.

'Now green soap,' Pete said, 'to one inch above the elbow. An extra inch for luck. Brush it right in. Like this. Three minutes. I'll keep talking while we work. Where did we leave off? Stanley's experiment. The protein crystals. They were tested in all kinds of ways, including the very delicate precipitin and anaphylactic reactions. It seemed clear that the virus wasn't simply a part of the protein crystals. It was the protein—or seemed to be. Anything that would destroy the protein destroyed it. The crystals behaved exactly like pure proteins. So far as anyone could find out they were simply chemicals. Nothing else.'

'Couldn't you call them dead?' I objected. 'After they'd been through all those wringers?'

'We'd reached a point where dead-or-alive didn't seem to apply. That's the extraordinary part. This pure protein material was rubbed on tobacco leaves. It infected them just as fresh tobacco-mosaic virus would. They showed the characteristic lesions. Very high infectivity, in fact, suggesting strong concentration. So you had what was by all odds a pure chemical acting like an organism. Invading tissues. Reproducing itself.'

I sighed. 'I didn't know they played that animal-or-mineral game any more.'

'It may bother you a little,' Pete said ruefully, 'but think what it does to us. Let's concede that these tests aren't final, that they're much too limited in scope so far to justify changing our basic definitions. Too, we haven't managed to crystallize any so-called animal viruses. Only plant viruses. Even so, we've got to face the possibility that we may have to change our tune in the next few years.'

My arms were red with the scrubbing. Miss Felton led me to another receptacle. 'Now put your hands in this.' It felt nice and cool, and smelled like alcohol.

'Five minutes in this and we'll be clear,' Pete said. 'Alcohol and Merthiolate, in a dilution of 1:1000. Merthiolate is a mercury-sulphur combination. We've found it works very well. Other people use Lysol or chlorine. Yep. We've known something about viruses for a long time. Even in the sixteenth century, Fracastorius made a good guess at them. Jenner actually did something about smallpox, of course, in the old-fashioned empirical way. Beijeriuck was an important early pioneer. Pasteur, too, had an idea there must be a few things we weren't catching with the microscope.

'By the way, if any more of these viruses turn out to be what we've been classifying as chemicals, it's going to hit Pasteur harder than most people. He usually gets the credit for establishing one of our most trustworthy little rules of thumb. How does it go? Omne——'

Miss Felton looked at the ceiling. 'Omne—omne vivum in vivo,' she said hesitantly, in what Niobe called the 'weevily Germanic Latin.'

Pete glanced at me and grinned. 'Just like "Information, Please." Didn't I tell you we had fine girls?'

She laughed. 'Oh, I happened to come across it in an old textbook yesterday. I'm not even sure what it means.'

'Yes you are,' Pete said. 'The principle that all life comes out of other life? Of course. We may revise that in the next dozen years. If we do, Stanley will be as big a name as Koch in medical history. A sort of grandson of Koch's too. Direct line. You can take your hands out now, Jim.'

They looked a little shriveled. Miss Felton came back with sterile gowns, tied the tapes, and snapped rubber gloves on our hands. Then she put a surgeon's cap on my head, laughing as she pressed it down. She tied a gauze mask over my nose and mouth. Why did it smell so rubbery?

'Rubber in there,' Pete said, the words blurred in his own mask. 'A sheet of latex foam. We're experimenting with it. These things aren't very efficient, you know. This is about the best made. Bleached 44-40 tobacco cloth. Very high count. Ready?'

He looked around and opened the door.

'Here we are.'

9

MY FIRST impression was a kind of dumb astonishment that all this had been going on behind that carefully deadened partition. I could shut my eyes and imagine myself back at the county fair in my boyhood. But not noisy. All muted. Dogs barking faintly,

other animals whining and yapping, motors and fans going, a sizable stir of people very earnestly engaged. It didn't smell much—
the ventilators were good—but you knew you were in a laboratory.
Down off the end of the big room somewhere, I could hear a tol-
erable mixed quartet working on the railroad. The patients.

Pete took my arm and tapped the wall on the right. 'Nurses'
conference room. The physics machines are over here. Straight
ahead is the zoo. We'll come back to them.'

The physics section was shielded off with what looked like some
kind of heavy rock wallboard.

As we came out into the long open part of the room a tall man
in a gown and face mask called to Pete. For a moment I wondered
what would happen if I lost Pete. They all looked alike, except for
the hair and eyes. This one's eyes were young and bright blue. Pete
introduced me. His assistant, Dr. Harold Wright.

'Rowan works for the city. He's hoping we can give him something to control the fever by—oh, five-thirty this afternoon at the
latest.'

Wright's eyes crinkled in a smile. He said something to Pete
about Janus green B and Rose Bengal, and something more about
Wratten "9" panchromatic. I remembered the words because they
were nice words and I remember everything. I still don't know
what they mean. Pete and young Wright talked about a cold
chamber. My tip from Dick Wirth. Wright made a little sketch
and put down some notes.

I nodded to him and we went on through the main part of the
laboratory. Men and women in gowns and masks working with
flasks and beakers and pipettes and Gradwohl colorimeters. It was
laid out, not in long rows, as I remembered the college laboratories, but in a series of three-sided cubicles or booths for separate
experiments, each large enough to accommodate five or six people
and their kit. Some were even bigger. They seemed to be arranged
about the pieces of apparatus in common use: sinks, cabinets,
small electric furnaces.

The sun came in at the tall windows and in one corner the long fluorescent lighting fixtures glowed rosy pink and white overhead. It didn't look much like the laboratories in the movies. It wasn't formal. The order it had was an order of convenience. Good hard use had knocked the glitter off things. They got stained or dented. It occurred to me—though I had a vague suspicion I'd read it somewhere—that what these people were doing was a very precise kind of mining.

A man with black hair and dark-brown serious eyes talked to Pete for a minute. One of the biochemists. He'd discovered some resemblances between the fever virus and the agent for lymphocytic choriomeningitis. Also a resemblance to the virus of something known variously as Pappataci fever, three days' fever, phlebotomus fever, sandfly fever, and summer fever.

Then a small well-set-up young woman with very pale red-blond hair and clear gray eyes like Niobe's. The eyes wandered to me occasionally as she talked. The psychosomatologist. She had a breakdown of hourly temperature data from the charts. Apparently it went up a degree or so late in the day, like other fevers. But there seemed to be a corresponding increase in motor activity too. I was beginning to develop an unholy respect for Dr. Seneca B. Jenkins. Also, I seemed to be stifling in the latex mask.

The little psychosomatologist and I bowed prettily to each other. Pete said: 'We'll stop in at L-6. I want you to see the Roncador people. A few more in there too. We're keeping the rest as controls in K-6. Eighteen all together. Getting them fast. We should have our quota of forty-eight in a day or so.'

He pushed a swinging door and held it for me. People seemed to be laughing in bursts. The pavilion was a long sunny room with beds down along each side, partitioned in fours. A big sunroom at the end. Just in front of us, two nurses were smiling in the doorway of the nurses' station. Straight down the middle behind them, a doctor's room, pantry, utility, linen-and-tray and treatment rooms.

Most of the people on the left had hauled their beds out toward the center of the room. They sat, sprawled or rolled on the ends, wearing those vague flannelette nightshirts that seem to be a kind of required Early American touch in even the best hospitals. Two or three of the girls looked worth while even in that getup and I noticed a very fancy old lady in a blue quilted satin bedjacket.

Out in the middle of the floor, a medium-sized rather pale blond young man and a small Negro boy of ten were putting on an act. Very spindly-legged in the flannelette shirts. The young man was talking with a dreamy look. He had what seemed to be a catheter knotted around his neck and held the other end out, waving it slowly and sinuously.

'—so the elephant, enraptured by the coming of spring, his great frame a-quiver with unrequited aplomb, advances through the jungle in search of *dum-dum, dum-dum.*'

He advanced through the jungle, galumphing. The boy watched him gravely. People tittered. He made a Danny Kaye face and turned quickly and lightly, waving the end of the catheter at the boy.

'The little hoola-hoola bird, who feels courage rising in his veins like the sap in the weeche-weeche tree, determines to test his courage against the biggest thing in the world. He attacks the elephant, jabbing at his tender hide.'

The little Negro boy, very grave, danced toward him, pecking. He really seemed to be a kind of bird. Wonderful sense of pantomime. The young man was good too. Sidling, he danced away, waved his catheter at the boy and made motions of brushing him off. The boy kept striking at him. Once the catheter went round the boy's neck but he avoided it gracefully.

The young man pirouetted. He did entrechats, twiddling his toes. It wasn't my kind of thing. The East Side night-club touch. For amateurs, by fake amateurs who wanted to give the impression that if the other amateurs were only a little better they could do it too. So clever. So witty. But strictly kindergarten. This thing, though, really had a lot of wild energy and balance in it. A good feeling, not in the stuff, but in the way they did it. The young man froze and held up a finger. The boy froze too.

'—the elephant cudgels his brains——'

The young man beat himself over the head with the floppy sleeves of his nightshirt.

'—trying to think of a way to outwit his little tormenter. Then, as the hoola-hoola bird comes at him again——'

The boy danced in and jabbed.

'—the elephant reaches around with his trunk, tears off——'

He slipped the catheter under the tail of his nightshirt and pulled the shirt off over his head. He was in the buff. The girls were screaming.

'—tears off his hide and flings it in the face of the hoola-hoola bird.'

He tossed the shirt over the boy's head. The boy did a scrambling dance under it.

'At that moment the elephant sights his intended mate——'

He stared at the nearest girl, who immediately sobered.

'—and *leaps* upon her.'

He did leap almost on her, in a standing broad jump. She howled, clutched him, and they rolled off the bed onto the floor. The others were kicking and shrieking.

In a moment the young man got up with dignity and helped the girl up. He walked out and shook hands gravely with the little Negro boy.

'Excellent, Sidney,' he said.

He looked at us, still clowning, and Pete introduced me.

'Is he a doctor?'

'No.'

'Then he's a spy. Girls,' he shouted dramatically, 'this man is a spy.'

They yelled and came rolling and tumbling off the beds and at me. Pete was trying to hold them off and I could see the nurses starting toward us. The girls were amazingly well co-ordinated. One of them jumped on my head from behind and I went down in the shrieking pile.

The mask got knocked down around my neck and the cap came off. A big good-looking brown-haired girl had me by the hair, shaking me. She said: 'Wait a minute,' twisted my head around, and looked at me. 'Wel-l-ll,' she said, and bent down to kiss me, slowly and with increasing pressure, still holding my hair.

One of the other girls saw what was happening, pushed her away, and kissed me herself. She gave me a little squeeze. 'M-mm-mh!' she said. The rest crawled all over me, kissing me one after the other. When I looked up, the old woman in the satin bed-jacket was leaning over me. 'My turn,' she said firmly, and took it.

As I got up, one of the girls asked: 'How did you like him, Miss Opdyke?'

She shrugged. 'Oh, so-so,' she said.

We got rearranged a little and Pete, still grinning, introduced us round. Two of the good-looking girls were Mrs. Baker and Mrs. Cherrill off the Roncador. Mrs. Baker's husband Hansell was the bright young man who had done the ballet routine and sicked the girls on me.

'Hello. Thanks,' I said.

'Oh, that's all right,' he said affably.

Then there was Mrs. Cherrill's husband Jacob, who looked cheerful enough but didn't seem to have the zip of the others, and the third or loose-ender girl from the Roncador, Cornelia Kelsey, plain but forward. The big brown-haired girl was somebody from Plainfield who had been visiting in town. They must play rough in Plainfield. The old-family woman had settled into bed again. Miss Wilhelmina Opdyke.

'Such a pleasure seeing you again, Mr. Rowan.'

'Thank you,' I said. 'I hope you've forgiven my presumption a while ago.'

'Indeed I have. I could forgive a great deal more of it.'

The little Negro boy was Sidney Reed.

'Hello, Sidney. You were very good.'

'Thank you.'

'He climbed the Venetian blinds yesterday,' Pete said. 'We had to threaten to roll 'em up to get him down again.'

'It was fun,' Sidney said.

'How would you like a pair of parallel bars?' I said. 'Or something else?'

'I'd like some paints.'

'You mean water colors?'

He nodded.

'Okeh. I'll see what I can do.'

I waved good-by to them. Pete led me out into the main laboratory and across to a row of lockers near the animal experiment house.

'We have a devil of a time trying to keep their relatives out,' he said. 'We've been promised lawsuits. Here. Put this on. These too.'

He handed me a long heavy rubber fireman's coat, boots, and a sou'wester. I began to get into them.

He said: 'I want you to see my pets. Don't forget that question of yours about experimenting on people.'

He was getting into a rig too. The animal house looked like a pretty big place, about seventy or eighty by forty feet, roofed over.

'The house is mineral board,' Pete said. 'Made from pyroxene. Flyproof. The whole thing is sealed. We keep the air pressure inside just a little higher than outside. Prevents foreign material from getting in when the door is opened. See that doodad sticking out up there? That's a small precipitron. An electron device. Washes the air as it's pumped in. Come right through behind me when I open the door.'

He unfastened a dog and swung the heavy insulated door out. I went in fast behind him and we were sloshing down a narrow corridor in about three inches of what he told me was a one per cent Lysol solution. I could hear the animals clearly now.

'The whole place is divided into two sections insulated from each other. We can close one up and disinfect it while the other is in use. The air pump leads through the precipitron, and then down through two separate ducts, one for each section. The air passes under germicidal lamps and out into the house. Step back a little and keep your head down.'

I did, and a shower streamed down all over me.

'Put your hands out.'

I did that too. The stuff ran off the dark-brown rubber gloves.

'More Lysol solution,' Pete said. He stepped under himself, then opened another tightly fitted door.

Instantly we were in the midst of more yapping, barking, whining, squeaking, and howling than I'd ever heard in my life. I noticed a battery of germicidal lamps high up under the roof. They made little rainbows with the fine spray of Lysol solution falling from sprinklers all over the central part of the room. The animal cubicles were laid out along both sides and brightly lighted. Sizes to fit. Rather smallish for the white mice, relatively huge for the St. Bernards and bloodhounds down at the far end.

'Doesn't it get damp for them in here?'

'The cages are nice and snug,' Pete said. 'They get a separate warmed air supply. I don't think I'd better open them up for you. You can't be sterile after all those girls.' He grinned.

We walked up and down, watching the animals. The mice were tremendously busy, though I couldn't make out what they were doing. They leaped over each other like kittens playing. Pete mentioned that his experimenters hadn't had much success trying to infect two of the commonest laboratory animals: rabbits and guinea pigs.

The prairie dogs, fine alert little geezers, were coupling two by two like the animals in the ark, quite gently, without haste. A lovely monomania. They didn't even take time to think it over in between, though I noticed they seldom made up to the same female again.

Pete reflected. 'You know, it's nice, for once, to be able to make them happy. Even if it can't last.'

We were looking at the ferrets. Something else entirely. The white hunters, quartering back and forth. Their small feet pattered silently and endlessly about the cubicle. Each on some imperceptible scent of his own. One of them looked at me steadily and unseeingly with his red-currant eyes and turned away. I knew what he wanted all right. I knew what would make *him* happy.

'They give me the creeps.'

'Don't they?' Pete said. 'We're glad to get them, though. They've been more or less canonized as laboratory animals—oh, since 1933. Since the British discovered what a fine subject for viruses they make. The Rockefeller Foundation flu vaccine just about clinched it.'

'In a case like this,' I said, 'I should think you'd pick your animals for temperament. Gloomy ones. When they're happy, it ought to show more. A hippopotamus, say.'

'Funny—your mentioning it,' Pete said. 'We're taking an extra floor for a hippopotamus house.'

'Or owls,' I said. 'A happy owl. Or how about some mules?'

Pete laughed. 'What's the matter with St. Bernards?'

We walked down toward them. Massive Victorian uncles, behaving with a total and scandalous lack of dignity. It was impossible not to smile at them. Two of them, faced up to each other, seemed to be playing patty-cake and another made love to a shy female, rolling over and over with little puppyish yelps and whines.

But the bloodhounds, the lugubrious liverish dewlappy bloodhounds, looked positively radiant. Wonderful to see them. They galloped around the cage with a sort of hop every few steps, their eyes bright and their tongues hanging out for pure pleasure. When they saw us, they leaped at the glass, wriggling their hindquarters for all the world like Boston terriers, their mouths one loud red gape of welcome.

We doused ourselves under the shower on our way out and peeled off the rubber coats. I was steaming. Pete glanced at his watch.

'Suppose we look at the machines some other time,' he said. 'I don't like to——'

'Sure thing,' I said. 'I've got a good start now. I'll drop over tomorrow. And thanks, Pete.'

'Don't—— Oh. One thing more. Dick Wirth may not know about this. We've found that getting plenty of fluids helps to ward

95

it off. The virus seems to do better in dehydrated tissues. Eating a little less than usual helps too.'

'I'll mention it to him.'

'And remember me to Niobe.'

I told him then. Pete squeezed my arm. He was very far from being a cold man but he had a New Englandish dislike of anything demonstrative. I was touched. I felt a little sick too.

'She'll live,' I said. 'She has a knack for it.'

'She has indeed,' Pete said.

10

WHEN I got out to the cab Nick was looking at Bill's map. He rolled it up carefully and nodded.

'Very good.'

'You're ribbing me, Nick. You don't know what it's for.'

'Me? Sure. I know Brooklyn like the palm of your hand. Where to, Commissioner?'

'Any bar along First Avenue. I'll buy you a drink. I want to phone.'

He found a bar. We ordered drinks and I put a bill down. The bartender, a hulking gray-haired man, leaned back and folded his arms.

'Put your money away.'

'Can I buy you a drink?'

'Nope.' He leaned toward us. 'I been tendin' bar in this neighborhood for twenty-five years. People come in here I don't like I have to serve them. That's the law. If they insult me I got to take it.' He shook his head. 'No more. If I like them they drink free. Like you. I liked you two fellows right away. If I don't like a fellow comes in I don't see him. I don't hear him order a drink.' He nodded. His eyes were bright.

I got some nickels and went to the phone booth. The afternoon light came in along the bar and the juke box rolled its captive rainbows and throbbed softly. Bing Crosby singing *The One Rose*.

I called home first. Elizabeth, the cook, answered. A Carpenter from the South County of Rhode Island. That wasn't like being an Adams of Boston. More like being a Crockett of Tennessee. If your ketch was in trouble off Quonochontaug and the Coast Guard came out in a motor surfboat, there'd be a Carpenter in the crew. And if you needed milk, or quahaugs, or a pair of those hand-knitted mittens the fishermen wrung out in salt water and put on to keep their wet hands from freezing, a Carpenter would have things like that too.

'Any word from Mrs. Rowan, Elizabeth?'

'Not a word. I told Rachel to change the sheets on her bed. Miss Booth telephoned you.'

'What'd she want?'

'She invited you to supper at seven o'clock.'

Supper was supper.

'Will you call her and tell her I'll come?'

'All right. And I roasted a chicken for you. There's cranberry in the icebox. You'd better have something to eat before you go to bed. If Mrs. Rowan comes home and finds——'

'Thank you, Elizabeth. You're a sweet girl.'

I could almost hear her blushing. Then she said: 'I'm going home now.' She had a room over off Lexington Avenue. 'I don't like to be out at night with all this going on. Is there anything else you want me to do?'

'No, Elizabeth. Thanks.'

I called Eunice.

'The same man. I talked to a fellow named Carson at the Weather Bureau today. He promised to help us out. Will you call him? Ask him if there's any chance of a break. Yes. Might do that morning and afternoon until we see—— And look, Eunice. How about you and Bill meeting me at Ada Booth's? About eight-thirty. I'm having dinner with her. We'll drive around town and see what's doing. Oh, and will you ask John Kane if he can get me one of the city's two-way radio cars tomorrow? Yes.'

I phoned Justin McKeogh. His voice sounded even grimmer over the phone. Did the police radio stations have emergency power in case New York Edison went out? If not, could we get power trucks?

'A storage-battery system,' Justin said. 'Forty-eight hours' reserve. What's on your mind, Jim?'

'I don't know yet. But we may need it.'

Paravecchio drove me over to the Astor bar. Polished black and cast aluminum, shuttered from the street. It was almost hot in Times Square—in the seventies, I should think—and the girls definitely were. I got a bad nervous shock as we were going in. A deadpan showgirl smiled at me. Or maybe at Nick.

Inside, people were sitting in other people's laps and a wide-eyed man wandered around looking at them. Nick and I ordered drinks and brooded. When the waiter came back he brought a drink for himself and sat down. Then there were three of us brooding.

A pith helmet. A topee. I got up after a while and called the Explorers Club. They consulted. No. No expeditions leaving or about to leave for tropical parts. I went back to the table and asked Nick to get the late papers. The *Post* had pages one and two reversed. Staten Island commuters were piling up at South Ferry. Only one boat operating. The Army had put the Governors Island ferry on the run. A reporter found the lost crews drinking in a bar on South Street. 'Too monotonous,' one of them said, winking. 'We're giving up the sea.'

The amusement ads. I went up and down the page and found it. The Roxy. An explorers' ballet in the stage show, to go with *Amazon Nights*, a jungle-hell picture. I went back to the phone. The ballet would go on in twenty minutes. I managed to catch George Romanelli at the Department of Docks. He told me they were diverting other ferries to the Staten Island run. I sat there for a minute, then called F. A. O. Schwarz, the toy people, and asked them to send a big box of paints over to young Sidney Reed at Kip's Bay. The line went dead just as I gave them the address.

Nick finished his drink and we nudged slowly through the traffic uptown. He pulled the cab in alongside a no-parking sign and we walked over to the Roxy. The box office was closed. No ticket taker. No ushers. I thought of talking to the manager, if any, and decided against it. He might tip her off. A full house. We found singles in the eighth row and watched a girl on the screen in something that looked like a cotton print from Best's fending off a crowd of blowgun natives with a revolver. Good work, sister. Or was it?

My heart was bumping as the lights came on. Not at the picture. The orchestra played something with lots of maracas in it and the precision line of girls led out onstage, dancing. Brown body paint, chalky sharkskin shorts and brassières, and tropical helmets. Niobe was in it all right, third from the end. The tall end. She knew the routine as well as any of them and did it as neatly. A terrific gift of mimicry, and those superb legs.

Something else. I hadn't caught it at first. She was burlesquing it. Just a shade. A tiny bit too much action in the leg throw. A little extra roll to the eyes. A faint idiot exaggeration in the smile. She seemed to be looking right at me. Maybe she could actually see me. I didn't know. Not a sign, of course. But even in that matched row of handsome girls, most of them years younger, she looked like somebody. Other husbands and friends might feel that way about the other girls. I had an odd miserable feeling I hadn't expected: that she was somebody I'd known a long time ago, that I was falling in love with her, and that I didn't have a chance.

The act was getting on toward the finish. I reached behind the man between us and tapped Nick. She might notice me when I got up. Better to take a chance than risk letting her get away first. I still didn't think the manager would be a good idea. He could phone backstage. The street was jammed. We pushed through the crowd, guessing at where the stage door would be. A girl got hold of me and wouldn't let go. When I got loose from that we found what seemed to be the stage door. Locked, of course. We waited.

It must have been five minutes before anybody came out. Two girls. Not Niobe. I caught the door. The blonde one said sharply: 'You're not supposed to go in there,' and the other one said: 'Oh, what's the difference? They're all alike.'

Inside I stopped a girl in costume. 'Where can I find the third girl from the right?'

She fluffed me off with a nice cute impersonal little smile and started away.

I stood in front of her. 'Tell me, please.'

She looked down me slowly. Another girl, already dressed, came toward us, and the one I'd spoken to first said indifferently: 'Where's O'Neill, Mona?'

'Gone,' Mona said without stopping.

I thanked the first one and she stared at me.

'You're all right,' she said. 'You're just a little excited.'

I found an assistant manager, told him who I was, and he hunted up the strayed doorman.

'Oh, Miss O'Neill's gone,' he said. 'She left as soon as they came off. I thought there was something funny. She didn't wait to change. Had her gabardine coat over her shoulders and her clothes in her hand. That's right. She said something about a taxi and dashed out.'

So she had seen me. She wouldn't be back. I was beginning to learn the routine. Play each stand like a pitchman with one eye out for the cops. A nice game for people married a dozen years. Well, sooner or later I'd catch her at it.

The street outside was like Eighth Avenue after a rally in the Garden. Nick wanted to go home to dinner. He promised to pick me up at Ada Booth's. As he churned away through the crowd, stumpy and self-possessed, a bunch of shrieking girls backed me up against a wall, dancing and jumping, eight or nine of them trying to grab my arm at once. I was having quite a time all round. Petticoat bait.

No more of a time than the other boys, though. The girls seemed to be doing the hunting. I've never seen so many people in the streets. A girl would plant herself in front of you and look up at you—'Mmmm! Definitely my type'—and the man she'd been with would wave good-by, take three or four steps, and find himself corralled again. It was all good-natured enough, though I saw a lone cop shorn of his buttons and two sailors blindfolded with their own neckerchiefs and led away, not unwillingly, by a group of hilarious women.

On Seventh Avenue a man took one of those big clove-studded hams out of a window and munched on it lovingly. Drinks were free in nearly all the bars, but nobody seemed to be drunk. Or how could you tell? Not much light in Times Square. Most of the signs were out and the lighted ones were mottled with unreplaced bulbs. When I tried a cab the driver said sorry, chief, he was taking his girl home to Hollis. We both knew where Hollis was because his girl lived there and I was head of the City Planning Commission. I shook hands with him and wished him *bon voyage*.

Going up to West Fifty-Fourth Street in another cab, I remembered what Dick Wirth had said that afternoon. Demonic possession. Possession by joy. The people in the streets were as irresponsible as buffalo in a stampede. I worried about Niobe for a while, and about the city and Pete's experiments and the control stations. Then I leaned back in the cab and stopped worrying.

Ada's place was a new adobe-colored building with the familiar corner windows. The automatic elevator didn't seem to be automatic any more and I walked up the five flights in the dark.

'But come *in*, Jim,' Ada cried. She looked very summery, all prettied up in something between a hostess gown and a dinner dress: a big full red chiffon skirt and a gauzy polka-dotted white blouse with pleated short sleeves. A dark-red brigand's sash. Lots of good bangles too. Ada was always a great girl for the bangles.

'I'm so glad to see you, Jim. Here, darling. *This* is my good chair. And how *are* you? I don't know why I'm not utterly *bushed*. I should be, Lord knows. We can't *find* anybody since this—it's perfectly ridiculous—but I came home from the office tonight feeling positively *exalted.* You've no idea. *I* suppose it's the fever,' she said resignedly.

She did seem all rosy and bright. A little taller than average, nicely built, dark-brown hair and very dark-brown eyes. Getting up to forty. She'd been married for years and years to Bob Stanhook, who ran an accountancy firm in the Grand Central district. Divorced in 1938. Niobe said she'd taken it pretty hard. The fly manner was part of her job. Ada had always impressed me as a pretty correct woman.

'It isn't doing you any harm,' I said. 'You look wonderful.'

'Well,' she said. 'That deserves—— Effie, will you get Mr. Rowan a drink? And make me one too, please. Scotch.'

'May I have one, Miss Booth?' Effie called gently.

A three-room apartment with dropped living room. Everything opening off the foyer. Effie brought the drinks. A tall bony Negro woman, about medium brown, and fortyish. Fine hands. Excellent rye for me. Ada knew what I liked. The big casement windows were open and the creamy monkscloth drapes floated in. The light seemed dimmish.

'I'm so disappointed,' Ada said. 'You haven't remarked about my new furnishings.'

I looked around. A big old-fashioned brass ship's hurricane lamp swung from the ceiling and an old flat-topped railroad stove had been set up in front of the fireplace, its pipe going up the chimney.

Effie took a genteel pull at her drink, stirred up the orange coal, and began to fry a batch of chicken croquettes. A rubberneck bus full of cheering people passed in the street and I couldn't make out what Ada was saying.

'—made up my mind we'd have to take *action.*'

She did too. No gas, and about an hour and a half of dim current every now and then each night. She'd gone down to Allen Street and poked around with a nice sense of the utilitarian and the curious. When she dragged out the big hurricane lamp, the man didn't even seem to be very sure what it was. The stove came from a Sixth Avenue elevated station. Ada had got it from a scrap-iron dealer.

So she had lots of historical interest too. Finally she'd ordered a drum of kerosene and a half ton of briquettes. She harried the coal people until they delivered it. The oil man wouldn't budge, so she got a cab driver to load the drum into his trunk space and cart it home for her.

The dinner was plain and tasted good—Effie had the loving hand —and the stove felt cheerful in the heatless apartment after sundown, with the big lamp's circle of light on the ceiling. Ada told me that the men in the building were organizing to run the furnace in shifts. Effie ate with us, getting up to serve, and Ada talked about Niobe.

She'd dropped in at Niobe's rehearsal Tuesday. Niobe seemed terribly low and that in itself was odd. 'Nobody could be more— more equable,' Ada said, looking at us, and Effie and I nodded. Mallett, who liked to run everything himself and hired a director only for form's sake, put her through the second scene three or four times. He'd been very gentle. Always was. But Ada said you could see how hard she was trying, and the third time she just covered her face with her hands and cried. Mallett was so shocked—no one had ever seen her, well, helpless before—that he dismissed everybody and took her out for a drink.

The next day she was radiant, Ada said. Positively glowing. Looks. Carriage. Voice. Wonderful timing. And the last scene, the one they'd always had trouble with—she went through it and pulled it all together and simply flung it at you. Ada made a scooping motion.

Effie nodded with a sort of earnest awe. 'She come home with Miss Booth afterwards. I've seen Mrs. Rowan a thousand times. I like her. I nev-er seen 'er like that.'

We sat on the couch and I told Ada how I'd got a glimpse of Niobe twice that day. Effie cleaned up and went home and the lamp swung gently in the breeze from the open windows, as it must have swung in some cabin in the Trades long ago, and I talked about the City Hall pigeons and the old woman in Vandewater Street. It just didn't occur to me, even when she sat over close and took my arm; and when she said 'Jim,' and I turned, and we were kissing, it wasn't anything about sympathy for her friends. Or it might have been that to start with.

Poor Ada. What the hell could I do? I didn't have any scruples. I had no feeling at all about it except that I was sorry. It wasn't as if she were some ordinary lollipop on the make. But Ada the correct woman. Ada the family friend in trouble. A queer kind of trouble, but trouble all right. You couldn't tell a woman who knew what she wanted that it was better for her not to have it. And only a damn prig would get up on his horse and ride away. But I didn't want to get mixed up in this at all.

We were beginning to get mixed up in it. I could smell Ada's perfume and her bracelets were cutting into my neck. And the impossible phone rang. Wonderful Bill, I thought. Celestial Eunice. Probably the first time since Alexander Graham Bell that a man had been glad to hear a phone ring at a time like that. Ada moved her mouth back and forth, meaning never mind, but I drew away gently.

'It's probably Bill Cornbill and my secretary. I forgot about asking them to call for me.'

'Oh,' she said.

I got unlimbered and went to the phone.

It was Eunice. 'Are you ready? Bill is here with Marguerite. We're holding him up.' They were laughing.

'Holding—— I'll be down in a minute.'

Ada came to the door with me. I kissed her gently.

'Never mind, darling.'

'But I do mind,' she said. She looked at me. I shook my head. 'I may be working all night.'

She closed the door softly.

11 Downstairs in the lobby Eunice was laughing at Bill, and Marguerite giggled gently, her tongue between her teeth. The

superintendent or somebody had left a big yellow candle burning on a marble table and Bill was trying to straighten himself out in front of a wall mirror. His dark short hair was up on end and his brown eyes looked round at me reproachfully. The joke was that you couldn't really ruffle Bill. He'd look tall and slatty even in a nightshirt.

'Terrifying,' he said mildly, with a shudder. 'Terrifying. And I used to be so fond of women. Gentle creatures.'

They laughed again. Eunice said: 'We had to defend him. We were coming up Sixth Avenue and some girls ran across the street and mobbed him.'

'Girls!' Bill said in his deep voice. 'Devils from the nethermost pits of—— I've always been nice to them. Haven't I given them freely of my substance? But these—— And Marguerite was right in there punching.' He imitated her girlish little straight-arm jab. We laughed. 'And Eunice was saying: "Oh, no, you don't," grabbing them from behind and whirling them out of the way. Saved my life.' He put his arms around them.

Nick had come in and was listening. Don't nobody make passes at me. I just come all the way down from the Bronx. Nobody even whistled at me.'

Marguerite whistled softly and giggled.

'Now I feel better,' Nick said.

Eunice had my brief case with the department reports and the investigators' notes on the control-station buildings. We sat on an Empire striped bench in the lobby and looked over the station data. Mostly favorable. Three or four of the places seemed doubtful and two were definitely out. Bill got his old map from the cab—I didn't want to mark the new one—and we traced a route lightly in pencil. We could go over the doubtful stations, try to find new buildings, and get a line on how conditions looked in general.

We piled into the cab. Nick opened the hatch and we started up the West Side, not hurrying. Central Park seemed to be full of laughing shrieks, wild small boys on bicycles, and horsemen flying across the lawns at full gallop. We didn't find out until the next day that the black panther had got out of Aymar Embury's handsome zoo and was loose in the park all night. Probably scared to death.

A policeman sprawled on a bench under a light. He watched, amused, as a tight-girdled high-heeled dryad went by at a clipping run, holding her black net evening dress above her knees. A top hat went racing after her.

Up the magical lighted northern escape of Central Park West, where the air always seemed to be clearer than in other parts of Manhattan, the traffic lights were out of sync and cars moved in a staggering involved dance. We got through to Broadway and went north, picking out one new station on the way. In Straus Park, the little triangle at Broadway and 106th Street, people were holding a beach picnic in the mild air, roasting frankfurters over a fire of packing boxes at the rim of the Lukeman fountain. Girls in beach pajamas and men in trunks splashed each other in the cold water.

Stray whoops and rebel yells on Morningside, rather like a Saturday night in the twenties. The street lights were fading and brightening, though the free movies seemed to be open anyhow. We nudged through the careless crowd that flowed out into the street. The weird light gave their faces the look of people watching an eclipse.

Washington Heights was fairly quiet, except at 145th Street, but there were watch fires on the high rocky crest of Fort Tryon Park, as there must have been in Washington's time, when the Americans were taken in the bitter crossfire of the guns. We cut across the Harlem at 207th Street and out Fordham Road. The whole Bronx was sedate enough, except for the noise of occasional parties through the open windows. We passed three or four abandoned streetcars.

I began to think it might not be too bad after all. Eunice was needling Marguerite to get her some dresses at Saks Fifth Avenue, and Bill and I tried to pick flaws in the control-station plan. Bill thought the problem of getting enough skilled men—and keeping them—was the weakest part of it. I did too, but there wasn't any way around it unless we pulled out some of the badly needed men and used them to train reserves. I made a note that the police and fire schools might be converted to give emergency courses.

Nick pulled up in the middle of the Bronx-Whitestone Bridge. All along the high slender roadway, men were fishing on through the night. Nick talked to a few of them. I couldn't make out how they could feel a bite with all that line—it was a good hundred and thirty-five feet down to the water—but Nick said yes, sure, and pointed out a fish here and there to prove it. One ingenious devil had rigged a little fair-lead on top of the bridge rail, with a big wooden clothesline reel to take the line up quickly.

We stopped for a free beer on Main Street in Flushing. It looked very much like a small-town Main Street anywhere, except that it had the electric feel of the city. The street was packed with families carting home bridge lamps, bed sections, mattresses, toys, and God knows what else. We watched a shoe clerk fretting over sizes, as careful as if he were actually getting money for the shoes. One merchant, true to the competitive tradition, had big stickers in his windows offering one free article with each free article taken. The storekeepers who didn't want to give things away had closed up, as they did in other parts of town.

The bar was three deep, with half a dozen bartenders drawing them as fast as the stuff would flow. Everybody seemed very amiable. The people in front passed beers to us one by one, and as we stood there looking at each other a man murmured in my ear: 'They're handing out money over at the bank. Better pick up some for the girls.' He nodded as I thanked him.

We finished the beers and strolled down to the bank at the corner. It was true all right, but not many people seemed to care. Smart people. The lights all on at ten-thirty in the evening. Every teller in his cage doing business—though not business as usual. We got into a short line and watched. It seemed to be one pack of bills to a customer, and whatever came first. I got tens and gave them to Eunice, who was stuck with ones. Nick drew a sheaf of hundred-dollar bills and distributed about half of them to the girls.

'Save the rest for my old woman,' he said. 'She be tickled. Maybe she'll even kiss me good night.'

Bill and Marguerite both got fives. Bill, the wolf, insisted that this was a good omen. Two of a kind, he said.

We crossed Flushing Meadow Park—Moses had done a good job in his time—and went out Grand Central Parkway to Jamaica. On Ninety-First Avenue the kids were having a parade. Dressed in bright yard goods wrapped around and around, with trains half a block long. One kid was wearing a white girdle as a helmet, the garters dangling at his ears, and a portable radio full out made the music.

We went east on Jamaica Avenue, alongside Forest Park and the quiet bare lift of Highland Park, into Brownsville on Pitkin Avenue. A little park like the one at West 168th Street in Manhattan, and Loew's Pitkin behind it, the marquee still blazing and people going in and out. The dun buildings had a blended quality of the lower East Side and Sixth Avenue and Harlem. Probably the latest big Jewish district in the Western Hemisphere. We had two large housing projects mapped out for it but Lord knows where the money was coming from.

Crowds around the pushcarts on Belmont Avenue, trading vigorously, though everything was free. Bargaining could be a passion, I thought, like Nick's fishing or the ex-Mayor's toy trains. Why not? I was Scotch enough to understand that. It was get-together and schmoozing and making sure you got what your labor was worth in exchange. Racketeering too, but less and less of that. It got monstrous only when it perverted the human relation into something huge and abstract. This way, without money, it was as purely social as dancing.

And that was the next thing. On Livonia Avenue, under the IRT pillars, the Moors were having a festival. Real Moors. Moroccans. Other North Africans, and the Spanish ones. The street lights out. A yellow bonfire sparking up through the tracks, and bare bulbs strung from pillar to pillar. Kitchen chairs for the jouncing musicians. Sharp yells, and the vivid full skirts whirling, whipped about the smooth thighs in a folding corolla, and the easy subtle balanced rhythmic interplay of the drums, the rhythm that comes up through flamenco and rumba and Calypso and samba and New Orleans jazz.

We watched a while. The girls wanted to join in, but Nick and Bill and I weren't up to that. We got into the cab again and drove on through a dimly lighted section of Flatbush. Two more stations relocated and one to go. We cruised a dozen blocks before we found something that would do for the last one. What we saw of the rest of Brooklyn seemed fairly quiet, but at a small electric-fixtures plant in Greenpoint, off Manhattan Avenue, a picket line was snake-dancing. The owner had just given them the plant.

In the Queens Midtown Tunnel the lights flickered and went out for a while. We dropped Bill and Marguerite at Bill's place, with our blessing, and Eunice and I rode up to East Sixty-Eighth Street. I picked up a copy of *Time* and the late papers on the way. When we stopped at my door, I told Nick I'd be using a city car after this and asked what I owed him.

He looked around. 'Nothing. I like to do it. Forget it.'

I settled the checkbook on my knee, fought off my Scotch ancestors, and wrote something a little better than was strictly necessary.

'Go ahead and get sore with me. This is for your wife. With this and what you got at the bank, maybe——'

He laughed, a little embarrassed, and took it. 'Okeh, Commissioner.' He reached in, shook hands with me, and turned back to the wheel. He was shaking his head. 'Life is a joke. You're only here as a guess.'

The next time I saw him he was a seagoing man.

I said good night to Eunice and she put her hand on my arm. 'Get to bed, Jim. It's two o'clock.'

Upstairs, I dumped the reports, maps, and newspapers on the divan and put on the lights. Dimmish but fairly steady. The Fred Becker prints of jazz musicians on the white wall. I'd been seeing them for years now, and talking about them, and I was more than ever convinced that two or three of the best ones were just about the finest things we'd done in America. I looked at my favorite again: a guitarist with the teeth of a wolf and a pick in his hand as black as the last morsel of coal in the world, swayed up on two legs of a rehearsal chair, his big spatulate fingers on the frets. A wild loose wonderful thing. The unerring intricate line and the balance as tender as a gyroscope's, but far more subtle.

I got the chicken out of the refrigerator and carved for one. A prize. The liver. I spooned out some dressing and cranberry, poured a glass of milk, and got settled with the department reports.

You could feel the man in each report: Justin's like a pocketful of marbles, Dick Wirth's telegraphic, John Hickey's a little disjointed. I did begin to get a coherent impression from the whole day. The reports made a set of footnotes to it.

I sat back, finishing the milk, trying to gauge my impression. Some bright spots. Feuerman's markets seemed to be holding up well. In general, as of yesterday morning, you could say that things were critical but not yet entirely out of hand. The bad point was the speed of it. A toboggan slide.

Restless, I got up and leafed through *Time.* They'd slipped in a piece about the New York situation. Terribly excited. It began:

No ordinary sun rose over New York City on the morning of February 16th. It was red, sweltering, awesome. Traffic lights flushed, went out for good. Transport planes paused in midair. Hanky-panky peddlers rang their little bells. Ducks in Central Park looked at each other, climbed, burrowed. Across Grand Army Plaza, whose full name is known to few, seldom mentioned, beyond the statue of flashing, golden Sherman eternally in tow of his long-skirted angel, five madcaps tripped like adagio dancers along the 28th-floor cornice of the old (1928), sedately swank Savoy-Plaza Hotel.

I put that down. My feeling about Niobe, in the empty house, ran like a gray motion-picture film between me and whatever I was doing. Someone was having a party upstairs. I could hear the yelps and the piano and the East Side women's voices like no other voices in the known world. I put the *Figaro* Overture on the Scott combination. Everybody liked it, and that was just fine for everybody. I listened sadly to the lovely wild glittering music. In the midst of it the telephone rang.

I shut off the record and picked up the phone.

'Hello.'

Five seconds. Nothing. Then Niobe's voice, warm and close. 'Good night, darling.'

I heard the receiver go down slowly. The girl traced it for me. A pay station in an all-night diner on the Sunrise Highway in Rosedale.

I went to bed with the newspapers. When I dozed off finally I dreamed there was a lion on my back. He had me all right but he was playing with me gently, opening and closing his claws, which were stretched out in front of me. He weighed a ton. I didn't seem to be very frightened. He was just a rather menacing nuisance. When the claws went into my arm a little I grabbed his paw and bit it, not too hard. Very shaggy. It tasted like an old polar bear rug. He whined and let go a little and I woke up.

THREE

1 I GOT out fairly early in the morning and made it downtown by nine-thirty in spite of a subway motorman who got tired of his job between stations and had to be coaxed. I hadn't slept much. Spent the time making notes on the control stations. My head ached. The sun had a misty glare, the favonian wind blew steadily from the same quarter, and the streets were dismal with uncollected refuse.

In the early New York days the town had been full of scavenger pigs. Might be a good idea to have some sent over from Riker's Island. I was fooling—or was I? Hard to tell what made sense any more. I realized how much of what we called reality was simply a general human agreement that certain things were so. They might be or they might not. I felt too gloomy to think about it.

The Municipal Building elevators out. No current. My office was on the twenty-seventh floor. Need an alpenstock to make that. Then I saw Eunice, up on tiptoe and yoohooing to me in the crowd. Bill came in later, and young Joralemon. After three-quarters of an hour the current went on again. I asked Eunice to take Joralemon along and buy coffee and a raft of sandwiches for our crowd upstairs, in case the power failed again. They did, and it did. They got up just in time.

John Kane had sent over most of the new department reports. As of Wednesday night. Worse. Much worse. Hickey had only

113

one trained man for every three of the two-man sanitation trucks. Feuerman's report showed that the food situation, pretty good on Wednesday, had fallen apart overnight. The trouble there was a trucking failure too. Only one day's supply of fresh food on hand. But the wholesalers had a backlog of staples. Enough to last a couple of weeks. Hanauer, the Fire Commissioner, was cheerful and blunt. Water pressure low here and there, the alarm system out of whack, the trucks short-handed. A bad fire that got out of control anywhere in the city, but especially in Brooklyn (it seemed to be harder to keep firemen on duty there, for some reason), might run over whole neighborhoods.

I spent the rest of the morning with Bill and Rich Jones, the Board of Estimate engineer, and some of our own engineers and statisticians, ironing out the kinks in the control plan. Most of it was the job of getting a clear and workable division of effort for all the things that might pop up, but part of it was setting things up in such a way that we wouldn't be walking all over the corns of the various departments. If you were in public business, being a poor politician was almost as bad as being a poor administrator. Sometimes it added up to the same thing. Even so, we managed to keep the main points clear, and flexible enough to take care of any surprises.

Bill had the map-makers busy getting out big district maps showing the boundaries, and Eunice bossed the job of mimeographing a sheet that summarized the main features of the plan.

She called Carson for the weather dope and imitated his flat-calm civil-service tone: 'No change. Be cloudy tonight. Nope. That doesn't mean much in the general situation.' She'd checked Niobe's bank and the other places again. The hairdresser said Niobe had been there and gone.

I had a minute before the committee lunch and glanced through the Public Notices in the *Times*. Niobe always read them. An unsigned one: MILTON AVEUGLE DICTANT 'LE PARADIS PERDU' A SES FILLES. That was all.

Plenty of time to think about it as I walked down the twenty-three flights to Hickey's office. Nothing to go on, of course. But it sounded like her. It was the kind of thing she might do. What the devil did *aveugle* mean? *Blind*, of course. The rest was easy: 'Blind Milton dictating *Paradise Lost* to his daughters.' I seemed to remember that it was a picture.

Downstairs in Hickey's office I waited until I got my breath and called Romana Javitz in the print room at the Forty-Second Street library. She knew everything. All the young artists and cartoonists went to her when they were stuck for ideas.

'That isn't very hard,' she said. 'The picture is here in the library.' She told me just where.

The Board of Estimate had sent over two of the official secretaries and Ellen was back at her desk.

'Whew! Am I glad to get rid of that,' she said.

'How's the baby behaving, Ellen?'

'He slept all night. Not a peep out of him.'

'That's better than I did,' I said, and she looked after me as I opened the door. Pretty low. All the way down to self-pity.

2

A FULL house up and down the long table, and some new faces. John Kane introduced me. I'd met a few of them. The City Sheriff and the City Register, both opposition party. Fornaro, Norton, and Grady, the opposition councilmen. Cecil T. Hart, a downtown lawyer, one of the representatives for the public. The others were Rabbi Felix Castro and Walter H. Emmanuel, head of the Inman Foundation. I recognized Dr. Leeson, the psychobiologist I'd seen elected chairman of the Advisory Commission to Wirth's department. Things a little soberer than the day before. More trouble, of course, but we had outsiders now too.

Romanelli, coming in briskly behind the chairs, called out: 'Run for your lives. The millennium is here.' He saw the new faces, put his hand over his mouth, and sat down quietly. Even Arnie Genovese wasn't doing much talking. Not then.

I don't remember what we had for lunch. It might have been old paper boxes for all I cared. My head was banging away, and I felt as if I'd come all undone inside, as if all the nerve circuits had been gently disconnected. And I had to lay out the control plan and get a go-ahead on it. Unless somebody else had something. Even then, it didn't occur to me that my trouble might be the fever. The medical boys hadn't found out much about the prodrome then.

John Kane talked over the news releases with me. They'd been good so far and I told him I thought so. He was pleased. Chase MacDevitt of the Port Authority seemed to be missing. The fever. Hickey was solemnly jovial and once Mason Emery gave me a reassuring look from down near the foot of the table. When the coffee was served I asked John Kane to preside and told him why. He got up slowly.

'Jim feels I ought to take the chair today.' He smiled down at me and I did my best to smile back. 'He has a proposal to make later on and doesn't want anybody to feel that he's making an improper use of the chair's authority. That right, Jim?'

I nodded. Didn't make much sense, but that was the way I felt about it. I slid the penciled agenda over to him and he began to call on the department heads one after the other for summaries. I made notes. It was all clear enough. Everything was just getting worse, and fast.

A few of the boys made detailed reports. Dick Wirth got up, looking pretty gray in the face. He lived in his head, very detached about any mere organic lesions of his own. I wished to God he'd take better care of himself.

The U. S. Public Health people, he said, had sent out routine requests for information to all the Caribbean ports the *Roncador* had touched at. He had a memorandum sent up from the Public Health office in the Subtreasury Building. They had answers from three places in the West Indies: Eleuthera in the Bahamas,

Kingston in Jamaica, and Guadeloupe in the Leeward Islands. The first two had four and six possible cases respectively but could give no information.

Dick laid the papers down. 'Anybody know anything about Guadeloupe?'

Some shaking of heads. Leeson, a thickset man, looked tentatively toward Dick and held his lapel between thumb and forefinger. 'I've been there,' he said quietly. 'It's very populous. About all I remember is the tangerine toddy at the Café Gréaux in Point-à-Pitre, the main port, and a group of little islands called the Saintes. The fishermen wear big round hats like coolies.' He paused. 'Now we can get on to something useful.'

His maiden speech. He looked around, his eyes wide, and we grinned at him.

Anyhow, Guadeloupe had come through with the first real outside news. The USPHS people said: 'We consider the report of the Guadeloupe health officer, Dr. Sylvain Martineau, rather pleasing——'

'Nice government word,' John muttered.

'—and we are forwarding the translation entire.'

Dick read the thing. It was a wonderful letter, the letter of a post-Hugo French novelist manqué. I could see him. A silky spade beard. He began with a little salute to New York: 'The exquisite pandemonium of that great city has its sister in the delectable madness of my poor burning islands.' He called the fever *hlehhana*, putting a Latin feminine ending on the Asiatic root of the verb *to laugh*—the happy or laughing disease. 'If I may be permitted such a hybrid.'

Later, with rough justice, it was also called Martineau's disease. He hadn't found an agent or vector but he had a clear idea of the syndrome. Incubation period evidently short. Two days at most. Acute depression the previous day. Exhilaration at onset, eyes also sometimes affected the first day, slight soreness at base of skull continuing for duration of attack. Runs its course in from eight to ten days. Dick Wirth looked up at that to be sure we got it.

Treatment unknown. The disease had first appeared in the islands less than a year ago. Martineau made a number of suggestions, most of them ingeniously literary rather than scientific. Dick's people were following up the more likely ones. But Martineau seemed to think, for example, that the fever might be caused by a mutation of the agent responsible for the dancing manias of the Middle Ages. Wirth scotched that. He said medical men were pretty well agreed that tarantism must have been a case of mass psychosis.

Hanauer said in his heavy direct voice: 'What the hell was a United Fruit liner doing in Guadeloupe?'

'A one-day courtesy visit,' Dick said. 'They landed some official from Grenada and waited for him to do his business. The passengers spent the day ashore.' He shook his head. 'Ironic—happening to them. The United Fruit people have one of the best private medical systems in the world.'

Justin McKeogh got up and spoke his piece. Six fever cases in Boston—the unconscionable horror of instinctive behavior in Boston—St. Louis three, Chicago seven. All isolated. Justin read from the police teletype sheets. Five more cases in Omaha, fourteen in Philadelphia (including the policeman and intern who rounded up the others), eight in Salt Lake City, six in Cheyenne, fifteen in San Francisco. The San Francisco, Omaha, Cheyenne, Salt Lake, and Chicago cases accounted for the crews and passenger list of a main-liner transport plane out of New York. The pilot had stunted over San Francisco for twenty minutes, with that big gas reserve they have, before he came in to land. The passengers were delighted. All over the country, of course, it was being called the New York disease.

Justin quoted a few more figures and sat down. We had it all wrapped up now and it was really snafu. John looked down at me. I nodded and he called for suggestions. Grady from the City Council did some talking that didn't amount to much. Then Lester Long of the Department of Finance got up. He lived in a more or less continual exasperation at the human elements that kept horning in just as he got his mathematical house in order. Made him cynical. He would have been outraged if you'd told him that the human factor could be figured into the equation.

I knew Lester pretty well—I'd worked on the budget with him —and I was amused by him in exactly the way you're amused by old maiden ladies who tell young girls to pull their dresses down. I was wrong. He showed me.

He talked hard, as if he were trying to pick a fight. A wiry dark man, about medium size, in a banker's-gray sharkskin suit. Glasses. His face twisted up as he talked.

'We got together here yesterday and elected a representative to put through emergency measures. This is twenty-four hours later. The city's going to hell in the meantime. What's been done? Nothing. Why?'

I saw some of the boys look at each other. He sounded as if he had backing. I could feel my ears getting red. He might be right. It might have been better to try something right away instead of taking time to figure out what could be done.

Arnie Genovese turned in his chair and pointed down the table at Long. John Kane raised his hand to stop him, but didn't.

'Wait a minute. Let's keep the record straight. Rowan told us yesterday'—his other hand pointed back at me—'that he wanted twenty-four hours to get a line on things and recommend something. We agreed to that. You were here. You heard him. You didn't open your yap. Think it over, Lester.'

People were nodding. I saw Dr. Leeson's mouth gape slightly. Evidently never seen us in action before.

Long was really hot now. 'And let you vote us down again?' That was out now. Us. 'I wanted you to find out for yourselves. We're on the skids and we sit here arguing. Most of us have sworn to keep public order. Well, why don't we? Why don't we swear in a few thousand special police and deputies from the Sheriff's office? Or do you want people to take things into their own hands?'

He sat down. The opposition boys and some of the others clapped. Penforth Reger was one. The putative CP. Why the shift

119

overnight? A little directive from East Twelfth Street? Or just a run-with-the-hare-and-hunt-with-the-hounds game? I didn't know. But obviously, in the long view, they couldn't afford to have progressives taking effective action in a crisis.

Kane and Wirth and the rest of us were pretty grim. Long sounded like the mayor of a struck company town. But more than that. We could feel the weight of opinion behind him, in that room and outside. All the people who believed that order was a stamp press, a mold, an Iron Maiden, a double file of troops you were commanded to walk between. The people who couldn't get it through their heads, by God, that order was a ball game, order was the free and healthy growth of a child. It was the means liberty took to express itself. It was the chance people had to find a way to do the things they wanted to do in common. Not holding down. Bringing out.

I hauled back on the reins and kept my mouth shut. I was an interested party. The other boys could handle it. Anyhow it wasn't open and shut. We did have to restrain people from getting in each other's hair. It was our good luck, even allowing for gaps in the police reports, that petty crime had fallen off some twenty-three per cent in the last few days.

A dozen people were trying to get Kane's attention. He nodded to Hugh Onderdonck and Hugh got up slowly. He took off his glasses and held them by the bridge, his hand quivering a little. Most of us felt that way.

'It's true,' he said quietly. 'Long is right. We have got to keep order. Is this an end in itself? I think not. By preserving public order we preserve the rights of each citizen. What are these rights? Social rights. They make it possible for him to live with other people and that in turn makes the city possible. You know this. If we begin by cutting those rights from under us—by extraordinary police powers, or martial law, or whatever—we fail twice. We take away the citizen's rights and we prevent ourselves from doing what he has empowered us to do.

'As I see it, our job is to keep the city running. When we fail at that, it will be time enough to try shutting it down.' He fingered the papers in front of him. 'I was reading Jefferson the other night and I came across this sentence: "I am persuaded myself that the good sense of the people will always be found to be the best army." ' His tight face turned up and down the table. 'Yes, even if the army has *hlehhana.*'

Charley Regan of Queens jumped up in the midst of the applause for Hugh and shouted above the other voices: 'Wait a minute. That's a fine speech and we all agree in principle. But it's about time we did something practical.'

'What's practical?' Dave Klingerman yelled across at him. 'Swearing in a lot of deputies so the Sheriff can cross their palms with silver?' The Sheriff was an opposition man.

It turned into a dogfight then—Regan and Long and Arnie Genovese and Conover and Elias yelling back and forth—with the tremendous bellow of Miles Norton, the councilman, coming through it: 'I want to put Long's idea in the form of a motion.'

He did, and Young, the Comptroller, seconded, and it was lost on a show of hands. Eleven in favor. Reger was one of them.

Things quieted down a little, though the heat was still there, and John Kane said: 'Any more suggestions?' He got two or three vague ones. The sponsors piped down in the face of a little amiable headshaking. Then Maurice Satin of Public Works came up with what sounded offhand like a fairly good idea for keeping people in their own neighborhoods.

He wanted to cut the Staten Island ferry to a few trips a day, close the Harlem bridges and the East River bridges and tunnels.

Somebody asked: 'What about the people who live out on Long Island?'

Nobody mentioned how hopeless it would be unless you quarantined the city itself.

It was voted down, and Regan called from the foot of the table: 'Let's hear what you've got.'

John said: 'Your cue, Jim,' and sat down.

As I got up I could see the yellow-and-blue flag in front of

City Hall, spreading in slow ripples toward the northwest. No change. For an instant it looked like the yellow jack of quarantine, waving over a pestilential city. I didn't seem to have any feeling in my legs. I was looking for an opener, but all I could think of was the kind of signal Captain Hornblower used to run up when the enemy's trucks poked over the horizon: SUBMIT WE ATTACK AT ONCE. Not my style, but what I meant. The *submit* and the *attack at once.*

'We've got a plan for you all right but I want to sum up a little first.'

Dave Klingerman called: 'Louder, Jim.' I hadn't realized my voice was so low.

'I've got to make sure beforehand that we all agree about how bad this thing is,' I said. 'If I don't, you'll start by tearing the hide off the plan. It'll seem too drastic to you.'

'Not unless you want to jack up the whole town and move it to Nevada,' Romanelli said in a matter-of-fact tone.

'Okeh. You remember yesterday Dick Wirth mentioned that a little cold weather might choke the fever off?' I told them what I'd found out at the Weather Bureau. Nothing in sight yet. Martineau's report seemed to show that the fever ran its course in about ten days. Even so, the cases would overlap. And we couldn't wait.

'Dr. Leeson's committee is studying the epidemic. They'll make recommendations. You know what Dick Wirth is doing. A Medical Co-ordinating Committee was set up yesterday to keep people digging along complementary lines.' I sketched in a little of what I'd seen at Pete's laboratory. 'I hope you medical boys will correct me if I get off the track. It doesn't look to me as if we could sit on our cans and expect the bacteriologists to come galloping to the rescue. They'll get results all right, but we damn well can't hope for them in time to affect what we've got to do today. It might be a week or a year. Why not? It's almost as new to them as it is to us.'

Dick and Leeson and Onderdonck gave me an amen to that.

My legs were quivering. I tried to show how the spotty transportation picture hooked in with shortages in food and gasoline and coal and fuel oil, and how the lack of fuel might cut out the water-supply pumps and put the Fire Department out of business. If the water failed entirely, we would have to jack up and move to Nevada.

I kept hammering away to make them see, if they didn't see already, how everything tenoned into everything else. Foolish to try piecemeal attacks. We'd only pull the whole thing a little more out of true. This was an over-all job. Our problem was to get skilled men to the right spots and keep them there, come hell or high water. I tried to suggest a little of the runaway human feel of the city as I'd seen it the night before, and topped it all off with the estimate Dick had given me that morning: total *hlehhana* cases in the five boroughs, about 1,045,000.

'Is that a fair statement of the case? I hope to God you'll pick me up on anything you don't agree with. If we don't——'

'Jim,' Hanauer said. A literal man. 'That point about evacuating the city. Isn't that a little strong?'

'Maybe it is,' I said. 'I'll take that back, Adam. But they say good generals always try to anticipate the worst. How about the rest of it?'

They nodded and clapped soberly. I had to sit down. My legs shook and my head was thumping like the inside of a Diesel cylinder.

'Okeh. Here's the plan we've tried to work out. We had it in rough form yesterday but I wanted to look around and see if it had any chance of working. I think it has. Rich Jones helped us out with it. You can shoot it full of holes or dream up a better one. The plan is this.'

I talked to them as I'd talked to Bill the day before. Consolidate the maintenance services—police, fire, medical, public works, water supply, emergency squads, gas, electric, and transportation repair men—into control stations centralized in mapped districts all over the city. About thirty-five in all. Three-platoon crews to live at the stations, which would be set up under the Chief Engineer of the Board of Estimate. He'd be empowered to commandeer personnel, within reason, and set up a labor pool for reserves. Also he could take over trucks, gas, supplies, beds, food, etc., from the other departments or wherever he could get them. As I warmed to it I forgot about how I felt. The police two-way radio system would be the main line of communication: WPEE, WPEF, WPEG, and WPY.

I said: 'Here she is,' and shoved the big mounted map down the table. They got up and crowded around it. I leaned in on the table and showed them where each station would be. A police station, firehouse, or school wherever possible. A big garage or parking lot close by, where the prowl cars, emergency wagons, fire apparatus, ambulances, and repair trucks could be taken care of. In some cases the stations didn't seem to be centered geographically. I explained that this might happen where an express highway or some other factor made one part of the district more accessible.

They buzzed over points in several areas and I brought out the detail maps and the mimeographed circulars. Then the objections began to fly. Why is this more effective than keeping the services in their regular groupings? Because they're dangerously thinned out and badly undermanned in many parts of the city. What I'd said to Bill: we've got to shorten our lines.

'The second main point,' I said, 'is that we can't depend on the regular communications. Telephone, police- and fire-signal systems. The third point is that we can be pretty sure of reaching all these stations, all these varied services, with one system, the most foolproof one. And they can talk back to us.'

'This is going to play hell with our regular organization, Jim,' Justin said sadly.

A few of the other department heads looked at me reproachfully too. I'd hoped they'd mention it first. When you've had your wallet taken, it's wonderful to find a dollar bill in your vest pocket.

'I was hoping it wouldn't, Justin,' I said. 'I thought we could keep the crews in each station under their own officers and fore-men. Have all the men elect a station leader for each of the three platoons. What do you think?'

They nodded. They were pleased. 'That sounds all right,' Hanauer said.

Bob Porter, the Director of the Budget, howled with discovery. 'Wait a minute. Fourteen of these places you've got listed are lofts and private schools and office buildings. Why, these people would raise hell if you tried to requisition them. And how could we pay for them?'

'We'll beg 'em,' I said, 'or borrow 'em. Get quitclaims. Can't we do that?'

I looked at Brownell, the Corporation Counsel.

He shrugged. 'Why not? It'll take a little tact. Maybe we can dig up emergency powers to cover it. I'll ask my office to get up the forms and send them over to Jones. Then Jones can have people sign them before his men take over the properties.'

'Jim,' Arnie called down to me. 'I want to get the picture. A car turns over on Shore Road in Brooklyn. Out near Bay Ridge Park-way. People are hurt. The car catches fire. What happens?'

'All right,' I said. 'Here's your district station. A prowl car comes along, reports by radio to WPEE at Police Headquarters in Man-hattan. We probably couldn't depend on the control-station re-ceivers to pick up the weak car signals. So WPEE transfers the call by radio to the district station. The station sends out a fire truck or an ambulance and makes an all-clear report when they come back.

'Or some ordinary citizen sees the accident and gets to a tele-phone. We'll put on a campaign asking him to do this. WNYC and the regular radio stations. Newspapers. Car cards. We'll urge people to keep the station list on hand, report things to those points. Lots of them won't pay any attention, of course, but you've always got a few people who make a business of being mamma's little helpers in a crisis.

'All right. If the phones are working, the operator gives the call clearance and turns the man over to the district station. If not, he has several choices. He can get a message to the station or to the nearest police station. A passing car, or a kid on a bike. Anything. We'll keep an operator in each abandoned police station on the chance that messages can be relayed by phone or teletype. He'll try to get the report to WPEE.

'We'll sign up the DX'ers all over town. The radio hams. List their addresses in the newspapers. Have them relay things. Maybe we can needle the telegraph companies into using their messengers. As a public service. We might even be able to get some walky-talky sets for cops on post—if we can spare the cops. Or train them.'

I inched back off the table. Some of the others sat down again. I could feel that most of the boys were with me now, but Lester Long and a few more held out. He said it was a lot of damn foolishness to talk about abandoning the organization we had for a hit-or-miss scheme. Might take days to set it up.

'We all know it's a long chance, Lester,' Hickey said persuasively. 'It might surprise us all. It might work.'

He winked at me, but I could see that was about it. We took the vote. It passed, with what was beginning to look like the usual margin. They voted two or three changes in the map and we began to talk about setting it up.

Rich Jones and Harold Brownell came around to the head of the table.

Harold put his hand on my shoulder. 'We'll duck out now, Jim. Get things started.'

'Luck,' I said.

John Kane took over the job of publicity for the setup. Leeson promised to round up a psychiatrist and a crowd psychologist to advise him. The other commissioners and heads of boards would collaborate with Jones. Then we settled a routine for some of the less hard-driven departments: Welfare, Purchase, Parks, and so on.

'Okeh,' I said. 'Now I've got my neck this far out, what about quarantine?'

126

That started a real bobbery. Long said it would cost the city millions of dollars a day and Porter mentioned suits for restraint of trade.

Dick Wirth led the argument for. He said medical men were pretty well agreed that it ought to be tried in cases like this. Probably wouldn't be very effective anyhow. 'But we owe it to the rest of the country,' he said with a faint grin.

McKeogh shook his head. The police were down to eleven thousand men. It would mean splitting even that force between control stations and quarantine lines. But Dave Klingerman said we ought to be able to get plenty of service from the neighboring cities and towns in Jersey, Westchester, Connecticut, and Long Island. Their grief if they didn't co-operate. The Coast Guard and quarantine service would help too. We'd have to divert river and harbor traffic to Jersey or to other ports.

I got out a rough quarantine map we'd made up and they pushed it around as they talked.

Maurice Satin called: 'What about commuters?'

'Ah,' Hickey said, 'let the Immigration Service handle them.'

Mason Emery thought we might put them up in hotels. The maids would catch it, though. Or we could just lock them out some fine morning.

I didn't try to push it too hard. I wasn't so sure myself, and I could see a lot of the boys were doubtful. Even at that, the show of hands surprised me. It went through all right but the margin, nine votes, set me right back down where I belonged. We might have lost it altogether if I'd fumbled the presentation just a little more. The boys weren't backing me or anybody else. They were voting for keeps, and a damn good thing too. They picked Justin for the quarantine job. He and Rich Jones on the control stations would report to me.

We broke up then. As we were crowding out, a row of some kind started down the room. Arnie and Regan were in it. Somebody said they were quarreling about South Brother Island. It took me a minute to place it—a little empty seven-acre patch in the East River off the Bronx, twin to the bigger North Brother Island.

I remembered vaguely that the Brothers and Riker's Island had originally belonged to Newtown in Queens—Regan's bailiwick. Regan wanted South Brother. He said Abraham Riker had claimed it for Newtown in 1664. But New York City had annexed Riker's from Queens in 1884. Where did that leave South Brother?

Arnie wanted it for children's outings from the Bronx. It was called Bareass Island locally. The boys got out there somehow and went swimming that way. Regan didn't say so, but he was planning to hold it for sale to the city. Neither he nor Arnie had looked up the land maps.

The word had got round by this time and people were grinning.

'Take it easy, Arnie,' Cincione of Purchase said. 'This is no time to start fighting over a hunk of mud.'

Arnie turned and tapped him on the chest. 'Listen, Andy. I was a labor stiff too long not to know the best time to raise hell is when the heat's on. This smart one'—he jerked his thumb at Regan—'knows that too. So what do I do? So here's what I do, Regan. I take the island. Then we won't have no more trouble about it.'

He waved and began to push his way out.

'Why, you conniving little land pirate!' Regan roared after him.

Arnie made the finger sign. 'Claim-jumper,' he said with a deadly contempt.

They calmed down a little when we got outside. Wirth caught up with me. His people at the health stations were using sulfanilamide, sulfathiazole, sulfaguanadine, promin, and a few more of the two thousand or so sulfa drugs. Trying out a special atomizer designed to handle the rather heavy powder. Originally developed for vaginal treatment, he said. They were testing its effects in the mouth and nasal passages. Results mixed. Keeping the patients under observation, of course.

His eyes were nervous and prominent.

'You might try looking out for yourself a little, Dick.'

He shrugged.

3 Downstairs in the lobby, I tried to get the city garage on the phone. Nothing doing. Rich Jones's number didn't answer either.

I was walking out to get a cab when a big red-blond Irishman about my own age came up, made a saluting gesture, and said in a half-humorous tone: 'Mr. Rowan, I believe. My name is Dennis Harrington. I'm the driver for the Mayor's car and I was sent down to pick you up.'

He grinned at me and I grinned back.

'Yes, sure. How'd you know me?'

'Oh, I've had you pointed out to me. Mr. Jones's office sent word.'

We walked out under the colonnade into the muggy warmth of Centre Street. The girls walking in their light dresses. Three of them, giggling, pulled up their skirts and played leapfrog over a hydrant.

When they saw me they rushed over shrieking and grabbed my arms. 'Take us with you, Mr. Rowan. See? We know who you are.'

I was so low I actually felt embarrassed. Dennis glanced at me and shushed them away gently as if they were so many chickens.

'Mr. Rowan has work to do, girls,' he said firmly and opened the car door for me.

A late-model eight-cylinder closed job. Very clean lines. NYC 1, and the radio call was No. 1 too. The girls looked over Dennis's shoulder as he explained how the two-way radio telephone worked.

I leaned back and the car moved uptown. For the first time I wondered seriously whether I could be getting the fever. What then? Would they take me off the job? I was too listless to think. The streets looked changed but it was hard to say how. Traffic lights out. Rubbish blowing across the roadway. Cars driving half up on the sidewalk. But more than that. The unmistakable feel of a place with its hair down and a flower dangling over one ear.

Dennis got past a zigzagging car with no fuss. I talked to him a little about Niobe. My hunch about the library painting. He nodded sympathetically.

'I told my wife I'd lock her up if she got it. Yes, sir.'

The Forty-Second Street steps of the library crowded with smokers. A crush inside. The elevator went up as slowly as a rain barrel filling. I decided the picture must be downstairs and found one of those X-shaped stairways, a bright little fancy of the planners, Carrère and Hastings. The fashionable architectural revenants of the 1900's.

There it was, over the landing at the foot of the stairs. A large dark rectangle, the Milton girls in Quakerish gray. I let people go past while I looked things over.

Fifteen or twenty kibitzers around the picture, watching a dowdy black-haired woman copyist on a campstool. I went over everything in skirts or slacks very carefully. Height first. Not so many five-foot-ten women in the world.

A tall red-haired girl in black, with a snazzy white hat, drifted to the edge of the crowd. Her face was turned away. I started down as I saw her. She got up on tiptoe to look at the copyist's picture, then turned away and out of sight.

I came out on the corridor overlooking the enormous vault of the Fifth Avenue entrance hall. The white hat. I saw it, well down the right staircase, and went after it through the crowd, muttering apologies.

Almost at the foot of the stairs I caught her, said: 'Wait.' She turned, her eyebrows up. Not Niobe. The faces around us stopped to watch.

'Won't I do,' she said, and very low, 'darling?'

I shook my head glumly. 'I only wish you would.'

She made me a gay little salute. Halfway back up the stairs, I looked around. The white hat was just going out the door.

On the landing below the Milton picture, the woman painter was gone, the kibitzers melted away. I stood there a moment, then started down, trying to analyze the faint sensation of familiar pleasure I'd had. It hit me. Niobe's perfume. Called Chemin de

Fer, for no reason, and made up especially for her by a friend in the trade.

Niobe was the copyist. Only a hunch. I couldn't be sure and she didn't tell me until long afterwards. The black hair. Why hadn't I asked Eunice to find out what Niobe got done at the hairdresser's? One thing was sure. I'd never make a detective.

Downstairs I got buttonholed by an agitated little plumber. He didn't want anything. He'd invented a vacuum toilet bowl as an aid to the constipated and he was dazzled by the vision of his own universal gift to mankind.

I called Rich Jones. He and Brownell and Cincione of Purchase had been working fast. They had quitclaims on seven private properties for stations. Twelve city properties cleared: four schools, two college buildings, two fire stations, three police stations, and a Queens dental clinic, besides three state armories.

'Good work, Rich,' I said. 'Only seven or eight to go? You have the lists of personnel and equipment. We'll begin setting them up right away. I'll get Cornbill. Look. Would it be too hard on you if I asked for Charley Roach?' Roach was Jones's assistant. A good bright boy. 'Thanks. We'll need him. Yep. You can begin routing things out to No. 1 in about twenty minutes. We'll——'

I was cut off. I tried to get him again. No use. He'd told me that he was shifting over to Police Headquarters. His people would keep things running day and night from there. I got Bill, told him I'd pick him up outside the Municipal Building.

Dennis and the Mayor's car were getting a looking over. Another little boner of mine, I thought as we started downtown. Why hadn't I asked for a less conspicuous kind of barouche? They had me listed for it now.

We flagged Bill on Centre Street and he got in. He was winded. He'd tramped down twenty-six flights singing: 'She'll be comin' round the mountain when she comes.'

We got over to Church Street just north of Fulton. Station No. 1. The second and third floors of an old office building. I asked Bill to see that the garage around the corner was cleared. Check the station vehicles in. Dennis got to work tacking up one of the signs our map-makers had roughed out: the blue, white, and orange colors and NYC CONTROL STATION NO. 1.

Upstairs, I looked around and hauled some old workbenches out of the way. Men and materials began to come in—at first in a dribble, then fast. I checked them at the door. The police emergency squad. Firemen. The regular cops. Two doctors. Water-supply men. Dennis took over for me at the door. I showed the boys where to set up the short-wave radio. Reserve batteries. They nailed the district map up behind it and rigged lights. I was helping get the beds spaced when the first call came in. A rubbish fire on lower Washington Street. The firemen ran clumping out and in a minute or two the truck wailed past the windows. It had taken us thirty-eight minutes to get shaken down into rough working order. So far so good.

When the men reported back I got everybody together to elect a platoon leader. They'd sized each other up fast. A well-known brain surgeon was voted in, partly as a compromise candidate between the cops and firemen. Bill came back then. All the horses were in the barn.

The brain surgeon got me aside and suggested that we might ask the medical men at each station to watch for signs of pronounced depression in the men. The station leader ought to relieve a depressed man at once and ask for a replacement.

'Thanks, Doctor. A good idea,' I said.

He watched me while I made a note and gave me a queerly professional look as he shook hands.

On the way uptown with Bill I got Rich Jones on the car radio and reported No. 1 operating. He said Charley Roach had Station No. 2 well on the way and sent us on to No. 3. A fire station in the Village.

We were almost there when the dispatcher's voice came through again. 'Calling Car No. 1. Car 1. Commissioner McKeogh requests that Commissioner Rowan meet him immediately at the emergency ward, Bellevue Hospital. The emergency ward, Bellevue Hospital. Please acknowledge.'

'This is Rowan. I'll be there in about five minutes.'

'Thank you, Mr. Rowan. That is all.'

4

WE DROPPED Bill at No. 3 and Dennis put the siren on for the run to East Twenty-Sixth Street. He showed me what he could do. It was like broken-field running down a corridor, with tacklers leaping at you from every doorway.

On Fourth Avenue we nearly climbed a truck. My head went down between my knees as Dennis pulled up and all the time I was thinking: It can't be Niobe. She was at the library. Not enough time. Time for what? An accident? An elevator the inspectors didn't get around to this week? An explosion? It can be anybody. Anytime.

Justin was waiting. 'Now take it easy, Jim,' he said. He took my arm and his blunt fingers went into the muscle. 'It probably isn't Mrs. Rowan but we've got to make sure. The girl has good clothes. Bonwit Teller labels.'

The Germaine Monteil dress I liked. Very soft thin wool, black, with a shiny peplum.

'We've compared the pictures,' he said. 'The ring finger is crooked.'

My face felt like stiff leather. 'Is she dead?'

Justin shook his head. 'They fished her out of the river. If she comes round she'll be all right.'

'How long ago?'

'About half an hour.'

'I think I just missed her at the library an hour ago. She couldn't——'

133

My stomach felt as it used to when I was a kid and swallowed a chunk of ice I'd been sucking.

He beckoned me. 'Better have a look.'

We went inside—I was tiptoeing, I remember—and stopped at the foot of a bed. People were laughing in the room and down along the row a man with a fractured skull shouted and mumbled. A soft hissing sound. Oxygen. Justin led me up to the bed and motioned the attendant to take the mask off.

I stared at the girl's face, the blue eyelids. Her head looked childish on the pillow, as all women's heads do, and I remember wondering how people could have the heart to cut their throats, as people did sometimes. The eyelids stirred. A nurse murmured and took the girl's wrist. The eyes opened and looked at me for a long moment, then closed again.

It was very like Niobe's face, but not Niobe's. I shook my head, Justin nodded, and they began to work over her again. He tiptoed out.

'Poor babe. I hope she'll be all right. Let me know, will you? And thanks, Justin. Wait a minute.'

I went back and left something with the nurse for her. The nurse smiled at me.

When I caught up with Justin we grinned at each other and went out together, talking about the quarantine. Good progress. A skeleton force already lined up along McLean Avenue in the West Bronx and Park Drive in the East. Langdale Street, Jamaica Avenue, Hook Creek Boulevard, and down along the capillary squiggle of Hook Creek to the Jamaica Bay marshes.

The water approaches were harder. The shores of the Kill Van Kull and the Arthur Kill. North River traffic shunted over to the west bank. Volunteer yachtsmen blocking off the Sound east of a line between Little Neck Bay and Hunter's Island. Some necessary freight lighterage, of course. The Hudson tunnels and the George Washington Bridge closed. Food trucks and supplies by rail being taken over by New York drivers at the city limits. The harbor itself would be cut off from seaward by the Coast Guard, except for permits to the Jersey ports.

Justin said they'd turned back two fourteen-year-old boys and a girl in a Star boat. The kids were beating through the Narrows, outbound for Bermuda. They had a case of Campbell's beans, a Boy Scout compass, an azimuth circle made out of the girl's brace-let and two bobbie pins, and an *American Practical Navigator*.

5

Dennis drove me back down to Station No. 3 in the Village. Children's faces outside all the windows, and what the hell were we doing with their school? Not that they wanted it back. Bill had the job about cleaned up, except for a dozen beds not checked in yet. He went ahead to No. 5—Roach was at No. 4—and I started downtown to compare notes with Rich Jones at Police Head-quarters.

Up in the crow's-nest of the old French baroque pile on Centre Street, in the Telegraph Bureau, Rich looked harried but all there. First time I'd ever seen him with his jacket off. He showed me around. They were stringing a battery of extra telephones for in-coming calls. The regular police operators taking incoming stuff by radio, teletype, and telegraph.

All calls cleared through a routing desk. A man each for the sta-tions in the Bronx, Queens, and Staten Island. Two each for Man-hattan and Brooklyn. A couple of the boys were topographical engineers from Rich's office. They had mounted maps in front of them, pricked with colored pins indicating the character and whereabouts of each unit at the stations.

When one of these boys got a call he picked out the nearest available unit, wrote out a chit and handed it to a messenger. The dispatcher at his desk mike initialed it and sent it out. Not very different from the regular police routine. Rich had assigned a block of control stations to each of the three transmitters. So far, it was working.

I praised the job he'd done—it was a good job, but Rich was an uneasy man who needed praise—and started uptown again with Dennis. I was draggy but fair enough while I kept moving. When I stopped, I felt low enough to crawl.

A huge poster slapped across a building front on Broadway, windows and all: COME OUT COME OUT WHEREVER YOU ARE: PARADE TO THE END OF THE WORLD: MONDAY FEBRUARY 23, 194–: LINE FORMS WASHINGTON SQUARE PARK AT ONE P.M.: MUSIC FOOD LIQUOR GIRLS ANIMALS BABIES FUN: THE WORLD IS YOURS FOR THE ASKING. All superimposed on a tremendous design of rearing dappled horses hauling a circus wagon.

Trouble for us. Dennis went back and we looked at it. I recalled the man with the sandwich board in Times Square. The same slogan: THE WORLD IS YOURS FOR THE ASKING. No organization address or printer's name on this. But style was a signature too. The slaty colors and the humorous chunky surrealism looked like Bill Wheatley's work. I called the dispatcher and suggested tracing it.

We drove uptown in the yellow warm sunset. Nothing to remind you that this was February. It felt like a windy late April. We cut across to the station Bill was working on in the East Seventies.

As I got out, a very handsome black-haired woman gave me a fluty how-do-you-do and her gloved fingers. About thirty-five or so. Swishy clothes. I thought vaguely that she must be one of Niobe's less theatrical women friends and asked Dennis to tell Bill I'd be in a little later.

She took my arm. 'Now come along. You're having dinner with me. Busy? But of course you're not busy.'

We walked four blocks, turning twice. She chatted away about the fever and how hard it was to get anything at the stores and so on, with neat little offhand touches that reminded you you were a male, and big, and probably wicked. I was amused but also preoccupied. Who was she, for God's sake, and why couldn't I place her?

136

We walked up three flights in a narrow good apartment building and she opened the door with her own key. She closed it gently behind us, took my face in her gloved hands, and kissed me. But personally. A friend of Niobe's? What friends.

'That's for being a good boy and coming quietly. Now we'll see what they've sent up. You can't imagine how difficult——'

She beckoned me into the pantry and we lifted covers on things from the Colony. Good to know the Colony was still on deck. Roast beef, which I didn't much care for. Brussels sprouts in Polonaise sauce, the bread crumbs nicely browned in butter with lemon juice and parsley. Cheese. Rolls. A *bombe* with magenta raspberry ice cream.

She got me settled with a drink, put on a tiny fluted apron, and began to lay the small table.

'My maid has gone where the woodbine twineth. *All* the maids have gone where the woodbine twineth. What *is* woodbine?'

A city girl, or just trying to draw me out?

'Sort of a creeper. A vine. It clings to things. Very handsome in the fall. Very vivid. Like you.'

My best offer, sunk as I was.

She laughed. 'Am I red? It must be the heat from the tureen. Oh, and you must try my darling wine. From the Finger Lakes. American, no less, and good. Come sit down.'

I helped her with the chair.

'I don't like to seem inquisitive,' I said, 'but I feel a little low, and when I'm low I'm literal. *Should* I remember you? I mean—should I know your name?'

'Never seen me before in your life, I'm sure. Eat your cabbage.'

She was eating away briskly herself and there were no rings on her left hand. But the place didn't look solo. It was standard upper East Side family kitsch. Too much of too many kinds of things in the living room. A vaguely English clutter.

Well, at least I had an even chance of not being shot in the back. They probably didn't shoot any more. What the hell did they say? 'Don't move. I just stopped by for my golf bag.'

The wine was good and I could see Bill waiting at the fire station. We attacked the *bombe*. Her cheeks curved in under the cheekbones and there were small pearls in the lobes of her ears. Tanned skin, flushed a little, and startling dark-blue eyes. She smiled at me gradually with her small teeth, like a werewolf.

We had coffee in the big chairs and she put a string quartet, Cherubini, on the phonograph. A clear and ingenious simplicity. The relaxed attack we used to talk about in jazz, the thing the romantics had thrown away.

'That was lovely.'

'It was lovely,' she said. 'But now you're going to bed. You look fagged out. There's a new toothbrush in the medicine cabinet.'

'Thanks. I must go.'

'But of course you're not going.'

She led me into the bedroom and got my tie off very efficiently. A Kindel Queen Anne dressing table and twin beds.

I said: 'Look. Are you sure you——'

She nodded. 'Of course I'm sure. I know *just* how you feel. Yesterday I was low enough to cry.' She lifted her hands. 'Today I'm fine. Now brush your teeth and get into bed. I'll be back in a minute.'

She was back in five, wearing a limpid chalky tailored nightdress that showed off her dark skin. She slipped off her mules, got into bed with me, and stretched.

'I don't know when I've felt so beautiful.'

'Or looked so beautiful.'

'Thank you, Paul, Freddy, Jack, Timothy, Donald, Henry, Carl, Daniel——'

'Jim.'

'Thank you, Jim. The woodbine twineth. The blessed, blessed woodbine twineth.'

I stroked the back of her neck. It was one of the things I'd always done and I did it without thinking. She flinched a little.

She was cool and expert. She tried to take the play away from me, as some women try to lead in dancing, and when I crushed that her round hard thighs worked in revolt. The nervelessness I'd felt all day gave me a kind of advantage. She fought back wickedly and cunningly, trying to snatch the bit. At first it was conscious and then it was not conscious, it was possessed and blind, as impersonal as wringing a chicken's neck, and I had her lifted from the bed with her teeth in my shoulder.

She rolled and beat my chest with her fists, whispering, then stretched and closed, and ruffled my hair.

In a little while she asked for a cigarette, with a kind of indifferent arrogance.

'Please, woman.'

'Please, you devil.'

I got up and had a shower and she came to the door with me in a white bengaline house coat. She kissed me good-by and it took me an instant to realize that she was knuckling my spine. An old schoolboy trick.

I bent her arm away. 'Where did you learn that?'

'We used to do it to the younger girls at boarding school.'

She gave me the gradual smile with the small white teeth.

I said good night. No name on the door. No elevator man and no doorman. Well, if I didn't get the fever now I never would.

6 SOMEONE called to me in the dark street. Dennis. He'd trailed us.

I grinned at him. 'Sorry, Dennis.'

'That's all right, Mr. Rowan. I see you were detained in a good cause. They've been calling you on the radio. I told them you'd be along in a few minutes.'

I asked for Jones and told him I'd been having dinner.

'We've got to do something, Jim,' he said. 'We're being besieged by the Boy Scouts. They want to help, and every last man of them is pretty hurt because we won't give him a job.'

139

I thought. 'Why not? We can use them for daytime work. Can't keep the little tykes out all night. Let's give 'em police whistles and put 'em into the quarantine lines. It'll be mostly open country anyhow. They can use their woodcraft. And, Rich. We'd better keep them close to home too. We don't want some kid from St. Mary's Park getting homesick pounding a beat in Tottenville.'

We were both laughing.

'Give 'em to McKeogh,' I said. 'Tell him it's an order.'

I could see Justin's face as the troops reported. They'd probably make him an Eagle Scout.

Bill was at No. 10 in the Bronx. Baychester. Roach and the others had about finished setting things up in Queens. Brooklyn and Staten Island still to go.

'How's it working?'

'All right so far,' Rich said, and sighed. 'We've answered all but five calls—the calls we got. Even the false alarms. We've had seventy-three of those. Not bad, considering. We set up an extra switchboard but if the phone exchanges were really working full time we'd be snowed under. The logistics situation is getting tight.' Logistics. He'd been a major in the 1918 war. 'We've kept up so far but things are beginning to run out. Trouble about kitchens and we're short five ambulances. Scully-Walton turned over the whole fleet to us but some of the private hospitals are holding out till they see how the thing works.'

'I'll get the ambulances,' I said, thinking of Pete. 'Where does Cornbill go next?'

'Station 17 in Greenpoint.'

'I'm going over to Kip's Bay Medical Center. I'll be in Greenpoint in—oh, about an hour. Thanks, Rich. And don't worry about the logistics. You're doing fine.'

I telephoned Pete and listened to calls on the way over. I felt worse than I had all day. The reaction. Sleeping with women while the town went to hell. Niobe bucketing around. No slouch herself once she got started. Oh God. I couldn't do anything about her until I caught up with her.

I stopped at a drugstore and asked for a prophylactic. The clerk spilled a half dozen out on the counter, said: 'Help yourself,' and waved me away when I offered him money.

The tall piers of the hospital glowed here and there with soft fluorescent lights. An occasional orange shade. A courier took me up to Pete's unit. There was another man in Pete's white office, a big pink baby-clean man in a white jacket. Looked like a youngish eighteenth-century hunting squire. What they used to call the sanguine type.

Pete introduced me. The psychiatrist, Dr. Rowland Hutchinson. They seemed strained. We talked a minute and Hutchinson said: 'Well, I'll be getting on.'

Pete leaned back in the chair. He looked tired and pale beside the other man.

'Hutch,' he said. 'Jim Rowan is in charge of control measures for the city.'

Hutchinson glanced at me.

'But I'd like to keep it quiet, if you don't mind,' I said.

'Jim is in on this,' Pete continued. 'If we're neglecting some promising line of treatment, he's entitled to know about it. I don't see why we can't get it settled now.'

'You people sound ominous. What's it about?'

Hutchinson shrugged. 'The fever. Pete and I have been having a little wrangle about it. My feeling is that unless we get a lot more bacteriological evidence than we have now, we're justified in treating it as a mass psychosis.'

I said: 'You mean something like crowd hysteria? Group suggestion?'

I looked at Pete. He was listening.

'Well, something like that,' Hutchinson said. He was striding up and down. Plenty of free nervous energy. 'What one of Strecker's patients called "a lovely little excursion into unreality." You realize there's a delusional system here. Precisely the sort of system we run across in individual cases. In fact, some psychiatrists think that crowd delusions may correspond to the two main individual reaction types—the schizophrenic and the cyclothymic.'

He turned suddenly. 'Of course this isn't extreme—not what we call massive. It seems to be a means of escape from what's known as cenesthetic discomfort. Discomfort caused by the part of the personality that's kept on a chain by convention. I grant you that's a fairly large part of it, for a good many people.

'Even so, I should judge that this derangement falls into the schizophrenic class. People withdraw instead of getting violent. Secede from the human race, as someone put it. But mind you, they're doing it as a group. In certain typical ways. Evading responsibility at the same points. Job responsibility. Sex responsibility. Financial responsibility and so on.'

'So does a pneumonia patient,' Pete said quietly.

Hutchinson looked at me with his eyebrows up. 'That's it. Pete feels there's some evidence of organic damage. I don't. Or not enough.'

'Not very much,' Pete agreed. 'But the cortex of the hypothalamus shows fairly definite lesions. If you can call a more or less acutely inflamed condition a lesion. The pictures seem to indicate virus invasion of the cells.'

He said to me: 'Viruses tend to be selective. Some are neurotropic, for example. This one seems to have a special liking for the covering of the hypothalamus. Down at the base of the skull. We've been using tissue from the animals.'

'I don't question that at all,' Hutchinson said. He looked closely at one of the Detrand sketches and turned back. 'My point is that the tissue damage is so slight it can hardly be credited with these— these extraordinary behavior changes. As a predisposing factor, as an excitant—yes. It probably creates a state of hyperesthesia that makes this—this mass excitement irresistible. But'—and he tapped his big square fingers softly in his open palm—'the behavior itself is a *functional* personality disorder and can be treated as such.'

Pete nodded. 'I'd agree to some of that myself. It's a good working hypothesis, at any rate. I'm not so sure about the last part.'

'If you gentlemen will forgive me,' I said, 'I don't quite catch. Why can't you both go along on your own lines?'

Pete was doodling again. 'We were coming to that,' he said, very low. 'The reason is that Hutch wants to try the shock treatment on our patients here.'

He looked up, waited for Hutchinson to explain. The big pink man stopped pacing, looked at me, then gestured and sat down. He said very earnestly: 'I don't know quite how to put this. It involves medical judgment and—oh, medical ethics generally. I don't know what ideas you have about us. A good many people believe that because some of us have offices in the Sixties and——'

It sounded naïve. I looked at Pete and smiled. 'I guess I'll waive that point.'

They laughed.

'We have a problem,' Hutchinson continued. 'We've had it, in fact, for several hundred years and it's getting worse. Schizophrenia. You know about that. In the Middle Ages, schizophrenics were burned as witches. In New England too. In east Asia, Siberia, they became shamans. Priests. Their hallucinations were thought to be divinely inspired.

'You probably know too,' he said, offering me a cigarette, 'that our hospitals are full of them. I'm not sure it isn't our worst public-health problem. We've had some success with the regular psychotherapy but a good many cases don't respond. Thousands and thousands of cases.

'Then, during the twenties, Sakel tried insulin. First in Berlin, later in Vienna. He got extraordinary results with patients who would have been considered hopeless before that. The insulin causes deep shock and convulsions, followed by coma. It's used in a series of treatments. Later they tried metrazol. That seemed to get even more striking results. Electroshock. Freezing in refrigerated blankets. Even surgical treatment—prefrontal leucotomy. We've had some remarkable recoveries with all these methods.'

'I've seen some of the newspaper stories,' I said.

'Yes. Of course they must sound very drastic to a layman. Actu-

143

ally we don't understand the mechanism of schizophrenia and we're not sure what precise effects these treatments have. Except that they do work in a considerable number of cases. It's frankly empirical and sometimes it causes injuries. We've learned how to cushion these injuries to some extent by administering curare or some other drug before treatment.'

I said: 'And you wanted to use these treatments on the fever patients?'

Hutchinson nodded.

'What Hutch told you is substantially true,' Pete said. He was white and grim. Unconsciously he made deep jabs with the pencil at each sentence. 'He didn't explain what these things do to the patient. The metrazol especially is about equivalent to being dropped off a bridge once a day for four to eight weeks.'

Hutchinson protested: 'That's hardly very——'

Pete didn't look up. 'Let me finish, Hutch.' His voice got quieter and quieter. 'In the convulsions, people often break their arms and legs, fracture vertebrae, or cause internal damage. Some patients go on having convulsions after the treatments are finished. Brain damage in almost all cases. Cobb's people at Massachusetts General experimented with animals. They found it destroyed great numbers of ganglion cells in the brain cortex. The patient's terror of the treatment is almost worse than angina fright. In the years since I've been out of medical school, I've never seen anything so pathetic as the delirious begging of one old woman being taken in for metrazol shock.'

Hutchinson was white-lipped now. 'Aren't you claiming a monopoly of human sympathy?'

'I don't think so,' Pete said. 'It's an assault on the organism and personality of a helpless patient. You could probably get the same effect by having him beaten up once a day. They do that too in a good many psychiatric institutions. Not officially, of course. Now. Today. In spite of Beers's book, and all the reforms since.'

Hutchinson looked hurt and angry. 'I don't know about that. I guess you know we don't. In any case, the shock treatment is routine in most reputable mental hospitals. You're talking against an established practice.'

'Yes, I am,' Pete said. He spoke so low I could hardly hear him. 'I happen to believe it's criminal assault.'

'Why, God damn it, Jenkins,' Hutchinson burst out. 'We're trying to help these people. Everyone knows it's heroic treatment.'

Pete looked up. 'I like my heroes voluntary. With no broken bones.'

They stared at each other.

Hutchinson said: 'Do you mind if I pull out of the experiment?'

Pete considered. 'I'd like you to stay. There are other methods of treatment.'

'Thanks. I'm afraid I can't. I'll call you. Good night, Mr.— Rowan.'

He shook hands with me. When he was gone I looked at Pete. 'You're a tough Calvinist, Jenkins.'

That was it too. I knew the feeling. My family were all Ulster or Scotch Presbyterian. The sword of the righteous.

He smiled faintly. 'Maybe so. Maybe they are too. I have a feeling that behind it all there's an unconscious assumption—the assumption that these patients are trying to evade moral responsibility. That justifies the use of force to bring them back to it. Punitive force. If you think that's naïve you should talk to some of those boys. Not the best ones, of course.

'Something else too. Something a little more practical. Most of the state institutions are using this shock business. They can clean up a lot of formerly hopeless cases and send them home. Cured. A little brain damage, of course, that can never be repaired. But it does cut taxes.'

'That's all there is to it?'

'No. Lots of good honest physicians trying to help their patients. But my God, you can't expect a bacteriologist to be impressed with a risky hit-or-miss procedure like that.

'How can I take a chance with it? We know cortical damage can be traced to it. How do I know it wouldn't cause all sorts of lesions

—even fatal ones—in an already inflamed hypothalamus? The optic thalamus too. Lovely if we had a few cases of blindness on our hands.'

He got up. 'Let's take a look around. Some new things you might like to see.'

7 WHILE we went through the interminable business of scrubbing up, Pete told me about the lines of research they'd been following.

A rank failure with gramicidin, the powerful bactericide worked up from soil organisms by Dubos at Rockefeller Institute. He said they hadn't expected much. The stuff was murderous with Gram-positive bacteria. The *hlehhana* virus wasn't a bacterium, of course, but it seemed to be able to hold on to some of the gentian violet in the Gram staining method.

This made the theory that the virus might be a degenerate bacterium a little more likely. So they tried gramicidin. The trouble with it was that it acted very ravenous with red blood cells. That prevented it from being used internally. But young Wright had had the idea of combining it with a detoxicant, methionine. He tried it on a few of the prairie dogs.

'What happened?'

'Poor little beggars,' Pete said. 'No more love. Miss Felton and the other nurses gave them a fancy funeral at the incinerator chute. I suppose you've noticed women admire——'

'Yes,' I said.

They were working with penicillin, a chemical from one of the ordinary penicillium molds found on cheese or bread. Dawson's experiments at Columbia showed that this might be even more effective than gramicidin and it could be given subcutaneously, intravenously, or by mouth. Damned hard material to get pure in any quantity but you didn't need much for experiments. It seemed to work well in dilutions as high as 1:500,000. They were making progress.

'I suppose you know about the stale-beer bacillus?'

I nodded. 'A sad thing for barflies. Here they've been drinking steadily all these years, imagining they were poisoning themselves, and it turns out the stuff is good for them.'

Pete grinned. 'Well, perhaps. Bacillus alkaligenes. We don't know how good it is actually. We've had very mixed results so far. But the alkalizing effect has all sorts of possibilities. What interests us mainly is that it might be used to treat the portal of entry. The nose or mouth or whatever. That's a very promising line of attack with an invader like this.'

My back ached and the scrubbing was an effort.

'Have you found the portal of entry yet?'

'Not quite. But in a case of this kind, with a highly selective agent—call it thalamotropic—the evidence is pretty strong. These viruses have regular routes of passage. One is the Overland Trail up through the nasopharynx.

'Right up at the top of the nasal opening, under the brain, is the olfactory area. Ideal. It keeps moist. Temperature stays pretty even. A nice cozy little hothouse. The trick, from the invader's point of view, is to get there. The mucous drainage is downward and away from the area. The ciliary current is too—the little hairlike proc- esses that stream like eelgrass in a riverbed.'

We'd got to the alcohol-and-Merthiolate stage.

'You ought to teach this,' I said.

The nurse, a tall gray-haired one, smiled discreetly.

'I do,' Pete said. 'This is Lecture No. 4, much simplified. So if the virus can get up to the olfactory area, that's the first and most important way station. From there on the trail leads straight into the cranium. Some experimenters have gotten through with col- ored test materials.

'The primary neurones of smell have little hairy processes that extend out to the surface of the mucosa. The virus goes up along them like a spawning salmon, following the olfactory fibers right up through the epithelial and the turbinates and the bone strata and the cribriform plate and the olfactory bulbs. These bulbs stand in a more or less vertical series and lead right through to the brain area.

'We're not very sure of the route from there. Probably it runs on back along the subarachnoid space between the dura mater and the pia mater—all layers of brain covering—and eventually to the cortex of the thalamus. One of the odd things about this *hlehhana* virus—yes, I got that too—is that it makes so little trouble on the way. Most infections that go through the nasal passages kick up at least a minor disturbance. Not this little character. Or rather, not enough to be noticeable.'

We were being bundled into the white gear. His voice sounded flat and nerveless.

I said: 'Maybe I ought to set up a doctors' bureau to watch the doctors. Dick Wirth is trying to knock himself out and it looks to me as if you're playing that game too. How many hours do you work?'

He glanced at me as the nurse slipped my mask on. 'I'm around most of the time. I was just thinking you didn't look up to scratch yourself. You don't suppose——'

'I don't suppose anything, Dr. Jenkins. Neither do you.'

He nodded slowly. 'Well, I'll bring you up to date on our little chamber of horrors and let you get back to your job.'

I smiled. 'In a way, this is my job too. I'm official kibitzer-in-charge-of-everything.'

The main laboratory seemed busier, if anything, than the last time I'd seen it. More of an industrial-plant look now, with all the fluorescent lights overhead. A pretty big place.

Pete said: 'I don't know whether I told you or not. That point about the lack of nasal irritation almost had me fooled. My original hunch—we'd been working with encephalitis—was that this stuff might be one of the postinfection encephalitides. Postinfluenza seemed most likely.

'Must be about a dozen of the known ones—postrabies-treatment paralysis, Schilder's disease, postmeasles, postvaricella—all showing inflammation as the main pathological change. They seem to eat off the fatty sheath of the nerves—perivascular demyelinization, it's called. I looked up the records and the influenza and measles percentages seemed to be a little below normal, if anything, this winter. Good thing that wasn't it, though. What I've told you comes pretty close to being all we know about it.'

People were stopping him to consult about this and that. He introduced me to a few of them. One man had what seemed to be a pretty good lead about the resemblance between *hlehhana* and the louping-ill virus in swine. Louping ill didn't appear to damage the nerve cells. In between Pete told me that he'd got his full quota of forty-eight patients.

'They've organized,' he said. 'Yep. The Prairie Dogs, Inc. A young lawyer in K-6, the control pavilion, drew up the papers. The secretary from his office came to get them and made a tremendous row when we wouldn't let her in to see him. Got very personal about it.'

'Sounds like love,' I said.

'Oh, and speaking of love,' Pete said. 'I didn't show you the poor kids in L-6. A little triumph for monogamy. Come along.'

The pavilion seemed fairly quiet—most of the people were in the sunroom down at the end—and a nurse came along with us. Down on the right, a bed with a canvas curtain around it. Pete drew the curtain back a little.

Two kids in the bed, the boy seventeen or eighteen, the girl sixteen or so. They were lying relaxed and close together, mouth to mouth. The complete absorption of suckling infants, wet with bliss. Their eyes were closed and the girl's dark hair was feathered out on the pillow beside the boy's sandy close-cropped head.

Pete and the nurse had the look of people watching a sleeping infant and I suppose I had the same feeling. Pete settled the curtain down around them and we went out.

I thought of all the kids in the city aching for each other, with

149

no place to go: the flurries in dark hallways, the listening for cops in Greenwood Cemetery, the little shrieks coming up from the slope of St. Nicholas Park.

'At least we had the open fields,' I said.

'But the mosquitoes were terrible.'

'They were indeed. Tell me about these kids.'

'Well, they came in yesterday and asked to be admitted.'

'Why?'

'Didn't seem to know exactly. In a cloud. They'd been wandering around. Wanted some place to be together, out of the storm. The human storm.'

'Well put, Doctor. But couldn't they go to a hotel?'

'The girl thought that wouldn't be nice. They seemed to have the fever—or both fevers, each reinforcing the other—so we took them in. They've hardly left each other long enough to go to the toilet. The other people are very protective. Young Sidney is a favorite around here but he went and peeked this morning and they ostracized him for an hour. By the way, he's doing some fine pictures with those paints you sent. Talented kid. He wanted me to thank you.'

'Good for Sidney. I'll come by and see them next time. Maybe we can get him into a school or something. I've got to——'

'I'll show you two or three things on the way out. You probably ought to know about them. We tried oxygen treatment and got what seemed to be partial recoveries. About forty per cent, I'd say. But it's too costly to be used on a mass scale.

'Then we're working on a group of detoxicants developed over at Warner Institute. The ascorbic acid-choline-cystine-glycine-glucuronic acid combination. Some are vitamins, some organic compounds. Part of the virus effect is toxic, of course. It may help there. Or we may be able to use it with some specific drug. But look at these.'

A cabinet full of broad flat-bottomed flasks leading up into smaller, high-necked flasks plugged with cotton and tinfoil. A little liquid in the bottom.

'One of our virus-farming methods. Those are collar flasks. The stuff in them, doused in Tyrode's solution, is minced tissue from the thalamic cortex of mice. The viruses are feeding on it. But this is what I really wanted you to see.'

Another cabinet. Rows and rows of nice clean hen's eggs. Each had a small transparent disk attached to the shell.

'I've seen those,' I said.

'Ten to one you haven't. These eggs are pretty well along. Developing chicken embryos. We pierce the shell and inject the virus with a special syringe. Then we close the opening with one of those cover slips. The chicken goes right on growing inside and we can watch the virus multiplying on the chicken membrane.

'This is fairly fast but we've got to speed up our methods if we expect to get anything in time. We're setting up two new experiments tonight.'

We were walking toward the outside offices.

'Too bad,' he said. 'I haven't shown you how we identified the virus. Size and weight and the rest of it. You haven't had a look at the machines yet either. Well——'

I felt pretty grim. It had just struck me that all this shining ingenuity and devotion might not work after all. We could hold the thing together for a day or so. Two days. Even three. After that——

'Pete,' I said, 'what actual chance is there?'

He closed the door gently behind us.

'We'll get it,' he said, and looked at me. 'You mean when?' He shook his head. 'I don't know.'

8

DOWNSTAIRS I remembered about the ambulances and called him back on the phone. He said it might be ticklish business but he'd do what he could.

Dennis drove me over the Queensboro Bridge and down along Vernon Boulevard into Greenpoint. Station 17. A small warehouse. The neighborhood kids darting around the door. Across the street, trucks and ambulances backing into a vacant lot. Their lights on the front of the building made the whole thing look like a fire or a movie opening on Broadway.

Bill was checking in the kitchen equipment and supplies. We watched a man installing reserve batteries for the radio. Very quick and handy. A cop at the door turned away two firemen's wives. No women. We'd made it a rule. Aside from the ordinary troubles, we couldn't take a chance on avoidable outside contacts.

One of the wives pointed through the doorway. 'There's a woman in there now.'

The cop didn't look around. 'She'll be out in five minutes. She's helping to set the place up.'

I glanced at Bill. 'Who is it?'

'Marguerite.'

'Well, hey. She's got the fever.'

'She's leaving when we finish up here.'

Bill was looking pretty travel-weary too.

I went back to see her. She and two gas repair men were making the beds. Army cots. The loft was nothing but bare black wood and a splintered floor. Have to get some whitewash.

Marguerite saw me and beckoned me over to a corner. We sat on the edge of a cot.

'I got a telegram from Palmer this morning.' The Pan American Highway boy friend. 'He heard it on the radio and he's worried about me. Says he's coming home.'

'What about Bill?'

'That's what I don't know.'

She took my hand. I had an impulse to laugh but I was fond of her and much too depressed. Not exactly a big problem, the way things stood, but I supposed lots of people must be having them. Bill hadn't been divorced very long. A poor risk, if that was what she was after.

'What do you want?'

'Both of them,' she said with the fever's candor and brushed her dark hair back. 'I'm going to marry Palmer but I guess I've sort of got a crush on Bill. I never met anybody like him before. He's sweet. He does everything for me, yet at the same time he's—he's indifferent. You know?'

I nodded. 'And you want Uncle's advice?'

'Uh-huh.'

I waved. 'That's easy. Just do what you want to do. I don't need to tell a lady the rest of that rule, do I?'

Nice talk for a man who was hunting his wife all over the bailiwick.

She kissed me.

9

BILL sent Marguerite home in his car and we started for the next station in mine. Dennis said they'd been calling me again and it came in just as he spoke.

'Car 1. Car 1. Commissioner Rowan. Come in, please.'

'Yes? This is Rowan.'

Rich Jones said: 'Here's Harry Conover.' Commissioner of Water Supply, Gas, and Electricity.

'Hello, Jim,' Harry said. 'We're in trouble at the Hill View Reservoir. You know—the West Bronx. Got a report there's nobody there. A phone call. The woman wouldn't give her name. Almost everything goes through it—the stuff from Schoharie, Esopus, everything. If it goes out we're licked.'

'What do you want me to do?'

'We've still got pressure. We don't even know whether anything's wrong. We chlorinate the effluent up there. Got a couple of downtake chambers and one uptake. The boys from the control station went up there but we can't get a report from them. I'm stuck with another job. The private wells over in Woodhaven. Water isn't feeding at all. I'm taking the men I've got here.'

'Okeh. I'll look at Hill View and report back.'

We dropped Bill at the next station, turned the siren on and went wailing over the dark Triborough Bridge. There were street lights in the Mott Haven district and all the way north. The lights were on in the water-supply building as we pulled up at Hill View.

Dennis shut the motor off and we could hear peepers. An April night. I noticed the service truck.

A little man in a windbreaker came out and I saw him catch the car license.

'I'm Commissioner Rowan. Everything all right?'

The little man's voice was so quiet it made me feel as if I'd been blustering.

'Seems okeh. My name's Hendricksen. From the No. 9 Station in Woodlawn. Funny thing. I'm a great admirer o' Joseph Conrad. *Post* had an offer on his books a few years back and I bought 'em.

'I see the atmosphere right away. We made a fast run over, and here she is blazin' away with nobody in sight. We went inside and hollered. Nope. Not a soul there. Just dropped everything. Valves open, pressure about right, the whole damn thing workin' away like a ship all lighted up with nobody on 'er.'

We went in and looked around. A nice clean shining orderly place, with a smell of cool water. Like a Victorian church. Dennis and I had a cigarette with the men and I asked two of them to stay until we could get replacements. On the way back I called Jones and told him.

'Wait a minute, Jim. McKeogh wants to talk to you.'

Justin's voice, grim as grit. 'You and your Boy Scouts!'

I laughed.

Bill was at No. 19. Crown Point in Brooklyn.

'Hill View is fine,' I said. 'Do you know what they do up there? They chlorinate the effluent.'

'The what?'

'The effluent. By the way, where's Eunice?'

She'd gone home from the office with a thumping headache. Must remember to call her.

Someone brought in a morning newspaper and I gave the weather map my earnest attention. The local forecast was: 'Light rain. Not much change in temperature.' I looked up toward northwestern Canada. Certainly something stirring there. A little flat-circle isobar with 'High' in the middle of it. So high. Cold up there now. Wind and clear stars. I remembered cold as you remember last summer. But Carson had said the winter highs sometimes veered off to the southward.

Jones called Roach back to spell him at headquarters but the other people seemed to be well along in Brooklyn. Bill and I did two more stations and headed for Staten Island. Dennis was very good at finding his way around. We turned down Shore Road Drive under the high dark shoulder of Owl's Head Park above the Narrows.

I recognized the four silvery stacks of the Brooklyn Edison plant and we went over to have a look. The foreman blinked at us out of a gray face. He nodded when we told him who we were.

'We need relief here. This crew has worked right through for thirty-one hours. Wives been bringing 'em food. I been here since Wednesday myself. We can't get in touch with the company. If they don't get help soon you're going to have some pretty dark nights around here.'

'We'll get help,' I said. 'And you can tell the boys I'd make it a medal too if I had anything to say about it.'

He shrugged and smiled faintly.

When we got back to the car I passed the word along to Roach.

'Oh, and John Kane might want to give it to the newspapers,' I said. 'A damn good object lesson. May keep a few other people on the job.'

Bill patted me on the shoulder. 'Well done, Scoutmaster.'

We rolled aboard the Bay Ridge ferry, got out and went forward, leaning on the bulwark. Mist was blowing in through the sea arm, under the low clouds that shone faintly. The ferry hooted once and thrashed out.

Bill began to sing, keeping time with his finger in the air:

We're sailing over the effluent, the effluent, the effluent,
Ohhhh, we're sailing over the effluent——

'I'll stop if it bothers you,' he said courteously.

Dennis laughed.

'Oh,' Bill said, 'Mason Emery told me a story on the phone yesterday. Supposed to be about a fellow in the hospital with a fractured leg. Did I tell you?'

I shook my head. The wind was blowing the sea mist in our faces.

'This fellow had been riding home late on a Fifth Avenue bus one night. He noticed a girl across from him, wearing old-fashioned clothes. But good clothes. A beauty, in a rather strange way. Very —very overbred. Like those Mary Petty girls in *The New Yorker*.

'So—when they got to Eighty-Sixth Street she smiled at him and got off the bus. He followed her. She didn't turn around until she got to the steps of an old brownstone house. Then she took out her key and beckoned to him.'

He beckoned gently to Dennis.

'Like that. So he followed her in, still without a word, his heart pounding, up one flight and then another. She leaned on the banister and looked around at him. He thought she looked strange. Her neck seemed a little crooked. But she smiled. Very beautiful.

'So he followed her up the third flight. She looked around again and walked down to the end of the hall. He was beginning to think she must be a maid in the house. He was right behind her, so close he could smell her perfume. Like old-fashioned smelling salts. She opened the door. He went through behind her and felt himself falling. He clutched at her. Nothing. Nothing there. As he

156

fell, he said he heard a little well-bred giggle, the kind a nice girl might make if you stubbed your toe.

'He came to in the courtyard three stories down with a broken arm and fractured leg. The neighbors said a young girl, the last of her family, had lived in the house. She'd been dead three years. Fell and broke her neck.'

We could hear gulls over the noise of surging water as we fetched round toward the slip.

'Is that a fact, Mr. Cornbill?' Dennis said in a voice of holy awe and we laughed together.

The trucks were waiting for us at the control station in St. George. We cleaned that up and by one-thirty in the morning we had the last of the Staten Island points rigged and working. That was in Tottenville. The grimy small-town houses in the night quiet. Quarantine barriers at the Outerbridge Crossing and guards strung along the Arthur Kill. The car radio went on talking. Pete had evidently got the ambulances and the job was licked in Brooklyn.

We sat on the backs of our necks with the car doors open and the mist blowing in from the sea. Dennis went looking for food and came back with thick cheese sandwiches, crackers and cartons of milk. He'd found a little grocery all lighted up with nobody inside. Made sandwiches and left the money on the counter.

I propped the milk between my feet and called headquarters.

'This is Rowan, Car 1, calling Mr. Roach. Car 1.'

The dispatcher said: 'Okeh, Mr. Rowan.'

Roach's voice: 'Where are you, Jim?'

'Tottenville. We're seven men short at Station 29 in Port Richmond. Two ambulance drivers, four firemen, and a doctor. We cleaned up Station 31 about ten minutes ago.'

He knew it was the last one.

'All lights burning?' he said.

He was a kid and he was thrilled. He'd been running his legs off.

'All lights burning,' I said.

10

I MADE sure he had relief. They held the ferry for us at St. George and we went back to Manhattan with the trucks. We dropped Bill at home.

'Like to have a drink and hear a little music, Dennis?'

'The night is young, Mr. Rowan. Yes, sir.'

He pronounced my name as if it were a brawl instead of an excursion on the river.

West Fifty-Second Street looked like a big-game rally. Packed from one building line to the other with young people and a few older ones. A bonfire halfway over toward Sixth Avenue. Having some mulled Coca-Cola, no doubt.

Dennis pulled the car in over east and we wormed down through the shrieking kids. A two-beer bacchanal. I felt old and strained and awkward. All the little music boxes were jammed tight and whooping.

We edged into Jimmy Ryan's, a long dim silvery cave with the bar in front, tables and a postcard dance floor in the middle distance, and the band at the rear. Henry Seaborn's band.

A taffy-headed kid with a small white ribbon in her hair pulled my face down and kissed me. Couldn't have been more than seventeen.

'Hey,' I said.

She laughed. Dennis was mobbed and could make progress only by picking each one up, kissing her, and setting her down out of the way. Inventive.

He talked to me over his shoulder. 'If my wife could see me now she wouldn't like it. Nosir. She wouldn't like it at *tall.*' He shook his head and kissed another one. They were squealing. 'But *I* like it. I haven't had so much fun since we give it to the Black-and-Tans. *Oh* boy.'

Henry Seaborn, Big Henry, finest of the great New Orleans drummers, hunched over the sticks, his contemplative brown head nodding against the faded gold damask. Hunched easily in his chair, riding the chair with an almost imperceptible lift. The contemplative look. Henry wasn't thinking. He was listening and judging. Listening for the definition of Joe's left-hand chording at the piano and judging how it worked out with Crozat's bass runs. Listening to the pressure-squeal of Victor's muted trumpet, pinking out a new melodic line, knocking the tune off balance, so that you had a three-cornered tension between rhythm and tune and trumpet.

They moved into the last chorus. Henry was doing long rolls now, building up the solid onset of the band. He looked around and saw my head over the crowd, raised his right stick and brought it down in a little three-beat salute.

For ten seconds, as we inched along toward the back, we could hear the kids' chatter. They were passing trays of drinks overhead and shrieking when they spilled. Henry took a slow beat that went on for a minute, two minutes. Then he leaned toward the clarinetist and I saw his lips move: 'The blues.' He glanced over toward me and his serious heavy-lidded eyes looked down at the drums. The beat went on. This was for me.

The open trumpet took it in a long meditative downward phrase. Dennis and I were against the wall now, back near the kitchen door, behind Joe at the piano. Splitting a beer. It was all we could get.

The shiny new kids weren't there. I was home again. Wherever I lived and as long as I lived. The motion of the dark years and the lost girls' faces and the sun of the twenties that would not come again. Sick all day and walking home last night. Yes, Lord, sick all day and walking home at night. I come to the door but I couldn't see a light.

Crozat the bass player hiked the microphone over and sang. The little bony humble face. A gentle delicacy in his enunciation. Creole Negro from the Felicity Street neighborhood in New Orleans. Lived fourteen years with a woman that don't love me. Said fourteen years with a woman that don't love me. The old dog died left me in my misery. Said take me put me in your big brass bed. Now take me put me in your big brass bed. And then you rock me rock me till my face turns cherry red.

The clarinet lifted and hung, a round wailing. The beat was strict and dark now against the lunge of the trumpet. Henry's face had the look of austere concentration that came over it when the feeling opened up in him and the blues moved on and out on a fifteen-stroke roll.

I got over close enough to say hello and thank him. There were new little girls pushing in at the door. New girls to swing on Dennis's neck. They got to me too but by that time I didn't care. I'd been low all day and the familiar music had changed it into a kind of comfortable sadness.

Dennis was still laughing when we got around to the car. 'I'm going to put this down in my little red book. Yes, sir.'

He took me home and I suggested that he might as well stay with me.

'Thanks, Mr. Rowan,' he said. 'Thank you very much, sir. But I only live over on East Sixty-Fourth Street. Yes. Yes. And my wife will be waiting up for me.'

I felt empty again as I let myself into the apartment and snapped on the light. My heart jumped. A red-haired girl in a gray dress sleeping on the couch. For a tenth of a second I thought it was Niobe. Face to the wall, knees up, shoes off, and the toes curling downward. I went over and looked. It took me a second to place her. The girl in the emergency ward at Bellevue.

I shook her gently by the shoulder. She started awake and sat up. Big apprehensive gray eyes.

'Hello,' I said and sat down across the room to give her a chance to latch on.

'How long have I been—— Oh.' She shook her head. 'I'm sorry. Your maid let me wait and I must have—— You're Mr. Rowan, aren't you?'

'Yes. It's all right.'

She looked down, saw her stocking feet, and tried to smile at me.

160

'Not very nice. Do—do you remember me?'

I nodded. 'You and I had a bad quarter of an hour.'

'Yes,' she said in a low voice. 'When they revived me I remembered seeing your face. I remembered because you looked—you looked haunted. The nurse wouldn't tell me who you were at first but she gave me the money you left. Then I told her I wanted to thank you and she did tell me. About your wife. I knew how—how you must have felt. My husband has been gone since Tuesday. That's why I——'

She was looking at me with the huge eyes. Trembling. Shock. I went over to her and put my arm around her shoulder.

'Lean back. I'll get you some brandy.'

She held my sleeve. 'No. Please. I'll feel better if I talk.'

'All right. Lean back and close your eyes. I won't go away.'

Close up she didn't look very much like Niobe. The same height and type of bony structure. But much paler hair. Red blond and the skin that went with it. The translucent skin that took freckles and showed the tender veins.

She was murmuring. 'What I felt first. I knew you were frightened and yet you thought of leaving——'

'It was an impulse. They said you had good clothes. I didn't even ask whether they'd found any money. Maybe I was trying to buy off fate. I don't think so, though. I had a feeling. Almost—almost not personal at all. You seemed pathetic but not like a girl in trouble. Like—like womankind in trouble.'

She opened her eyes and we stared at each other.

'I knew that,' she said slowly. 'No, I didn't know. But I had a feeling too. I knew that we could—we had the same *kind* of feeling.'

'Maybe a lot of people have these days.' I smiled.

She sat up. 'Yes, but I felt that—— Well, it's almost the same thing. I thought if most people were having a time like us there'd be a little more—more human sympathy.'

'I hope so,' I said. 'You're better now?'

She nodded.

'Brandy first, then. Some hot food. After that I'll find a cab and take you home. Okeh?'

She didn't answer. I poured a manful slug in the balloon glass and handed it to her.

She looked at me. 'I'm afraid to go. I keep thinking of Gordon and——'

'But my God, woman. Haven't you any friends?'

'Yes, we have friends,' she said in a voice that made me ashamed of myself. 'They think I'm making a fuss because he decided to leave me. But he didn't. Not that way.'

'The fever?'

She nodded.

'Okeh,' I said. 'We'll put you up here. Drink your brandy and I'll see if I can't get a little work——'

A note from Jerry Cobb in Washington. What the hell was going on? He wasn't sure a telegram would get through and felt it might be safer to write me at home. There was a chance the East Side site could be wangled. The Western end was clear now.

'I didn't tell you,' the girl said softly. 'My name is Marjorie Grow.'

I looked up and smiled at her. 'Hello, Marjorie Grow. You're looking very sweet. Maybe your husband was damn fool enough to leave you but I'm pretty sure he won't be damn fool enough not to come back.'

She gave me a faint smile but the tension was there.

The two bottles of Chilean wine on the mantelpiece. Niobe's present from Washington. It seemed a year and a half ago now.

More mail. Ads. One of the architectural magazines wanted an article. Title: 'A Physical Plant for the New Community of Man.' The editor said blandly that since we had entered on a new and evidently permanent era of harmonious human relations, we must begin to build for it. Might he take the liberty of suggesting what seemed to him a very attractive idea?

We must immediately replace all highways and railroads with a single great conveyor-belt system articulated out to the ends of the

162

earth. Dwellings would no longer be tied to the ground. They would be fluid, mobile. Set up directly on the conveyor and traveling with it. Hereafter the great world regions would exchange not only goods and ideas but populations too.

Thus for several weeks at a time Peruvians would be Latvians and Americans Chinese or Arabs. This would be good for them. In any case, they would have no choice. It would solve at one stroke the problems of cities, countries, and continents—by abolishing them. Remove forever the abomination of the local. He had a plan for bridging the oceans by taking advantage of the surface tension of water but I didn't go into that.

Another envelope, a squarish one. Printed card. 'You are cordially invited to attend services and the placing of a wreath on the grave of Bloodgood H. Cutter, the Long Island Farmer Poet, at Zion P. E. Church, Northern Boulevard and Douglaston Parkway, Douglaston, Queens, on Friday, February 20, 194– at eleven A.M. The Bloodgood H. Cutter Memorial Association. Amanda P. Drew, Sec'y.'

I almost crumpled it up but hesitated and put it in my pocket. Marjorie's drink stood half finished on the end table. I listened. She was in the kitchen, doing something with pans. Good girl.

The phone. Ada Booth. 'Darling!' she cried. 'How are you? I just wanted to tell you that I heard something. Yes. Louise Bellamy called me this afternoon. She'd been in the Benjie Harrison Cotton Shop—yes, you know, up on Madison Avenue—and she's never met Niobe exactly but she's seen every play she's ever been in and admires her enormously.

'Louise was absolutely certain it was Niobe. Clerking in the store. Hair brushed back, shell-rim glasses and all. She asked her. "Aren't you Niobe Lloyd the actress?" Niobe just laughed. Said, "I'm afraid not." Isn't that simply—— I can tell you this. When I heard that I flew into my tippet and went bouncing over there. But of course she'd gone. Trust Niobe, the blessed idiot.

'Well, darling,' she said. 'Look. I have an idea and I'm not sure you'll like it. But I thought with you over there with nobody to

163

look after you and me here with Effie and all, why couldn't you just move into my place? After all, somebody must look after you and Effie's here all day and—— I know Niobe will never forgive me if I don't do something to——'

Poor Ada. Nicely put too.

'That's damned sweet of you, Ada,' I said, and meant it both ways. Why not? An invitation to the waltz was a compliment, wasn't it? My head was banging away again. But of course I couldn't, really. Bringing work home every night, work that needed references. Elizabeth and Rachel had been coming in every day so far and actually it wasn't much worse than if Niobe had gone on the road. She had, in a way.

'Well then, you will manage to come to dinner, at least, my pet?'

But she knew it wasn't much use.

'I will not,' I said. 'But I'd like very much to take you to dinner. If I can manage to get loose some evening.'

We left it at that. A fine day all round. Thank God for Eunice, who never went off any deep ends. I thought of calling her but it was past three.

Marjorie came in with a big tray loaded down and I set up the card table.

'My, my,' I said. 'Marjorie Grow is wonderful!'

I helped her with the chair.

She didn't smile but she said: 'I just can't understand why his wife left him. James Rowan——'

'Jim.'

'Jim Rowan is—he's such a darling. So appreciative. I had him to lunch last week and you'd—you'd almost think I'd been out all morning hunting plovers' eggs.'

A little lame. She was tense and preoccupied. Rather like people sharing the special community of a hangover.

How Elizabeth had managed to simmer chowder on a Sterno stove I didn't know. Marjorie had it good and hot. Pilot biscuits and butter. A mixed salad. Beer for me and milk for her.

164

I tuned the short wave to one of the police radios and we listened. Things seemed to be working out all right. The calls weren't being repeated too much. The dispatcher ordered one of the Harbor Squad launches to South Brother Island. The information was vague. Rockets had been seen coming up from there. Some gag of Arnie's, probably. I switched it off.

'Now I suppose we'd better see about getting you to bed.'

I turned on the light in the guest room and grinned. Black satin sheets and pillowcases on the beds.

'Can you stand that?' I said. 'Little gift to Niobe from some friends on the West Coast. They turn up every time the laundry gets short.'

I rummaged around and got towels and a toothbrush for her. Ought to be a nightdress in one of the drawers. But she shook her head.

'Pajamas?'

No.

'Okeh. Good night, Marjorie Grow. If you get feeling bad call me. Promise?'

And if I feel any worse I'll call a cop.

She nodded. 'Good night—Jim Rowan.' Very subdued.

Queer business, having a strange woman in the house. I heard her in the bathroom and then forgot about her. The newspapers. We'd got so worked up trying to keep the city glued together we hadn't been paying much attention to the outside effect. Bad, evidently. A statement from the Governor, who sat in the other pew. If the municipal authorities failed to clear up the situation by Monday, troops would move in. The implication was clear. We were gold-bricking. Moral deficiency and low types besides.

The U. S. Senate talking about a special investigating subcommittee. They had a case all right. The whole thing must look very slack from the outside and there was some danger that it might spread in spite of the quarantine. But Senator Glenn B. Rowley, my distinguished friend of the Union Station in Washington and an old metropolis-baiter, seemed to be the principal thunderer.

I took a shower, remembering to use the prophylactic, and got into bed. Lying down seemed to bring the headache to a peak. I read John Kane's statement with throbbing eyeballs. Just dramatic enough. 'We have dropped the keys of the city into the middle of the Hudson River. . . .'

The control stations didn't get much notice but the instructions were boxed on page one of the Times. Good deal of low moaning about the quarantine. Some helling too. The railroads and a few of the firms that moved goods in and out were definitely helling. PM had interviewed five hundred people at the Times Square subway exits. Do you favor the quarantine? Two hundred and three hadn't heard, one hundred and twenty-seven liked it for various reasons, forty-seven thought it was just politics, two men and a woman wanted the city to apply for admission to the union as the forty-ninth state, and a youth from the Bronx said: 'My girl lives in Weehawken and you know love.'

I opened the window. Rain falling softly out of the warm sky. I put out the light and lay there with my eyes open, feeling bad. All this running around. The emergency system wouldn't hold up. How could it? Something must have happened to Niobe. She'd called me the night before. Probably too late now.

The door opened a little. Marjorie standing there in her slip.

'Are you awake? I—I can't sleep. I feel terrible.'

Her teeth were chattering.

'Feel my hands,' she said hopelessly. 'I'm so cold. It must be shock.'

'I think we've got some triple bromide. Wait. I'll see.'

'No. They gave me stuff at the hospital today. I don't want any more. It isn't only that. I feel so awful, so God damned alone, and I can't stop shaking. Can I——'

'Yes,' I said, and held the covers for her. She got in and crouched beside me, hands crossed on her breast. Shaking as if she had a bad chill. I held her, smoothing her silky hair back.

'Poor Marjorie Grow.'

She murmured with set teeth: 'It isn't that I just want to——'

'I know. Never mind.'

'But I feel so awful. I've got to be close to somebody. I never thought Gordon would——'

'Don't you realize what's happening to people?' I said gently. 'Yes,' she said between her teeth. 'Yes. That's why I'm afraid.' Still shaking, she fumbled up to my face, kissed me with her wet silky mouth and began to cry.

'You thought of me this morning when they took me out of the water. Oh God. I was afraid. I haven't thought of you, have I? Not once. All I thought of was—was somebody to help me. That's why I came.'

'Never mind.'

She was twisting in my arms. 'Oh God. Oh God. Why can't people be good to each other?'

Without noticing what I was doing I stroked the back of her neck. I could feel the wide glimmer of her eyes looking up at me.

'Please,' she said in an apologetic voice. 'You're hurting me.'

'I didn't mean to hurt you.'

She was quieter now, crying with her eyes closed. 'I know. Oh I know you didn't. I want to be good to you. I—want to comfort you. Please. Please let me.'

She kissed my eyelids and temples. My throat. Delicate. Gentle and delicate, exciting herself with pleasing me. Light hands on my face. All light sensibility. Her whole body.

Marjorie Grow. Marjorie Grow. Shivering now, but relaxed and delicious. Expectant. The silky skin of her flanks and breasts. She lighted quickly but I waited until she stirred, moaning a little. The rapid shallow breathing like Cheyne-Stokes breathing.

The two kinds of death she had known that day. The two fugues of entry into the warm forest and the slow wandering, quickened by an intimation of some unknown errand, urgent at a glimpse of light beyond the trees, then hurrying, running, driving, bursting into the light. I helped her while the fading tremors ran down her thighs. Then she was crying luxuriously in my arms and we could hear the rain.

FOUR

1   RACHEL, the maid, woke me in the morning and pulled up the blinds.

I blinked at her. 'My God, Rachel, you're beautiful!'

She *was* beautiful—a tall gracefully knit brown girl with a clean coppery glow to her skin. I'd noticed it before, of course. We'd always gotten along fine. She knew I had musician friends in Harlem, for one thing. She lived over on Sumner Avenue and she was gunning for a civil-service job. Niobe had tried to get her to stay but the post-office job was what she wanted. 'If I can only get fixed,' she said. So I talked to Phil Givens, which was about all I could do, and got somebody to coach her.

But there she was looking like a very modern angel in a stained-glass window. A finely stylized effect in the bones of her head and body. High style. Breeding. I knew enough anthropology to know that it probably didn't come from the white blood. I remembered something like that same look of a strongly distinctive culture in the photographs of Bantu and Ashanti women.

She stared at me, nodding solemnly. Then she tiptoed over, shut the door, and came back.

'Never mind about *me*, Mr. Rowan. *I* got a husband. Fine talk.'

She watched my face.

'I come into the bathroom this morning and look on the floor and I say, "Why, *Mrs.* Rowan's come home." Then I look again and I say, "*Oh* no she ain't. *That* ain't Mrs. Rowan's." An' I pick *this* up.'

She took a small strawberry-colored handkerchief out of her apron pocket and held it up, rolling her eyes toward the ceiling, waiting for a cue from me.

'Marjorie,' I said.

'Yes, Marjorie,' she said in a deep voice and almost at the same instant we burst out laughing, her voice restrained but going up and up. I fell back on the bed, looking at her, both of us laughing. Suddenly she turned sober and pointed her finger at me. 'I picked up the bathroom quick so's Elizabeth wouldn't see it and made the bed in the other room *like lightning.*' She whispered it.

'*Like lightning?*' I said, imitating the whisper, and we were off again.

I caught myself staring at her. The long supple body in the faded house dress.

Her eyes widened. She said in a high soft half-comic whine: 'What you looking at *me* for? You after *me?*'

I was startled. 'I—I guess I am.'

'You *guess* you are?'

She leaned her hand on my naked shoulder, firm and comforting, kissed me gently, and straightened up.

'Poor Mr. Rowan. You better wait for your mummy.'

We looked at each other with our eyes widening and laughed uncontrollably again.

I stretched. 'I feel wonderful, Rachel. Everything looks so fine. The paper on the wall, the colors in the carpet. Look at the sun.'

She stared at me. 'I know what you got. You got the fever.'

'Maybe I have,' I said and felt the back of my neck. It didn't actually hurt much. Felt as if I had a good deep bruise.

'Yep,' I said. 'I probably have.'

Elizabeth knocked and came bustling in with breakfast and a late edition of the *Herald Tribune.* You got breakfast in bed from Elizabeth about as often as you celebrated your one-hundred-and-third birthday. I didn't like it anyway—seemed a messy female business to me—but it just showed where I stood.

'What's there to laugh about?' Elizabeth said. 'Rachel, those books ain't been cleaned in a week.'

Rachel opened her eyes at me and marched out. I told Elizabeth about hunting Niobe the day before and about the girl at Bellevue. All except the last part, of course.

She listened and shook her head. 'Haven't slept a wink since she left. I wrote Horace last night about it.'

Her husband. A licensed boatman. He'd taken an Elco down the Intracoastal Waterway to Florida for the winter.

She said: 'I almost get frightened of myself sitting over there in the midst of this. S'pose *I* take to actin' that way?'

I had a curious rush of feeling for her: a blue-eyed, plain-faced woman of forty-five or so who knew her own mind and was no doubt strong-minded enough not to regret it. She'd been good to us.

'Look, Elizabeth. You'll get yourself all bothered. Why don't you just move your things into the guest room? You know that's what Mrs. Rowan would want you to do.'

We spoke of Niobe as if she were lost in the Arctic.

Elizabeth said no and then she said she'd think about it.

'And thanks for that wonderful chowder you made.'

She was pleased. 'Wasn't it good? Come just right for once.'

Breakfast on the tray. Orange juice, whole-wheat cereal, a poached egg on toast, and coffee. But my God, what a mortal luxury of sharp sweetness in the orange juice. Like the first fruit of the Bahamas in Columbus's salty mouth. That breakfast was to eating what love, the several kinds of love, is to a quick trick.

I'm not being fancy. That's the way it was. It struck me more the first day, of course, but it went on like that. I'm a Middle Westerner at bottom and we go in for hearty rather than subtle or accomplished senses. Though God knows mine aren't very hearty. In any case, all I'm willing to claim for myself is a good

171

enough sense of the shades of feeling and an old-fashioned liking for other people.

Not much to go on. I found nothing to compare it to and didn't try. I was too damn busy being alive. But afterwards it seemed to me there were a couple of things that came pretty close. One was the delicious feeling I remembered in the first few weeks of a convalescence from pneumonia. A good analogy in some ways. The springtime feeling. The freshness of the senses and the gentle euphoria and the flooding of hope. It was unlike the fever in the sense that it took its tone from bodily weakness, or at least the slow return of strength.

The other was nearer in that way. I suppose we've learned a little about danger in this century. Some of what we've learned is mere pathological nerve tissue for the psychobiologist but a good deal of it adds up to a common experience. There is a moment when something begins to happen. You don't think. You know. This is the one. You may be moving in the anesthesia of violent action. The world turns to quivering gray glass. But more often it doesn't. It shines as if you'd never seen it before, as if there were a light behind each separate particle of it. It looks and smells and sounds and tastes intolerably bright. You feel that you can see the structure of it as you see the veins in a leaf against the sun. It has a new unearthly value.

That's what I'm talking about. Like the vision of a great painter. Nothing but the quick charge of adrenalin in the blood, probably. The organism startles you with what you need to know. The awareness I got with the fever was very close to that, but it lacked the tension, the screwed-up clench. No strain at all. A little giddy the first day and after that high and serene.

Convalescence and danger. Both death. One going away, the other coming close. But it didn't feel like death. It felt as if you were lifted up on some harmonious and inexhaustible level of vitality. Not mere energy or vigor. Vitality. The damn thing sang.

But the point I remember best about that morning and the whole time afterwards was the sense of happy expectancy I had.

Expecting what? Oh, everything, nothing, me, you, the United States of America. Something wonderful was going to happen and I'd be there to meet it. No hurry. Nothing anxious. It was there waiting, like the girl you have in your mind's eye at fifteen. The essence of it was safe inside me. I knew that. And of course it would go on forever.

I had breakfast and read the *Herald Tribune*. A note about the Bloodgood H. Cutter services in Douglaston. Mrs. Bertha K. Hollings, a grandniece of the poet from Butte, Montana, would speak. I decided to go. If Mrs. Hollings wasn't Niobe it would be only because Niobe couldn't be everywhere at once.

No mistake about my lovely wife and South Brother Island. A front-page story. Some background on Arnie's fight with Regan. The island *had* been attacked the night before. Taken by a landing party armed with flashlights and Buck Rogers guns and led by an unidentified tall red-haired woman. The invaders had planted a sign, taking possession of that floating scrub patch in the name of Bronx County and the Society for the Preservation of Happiness. They decamped before the police launch got there. But not before the woman had made what the reporter called "an impassioned speech."

That's her, I thought. That's the Wabash River hellcat. The woman who tried to scare me to death the first time I ever laid eyes on her. That would be during the other war. I was pretty sure it must have been 1918. A nice hot clear afternoon in the summer of 1918.

I'd got my work done early and the battered green Old Town canoe was mine by default. My older brother Bruce had given it up. He had plans for the family's new National. I stood a moment at the rim of our corn, at the edge of the bluff below Merom, the paddle and sails and outrigger in my arms. Thirteen years old. Happy. Looking upstream toward the old bandits' island of Civil War times and out across the hazy farmlands and down along the shining kinks of the river.

Tacking down with the stream. A short tack and a long one. The ripples on a sand bar flashing like a joggled mirror. I wasn't thinking of anything. Just gliding nice and quiet in the bottom of the canoe. Free.

Then I heard kids' voices under the far bluff and tacked over near them. Four girls, swimming. The two Haley girls and Henrietta Behrendt from Oaktown. Another one, a strange girl, tall and bony. Thick dark-red hair.

They didn't speak. They were giggling among themselves, halfway out of the water, watching me. I ignored them. But as I came in close the red-haired one dabbed a little water on me. Looking at me all the time. It was cold.

'Hey,' I said. 'Don't do that.' Sullen male dignity.

She mimicked the dignified tone exactly, surged over and began scooping water all over me with both hands. 'Don't do that! Don't do that! Don't do that!' she chanted.

The canoe was half full of water. I scrambled up, dropped the old gear we used for an anchor overboard, then leapfrogged over the stern and after her. I caught her in the shallows and dragged her back. She didn't yell. Just looked at me with those bugged gray eyes.

I pushed her under by the hair. She didn't even swallow any water but when she came up she let out a scream you could have heard in Terre Haute. Awful. 'Help! Help! He's trying to drown me!'

There were a lot of girls who might be mean enough to do that. I didn't think she was being mean. I thought she meant it. I didn't realize until afterwards that her eyes hadn't changed. Watching me all the time to see what effect it had.

The girls on shore were blubbering now. The Haley house stood just back from the lip of the bluff. Niobe's folks had been up there visiting from Vincennes and her old man came down the path in the side of the bluff roaring like a lion. I let go of her, got the gear back in, and shoved off. But just as I got started she gave me a little gentle parting dab down the back of my neck.

She must have been about eleven then, though she looked older.

174

The next time I saw her was at a high-school dance three or four years later. I didn't recognize her but when somebody introduced us she gave me the big gray stare and screamed so loud you could hear her over the trumpet. Her father never liked me after that first time. Always suspected I had a homicidal streak.

2

DENNIS came in. I called to him to put the short wave on and got up to take a shower. I was a little dizzy and my back ached like an ambitious bridegroom's. But it was nothing. A detail. Everything was wonderful. The shower water felt fresh and bland and shaving was a pleasure. My glum face looked almost handsome. Warm and excited, as if I'd just fallen in love.

A good many of the control-station calls on the radio seemed to be hanging fire. We'd iron that out. Problems were a pleasure too. A promise of action. I looked forward to the commissioners' lunch. Might pry something out of Arnie about Niobe's little raid. He must have been in on it.

I told Dennis that he was looking very fit and he returned the compliment. Rachel lifted her eyebrows at my bow. The city looked incredibly bright on the way downtown. The porous textures of building brick. The whipping summery dresses of the girls. The clean glass glinting in windshields and store windows. I was dizzy with happiness.

The Society for the Preservation of Happiness had big red-white-and-blue spectaculars rippling across Times Square, announcing the Parade to the End of the World on Monday. Dennis got the name of the sign shop. It struck me as a delicious idea. I caught myself thinking of joining.

It would never have occurred to me that what I was seeing were the first workings of a vast good-natured humming conspiracy. Against me. Against all of us who were trying to hold the city

175

together. Or that the Lord of Misrule was a woman and the woman my wife.

Why not? The male principle of controlling intellect against the female ascendancy of emotion. Very neat. It was never quite that, of course. The city could have done very well without us. Either way. But toward the end, it did become something like that for the two of us. A grimly comic domestic duel. Or it amused me afterwards to think of it that way.

The Municipal Building elevator felt as if it could lift its weight in wildcats. Pop Mancini grunted at my cheerfulness and Carlotta Breyer perked up like a watered geranium as I went by. Breezy.

'Good morning, darling,' I said to Eunice. 'You're looking very radiant.' She was.

'*Well*,' she said, and fluffed her back hair, walking a little out of joint at the hip.

'Where's Bill, my sterling assistant?'

'He doesn't steal. Jones asked him to drop over. He wanted to explain the breakdown on yesterday's operations.'

'Good or bad, did he say?'

'They're losing a lot of men.'

'What about the commissioners' reports?'

Most of them had come in and I spent the next half-hour piecing them together. The most optimistic thing you could say was that we were beginning to show a little braking action. The quarantine had cut down the normal daily load of commuters and visitors, though it caught some of them in town. But it was having a temporarily bad effect on other things. Supplies, for instance. Trouble with the milk companies about the transfer of trucks.

I looked at my watch as Eunice came in with a load of papers.

'When am I going to see you about all this stuff?'

I scooped them up and grabbed her hat and coat.

'Come on.'

Dennis was waiting. The Queens Tunnel, then Jackson Avenue and Northern Boulevard to Douglaston. 'We've got to make it by eleven. It's—ten twenty-seven now.'

'What an impetuous man,' Eunice said.

'Plenty of time, sir,' Dennis said and pulled uptown.

I talked to Jones on the radio. Nothing serious during the night. Very few fires, thank God, Rich said. The newspapers had just about all the dope on South Brother Island. Heavy turnover of personnel at the stations. Two hundred and thirty-one people missing. They hadn't replaced all of them yet and of course the replacements weren't all fully trained men. The doctors had done some weeding out too.

Wait'll they see me, I thought.

As I was talking to Bill a cop flagged us down at the tunnel approach and saluted.

'Got a wreck in there, Mr. Rowan. Won't be cleared for twenty minutes.'

It came in on the car radio while he was speaking.

We pulled around and went up to Queensboro Bridge. A wonderful morning on the river, like May in heaven.

'Fascinating bridge,' I said expansively. 'I never liked it but now I find those rococo piers enchanting. Think of the subtle financial imagination that went into them. Yes. Delectable bridge, delectable river, delectable driver——'

Dennis nodded. 'Thank you, Mr. Rowan.'

'—delectable car. And not least——'

I squeezed her shoulder.

'—delectable Eunice. Ah, *Life*, *Time*, *Fortune*, *Mademoiselle*——'

'You'd better stop,' Eunice said, looking at me.

'Bright eyes. Why?'

'I might believe you. Never mind. Look at this.'

A memo from Reger at the Department of Investigation. They'd tracked down the circus poster I reported the day before. Bill Wheatley all right. He'd turned it out on five or six hours' notice for a woman he didn't know. Looked like an upper East Side matron. Tall. Black hair. She'd paid him. Said it was for some charity blowout.

It could be true. He didn't know Niobe. She'd talked the printer into cutting his price. Charity again. Nobody seemed to know who had slapped the posters up. The space hadn't been paid for. After all, you don't rent space on the Public Library steps. I was beginning to have my doubts, though. Even Niobe couldn't get around that much.

Eunice had a draft of proposed changes in Article V of the Zoning Resolution. People were always chiseling away at that and when you fought them you got hell from all sides. But I was pleased to see that the boys were carrying on.

I told Eunice and Dennis where we were going, and why. They laughed. We were sailing through the Murray Hill district in Queens and out along Northern Boulevard. Kids stared at the car, as they usually did. One of them, who must have been out of town a long time, yelled 'Butch!' after us. Nostalgic.

Down the hill, across Alley Creek, and up the opposite hill. Douglaston Parkway. Very close to the fringe of the city. It felt open, almost rural, stringing out toward Great Neck. Big comfortable houses. I seem to remember cypresses. We could smell the Little Neck Bay marshes in the warm air.

The high retaining wall and a glimpse of the church beyond it. Dennis turned left between carriage-era gatepost lamps, up a long gravel drive. I stopped him.

'Better pull out and go round in back, Dennis. I should have warned you. If she sees the car——'

'Right you are, Mr. Rowan,' Dennis said cheerfully.

He drove around the corner and up a steep little slope behind what looked like a parish house at the rear of the church. Eunice and I got out.

'You might turn the car around and wait in it,' I said. 'If we see Mrs. Rowan, I'll try to get her, and Eunice will tell you what to do. Okeh?'

They nodded. Sounded as if we were chasing a strayed heifer. Or even Aunt Amy, who couldn't remember who she was.

A little after ten forty-five. Most of the people seemed to be in the parish house but two or three middle-aged women were wandering around among the stones.

We scouted the place thoroughly. All high ground, except for the road up from the boulevard. The one we'd nosed into. This led straight to the church and divided the long easy roll of churchyard to either side. Wineglass elms budding and new grass among the dark stones. The retaining wall was too high to drop over and things looked fairly open toward the north.

On the south side, a steep drop to skylights and a courtyard. But farther along, there was a seven-foot brushy hedge with a gap in it, evidently leading down to the white rectory. The rectory lawn flowed open down to the street.

The church was white clapboard in a sort of late county-Wren carpenter-classic style. White spire. Erected A.D. 1830. A Dutch feeling in the proportions. Definitely Long Island. Good sense of ornament. A little too boxy to be really fine. But very nice. Very clean and pleasant.

A woman in a black satin hat showed us where the Matinecock Indians were buried and told us that Bloodgood H. Cutter had been the 'poet lariat' in one of Mark Twain's books. She couldn't remember which one. Mark could pull a real stinker when he tried.

People were beginning to gather in a little clump at the south side of the church. We went over and stood facing them across the writer's last line: the single word CUTTER in bold block letters on a big rough marble topped by a cross. In its shadow, a small delicately curved iron-gray stone with a few blanched crocuses up around it and a thornbush to the left. His wife Emelin, poor girl, who had lived with a man whose wit had been canonized by Mark Twain.

People seemed to be waiting. Eighteen or twenty of them now. A man finally began to talk about Cutter and quoted some of his verses. Jocose and not very good.

Someone whispered to him and he said: 'I now present to you Mrs. Bertha K. Hollings of Butte, Montana, grandniece of the poet, who will say a few words.'

There was a little polite handclapping. A woman stepped from the back of the crowd, cleared her throat nervously. Eunice gasped. Niobe. In brogues, dowdy hat over dowdy hair, rimmed glasses, and the standard suburban oatmeal tweed coat with a wolf collar. The notes in her hand trembled and she peered nearsightedly at them.

'It—it is a great honor,' she began in a high-pitched, rather sing-song, definitely cultural voice. 'It is a great honor to be here with you today to honor the memory of——'

The notes fluttered down out of her hand in the sunny silence. She whistled on her fingers, turned, cut between two men and around a stone at a dead run.

I said: 'The car' to Eunice, saw her running, got tangled in the thornbush, and pulled away. The women huddled. I got between two of them and heard the first one say: 'Why, he pushed me,' and the other: 'He must be crazy.' A man said: 'Here!' caught my arm, and when I jerked loose there were two or three more women in the way.

Niobe was through the gap in the hedge, a good thirty yards in front of me down the long slope of lawn, running hard without a sound. She could always run, the devil. A white house with a big gray gnarled oak. A man in a clerical collar came out the side door and called: 'Don't you think——' I was going full out, pretty short of breath but taking it up a little.

I was less than twenty yards behind when she hit the street. A car came down left with the door open and she jumped, sprawling in. I almost touched the right rear fender as it pulled away. Wheeled down Northern Boulevard, going very fast, with the door gradually closing. People were streaming down the lawn behind me and I could hear a man shouting.

Dennis pulled in hard, Eunice flipped the door open, and I went in on my shoulder. She wrestled the door shut. The car ahead leaped at the bridge over the creek and bored up the far hill. We were halfway down, the big car taking it up steadily. We sailed twenty feet at the creek bump.

'If he stays on the boulevard we've got him,' Dennis said.

It looked as if we had. But in Auburndale he screeched hard left in front of a car in the opposite lane. Into a side street. Dennis cut just a little and whisked in behind. Niobe's driver doubled right, then left, in the whirl of a residential neighborhood that seemed to have been assembled from parts of all the smaller American cities I'd ever known: Indianapolis, **Albany**, Cincinnati, Providence, even Cambridge.

Dennis made a neat job of the turns but the big car just wasn't nimble enough. We got to one intersection an instant too late to see which way they'd gone. Dennis picked up the tire marks and lost them again. We cruised around for a while. Nothing. The car was gone.

Dennis seemed inclined to be gloomy about it but Eunice was positively gay. She squeezed my arm.

'Never mind, boss,' she said in Chico Marx's honest accent. 'We catch 'em some day if they don' wait too long, huh?'

'If they wait for you, Revelli,' I said, 'they're crazy. Come to think of it, they are crazy.'

'Sure, sure, boss,' she said. 'We catch 'em. Come on. This way. They went the other way.'

3

DENNIS got us back to the office an hour or so before the commissioners' lunch and Bill and I spent most of the time going over Jones's report. Bill had had it right the first time. The weak spot was in personnel replacement. We'd have to do something drastic about that.

Bill stared at Eunice as she came in.

'Doesn't she look attractive?' he said. 'Our Eunice.'

She curtsied, deadpan. 'I just talked to your friend Carson again. He says the high—you know, the high—is getting larger.' She looked at her notes. 'Moved down through Saskatchewan from the Great Slave Lake district. Regina reports snow and clearing weather. Should be over southern Minnesota by tomorrow morning. The Swedes will like that.'

'Sounds good,' I said.

'Doesn't it?' said Eunice and went away again.

We'd about settled down to work when the phone rang. The operator said: 'Mrs. Grow calling you.'

'Mrs.—— Oh yes. I'll take it.'

Marjorie, very excited. 'He's come back. He's come back. Gordon's come back.'

'Who?'

'My husband. Oh, I'm sure your wife will too.'

'I'm glad.'

'Well. I just went out to the drugstore for a minute and I wanted to tell you how happy I am.' She said very low: 'Bless you, darling.'

I put the phone down gently.

Bill and Eunice promised to meet me for dinner. On the way out young Joralemon stopped me.

'May I talk to you a minute, Mr. Rowan?'

'Sure. Come on outside.'

Nice kid. Very earnest brown eyes. Lived with his mother uptown somewhere. He'd gone to the city-planning school at Harvard. The mother and Harvard made it pretty difficult for him to spit out what he was trying to say. I don't suppose he ever would have tried it if he hadn't had the fever.

What it came down to, when I finally caught on, was that he was crazy about the girls and mortally afraid of them, and what did I think he ought to do?

I thought. 'Any special girl?'

No.

'Come on,' I said and pushed the bell.

We went down in the tower elevator and walked toward the

main bank. A small blond girl came out into the corridor ahead of us. Neat pony shape. Not my type.

'Like that?'

He nodded.

I called: 'Just a minute, please.'

She stopped and looked over her shoulder negligently. Young Joralemon hung back as I caught up with her. Blue eyes.

'Look,' I said, very seriously. 'My friend has been carrying on a long-distance love affair with you for about six months. Waits in the lobby downstairs every night to see you go home.'

'Oh. Poor boy,' she said, half smiling.

'He's got it so bad now he's afraid to speak to you. So why don't you be a good girl and give him a date tonight?'

She ducked under my arm, glanced at him, and nodded, laughing.

I introduced them. She was demure but I could see she was pleased with her new power.

'I told Miss Bowitz you've been on her trail for a long time.'

He was startled but game. Determined to live up to me. They chatted a minute and he asked when he could take her out.

'Why not now?' she said with a gloomy pout. 'I'm all alone in my office. I get bored.'

Well she might. He looked at me.

'Why not?' I said and wished them luck.

Downstairs in Hickey's outer office I could hear the boys yelling long before I got to the door. Ellen rolled her eyes at me.

Inside, people were grinning down the long table and I could see Regan half out of his chair, shaking a napkin in his clenched fist at Arnie Genovese. John Kane was sitting there taking it like a good third act. The South Brother raid.

'Listen to this, you little two-bit shonniker,' Regan bawled. 'I'll get that lousy island back if I have to round up all the cops in St. Albans. And when I do I'll keep it.'

He shook his head in disgust.

'You heard him yesterday,' he said quietly. People nodded. 'I don't mind an honest crook. He told us what he was going to do and now he comes in here and tries to make us believe he didn't do it.' In a mealymouthed voice he said: 'I don't know *who* did it. I wasn't *in* on it. I don't know *anything* about it. Ahhhh!'

He flapped his hand at Arnie. Arnie was back on his heels for once. The first time in his life people had refused to believe him. Or pretended to.

'That's right,' he said earnestly. 'I said that. I was going to do it too but somebody beat me to the punch.'

He looked around at us.

'Yes, sure,' Henry Feuerman said. People laughed.

'Okeh.' Arnie was a little injured. 'I talk too much. I talked about it here. Uptown too. You read the newspapers. Do I look like a redheaded woman?'

'We thought you were looking for one, Arnie,' John Hickey said.

Everybody laughed that time. But I was convinced that Arnie really hadn't had anything to do with it. So were the others, for that matter.

We got down to business a little later with Rich Jones's report on the control stations. As of nine A.M. that morning. I gave them the story. All stations set up and operating by one-thirty A.M. We'd answered 196 fire alarms, of which 177 were false alarms, 302 police calls, 138 medical and ambulance, nine water supply, and seventy-four miscellaneous, including one to get a dog out of a rathole in Cunningham Park.

They clapped.

'If that's for me,' I said, 'I'll just pass it along to Rich Jones and John Kane and Bill Cornbill in my office and young Roach and the people at the stations.

'The rest of it is bad. We've had 364 replacements in the crews —walkouts and culls—in less than twelve hours. It may calm down a little. But we can't keep going with a turnover like that. Not unless we begin training new men.

'By the way,' I said, looking down, 'I've got it myself.'

The boys stared at me.

'I'd rather do what I'm doing than anything else I can think of. I'll stick with it if you say so. Wait. Keep an eye on me and vote on it before we break up. I wouldn't know myself. All I can tell you is that it feels fine.'

Two or three people made suggestions and we worked out a general replacement pool. They elected Maurice Satin of Public Works to head it. Good choice. Maurice was sharp, and a driver. He'd take charge of all the present reserves and the volunteers. John Kane got the job of drumming up enough volunteers.

Maurice talked to Rich Jones for a minute and waved good-by to us.

'I'm going to work.'

We gave him an ironic cheer. In spite of the way things were going, the boys seemed to be in much better spirits now than at any time since the whole business started. Taking action. Doing something. I hadn't trusted my first impression. I was feeling too good myself. But it seemed to be so.

A girl from Hickey's office whispered that Dr. Jenkins was calling me. When could I come to see him?

'About an hour,' I said.

'I'll tell him.'

Dick Wirth gave us some new figures. He really looked bad, gray in the face, and I noticed he didn't get up. The situation approaching a peak, he said. More than 1,200,000 cases. Estimated, of course.

The fever had caught on a bit in Chicago and St. Louis. The weather was unseasonably warm out there too. But a milder convalescent strain. He had a scatter diagram of the distribution in New York. The dots ran all over the map except for a bare space in northwestern Brooklyn.

Dick put his finger on it. 'Brooklyn Heights,' he said with a faint smile.

We laughed.

'Uh, Dick,' Mason Emery called. 'Did the West Indian doctor, Martineau—is that his name?—find out what happened to people when they got well? Aftereffects? That kind of thing?'

'We've been trying to check on that,' Dick said. 'He evidently didn't follow up very carefully. Hard to tell. So many other uncared-for diseases down there. He seemed to think there might be complications in some cases.'

Justin delivered a few grim remarks about the quarantine. All neighboring communities had agreed to co-operate. Some of them weren't doing much about it, though. He promised to needle them. The Coast Guard, the Power Squadron yachtsmen, and the Boy Scouts—he glanced at me—were handling their end of the job very well. Not much getting through so far. But he didn't have enough people to take care of a really serious attempt.

'We're having trouble with communications,' he said. 'We've been taking messages at the nearest control stations and using motorcycles to get them out to the men. We could probably do a lot better if we could take over amateur short-wave stations in a few districts and get two-way sets for the key points in the lines.'

I nodded. My God. How did I miss out on a thing like that? Playing with girls. We arranged to get the equipment for him.

'That's about all,' Justin said, 'except that we've got word that an underground railway is being organized. For a flat fee they'll smuggle people and goods in or out of the city. You give them a deposit and pay the balance after they get you through. May be only a rumor. We're tracing it.'

Young, the Comptroller, got up. 'I don't want to be a dog in the manger, but I'm surprised nobody's mentioned that business in Congress yesterday. Or the Governor's statement.' He stopped and looked up. 'Personally I don't see how we can whip things into shape in time to beat that deadline. It looks to me as if we'd better think about what to do when the troops come in. I'm not suggesting any—— I'm just asking a question.'

It was true, of course. Pretty long odds against us. We all knew that, though I found it hard to convince myself of it.

John Kane spread his hands. 'What can we do, Roz?' John called. 'If he sends the militia in we'll still have to keep up most of the organization we've got now. Have to take over again when they leave.

'We've been stalling all we can. Charley Porter has been up in Albany since Thursday night. You know how much chance we stand there. I've been keeping in touch with Holdsworth in Washington. Nothing's going to make any difference but what we do here. All we can do is stall and play for a break.'

That was the story all right. People nodded, John took the chair, and they gave my fevered brow a vote of confidence before we broke up.

I got hold of Dick Wirth on the way out.

'Dick,' I said earnestly, 'I wish to Christ you'd take a couple of days in bed. You must have a lot of incompetents over there. Can't they get along for forty-eight hours without you?'

That might fetch him.

'It's nothing, Jim,' he said quickly. 'I need a little sleep. Been taking benzedrine to keep going. No. The boys do better without me. Just my ego.'

4 PETE was alone in his nice clean white office. He asked me to sit down.

'Thanks for the ambulances,' I said.

He shook his head. 'I didn't have any trouble. Pleaded eminent domain.'

He swung half around in the chair and picked up a small card.

'Kelsey, Cornelia. Thirty-two. Address 121 East Sixty-Fifth Street, Manhattan. Admitted 2/18/4–. Remember her?'

'The odd girl from the Roncador,' I said. 'Tall dark girl.'

'That's right. This morning at breakfast she complained about

187

the food. Usually when people do that they're beginning to get well. Hospital food is all kinds, as you probably know. Ours is pretty good.

'I had a hunch. Went in and talked to her. She was cooler with me than she had been. She'd developed a certain hardness of manner. She had all kinds of requests. Wanted nightgowns and things sent over from her home and she felt that the nurses weren't looking after her properly. Special food. Oh, and a hairdresser.

'She talked about Sidney too. She said personally she liked colored people—they were so gay—and she thought Sidney was a nice boy. But after all you couldn't live with them. Besides, the place couldn't be a good influence for a young boy. People were so irresponsible.'

'Back to normal,' I said.

'Yes. That's what I thought. I looked up the records and found that from what the others said she must have been the first case on the *Roncador*. That would make the whole course of the disease about nine days.

'I was planning to put her through some tests this afternoon. Even when the nurse called and said she wanted a private room and that she was acting queer I didn't pay much attention. She *would* seem a little queer after the others.

'But about eleven o'clock the nurse called again and said she thought I'd better look at Miss Kelsey. Young Sidney was frolicking around and the Bakers and Cherrills were playing gin rummy on the foot of her bed. They'd tried to get her into the game. Thought she was sulking.

'She was lying there with her eyes open. Didn't answer when I spoke to her. I shooed the others away and examined her. Couldn't find anything obviously wrong so I asked Hutch to have a look at her.'

'He came back?'

'He came back,' Pete said. 'We did a little mutual apologizing. I admitted I might be wrong about the principle and he agreed that shock treatments might not be advisable in a situation like this.

'Hutch examined her. He couldn't be sure, of course. Needed more time. But he said it seemed pretty obvious to him that what she had was a well-developed case of schizophrenia. They moved her over to the psychiatric division an hour ago.'

We stared at each other.

'My God. You don't think——'

'I don't know,' Pete said. 'But you should have seen Hutch's face. "Call on me anytime, Pete," he said. "Just anytime at all. Always glad to help you medical men." '

I sat there. Niobe. 'When can you tell whether it's a typical reaction or just——'

'About tomorrow night. If we're lucky. From what the Bakers and the others said, Miss Kelsey was about a day ahead of them. In any case, I thought you ought to know.'

He was astonishingly cheerful. A little flushed. I realized that I felt the same way about it myself. Awed at the prospect. But not scared. Hardly even what you could call bothered.

'As a matter of fact, I've got it myself,' Pete said.

'So have I.'

We shook hands with solemnity.

'Is it—pleasant in the psychiatric division?'

'Oh, nicest place in the world,' Pete said. 'Just like mother. Except for that shock business, of course. Still, you can't have everything.'

'I feel as if I could.'

'So do I,' said Pete. 'So do I.'

We scrubbed up and he led me into the flat-topped shedlike structure where the machines were. Heavily shielded: roof, walls, and floor.

The first thing I noticed was Hansell Baker, who had sicked the girls on me, wearing a very fancy helmet. A broad oval band of metal around the head at the sides, with a curved piece over the top from front to back. Setscrews all over it. A black rubber tube led to the instruments on the bench beside him. He looked like a Byzantine saint.

'Well, well,' I said blandly. 'Cooking something?'

'Just a permanent.'

He paid no attention to us. He was going through what looked like a set of drawings.

'Oh, are those Sidney's pictures, Baker?' Pete asked. 'Do you mind if we look at them?'

Baker handed them over.

'The nurse is good,' he said indifferently.

Water-color sketches, done in long easy swoops, some with a darker bordering band like a Matisse. Marvelous flow. Couldn't be looser. They were full of a kind of giant glee. Everything in them was outsize and in motion. Wavering like figures underwater and deliciously tactual.

A scene in the treatment room. A woman getting a massage on what Pete said was a Kelly pad. Pneumatic. But the pad was a fat pink cloud and the woman was a fat milk-chocolate cloud. Woman and pad squashed down in the middle under the nurse's hands. As if she were kneading dough. Her yellow hair standing out in points around her head like the petals of a sunflower.

A scene out the window with a splashy blue pigeon in each corner. A food-conveyor truck with roast beef and asparagus and orange layer cake piled up to the ceiling. People playing cards, a man holding up an ace of hearts bigger than he is.

Two or three of the pictures were just splashes. Sidney hadn't had any feeling about them and didn't know how. But Baker, my smart young friend, was right. The nurse was a knockout. Probationer's stripes and big hands coming at you all over the paper. As if you were a mouse. Some girl who played with him, Pete said. Chased him.

Wonderfully happy. I'd seen children's work before and liked it. This was more than that. Of all the things afterwards that reminded me of that time, Sidney's pictures came nearest to the feeling.

I asked Pete about the gadget Baker was wearing.

'It's the contact for an instrument that makes photographic records of the pulse in the temple artery. Been used for migraine study. We're getting all the data we can on the Roncador people. Tomorrow may be their last day here.

'This is interesting. The calorimeter. Measures heat balance, heat loss, energy output. Very handy for fevers.'

He nodded to a technician at the controls alongside. The machine itself was raised about two feet off the floor. A large cabinet of what looked like wallboard framed with oak, sloping off in a gable at one end. Oddly Tudor effect. Lengths of rubber hose led out from the top and down into what seemed to be glass condensers on a stand.

We looked through the window in the demountable end. Lights inside. A girl's dark head on a small white towel. We must have made a shadow. She twisted around and wiggled her fingers at us. Mrs. Cherrill. She was sweating lightly.

Her mouth made the exaggerated shapes of words: 'I'm losing pounds and pounds.'

We grinned at her. The technician was shaking his head.

'You ought to sell tickets to this place.'

'We've been thinking of it.'

Pete led me down to a row of four or five cubbyholes along the far end. Each booth had an opening like a teller's window, covered with wire mesh. All the openings faced out on a long bench, on which a series of identical little machines were feeding out paper tape.

Full house. Somebody said: 'Hello!' The tall brown-haired girl from Plainfield, in one of the cubicles. Sitting there with electrodes pasted all over her head.

'They're discharging my batteries,' she called cheerfully. 'I've been doing my best to keep Dr. Hendricks's mind off his work but he doesn't seem to care.' She curred her r's.

Dr. Hendricks looked around. Bony and red-haired. Blue eyes

glinted at us over the mask. Then he went back to his tape-reading. A stop watch was running on the bench in front of him.

'This is part of the electroencephalograph,' Pete said. 'Registers the electrical impulses of the brain on this strip of paper.'

Two continuous wavy lines.

'In violet ink too,' I said.

'In violet ink. The normal brain potentials run ten waves to the second. Pretty regular. See it here? A second takes up about three-quarters of an inch on the tape.'

'Am I behaving well, Dr. Jenkins?' the girl called.

'Very dull and normal,' Pete said. 'Rather high voltage, though.'

She laughed. 'Then I am overcharged. I knew it.'

'Most of our fever cases have run about normal,' Pete said. 'The sinusoidal line. Easy and curvy. But ordinarily we get a fairly broad differential in the voltage from patient to patient. The *hlehhana* cases have shown a remarkably high *level* of voltages. Naturally we suspect they're above normal—for these people.

'We're using all these machines in the field of—well, physiological psychology. They study the patient. The other main approach, of course, is the agent. Now I'll show you my pet.'

Off in its own large stall, like a blue-ribbon heifer. The electron microscope. It looked like an automatic machine tool designed by Henry Dreyfuss. Shaped like an upright thick squared C, facing outward. Down through the middle of the C, a fat jointed metal column like the shaft of a big telescope. The top section of the machine was rounded off at the front end and finished in dull gray-green linoleum with chromium bands.

A man in a white coat working over it. He pushed some brown spears of hair back from his eyes and got up with slow courtesy as Pete introduced me. Dobson. The physicist. He didn't look to be more than thirty or so.

'Mr. Rowan wanted to have a look at the machine and see how it works,' Pete said.

Dobson cocked his head. 'Well, now, that's the kind of man I like.' Gulf Coast in his voice.

He took us around to the back of the machine. Tubes and gadgets and coils.

'Dr. Jenkins didn't happen to show you the electroencephalograph?' He poured it all together.

I nodded.

'Well, she's sort of a first cousin to this. Lots of things came out of the vacuum tube. Sound detectors. Radio and television. This baby is really the *daughter* of the vacuum tube—that's the source —and the light microscope—that's the principle of operation. In fact, she comes mighty close to being a mechanical equivalent of the regular compound microscope, except she uses a stream of electrons instead of a stream of light.'

'All clear so far,' I said.

'Now.' Dobson pointed to the top section. He was a natural spellbinder. 'Up here is all lead baffles around the outside. We don't want the electrons or maybe a few X rays to leak out. Got 60,000 volts up there too. Might give you a headache.'

'We build up our power from the regular A. C. lines. Had some trouble lately too. That's what I was working on when you came along. Well, the vacuum tube shoots off electrons from the cathode terminal. We squeeze 'em together and roil 'em round on a coil up there and they come snarling off the point of a little tungsten wire like a slew of wildcats. Going mighty fast.'

'How fast?' I said.

He looked up and squinted. 'Oh, about a hundred thousand miles a second.'

We all laughed. What could you do but laugh?

He pointed to the head of the metal column. 'That's where they come out. Into that tube. Shooting straight down. All high vacuum inside that tube. Very high grade of nothin'. Any air, gases from oil and stuff get in there we have trouble. When one of these little electrons is going someplace he don't want to push his way through a crowd.

'They won't go through glass. Instead of glass or quartz lenses we use magnetic coils. They focus the beam and crisscross it and act so much like regular lenses you can hardly tell any difference. Then, down here at the bottom, the beam hits a fluorescent screen that makes these little electrons shine just like light. That's where you get your image.'

'I wonder if you'd show us Dr. Wright's specimen?' Pete said. 'The one we looked at this morning.'

'Believe it's right here,' Dobson said.

'This is a surprise,' Pete confided to me. 'I hope you remember my monologue about Stanley's experiment with tobacco mosaic?'

'I do indeed. You don't mean to tell me we're going to cure the fever with some very special cubebs?'

He laughed. 'We haven't got that far yet.'

Dobson showed us the cartridge. The specimen was clamped in the nose, on a thin membrane of nitrocellulose.

He moved a handle. Down near the bottom of the machine. 'This is an air lock. Similar to a submarine air lock. When I move this first lever the cartridge we got in there swivels over on a movable tray into a little decompression chamber. Closes off the chamber too.

'Now I move the second little handle here.' It made a noise like opening a bottle of pop. 'That lets the air into the chamber and releases the outside door.'

It did. Very neat. He took out a cartridge, set the new one on the tray, and worked the lever again.

'Now we seal the outside door, close the air intake, and open up a pumping valve. Got a tiny pump that takes the air out of the chamber.'

'One handle does all that?' I said.

He nodded. He had a kind of slow dignity but he was obviously delighted with his little knickknack. So were we. We listened. You could hear the pump going. Half a minute or so. Then he worked both levers one after the other, carefully.

'That shuts the air valve, opens up the inside door, and swings the cartridge right out in the objective field. Ought to be pretty near in place. Next thing we'll see how the magnification is.'

He squinted into an oblique eye port halfway up the big shaft and monkeyed with some knobs on the control panel behind it. Looked like nice careful work.

'There,' he said. 'Guess she's pretty good now. Have a look, Mr. Rowan.'

I glanced at Pete. He got another chair and sat down with me. A broad metal collar on the tube, near the bottom. The face of the collar slanted up and in it were three sets of binocular eyepieces.

I looked. The photomicrograms had been a little disappointing. This was wonderful. A pale otherworldly light, like the first light of spring on a bland Arctic sea. All gray and black and white, but a pearly tone.

Floating in this light, the infinitely tiny cubes of what appeared to be clear gelatin. Some with little blobs attached. Shimmering daintily, as everything appeared to shimmer in that vernal world. I couldn't tell whether it was the Brownian movement or the action of the electrons or some slight mechanical vibration.

'Is it good?' Dobson asked.

'Very high resolution,' Pete said. 'I think one of the best we've had.'

He murmured to me: 'You may not know it, but what you're looking at may be the beginning of a revolution in biology. Can you guess what those cubes are? The *hlehhana* virus. Crystallized for the first time. The first organic virus of any kind to be crystallized.'

'Congratulations,' I said.

'Just a slight variation in the salting-out process. But the variation amounted to pure intuition. Might have taken ten years of methodical experiments to hit it. That and a small increase of alkalinity in the pH. Young Wright, my assistant, pulled off this little trick. You met him. His name will go on the paper.'

'Weren't you in on it?'

'Oh yes. All along.'

'You're quite a guy, Jenkins.'

We looked at each other.

'Now you're being sentimental,' Pete said evenly. 'It may help his career. I hope it does. I may even lose him. But the thing itself is what counts. Something we found out. We. All of us. It doesn't matter who.'

'Would you say that this attitude is general in your profession, Dr. Jenkins?'

I could see his eyes crinkle up. 'I wouldn't say, Commissioner.'

Dobson came back. We thanked him and strolled toward Pete's office.

'Does this bring us much closer?'

'Not much,' Pete acknowledged. 'What it means in the way of immediate help is that the *hlehhana* protein may be one of the organic-and-plant viruses. That might explain how we managed to crystallize it. There are double-duty viruses like that, of course. It opens up a new field for us. A field we've only skirted yet. The plant viruses.'

We got out of the white regalia and sat down in his office.

'We have a good concentrate virus culture,' Pete said, 'and in good quantities. The speed-up process worked.

'I wish I could show you the Svedberg ultracentrifuge. We have to keep it in the subbasement. Chambered in thick concrete. It's a little thing, about three inches in diameter, but it develops a circumference speed of around 1200 feet a second. Forces up to 300,000 times the pull of gravity. If we tried to use it up here it might drag the building apart.

'Then of course the collodion membrane filters. Thin membranes graded according to the sizes of the holes. We've got batteries of those working. Electrophoresis too. The Tiselius apparatus. Rather like silver-plating. A weak electric current draws materials of the same molecular weight and collects them in separate groups.

'The point is that we're using all these methods to get a supply of fixed concentrate. I think—well, we're getting hot. Definitely now. Unless I've got overconfident. I keep watching myself with this fever.'

'I do too,' I said.

'But we've got three—no, four experiments. Very close now. A matter of a couple of days. If the schizophrenia business doesn't knock it all down.' He glanced at me. 'I'm sorry, Jim. I keep forgetting.'

'What? Oh, about Niobe. I don't know. I feel too good to feel bad about her. And after all, wouldn't it be a great opportunity for an actress?'

Pete smiled faintly. His own wife had been dead five years now. Encephalitis. Of course he'd imagined he knew where it came from.

5 THAT Friday is the only day I'm a little scrambled about. My first day of the fever. When I could concentrate on something definite—Pete's gadgets, the relief station, the fire—I seemed to be all right. But when it was just a matter of getting around from place to place with Dennis, as we did most of the time, my mind worked sixteen to the dozen and I was giddy with a happiness as immaterial as music. But not cloudy. Not inside myself. The world. As if everything had been varnished with light.

That was the day Ernie Lankas, the national three-meter spring diving champion, went off the 102nd floor of the Empire State. He phoned downstairs first to give them time to rope off the street. The clerk said he sounded perfectly normal. A little excited. He explained that he'd never had a chance to do his whole repertory in one swoop before and he was 'willing to risk it.' That was the way he put it.

The clerk argued that a parachute drop from an airplane would do just as well. Ernie said he'd thought of that. But the gear on his back would throw his form off and the jerk at the end would ruin the whole effect.

'I hope I can make it good,' he said, and went out and climbed and dived. He cleared all the setbacks on the way down, turning slowly in relaxed and perfect jackknives, gainers, and half-gainers.

Dennis and I toured parts of the quarantine lines and a half-dozen control stations at one time or another that afternoon. I wasn't checking on Justin. He knew that. I wanted to see if they needed more help and I also wanted to show myself. People expected you to look around and listen to their problems, even if you couldn't do anything. They wanted to feel that you were behind them.

In Baychester a proud cop introduced me to young Arbelski, the Boy Scout who had caught a quarantine runner with a rabbit snare, and the Coast Guard people had me out looking at their system of night patrol. Relays of picket boats equipped with photo-electric cells. When any object—a boat, or even a swimmer—passed through the invisible beam, the lights flashed.

A rather nobby English volunteer in a control station on the upper East Side handed me a slip of paper.

'Say it, please.'

I looked at the paper. 'Shrimp wiggle.'

'That's it,' he said happily. 'I can't pronounce it at all. Whenever I try, it comes out *shrink wibble. Shrigg wimple.* That isn't right, is it? *Shring wickle.*'

'What is it?'

A chafing-dish recipe he was very fond of. We studied it and after a while I found I couldn't say it either.

'You see?' he said triumphantly.

The dispatcher notified me that a cop in a home relief station on Columbus Avenue had reported a woman who looked like Niobe. We drove over there.

An outside stairway, hooded with corrugated iron, going up to the second floor of an old brick building on the corner. A yellow bulkhead door at the top. 'They're all a bunch of crooks' scrawled up it in red chalk.

I went in out of the bright sunlight under a SMOKING PROHIBITED sign. At the information desk, a gray-haired full-faced man wearing steel-rimmed glasses and a brown suit. A neighborhood Tammany type. He pointed across the room at a cop standing near the exit door. They seemed to be the only two people in the place.

The cop's name was Creighton. An oldish man. He bent toward me as he listened. He had a bar over his badge.

'Yes,' he said. 'That's right, Commissioner.' As if he were humoring a child, but good-humoredly. 'I recognized her from the notice, and mind you, I wouldn't start the wheels turning unless I was pret-ty sure.'

A row of cubicles with frosted-glass door panels in the far corner of the room. The partition didn't quite reach to the ceiling. He looked at a closed door.

'Well, you'll have a wait now, Commissioner. Sit down here.'

He led me over to one of the long, knocked-together benches painted dark green.

A woman's sharp voice came over the partition. 'I won't stand for this. I'll stay here all day and all day tomorrow. I'll get up early in the morning to come here.'

She came out of the booth talking over her shoulder. Neat and spinsterish. A nervous face with a thin jaw, glasses, and a dark-green hat. A red cock's feather at the back. The interviewer came out behind her, murmuring.

The woman in the green hat was evidently working herself up. She kept talking in a loud voice. The information clerk didn't look bored or hostile or sympathetic. He looked as if he were being confirmed in something he'd been born knowing.

The thin woman went as far as the exit door. The cop murmured to her.

'But I can't talk to her. I can't explain,' she said. 'I'm too excited. I'm getting hysterical. I can't live on what they give me. This isn't living. This is dying little by little.'

199

The cop said: 'Well now, you're the first person we've had in here all day. People are doing pretty well for themselves, you know. Pretty well. Times have changed.' He nodded.

She stared at him for a full minute. He looked back dispassionately.

'What're you wearing that uniform for?' she said in a loud voice. 'You ought to take it off, advising people to take what doesn't belong to them. I'm not going out and steal like the rest, the way they're doing now.'

'I didn't say a thing, lady,' he murmured soothingly. 'Not a thing.'

She whirled on the information clerk. 'What are you staring at?'

We'd looked at her only in quick glances. He didn't answer.

'Don't stand there staring,' she cried. I could feel that she wasn't really hysterical. She was baiting him.

'Look at that man staring,' she said in a loud voice. 'He ought to be exterminated. I'm going to stay here until they do something. I'm not going to steal. I won't.'

She stood there. 'I'm going to commit suicide. I'm going to commit suicide right here on the floor.'

I went over to the cop and slipped him five dollars for her. She took it without a word, nodded, and we could hear her going down the stairs.

The information clerk said reflectively: 'She ought to be examined.'

'Examined?' the cop said mildly. 'Didn't your wife ever offer to kill you?'

The clerk and I smiled at each other. The cop nodded toward the booth. I went in and introduced myself. The interviewer called Blaine, the Welfare Commissioner, and asked me to talk to him before she gave out any information.

She told me about the woman the cop thought was Niobe. The interviewer said she'd been convinced of her sincerity. The description fitted Niobe all right, except that she'd given her age as forty. A daring touch. Mrs. Gustav Freeman. She had rent receipts and mail addressed to a rooming house on West 124th Street.

The cop stopped me on the way out. He said the thin woman made a scene like that about once a week.

'Tell it to the big fat cop,' he said with a sigh. 'Well, that kind's not as bad as the epileptics. We had one the other day. I said: "You shouldn't do that." Boy about twelve. Nice boy. She hit him so hard she knocked him bowlegged.

'He didn't do anything. In a minute she was on the floor. When we got her out of it she said: "Oh, pardon me. I sorry. I kiss your hand." I said: "That pardon stuff's not much good, lady. You mighta had seven of those women dead on the floor." Lots of 'em have got bad hearts. "Pardon's no good," I said. "How do you think these other ones feel? They don't come in here if they haven't got heavy hearts." Do you think it's Mrs. Rowan?'

I said it sounded like her and thanked him. Must have Eunice send him something. Dennis drove me to the address on West 124th Street. The rooming-house keeper said yes, Mrs. Freeman lived there. She'd be back for dinner.

6

DENNIS and I had a drink and a sandwich in a bar on Broadway near 110th Street. When we got back to the car the dispatcher had a message from Mr. Hilson at the *Herald Tribune*. Wanted me to call him. I tried the number three times.

'Yep, I've got it too,' Frank said in his deadpan voice. 'What's the difference? May as well rot here as anywhere else.

'Look, Jim. I talked to the girl at your office. This is only a hunch. Don't jump into your boots. But we have a release on a mass meeting at the Garden tomorrow night. A new evangelist. Been getting people all steamed up over in Brooklyn. Oleander Sanderson. The name's too phony even for that business. We have nothing in the files on her. I talked to the kid who covered it.' He paused. 'It sounds like Niobe.'

I thanked him and said I'd try to get a look at her. We drove downtown to Maurice Satin's office and I spent three-quarters of an hour going over the labor-pool setup with him. Then Dick Wirth put a message through asking me to meet him at the Lower West Side Health Center in Chelsea.

Dick was waiting when we got up there. He looked yellow and haggard in the sunlight. Eyes sticking out of his head. He introduced me to a Dr. Laird. Youngish and tired. We sat on a bench in the waiting room.

Laird said he'd tried giving small amounts of promin in a solution of ordinary baking soda and got what seemed to be effective cures of the fever. About twenty per cent in a group of fifty-four. Then, just on a hunch, he gave another group the sodium-bicarbonate solution without the promin. A level teaspoonful in a glass of water. The results were almost exactly the same.

I looked at them. 'It couldn't hurt anyone?'

Dick shook his head. We talked it over and they agreed that it ought to be tried. I took Laird out to the car and he gave it to the dispatcher. Hospitals, drugstores, bars, eating places to be notified. All citizens requested to co-operate by drinking one glass each day. Nothing was known about its preventive value but it might cure the fever.

The dispatcher read it back and I said something complimentary to young Laird. He shrugged. You couldn't expect very much from it but it might make people feel they were helping.

We stopped at the nearest drugstore and I called Dick Wirth's wife. We chatted a minute.

'I'm worried about Dick, Emma. He isn't looking well at all. I've talked to him but he says it isn't anything. I wish we could——'

I listened. She was sobbing.

'Emma. Please.'

'He's killing himself. I know, I know, Jim. I've tried to keep him in bed but I can't.'

She blew her nose gently.

'Jimmy, you can't take a man's work away from him just when he feels he's needed the most. Not even if he——'

I felt obscurely angry. 'That may be wise, Emma, but it damned well doesn't make sense. I'll see John Kane and——'

'No, no. Don't do anything, Jim. Please.'

'But we can't——'

'No. I'll talk to Dick tonight when he comes home. And I'll ask Dr. Mirenburg to look at him. Thank you, darling.'

She was sympathetic about Niobe.

We crawled up Fifth Avenue a block at a time and I tried to puzzle out the fashions. Men in hunting jackets and corduroys. Some with flies stuck in their rumpled hats, or wearing house slippers. Men in overalls and jumpers. Baseball uniforms. A few yachting caps. One old sea lion was sporting the three stars of a commodore.

Almost as many of these as there were business suits. Simple enough. The men from the small towns and the open country reverting to type. The others who just liked to be comfortable. The boys who made their living in the midst of private dreams about an afternoon at the Yankee Stadium or a morning off Seaflower Reef.

The showoffs were right behind them. Bathing trunks and mandarin robes and cowboy getups. A scarlet-lacquered palanquin went dogtrotting through Fifty-Third Street. I recognized Lucius Beebe in front of De Pinna's, tricked out in lilac butler's livery and carrying a magnum of sparkling Burgundy. He announced later (but in time for the Sunday newspapers) that he had made this drastic sacrifice as a protest against public disorder.

New York had always been a gambler's town but that week the boys were really operating. Everything from madhouse poker to the regular brace games at the hotels. The betting was about as universal as breathing and a lot more noticeable. You could get three-to-one that the next girl who came along would speak to you, side bets on whether her eyes would be blue, gray, green, or brown, and a birdcage that took the whole thing right on up to love. I don't remember whether they sent an inspector along for the love part or not.

Not very imaginative, on the whole. The male vanity came out in other directions, too. Horseplay, human-fly exploits, bullheadedness, a certain quiet but persistent boasting, and a tendency to collect the girls. Much slapping of female bottoms. The girls themselves puzzled me at first. Only a few of them went to such extremes as negligees or openwork girdles for street wear, though there was a flurry of sarongs and a number of women just gave up the distinction between wandering around the house in a slip and going out in it.

These were exceptions. The general change was harder to catch. Nobody bothered about conventions, of course. Not even about defying them. I remember one girl, on the open deck of a Fifth Avenue bus, who stood pigeon-toed, holding her pocketbook in her mouth, lifted her skirts and hauled her girdle down into place. The women clapped for two blocks but the men, I confess, were pop-eyed.

The other point was that just about all the stores were giving things away. A woman could wear what she liked—if she got there first. That meant a whole new brigade of mink coats but it still didn't explain the difference. I decided it came down to this: that the girls, most of them for the first time, were dressing and acting up to their own secret idea of themselves.

Obviously this would lead to a general playing down of ages, except at the bottom, where the fourteen-year-olds got suddenly mature. A few cases of houri trousers or mantillas. The general effect was more conservative than you'd imagine but striking enough. For one thing, they seemed to lose any sense of being inferior as women, or vis-à-vis other women. This made for free trade and a pleasanter time all round.

Some of the plain girls, who hadn't quite dared, turned out to be stunning clotheshorses. The good-looking ones, on the whole, got a little less uppity about it. There were some comic effects, of course. People who had odd ideas about themselves. And a good deal of infantilism. But the frank and almost universal vanity was on a give-and-take basis. I rather liked it, except for a certain effervescence of cuteness that went with it.

Still, I didn't actually appreciate the depth of the revolution until a girl on Vanderbilt Avenue swung round in front of me like a model, hands out.

'Darling, huh?'

'Delicious.'

She looked down her back. 'I think I've got the slimmest rear end in town,' she said complacently.

7 ABOUT five-thirty that afternoon the lone cop we'd been able to shake loose for traffic duty at the south end of Times Square called for help. The nearest we could get was Sixth Avenue. Dennis and I left the car there and hiked through.

Not many bulbs left in the street lights and signs. The place had the woebegone air of an amusement park the day after Labor Day, but it was roaring. We got through to the distracted cop on his bay horse in the middle of the square and Dennis boosted me up on top of a car to get a look at things.

A pretty sight. Cars parked solid through the square, up the fork as far as I could see, and down Broadway and Seventh Avenue to Thirty-Sixth Street. Nothing moving but a single line along the traffic island in the center. Cars still inching in from the side streets. Horns going, girls laughing, drivers calling as they tried to worm their cars out of the solid block. Everybody cheerful as hell. A picnic.

'My God,' I yelled down to the cop, 'why didn't you put that call in a little sooner?'

He shook his head. The horse backed delicately between cars.

'It all happened in ten-fifteen minutes,' he bawled over to me.

'One minute I had the stuff moving okeh. Next minute I was in a blizzard. Can't understand it. Going to the free movies with their girls. Look. Half of 'em are new cars. Dealers' plates.'

I told him to try to get help and block off incoming traffic from the side streets. Dennis stayed with him. I pushed back to the car. No time to find out where Justin's traffic inspectors were. I made a scratch map, looked at it, and called Bill at headquarters. He'd been working with Rich Jones all day.

I asked him to get a small map—Hagstrom's, Geographia, anything—and a red-and-blue pencil.

'Okeh? These boundaries are inclusive. Draw a red line around the area Thirty-Fifth Street, Fifth Avenue, Fifty-Fifth Street and Ninth Avenue. We'll block that off to incoming traffic. The main pressure will come at the ends of Forty-Second, Fiftieth, and the avenues. We cover those first.

'Got that? All avenues and cross streets in the area feed out. We'll shoo cars with drivers out both ends of the avenues, Forty-Second and Fiftieth. That's right. On the other streets, driverless cars move east and west out of the area. Single parking as far as the river, if necessary, on the West Side and as far as they go on the East. Might mark those streets blue.'

Bill mentioned Polyclinic Hospital at Fiftieth Street and two control stations in the district.

'Okeh. We'll have to clear those blocks and close them off. Police from the five nearest control stations. Emergency trucks. Better assign two radio cars to cruise each avenue. Ask them to keep reporting. We'll need all the wrecking cars we can get. I'll stick here. Northeast corner of Sixth and Forty-Third.'

That was about all I saw of the great Times Square traffic jam. I heard the orders go out and a few minutes later the wails of converging sirens. A radio car began to ride herd on Sixth Avenue. Two or three drivers turned and hurried south. Then a half dozen more. Still the cross streets were jammed tight. A wrecker backed in with his chain hoist. The key log came out. Two cops rolled an unlocked sedan around the corner and the mass began to stir.

I helped them clear the block between Sixth and Fifth. We shoved the Mayor's car into the parking lot on the corner with two or three dozen others. Dennis had the keys. Forty-Third east of the square and Fifty-Fourth to the west were the first streets to be cleared. We shunted the tow cars through them. The center lane in the square itself was free now and the upper and lower sections on Broadway and Seventh Avenue began to break off like the lip of a glacier.

A young man opened the door of the car next to me. 'Look at that,' he said in quiet wonder. 'I'm walking up towards Columbus Circle minding my own business and this schlepper grabs my arm. "You need a car," he said. A salesman. "Not unless you got time payments for a thousand years," I said. "Pay?" he says. "Who said anything about paying? This little job is a gift. Climb in and see how you like it." I thought it must be hot. A hot car. "It's okeh," he said. "I'll give you a bill of sale. Got a penny?" So I gave him the penny and he gave me the bill and the keys and slapped me on the back. "Good luck," he says and opened up the showroom window and I drove out.'

He shrugged and backed out carefully. I called the dispatcher and asked him to request all movie managers in the area to announce that the police were hauling cars out of the square. It damn near started a riot but the cars moved. In an hour and twenty minutes we had reasonable clearance. It was a little over two hours before we could open the district to no-parking traffic, and drivers were still wandering the back streets bawling for their lost cars.

That was what I got for being damn fool enough to believe we could get away with skimping on the traffic system.

8

WE PICKED Bill up and drove around trying to decide where to have dinner. Chatham Walk. A small sign: OPEN FOR THE

SEASON. In February. Flowers behind the tables. Pale-yellow table-cloths under the big flowery pink parasols. The loom of buildings all around.

The headwaiter found us a table and bowed slightly.

He said: 'Good evening. Are—the gentlemen working at their regular occupations?'

I looked at Bill and Dennis.

'Yes indeed,' I said. 'In a way.'

'Then the management wishes to congratulate you on your public spirit and suggests that you have dinner with the compliments of the house.'

We thanked him.

'What do you do if people aren't working at their regular jobs?'

He showed his teeth.

'Then we congratulate them on their freedom from business worries and invite them to have dinner with——'

We nodded all round.

Dennis and Bill decided to share a steak. I wanted pompano fileted and baked New Orleans style with crabmeat in a paper bag. The sauce was butter and wine and chopped green onions and mushrooms and truffles and a few other things.

All that time, in fact, I had a pregnant woman's hankering for foods a little out of the ordinary. *Forlorn skilpadde,* a kind of Swedish mock-turtle ragout. Periwinkles picked out with a lobster fork. Fig jam from the Mediterranean on hot toast. S. S. Pierce's honeydew pickles. And oysters. Robbins Island oysters on the half shell and Maurice River Salts pan-fried and Seawanhakas in a bubbling stew. Nothing ever tasted so heavenly before or since.

While we were waiting I phoned Eunice and told her where we were. Then I called the rooming house on West 124th Street. The landlady said Mrs. Freeman had come back an hour ago. When she told her a man had called to see her Mrs. F. packed her things and moved out. No forwarding address.

I sat there a minute, realizing how idiotic I'd been. No precautions. It would have been the simplest thing in the world to tell the landlady I wanted to surprise my wife. True too. But that was the ridiculous confidence the fever gave you. Anything you wanted couldn't help but happen. Why bother to think? It didn't seem to affect my thinking, such as it was. It did play tricks with my judgment, though Niobe's seemed to be all right. I decided to watch myself.

When I got back to the table Dennis was talking about the gas war in the Bronx. Two chains of service stations competing to see which could give away more gas. One chain decided to throw in a free tire with every twenty gallons but the customers complained that the tires weren't white walls.

Then we saw Eunice coming along behind the headwaiter. She yoohooed, obviously satirizing our swank. Short-sleeved white pique dress. Square neck, with rickrack. Little bright insectlike Guatemalan figures embroidered here and there on it. A big picture hat. I realized the women at the other tables were wearing hot-weather clothes too. Prints and cottons and summer blacks.

Eunice put out her white-gloved hands, limp wristed, to me and Bill and smiled at Dennis. We got up gravely. I said: 'Hello, dear,' and kissed her on the cheek and an elderly woman at the next table nodded and smiled at me.

We talked about the traffic situation. You pinned one thing up and something else let go. Bill said Justin had told him the American Legion boys were pretty sore because the Boy Scouts had been put to work and they hadn't. We could use them. I made a note to detach Justin's traffic inspector and a deputy or two and have them take a crack at reorganizing the system with volunteers.

Bill said the Department of Markets was having a hell of a time. Whenever one of Feuerman's trucks stopped, people would climb aboard and unload what they wanted. They were going to the central markets too—Bronx Terminal and Fulton and Washington. It was beginning to cause shortages in some parts of the city. We could give Henry some volunteers for guards, but they'd need to be damned tactful and good-natured.

When Dennis finished his coffee I asked him to try the car radio and see what was doing. He came back in a hurry. A fire at Bush Terminal in Brooklyn.

I sighed and got up. Eunice was just beginning on an orange ice. I picked up the ice and spoon and her gloves, Bill put a tip down, and we started for the car.

'I'll get you coffee later.'

'You're always rushing me,' Eunice said.

'How I'd like to,' I murmured.

We could see it from Manhattan Bridge. An aureole at first. It shot up into a bright light as we went out Flatbush Avenue. Bill and I hunched over a map. Bush Terminal was tremendous. Must run to something like 200 acres. Well over a hundred buildings. Warehouses, factories, sidings, lofts, and eight piers south of Gowanus Bay. Erie Basin and the State Barge Terminal just across the bay. The wind was blowing in that direction. Not very hard.

The body of the fire seemed to be down toward the piers. We ran along the row of white brick structures and found Adam Hanauer beside the glistening Commissioner's car. He looked bigger, red with command. This was his business.

He shook his head when he saw me. 'Not very good, Jim. Sisal, jute, pitch, industrial solvents. Funny thing. There's a whole bargeload of bulk asbestos down there. The fire went all around it.'

He and a deputy chief shouted at each other over the throbbing of the pumpers. People's faces massed behind the fire lines.

Adam came back. 'Pressure's low. If that wind gets up a little more the flames may carry across to Erie Basin. The fireboats are in there now, trying to head it off. I notified the Navy people at Fort Lafayette, in case the wind changes.'

Lafayette was a small naval magazine off Fort Hamilton.

'I'll talk to Harry Conover,' I said. 'What else do you need?'

He told me. We checked it off on a list of control-station apparatus. Four pumpers and three hose wagons from Staten Island on the Bay Ridge and Thirty-Ninth Street ferries. Another pumper and two hose wagons from Jamaica. The nearer ones had been called in. A water tower, six aerial ladder trucks, and a smoke ejector from downtown Manhattan.

I called off each item on the radiophone. Bill and Eunice standing in the glare of the searchlights. The dispatcher read the list back and we could hear the orders going out. Bill took over until he got the dispatcher's: 'All equipment on the way.' Then he began on the job of deploying the rest of the apparatus all over the city.

A cop took me through the lines and found a telephone. I got Conover and told him.

'It's bad. We'll need all the pressure you can give us. Even if it means a temporary shutoff somewhere else. If you have to do that, Harry, you might ask John Kane to give out an announcement beforehand to the regular radio stations. Save us some trouble.'

He thought. 'We might get it up to half again, Jim. That's about all.'

'That should do it.'

Hanauer turned the command over to a squat man named Tolliver and Dennis took us wailing across Brooklyn. We put the call through on the way and when we got to Floyd Bennett Field the police amphibian was warmed up and ready.

The pilot circled up over Big Channel and went straight downwind for the glow. Jouncy air. In minutes we were over it and the pilot leaned toward Adam.

'How high, Commissioner?'

'About five hundred,' Adam said, though he didn't seem to be listening. He stared down. The pilot snapped a switch, dialed, and put the microphone in his hand.

The smoke waved down toward Buttermilk Channel. Fire coming up from three piers and eating into a semicircle of warehouses behind them. It looked awful, rolling out now and again in streaked soft balloons of flame. The firemen on the aerial ladders seemed to be right in it.

Then I saw the fireboats. Seven or eight of them. Adam pointed out the *Gaynor* and the *Harvey*. Black hulls and pale deckhouses. The big one, the *Fire Fighter*, moved in like a puncher who liked infighting. Forcing it, getting in close, backing a little when the pressure got to be too much, then crowding in again, crowding hard, punching with the heavy white streams. It curled your hair to watch her.

Adam was smiling to himself. 'P.D. 1,' he said to the mike. 'Hanauer calling Deputy Chief Tolliver. Over.'

'This is Tolliver, Adam,' the squat man's voice said. 'Over.'

'I've got it now, Joe,' Adam said. 'Six aerial ladders between warehouses No. 7 and 8. Back them up with as many pumpers as you can spare from the other side. Twelve lines over the roofs at 5 and 6. Get No. 4 first. Is that clear?'

Tolliver's voice said: 'You're a genius, chief. I've got it.'

Adam chuckled. 'P.D. 1 calling *Fire Fighter*,' he said. 'Hanauer calling Miller. Come in, Al.'

Miller's voice came up to us. 'Damned hot weather for February, chief.'

'Everything on No. 6 pier now, Al. Signal the other boats. Pour it on. We'll have it in half an hour.'

It took a little longer. Almost three-quarters of an hour. I didn't understand how it was done and don't yet. But the pier began to darken. No. 4 warehouse died down, then No. 5. We circled slowly. Adam radioed a few more directions, nodded to the pilot, and we headed back for Floyd Bennett.

'That looked to me like a damn good job,' I said.

Adam chuckled to himself and turned half round to me. 'If you don't catch on in thirty-five years, Jim, you never will.'

Bill and Eunice were waiting at Hanauer's red car. We said good night and started back for Manhattan. I checked with the dispatcher on fires in other parts of the city. Everything about normal.

We dropped Bill at home—Marguerite was waiting for him—

and went on up to Sixty-Eighth Street. A cab at the door. The driver got out as we pulled in.

'Nick!' I called. 'How are you?'

He shook hands all round. I led them upstairs and poured drinks.

'What've you been doing, Nick?'

'Fishin',' he said. 'The weaks come up north already. Three-four months ahead of time. The shads are runnin' too. They're not supposed to come till them little white trees get flowers on them. My brother and me got nineteen shads today. Out by 125th Street.'

Dennis nodded. 'They're fine eating,' he said. 'Very fine eating.'

Nick got me over in a corner. 'Your wife come back, Commissioner?'

He watched me and shook his head when I shook mine.

'I was over with my brother today,' he said earnestly. 'Over Jersey. By the nets. We see a woman workin' on the lift with the men. She had hip boots and a sweater. Red hair.'

He took a newspaper cut of Niobe out of his pocket and tapped it with the back of his hand.

'I think it's the same woman, Commissioner. My brother too. Red hair she got. Pushed up in back. We was right over close. I looked.'

The Wabash Terror. In hip boots. I asked him a few questions. The description was about right and Nick was good at sizing people up. He made arrangements to meet me with the boat next afternoon.

'Damn nice of you to let me know,' I said.

He shook his head, finished the drink, and said good night. He was on his way home.

Eunice was restless. She asked me to walk her part way crosstown. I called headquarters before Dennis left and got good night.

We strolled toward Fifth Avenue. A warm darkness. Stars. We were laughing at a line in the *Herald Tribune*. Something about the unusual birds showing up in the city. Feathered. A golden eagle in Forest Park and a Pacific loon down along the water front. The smarty reporter said a young brown booby bird had been discovered perched on a limb in Bronx Park, studying William Beebe.

Right in the middle of it she said: 'What was the idea of kissing me tonight? At the Chatham.'

I couldn't see her face under the hat. 'A little gag. My God, you weren't offended, were you?'

I had a hunch and refused to believe it.

'No, I wasn't offended,' she said in a tight voice. 'Let's get a cab.'

I pointed at a driver as he went by and he swerved back under the light.

'Where to?'

'Where do you want to go, Eunice? Home?'

'Oh, anywhere.'

'Uptown. Just drive around.'

The grass in the park smelled like April.

'What's the matter, my sterling compatriot? Anything I can do?'

She slid into my arms and kissed me with a little gasp, then pushed me away. Her face and hands were hot.

That was what I'd refused to believe. 'Oh, Eunice. For God's sake. Me? Old me? You know I'm fond of you.'

She was huddled in the opposite corner. 'Yes, you're fond of me. God damn you, I could get better men than you on an off week end.'

She lashed out and kicked me in the shins. I twisted the front of her coat and shook her a little.

'Stop that.'

'You son of a bitch.'

'All right. I'm a son of a bitch. You've got the fever, that's all. So have I. Don't be so damned Irish about it.'

She lifted her hat off, put her face down in my lap, and boo-hooed, clutching me. In a minute or two she twisted around until she was looking up at me. She laughed and pushed my nose.

'Strong man, huh? I guess I must have come all undone. Come and stay with me.' She wrinkled her nose and laughed. 'Please. Go ahead.'

I smiled down at her. 'How can I help it, you devil? Where?'

'Oh, I don't know,' she said, sprawling luxuriously, and pulled my head down to her mouth. One hand unbuttoned my vest and slid through my shirt and tucked up my undershirt. The next thing I knew it was running up my side like a mouse.

I yelled, tickled her hard, and she landed on the floor in a shrieking ball.

We were just coming out of the park at the third transverse. West Eighty-Sixth Street. I helped her up and she got straightened out.

'We can't go to my place. The other girls.'

'How about the Ainsley on Broadway? In the seventies, isn't it? I always liked that big old barn. Hardenbergh designed it.'

'In our trouble we should think about architecture,' Eunice said. 'Why not? Tell him.'

'Want to find a drugstore first?'

'I've got something in my bag.'

'My forehanded compatriot. How'd you know you'd meet a man?'

'Didn't I?'

I told the driver. He pulled down Broadway and nodded as we got out.

'You two'll do all right together. Some of the people I haul you figure they won each other in a bingo game.'

'Is that a blessing?'

I offered him a tip and he pushed my hand away.

'Good luck. I wish I could get a friend and join you.'

'Why don't you?'

'With five kids?' he said, watching my face as he pulled out.

The elderly clerk at the desk fussed over us. 'No, that isn't nice enough for you. I can give you something on the fifteenth floor. River view. Three rooms. A Louis Quatorze suite.' He smiled at us. 'It was Mr. Ziegfeld's old suite. We haven't changed the furnishings.'

'That sounds very nice,' I said. 'Can you get us some food?'

I told him what we wanted.

'Good night,' he called as the bellboy led us to the elevator. It went up twelve floors and jammed. We walked up the other two.

A wonderful place. Big high old rooms with a gilt molding. Long brocade drapes. A huge gilt bed with cupids and things on the headboard. The bath was all black marble with gilt griffons for faucets.

As soon as the door was closed Eunice ruffled my hair.

'Last one undressed is a stinkfish,' she yelled.

The cartwheel hat sailed and she was wriggling out of the dress. I worked at my shirt buttons. I had hopes of catching up on the girdle but it had a zipper. Her slip wrapped itself around my head, she kicked her shoes up at the glass chandelier, and when I tossed my pants the change went rolling all over the room.

She was peeled like an eel before I could get out of my shoes. She whooped and leaped sprawling into the bed, bouncing like a rookie fireman on a trampolin, and came out neatly on her feet.

'Athletes we should have.'

'Captain of the girls' gym team, George Washington High School, Class of '34,' she said. 'Come on. Let's look out the window.'

I opened it. An ornamental iron guard. We rested our elbows on the low sill. Three o'clock. The river and the calm stars. It was so quiet I could hear the wild geese going north. In February.

I shivered. 'That's the loneliest damn sound. I used to hear it down by the river at twilight. October. It meant going away.'

'Oh, you're cold. What a shame,' she said and tickled me.

I yowled. She tried to tumble out of the way but I caught her by the ankles and hauled her back. Quick and hard and slippery. We were laughing and panting. She shrieked softly and fought me off as I tickled her. We were rolling all over the floor. Once she grabbed me from behind and said: 'Now I'll get back at the boss' before she worked me over. I got her down finally and made her beg.

'Pretty now. Say it nice.'

'You're a sweet man. You're a lovely man.'

She screeched as I got her with both hands.

'Say it pretty.'

'Ohhh. You're the nicest man I ever met. You do things to me.'

'Smart, huh?'

She yelped again. 'Oh. Oh. Please.'

'What'll you do for me? Talk,' I said.

'Oh. I'll do anything for you. I love you. I—I'm yours. I tremble when I see you.'

'That's better.'

She pulled me down by the hair. 'Louse,' she said as she kissed me. 'Stinker. Bum. Shiker. Rat. Big Mean,' she murmured slowly.

The bellboy knocked. She relaxed on the floor out of sight, laughing to herself. I took the food, found a half dollar and a quarter on the floor and gave it to him.

'What'll we do with this?'

'The window ledge,' Eunice said. 'That's where we kept the butter when we lived in the brownstone. When I was a kid.'

'We kept ours in the well.'

'I don't know about you,' she said, 'but if I had to climb down a well every time I wanted a pat of butter——'

We had a shower and got into bed. We jounced a little. It was a wonderful bed.

'Oh my,' Eunice murmured. 'That Ziggy.'

'Must be ten feet wide. I could go way down there where you could hardly see me and make love to you, and you could——'

'I'd miss you. I miss you now.'

217

She sighed. 'Big Mean.'

'My fond compatriot.'

The strange thing was that we made love as if we'd known each other for a long time. We had, of course. But as if what we'd learned about each other by working in the same office could be applied to anything we did together. I seemed to do just the right things to get her bothered. They weren't the same things for everybody, or not in the same order. And once when I shivered at her tongue she laughed gently, like a woman laughing in her sleep. But also as if she were pleased at having known the secret in advance.

When our troubles were over for the moment I lighted cigarettes.

'Why, Eunice. There's a little pool of water in your belly-button.'

'I keep goldfish,' she said primly.

We noticed the light in a room across a narrow court. Four or five men sitting around talking. The windows were open and we could hear the voices clearly.

An oldish man with a full bristly mustache said: 'I don't agree, Walton. I don't see why this couldn't be the beginning of a revival of sensibility. Of course you despise Rousseau, don't you? Well, it's understandable.'

One of the others laughed.

'But after all,' the mustache said earnestly, 'he did provide a voice—a mixed-up voice, if you like—for the fresh level of feeling in his time. He made everyone conscious of it. These things usually begin on the feeling level.'

A heavy somber man said: 'And what did it lead to? How many years of war and civil war?'

'Yes, and about—about sensibility,' a thin brown-haired man said. He seemed to twitch with his ideas. Had a sort of mental stutter. 'Sensibility? The Japanese. The Japanese are *teeming* with sensibility. They hold looking-at-the-moon parties. Yet they've committed some of the most extreme——'

218

'So did the French Revolution,' the somber man said. 'Obviously there's a connection. I'll take reason.'

'The French had reason too,' another man drawled. They laughed.

'I think you're taking sensibility as a thing in itself,' the mustache said. 'It's that too. But in the main it's a signal. It shows that a certain phase has been reached. It doesn't determine the next phase. In fact, it doesn't even determine the quality of the social context it appears in. It does announce a new departure of some sort. Now if, by the accident of a little virus that happened to be carried here, a revival of sensibility—already latent, mind you, in the social situation—were to be set off, then I think it might——'

We got up and found glasses for the milk.

'What the hell are they talking about?' Eunice whispered.

'Us,' I said, and laughed.

We left the light on in the bathroom and carried the food back to bed. Big delicatessen sandwiches on crusty rye. We lay there in the dark, eating and listening.

FIVE

1 I woke up in the first fog of dawn. The river air came in cold at the open window and Eunice was wrapped around me like a very chummy boa constrictor. My leg ached. They were still talking in the room across the court.

The twitchy man said: 'But don't you think—— The reaction. We're sure to have a reaction. I mean the party must be over some-time.'

'Isn't that an ethical superstition? After the crime the expiation?' the drawling one put in.

'I wouldn't say so,' the somber man objected. 'Call it an experiential observation. The flood and ebb of energy. Most phenomena have a cyclic pattern of some kind.'

'Did somebody mention the—the crime? Of happiness?' said the twitchy man.

'Exactly. Yes,' said the mustache. 'Or don't you agree that happiness is anarchic in our society? A disturbance of the peace. Aren't we having a little demonstration right now?'

'Wait a minute, gentlemen,' the drawling man said. 'Let's define our terms. What's happiness?'

I tried to pull my leg away gently but Eunice's thighs clasped on it. She stirred against me, eyes closed, and her drowsy open mouth twisted back and forth on my mouth.

The switchboard girl called us at eight. One of those mornings like the mornings you wake up a little too early after a night out and everything is weird and very, very funny. We laughed at the pink cupids, and the pennies on the floor, and took a shower together, giggling, in the black marble tub.

Eunice looked over her shoulder as I scrubbed her back. 'You don't suppose this is where Anna Held had her milk baths?'

I went out and got the milk carton. Shook it. About a jigger left.

'There you are,' I said, pouring it gently down her back. 'Anna Held wasn't any better than you, my friend. Confidentially, I don't think she was half as good.'

Eunice gaped at me and laughed so hard she sat down in the tub.

We went back to bed still damp and that was one of the few times I can remember it as being pure comedy. No organic seriousness at all. The only rule in the game was that each of us had to submit to the other's tricks. If they didn't hurt. We ended up hanging off the foot of the bed, played out and gasping.

When we got settled again with a cigarette Eunice sighed. 'Just think. This could go on forever. First a shower and then back to bed and then a shower——'

'Like hell it could. My back aches like blazes. I'm an old fool. If I ever see another woman I'll——'

'You'll be sorry.'

'Let me give you a piece of advice, young lady. I'm old enough to be your aunt. Finish that cigarette and take a shower. Alone.'

'I want a towel.'

'I didn't say I was your aunt. Ask room service for it.'

In about fifteen minutes she was looking very trim and sedate. We smiled pleasantly at each other as we went down in the elevator.

I dropped Eunice off at her place and went home. As I got out of the cab, the girls were chattering into the newish Hunter College building across the street. As good a job of architecture as anything in the city. All glass and cement.

I felt lightheaded in the sunlight. A motto in bas-relief, handsomely spaced down the slab of cement wall: 'WE ARE OF DIFFERENT OPINIONS AT DIFFERENT HOURS BUT WE ALWAYS MAY BE SAID TO

BE AT HEART ON THE SIDE OF THE TRUTH.' RALPH WALDO EMERSON.
Well, yes, sir, I thought, going up in the elevator, feeling good in spite of my backache. Indeed we are. But while you Boston gentlemen warble of the truth, your cool bedfellow, we ordinary mousers have to begin at the other end. The hind end, if I may say so, sir. Facing each moment the eternal need to grub the smallest damn stick of the truth, whatever that is, out of the woodpile of the actual and whittle it and make it fit. And the girls. Did you know about the girls, Mr. Emerson, sir?

Mail on the hall table. A letter from my mother in Indiana, who was worried about us. Bundle up well, she said. Rachel was in the living room as I came in. She opened her eyes and smiled at me. I said: 'Morning, Rachel,' and grinned, but as I walked in I'd felt Niobe there, as if she were in the other room and would be out in a minute. Down underneath the serene lift of the fever, I felt hollow and lonely, like a drinking man who remembers suddenly why he is drinking.

2

ELIZABETH gave me breakfast with some tacit disapproval. Honeydew melon and eggs and scrapple. I picked up the *Times*. In those days I had to read it from end to end, partly because things weren't in their usual places and partly because, like a bookie, I was backing the field.

Mrs. Landsman Hosgrave III on the front page. A well-heeled New Yorker who had made several expeditions to the South Seas, in the company of such ranking anthropologists as Buck and Rivers and Mead. She'd also done social-service work, mostly with adolescent delinquents, in New York. A husband in good standing and three grown kids. She looked like a big capable motherly woman.

She announced that she'd formed a corporation to take over

London Terrace, the block-long apartment unit in Chelsea. She planned to set up something to be called the House of the Young. The development would be thrown open free, all living expenses paid, to as many young people of both sexes in the New York area as could be taken care of. Ages sixteen to nineteen inclusive. Resident doctors, nurses, instructors, a birth-control clinic, a personality clinic, a social-problems clinic, and so on.

The house rules were simple. Good food prescribed by the dietitians for individual cases. One day a week, called Spree Day, for overindulgence in pickles, candy, cigarettes, and liquor. After the necessary instruction, each resident would be required to sleep with a resident of the opposite sex at least once every two weeks. Couples must not remain together longer than three days at a time. Thus each youth would sleep with each girl in more or less informal rotation.

Aside from its value as a sexual, emotional, and social apprenticeship, this would tend to democratize the special privileges of good looks or personality. Mrs. Hosgrave said she had been led to it by her observation of the youth houses in Polynesia and New Guinea and her experience with the guidance of adolescents in New York. She believed that rotation was the ordinary pattern of adolescent behavior, just as it was the pattern of the square dance, a taboo version of it.

The *Times* handled most of it in gingerly quotes. 'The pudding-headed idiots,' said Mrs. Hosgrave, 'who persist in regarding the crisis of adolescence as a dirty little joke—half masturbation and half puppy love—are pulling their own house down about their ears. Our prisons are full of youthful offenders. Our mental hospitals crawl with schizophrenic young people and our houses of correction are crowded with so-called delinquent girls.

'These complacent muttonheads are the real delinquents. They are the ones who must stand trial. The first job of any society is to show its young how to live and to give them a chance to do it. A society, like a royal family, must establish the succession. We haven't done it and we're not doing it now. I propose to show that it can be done.'

The last paragraph was a little sad. Registration figures for the first day at the House of the Young, Inc., offices. Total applicants: 2372 boys, fourteen girls. Six of the girls turned out to be older women.

Dennis called for me and I bored through the rest of the paper earnestly on the way downtown.

People racing dinghies in the Central Park Reservoir. An organization of amateur wreckers tearing down tenements in Harlem and Red Hook and Hell's Kitchen. Most of the people had moved into free apartments long ago. The Governor talking. Congress talking. The report of the Advisory Committee for the Department of Health. Two and a half columns. Not much we didn't know. Very little synergetic action between the virus and other diseases. That was a break. Recommendations: none. Or rather, more of what we were doing already. Especially more use of volunteer public-health nurses to help take some of the load off the badly understaffed hospitals.

Zolotow had an item about Niobe's opening. Postponed for two weeks, he said, 'because of the unfortunate absence of the star, the director, the author, and most of the cast, all of whom have migrated to parts unknown. Christopher Mallett, the producer, is holding the fort with a slightly wistful air.'

At the office, Bill wandered in as Eunice was giving me the weather report.

'Take a look, Bill,' I said.

'Carson sounded almost definite this morning,' Eunice told us. ' "We're pretty sure to have a change. Not really certain yet, though. It *could* veer toward the south." '

Lots of dope. Rapidly falling temperatures in the Dakotas and Minnesota. Pressure rising. At Minneapolis down to eight, twenty degrees lower than the day before. Huron, South Dakota, down to six. That was minus twenty. Bismarck minus ten. Snow developing at La Crosse, Wisconsin. Heavy fall at St. Louis. The low had

225

moved about 350 miles northeastward in the last twenty-four hours. Cold air farther south and east.

We looked at each other.

'Now we're getting someplace,' Bill said quietly.

I thought. 'Close, though. The deadline is Monday. We can't expect the storm to come booting in like the U. S. Cavalry and save us from the Governor's Indians.'

'It would be nice, though,' Eunice said.

Bill sighed. 'Our Eunice. My dream girl. Doesn't she look sweet today? All in black, with that cute little white doodad collar.'

I glanced at him.

'She always looks so *fresh*,' Bill said.

She did, too. The vivid mouth and the hair brushed silky and the pale glow you get from running it out a little. If you're young enough. She fluttered her lashes at him.

'Like a schoolgirl,' Bill said. 'I wish *I* had a nice girl like Eunice.'

'What about Marguerite?'

'Well, Marguerite is retired,' Bill said gently. 'Mr. Palmer Palmer, the Pan American boy friend, is arriving any day now and so—she said farewell. Farewell, sweet love.

'But I think,' he said confidentially, 'I *think*, mind you, that I may have a new little numero. A little Powers numero. Of course' —he shrugged—'as we all know, they must be in bed every night at nine o'clock sharp to preserve their beauty. But what is to prevent me from keeping early hours too? A little sacrifice for love?'

We were laughing. I spent an hour on the reports and caught myself getting drowsy over them.

On the way down to the commissioners' meeting I ran into young Joralemon.

'Everything all right now?'

He beamed. 'Everything is fine, Mr. Rowan. Thanks to you.'

A short session that day. John Kane had a telegram from Gordon Lummis, the Deputy Mayor, at Recife. Bad flying weather. I told them about the weather we might get if things held out and the bad news about Cornelia Kelsey.

Dick Wirth, looking terribly drawn, quoted the day's figures: 1,560,000 cases. Plus 360,000. Hardly slowing up at all, as it should if we were nearing the peak. We talked over the Advisory Committee's report.

Waldo Selby, the Department of Correction boss and a rather fussy animal, got up nervously. He said things were pretty much out of control. For a moment we had visions of medieval robber bands but it wasn't as bad as that. The big prison on Centre Street and the one on Hart's Island were fairly quiet. The Riker's Island plant running more or less on its own momentum. All the guards and prisoners who felt like it had sailed away on the ferry. A good many of them stayed too.

We looked at George Romanelli, who was in charge of municipal ferries.

'I don't know,' he said. 'I haven't been able to get a report from there in two days. The ferry isn't at the dock. I don't know where the hell it is, or who's running it.'

We patched that up by closing the island to everything but the Correction Department tender and assigning a police boat to the area.

'And there's been a great deal of trouble at the House of Detention for Women,' Selby said. The handsome modern building on Greenwich Street. 'Very disorderly. Sixty-five of the attendants walked out. We still consider it escapeproof but we have nearly 500 women there. Most of them spend their time on the exercise roof, yoohooing to the men in the street.'

In the midst of some general grinning Arnie said: 'Well, hell. Can't a girl even yoohoo?'

I watched the blue-and-orange flag on the staff at City Hall, standing out in that eternal southeast wind. Onderdonck said the hospitals were falling into a really dangerous condition and we arranged to give him priority on the volunteer pool.

Afterwards, downstairs in the street, I happened to look up as a small yellow plane formed the letter T in white smoke. Slowly it spelled THE WORLD IS YOURS, its wings glinting as it climbed. Then it leveled off and bored away toward Queens. About over the Williamsburg Bridge, a police plane came down on it and they played tag across Brooklyn. I got the report later. An ordinary commercial job. The pilot had been paid in advance by a man he didn't know.

3 I THOUGHT of calling Pete before I went up there, but didn't. Seems damned odd now. We were facing the chance that half the town, my wife and I included, might come out of the thing crippled in the head, and I was taking it without a flutter. It wasn't that I didn't care or that, like a paretic, I failed to realize the actual enormity of the situation. I did. In fact, I'd already considered the possibility of closing off certain parts of the city. Segregated areas, where the schizophrenic patients from other neighborhoods could be sent and confined to quarters until we got a chance to treat them or farm them out. Otherwise we might have a mass panic on our hands.

But I was utterly serene about it. If something human needed to be done, we could do it. The gyroscopic harmony that purred inside me from truck to keel was superior to heaven or hell. Or so I believed. Not that I discounted the howlers I'd pulled. The neglect of the traffic system and the rest. They just didn't signify.

Dennis drove me up to Kip's Bay and Pete chuckled as I came in.

'How are your nerves?' he said.

'I was just thinking about them. I don't seem to have any.'

'You won't need them. The Roncador people are as good as new. Or better. So far, anyhow.'

I sat down. 'Praise the Lord.'

He wanted me to see them. As we scrubbed up, I complained that his noxious fluids were turning my nails black.

'Look at mine,' he said. 'We may start a new fashion.'

The clinic seemed to be in its normal cheerful hubbub of men, women, children, and animals. We went straight through to L-6 pavilion.

The Bakers and Cherrills quarreling. Both intramural and intercollegiate. Baker slouched on one of the beds, looking indifferent, but he was getting in a dig every now and again. Mrs. Cherrill was packing. She'd straighten up, flip her hair back, and let go with a broadside. Once she sank poor Cherrill with a remark about his manhood. She said she'd found him deficient in it. Mrs. Baker's steady drawling monotone kept the ball rolling. The Plainfield girl was trying to smooth things over and young Sidney stood on one foot looking bewildered.

They said hello but they weren't interested. We stayed only a minute or two. No doubt about it. They were back in their right minds.

'The beginning of the end for Prairie Dogs, Incorporated,' Pete said.

The charter members were leaving before dinner. Pete wanted to keep them for observation, of course, but they had other ideas.

'What about the Kelsey girl?'

'A little better, Hutch says. He thinks he may pull her back in time. The other news is that we should have something fairly definite on the vaccine tomorrow.

'We've had pretty encouraging results with the ferrets and we're trying it on some of the uninfected patients. Preventive, you understand. But I'm afraid it won't be of much immediate use to you. We won't be able to produce it in bulk for a long time. However, we have found out that the nasopharynx is probably the only portal of entry.'

'Then why wouldn't face masks do some good?'

He looked at me. 'For everybody? They might. A little. Probably not much. Good dramatic propaganda, though.'

I nodded. 'We can try it.'

He gave me some samples of a four-tape mask and suggested an even finer high-count filler. If we could get it.

As I was leaving he said: 'By the way, did you hear they had a baking-soda party at the Stork Club last night? All over town to-day. One of the doctors here was asked to a soda cocktail party this afternoon.'

I spent a half-hour with Rich Jones at headquarters while we rounded up some people to take action on the masks. We met later in the Department of Purchase office: Jones, Wirth, Onder-donck, Cincione, Brownell, and Young, the Comptroller.

Onderdonck said masks had been used since the Middle Ages. Pink masks in the London influenza epidemic of 1919. Never very successful. But he agreed they might be of some help, mainly in limiting the spread of the virus from already infected people. We'd ask everybody to wear one. Give them away.

Dick Wirth nodded. I remembered afterwards that he hardly said a word. Jones thought we might be able to put the Garment Center to work. They could convert stocks of bandages and women's sanitary pads. Brownell and Young would try to iron out the legal aspects.

We ticked off a few names and Cincione offered us his assistant, Danny Sabin, to run the show. Purchasing experience. He could get the figures lined up and keep an eye on specifications. We called him in and put the baby in his lap.

4 I PICKED Bill up and we went out Henry Hudson Parkway to Spuyten Duyvil. Paravecchio was waiting in a battered cockpit launch. One of the old ones. Low freeboard and a sheer like a little sloop. He had an old hat, pants, jumper, and an extra line for me. I didn't want to be recognized if I got caught breaking my own quarantine.

Dennis pulled the car into the bushes. I got into the old clothes and climbed aboard. Nick started the engine and Bill handed in the bow pennant with a flourish. He was laughing.

'Don't worry about bail,' he said. 'We'll take care of it.'

'Good luck, Mr. Rowan,' Dennis said.

Nick was up forward at the small wheel. We chugged out into the river, cutting sharply northward across the deep power of the current.

'Tie she's goin' out now. Halfway out,' Nick said.

There was a cloudy satiny glare on the water and when we got into midstream it broke up into ripples like a school of silversides.

In one movement Nick turned and shut off the engine. He said under his breath: 'Police boat comin'. Make like you're fishin'. Upside. This side.'

The bow fell off and I could hear the throb of the Harbor Patrol boat coming upstream. She looked dark in the glare, creaming along with her stem out.

'Fish,' Nick said. 'Don't talk. I can talk to 'em.'

The boat came up swiftly. Black topsides and white upper works. POLICE NEW YORK CITY NO. 12. A man in the pilothouse and two more in the cockpit watched us.

The boat throbbed upstream about twenty yards away and one of the cops funneled his hands and called: 'Keep over in midstream.'

Nick looked up without interest. The Italian closed look. He pointed toward the Jersey shore and yelled: 'Fishin's better close by.'

The harbor cop shook his head and called: 'Keep away from the Jersey shore. Midstream. Keep in the middle of the river.'

Nick gave them a dull nod. I'd been keeping my head down. Just at that moment I felt a pull on my line. I jerked and hauled it in. No bait on the hook, but I'd got a fat five-pound buck shad.

The cops in the cockpit grinned as the boat veered away toward the Bronx and went down the river close inshore. Nick waited until they were out of sight. Then he started the engine and bored steadily upstream, working in toward the Jersey bank about opposite Yonkers.

Down under the loom of the Palisades, two old barge hulks.

One of them had a line of wash hung out. Nick ran close in behind the outer one and made fast. On the foreshore bared by the
tide, a line of upright fifty-foot poles with the linen gill net strung
between them. Four or five men were mending it.

Nick called to them and they came over. Hip boots and sweaters.
He talked rapidly in Italian to one of them. The man answered
and shook his head.

'She's gone,' Nick said to me. The others stood around curiously. 'Said her name was Milly Osterman. He don' know where
she's gone.'

I took a snapshot of Niobe out of my pocket and handed it
around. They looked at it earnestly and shook their heads one after
the other.

'Nope, that ain't the one,' a fat blond man said. He wheezed a
little. 'This one told us her husband was dead. Said she had a kid
to look after.'

A quiet man with sad gray eyes said: 'She begged, didn't she,
Paul? Paul give her five dollars yesterday.'

The fat man shrugged. 'Good worker. She shot the net with us
yesterday and done a two-hour lift. That's hard for a woman.'

The others nodded. One of them said: 'Was it your wife you
were looking for?'

I nodded. The sad man went down the companionway and
came back with a gallon glass jug of beer. He offered it to me. I
cradled it on my elbow and took a good pull. They smiled slowly
and drank in turn after Nick.

'We've got to get back,' I told them, 'but how about buying you
a drink?'

They said okeh, thanks, and I left some money with the sad
man. We went downstream fast. Nick veered in toward Spuyten
Duyvil and we could see the police boat coming upriver again.
They passed us without a glance.

I changed my clothes and made a move to pay Nick but I could
see he'd be hurt. He waved to us as he pulled out for another turn

at the fishing and on the way downtown Bill and Dennis told me how disappointed they were that the cops hadn't tagged me.

5

THE town looked bleary and untended. The midtown streets were choked with people on foot and we tried to straighten out a near-riot in Thirty-Fourth Street, the women almost hysterical in their vast surge of free bargain-hunting.

I got hold of Danny Sabin and we arranged to set up the distribution centers for face masks. At first people looked at them curiously and dropped them in the gutter. Then a few girls wore them as a sort of game and the thing began to catch on.

For a while I helped to hand them out in front of Macy's. A thin black-haired youth nudged me.

'Get this,' he murmured. 'I walk up behind a girl and whisper in her ear: "Just slip your dress off, honey." Watch.'

The first one took two or three more steps before it hit her. She gasped and stared at him, pop-eyed. The next girl told two others she was with and they doubled over, giggling and shrieking. A little brown-eyed girl turned around and smiled at him, nodding gently, but he waved her away. Then along came Nemesis in an Oxford flannel suit. She wheeled and clipped him.

He looked at me and shrugged. 'I'll stick to billiards.'

We put up booths at Fifth Avenue and Fifty-Seventh Street, Grand Central, Borough Hall in Brooklyn, and a dozen other places. The stock of masks ran low in the first two hours and dwindled steadily after that until we began to catch up late in the evening.

About five o'clock I got word from Rich Jones that there were nearly a million people at Coney Island and the Rockaways. Nobody seemed to know what the situation was out there. I took Bill along. As I got out of the car on Surf Avenue with a mask on—it was damned hot but I thought I ought to wear it—a kid said: 'Hey! The Lone Ranger.'

Coney was in full midsummer bloom or a little better. All the concessions open and free. Very little swimming, but the beach was jammed and the love-making was love-making indeed. We hunted up the control station. They were snowed under with petty stuff: lost handbags, lost children, lost cars, lost husbands or wives. We helped to straighten out a little of that and Maurice Satin promised to send twenty volunteers. All he could spare.

I called Eunice when we got back to Manhattan. A note from Ada Booth. She'd bring it along. We arranged to meet her at Keen's Chop House.

We sat down gratefully around a heavy white cloth in the big room upstairs.

'Where's Dennis?' Eunice asked.

'Taking an hour off to visit his wife and children,' Bill said.

I looked at Ada's note. 'Dear Jim: I *really* shouldn't do this. But if you'll go to the novel class at New York University tonight I *think* you'll find out where Niobe is. And don't say I don't love you. Ada. P.S. For heaven's sake get rid of this.'

I showed them the note. Bill tapped Eunice on the shoulder and whispered: 'If you will crawl down the manhole at the corner of Fifth Avenue and Twenty-Third Street at eight o'clock tonight you will find something to your advantage.'

'What?' Eunice said.

Bill shook his head and put his finger to his lips.

I went down to the bar looking for a telephone. Ada didn't answer. I got Ray Forster in the office of the Assistant to the Dean at Washington Square.

'Ray, this is Jim Rowan.'

'Ah, my brilliant former colleague and esteemed friend, Mr. Rowan. I trust you are in good health, James. What can I do for you?'

I told him about Niobe and the tip.

'My God, Jim, that's too bad. Let's see. That would be Gilbert Paulsen's class. Just a minute.' I waited. 'Yes. Room 211. Twenty Washington Square North. I'll leave word at the office downstairs. You can pick up a guest card there. Good luck.'

I promised to call him for dinner.

Eunice and Bill and I had a bottle of Schoonmaker's Lake Erie Island Catawba with the Early American maenads on the label. Grilled shrimp on toast. Fresh leaves of lemon balm and borage churned into a green salad. A big slightly charred porterhouse and shoestring potatoes and little carrots and mushrooms broiled in butter. Water crackers and a slice of rather sharp Wisconsin cheese.

Eunice twisted the knee of my trousers under the table.

'What are you doing tonight, darling?' Bill said.

'Nothing,' Eunice said. 'Just nothing at all. And I'm going to keep on doing it. I'm pooped.'

'Me too,' Bill said.

'Why don't you go up and lie around my place?' I said. 'I'll probably be back in a couple of hours. Play some records. But for God's sake be careful. Some of those old Louises are priceless.'

'Louis Quinze or Quatorze?' Bill asked.

Eunice and I looked at each other.

'Pit in mamma's hand, Bill,' she said.

We sat around talking drowsily until Dennis came. I gave Bill my key.

On the way downtown Dennis stopped for a rush of traffic out of a side street. A wedding, alive with serpentines, fishhorns, and old shoes. I read the legend in white paint on the crosswalk: THE WORLD IS YOURS FOR THE ASKING. ASK FOR IT.

Revolutionary indeed. Well, happiness—whatever that was— would be revolutionary for most people. Right now it looked a bit messy, like most revolutions. But in twenty years, fifty, a thousand —why not?

If the German disease of idealism could be bred out of us. If we had to pay a forfeit—our lives, say—every time we proposed a social

235

end without working out the means, or vice versa. People could at least find out what the things they wanted were worth to them. Though you couldn't touch the serious wants in ten days or a hundred. Most of the good wants meant that you had to become what you wanted.

Dennis dropped me at Eighth Street and promised to call back at 9:45.

6

I WALKED around the corner to Washington Square North. Somewhere behind the rim of budding pin oaks and yellow locusts a loud oomphing band in the park played an old Tetrazzini aria. The street lights faded and brightened and there were throngs of people strolling along the north walk.

No. 20. A generous brick-and-limestone dwelling with a fanlight. One of the old shipmasters' houses. A family was a regiment in those days. I went down into the soft light under the graceful outside stairway and found the office. A blond girl said: 'Here you are, Mr. Rowan,' very pleasantly and handed me the guest card and a catalogue. I looked up Paulsen on the way upstairs. He'd written four novels I never heard of.

Room 211. I was a little late. A long narrow room with a blackboard down one wall and an upright piano, padlocked, at the far end. About fifteen people seated around a golden-oak table in sections. Must have been eighteen or twenty feet long. The instructor at the head.

Paulsen. He looked tall and alert. Gray chalk-striped suit and regimental tie. Thirty-five or -six. Brown hair cut short on a rather narrow head. As he talked, the mask drew in and out over his sharp nose and the gray-blue eyes widened and contracted.

About half the other people wearing masks. Two or three of them turned their heads and looked at me as I came in, but without seeing me. The room felt keyed up and intent. I laid the slip down beside Paulsen, who glanced at it, said: 'Thank you,' and went on talking. I sat down near the foot of the table.

I didn't look at the faces but I could feel she was there. A window open behind the instructor. The band in the park was playing the *Light Cavalry Overture* now, very loud, and voices came up from the street. Paulsen looked up at the ceiling and shouted the last part of his sentence with a kind of violent deadpan humor.

He got up, shut the window, and said quietly: 'I'll bring my own band next week. I know a better one than that.'

Then he went on with what he was saying. I began to look the people over. Their heads were all turned toward him. Two men, one thickset and dark. A woman sitting three chairs up from me on the other side, wearing a mask. My heart flopped over when I saw her.

Niobe, in a dreadful hat with lilies-of-the-valley and a veil. Very little make-up. She was wearing noseglasses. She kept taking them off and putting them back on. Her dress had idiotic fluffy touches at the collar. She looked healthy, a scrubbed color in her cheeks. The dark-red hair brushed unbecomingly back.

I was damned mad all of a sudden. It startled me. I wanted to get up and shout: 'Stop that, for Christ's sake, and come home!'

I didn't, of course, but I must have made some small movement. The black-haired girl just behind her turned slowly and studied me with her level cool gray eyes. I stared right back. I was in no mood to be studied.

Niobe took her glasses off and put her hand halfway up, diffidently.

Paulsen broke off, said: 'Yes,' and nodded to her.

'Oh, I—I didn't mean to interrupt you,' she said.

'That's all right,' Paulsen said gently. 'I hope you *will* interrupt me whenever you like. You might not remember the point later on.'

'Well, as a matter of fact, I wasn't sure whether I should ask a—

237

a question at all,' Niobe said. She looked around. 'I—I haven't registered yet and I didn't know——'

'That's all right,' Paulsen said quickly and lightly. 'Neither have I. What——'

'Well, it's about a novel that I—well, I haven't done anything much with it yet. But I wanted to get a crowd of people—about eight or ten people—and put them through some crisis. I thought the hurricane a few years ago up in Connecticut. That would be good. That kind of thing.'

The other people were watching her now.

She said in a quieter tone: 'I was up there. Up near New London, visiting with friends. We—we got out just in time. We drove south that morning. We'd been meaning to go on to Narragansett. If we'd driven north I don't know——'

She sounded vague and earnest and modestly self-possessed.

'Well, I've thought about that and made some notes, but then what's happened in the last few days—the epidemic, I mean—seems much better. I feel it would give me a much better opportunity to—to realize what a crisis like that means. To—to put the characters, the people, here now, with the busses and subways and people doing everything imaginable.'

She paused and looked around. Two or three of the others smiled.

Paulsen waited to see if she wanted to say anything more. Then he said: 'Well,' slowly. 'I guess people in this town always do do everything imaginable. But we're certainly doing it more so now. And it shows more.

'The point is, if you feel it hard, if it keeps unraveling in your head, then it may be the thing for you. People think a writer has free choice of all the subjects in the world—"if he's man enough," as somebody said. To a certain extent that's true. At least we like to think so. A professional should be able to do a capable job on almost anything.

'Actually, though, for our best work, the work most in character for us, we are somewhat limited by what—well, obviously, by what

238

we are, what we know, what we feel, what we think. I mean the store of direct experience we've got. The experience that's available to our imagination. Maybe it's even narrower than that. Call it the part of our experience we're ready to use at any particular moment.

'But about the fever. I can't advise you, Mrs.—Barnes, until I get a look at your material. But offhand, I'm afraid I'd say no. Too tough for a beginner. Probably too tough for anybody. It's a hell of an opportunity, of course. *Walking* with opportunity. But it brings you right bang up against that problem of *making reality*, making the thing stand by itself and be its own master, and the reader's master too.

'You make that twice as tough by choosing a subject that takes off, leaves the ground of what we *still* think of as quote reality close quote. You see'—he looked down at the table—'for the novelist, what we call *reality* is simply the broadest circle of reference common to his work and the reader. A kind of *a priori* agreement that life is like that, or could be. He'll grant you even a hurricane.

'But with this damn Mardi Gras, this fever, you've got another kind of hurricane. A hurricane in which the houses stand but the people blow away. That's bad, for our purposes, because human character is our talisman. The part of reality we use to make all the other parts come alive.

'So you'd have to ask your reader to accept a *double* convention, as in fantasy. But this is tougher than fantasy. Here he's got to believe that *both* your realities are real at the same time. First, the way the city and the people acted *before* this fever came along and, second, the new human logic *after* the fever got them.'

A middle-aged woman shook her head at him and he looked at her inquiringly. 'I don't understand that,' she said.

'Well, this isn't just a crisis, as a hurricane would be,' he said. 'Just a temporary disturbance of the normal order—though of course it *will* be temporary. This thing has been going on long enough now to give people a chance to *adapt* themselves to it. It's become a new *norm* for us, a new way of life. At the same time the old norm still operates to some extent, especially as a field of reference. That makes a pull between them, a tension. And there you have the principle of social change.'

'Then you think I'd better not——' Niobe said timidly.

He shook his head. 'I don't say it can't be done, or that you can't do it. Maybe you can. I can't judge that until I see your material. The point I'm trying to make is that it would be a damned hard job.'

They talked about it. The black-haired girl asked whether he usually advised against a subject simply because it was difficult. She had a nice low voice but I thought it sounded a little challenging.

He smiled in his mask. 'Hell no,' he said gently. 'But I try to make the punishment fit the crime—and the criminal.'

So that was the way they went on, I thought. Politicians, bacteriologists, firemen, actresses, shad fishermen, novelists. Everybody had his special pot-holder for grabbing the hot handle of reality. I was getting educated.

When the class broke up I got up first to block Niobe, sure I had her now. She hadn't even looked at me but I knew she knew I was there. Five or six people crowded around the instructor, talking. She moved around the other side to the door and tried to brush past me.

I took her arm. 'Hello,' I said softly.

'Hello, you,' she said, so quietly I couldn't be sure I'd heard her.

The next moment she snapped her arm away. Her face got red and her eyes popped like the eyes of a middle-class woman being accosted.

'What are you—— I don't know who you——'

I grinned. 'You know who I am all right, Mrs.——'

She cracked me hard across the face and yelled: 'Mr. Paulsen, this man is—— Won't any of you——'

The thickset man took his glasses off and pushed me hard in the chest. Tough people, novelists. I went back against the table. A woman shrieked gently with her hand to her mouth, Paulsen snaked through the people around him and had me by the arm, and Niobe was out the door and away. I could hear her heels in the corridor.

Paulsen drawled: 'It's all right.' He looked around and laughed and people quieted down.

'What *is* this?' he said to me.

'My wife,' I said and showed him the picture of us together.

'She spoke to him,' the black-haired girl said. I looked at her. Miss Big Ears.

'In the doghouse?' Paulsen said.

'No. A gag. She has the fever. I'm afraid she'll——'

He picked up his coat. 'Come on.'

We tumbled down the stairs and into a cab. I asked the driver where the other cab had gone.

'Around into Fifth.'

'Follow it.'

I suddenly realized that the black-haired girl was between us.

'Why, Miss Brandon,' Paulsen said ironically. 'You here?'

'I'm interested,' she said casually.

We pulled hard into Fifth. The other cab's lights were four blocks ahead. I saw Dennis at the corner of Eighth Street, looking startled, and yelled to him to follow.

The girl looked around at the car and then at me.

'Who are you?'

'Shhh,' I said.

We were full out, but Dennis in the big car came up smoothly to a couple of lengths behind and hung there. Three of us now, scattered for nine or ten blocks with a stray car in between.

A new Buick piled out of Eighteenth Street dead ahead. The wrong way. Our driver rode with it as far as he could and stamped on the brake. The Buick clipped our right front wheel, rebounded, and kept going.

I'd had my feet up on the jump seat. We landed on the floor with Miss Brandon, who smelled faintly of Yardley violet.

We helped her up.

'All right?' I said.

241

'I believe so,' she said in her cool voice. 'But you might feel me over to make sure.'

'My God, Paulsen,' I said. 'What do you teach these people?'

'Sinister, aren't they?'

Niobe's cab was out of sight. Dennis had pulled in behind us. He came over. Our driver had a bloody mouth and was trying a tooth thoughtfully. He got out and looked at the cab. Not much. A fender bashed in and the right front wheel out of line.

'We'd better get you an antiseptic for that,' Paulsen said.

We drove slowly down to the Longchamps on lower Fifth Avenue and found a table in the middle of that crowded red splendor.

The cab driver, who said his name was Brownie, ordered an old-fashioned.

'Mind telling me who that was we were chasin'?'

I said: 'My wife.'

He looked up and down. 'Congratulations,' he said.

He began to develop a theory he had, a theory that the grunts were coming out of their holes. He didn't explain who they were but we gathered that they must be a little out of order. He was apocalyptic about it, in a resigned way. His theory was that they were overrunning the earth. He cited lurid cases from his own experience. Dennis was laughing.

Brownie left to take his cab back to the garage. Paulsen was curious and I told him about Niobe's recent acting career without saying very much about myself. Just that I was the pro tem City Planning Commissioner. Miss Brandon listened with her chin in her hand.

Paulsen grinned. 'A wonderful woman. I didn't catch on. Not for a minute. But I still think it would be damned hard to do in fiction.'

The waiter murmured that they were calling for a Mr. Rowan on the car radio outside. Was I—— We finished the drinks and went out. Four or five people standing around the car.

'This is Rowan. Come in.'

Roach's voice. 'Mrs. Wirth wants you to go up there, Jim. 681

West End. You know. Dick is in bad shape, she says. The ambulance is on the way now.'

Paulsen said good night but when I got in Miss Brandon was right behind me. I could see him laughing as we started uptown.

'Look, Miss Brandon. What's your first name?'

'Deborah.'

'Well, look, Deborah.'

'That's a police trick,' she said. 'Calling people by their first names that way. It's supposed to mix you up and make you feel inferior. I didn't believe that story in the restaurant. You're probably the Police Commissioner.'

We were making time up Fifth Avenue and Dennis had the siren going.

'Okeh. I'm the Police Commissioner. I'm Haroun-al-Raschid. Now take that damn mask down and listen.'

She took it off and put it in her pocket. She was good-looking. Very good-looking. She looked gentle.

'All right,' I said. 'Dick Wirth is the Commissioner of Health. I—well, he's a friend of mine and I'm worried about him. I'm afraid he's damn sick. Not to mention the hole it puts us in. I've got to see that he's taken care of at the hospital and try to look out for his wife. So be decent. Where can I drop you?'

She thought. 'I'll wait for you.'

'That's silly. What if I meet you afterwards?'

'You wouldn't. You'd be too upset.'

'That's probably true. Where does that get us? Some other time?'

'No. Tonight.'

I laughed. 'Are you the cobra type? You don't look like the cobra type.'

'I'm interested in you,' she said simply. She might have said she was interested in horses.

'For your—book work?'

'No.'

'Thank you,' I said gallantly. 'I'm interested in you. Have you—any plans?'

'I'll follow you in a cab and pick you up when you're free.'

I looked at her. She meant it. That was what she did. Dennis was mildly scandalized at the hackie tailing us but I forgot about it for the next couple of hours.

They were taking Dick out of the elevator as we got there. He didn't look at me. He was barely conscious and his face was twisted up. Emma fussed around him and when she saw me she shook her head and her lower lip tightened. Her sister was there. I talked to Dick's doctor but all he'd say was that they might be able to do something even yet.

The doctor rode up with him in the ambulance and I took Emma and her sister with me. We drove into the little circle of the emergency entrance behind the pillbox at Presbyterian Hospital. They wheeled Dick in and lifted him onto a pallet in one of the canvas-screened cubicles of the receiving room.

In two or three minutes there was a heart man, the night head nurse, orderlies, interns, and nurses. The room had been half dark and empty as we came in. A nurse went around turning on the lights and another nurse led Emma and her sister to chairs on the other side of the room.

The doctors worked swiftly. I could see their hands moving in the light over the pallet. Dick groaned once. The head nurse passed me as she went into the cubicle. I noticed the white wings on her gray hair and the small gold pin at the V of her uniform. A gold cross on a red background. In the middle of the cross a red field and the initials *P. H.* in gold.

She came out in a minute and said: 'Mr. Rowan? Dr. Emmons would like to speak to you.'

He came out in the white coat, taking the lobes of the stethoscope out of his ears.

He nodded to me. 'He may come round for a minute or two but he won't last. We'd better ask Mrs. Wirth to come in.' He shook his head. 'Too bad. Right in the middle of it.'

I took Emma's hand and led her in. She was clutching me tightly.

Dick opened his eyes for a minute. 'Emma, don't cry,' he said softly, almost impatiently. 'It's nothing.'

He moved his head slightly and looked at me. 'Lick it, Jim,' he said.

As I touched his hand his jaw went up hard and his head went up and he died. Emma could cry now.

I took her home and stayed with her for an hour until the worst of it was over. But the thing I remember is what she said in the car on the way back.

'Now he'll never have the little son he wanted.'

They'd been hoping to the end.

7

DEBORAH was waiting in the car.

'How is he?'

'He's dead,' I said, and asked Dennis to drive south. I called Roach on the radiophone.

'Dick Wirth is dead, Charley. About an hour ago. I was with him at the hospital. He was gone before they got a chance to move him out of the emergency room. Come in.'

Roach said: 'That's tough, Jim. Tough for him and tough for us. If a guy ever died for this town, he did. Want me to notify John Kane? Over.'

I said: 'Yes. He'll want to release the story. Will you tell him I'll phone him? And you might get Dick's assistant. Dr. Barry. Tell him he's got to take over. And Dr. Leeson. Dr. Alexander Leeson at Cornell. Head of the medical advisory group. Ask him to get in touch with Barry. He may be able to help. Anything else?'

Roach said: 'More clowning at South Brother Island. A scramble. The police launch is up there now.'

Niobe couldn't have been in on that.

'The Coast Guard got a speedboat trying to run drugs into Coney Island Creek. Trouble out at Laurelton Parkway. Five motorcycles with sidecars hit the quarantine barrier at the city line. They were through all right but the Boy Scouts started shooting with .22 rifles. The motorcycle guys lost their nerve and went back over the line. I don't want to be around when the Boy Scouts really begin to give with the lead.'

'My God,' I said, 'does Justin know about the rifles? Better ask him to disarm them. But tell him to be careful. They're well-trained and formidable fighters.'

Dennis found a late drugstore and I talked to John Kane. Then I called Kip's Bay.

'Dr. Jenkins, please. But don't disturb him if he's sleeping.'

He wasn't. I told him about Dick Wirth.

He was shocked. 'That's what happens to us. If we *last* until we're fifty.'

'I'm sorry to hear that,' I said, 'because I was going to ask you if you'd consider the Department of Health job. Just a feeler. Nothing official yet.'

He laughed. 'With all this?' But he promised to think about it.

I went back to the car and got Roach again. Dr. Barry was taking over. Young Sabin reported that his people had distributed nearly 600,000 masks. It seemed fantastic that we'd started out to give away almost 8,000,000 of them. But every mask would help.

I said good night to Roach. We were on Sixth Avenue at Fifty-Eighth Street. I told Dennis he'd better go home.

'I'll take you anywhere you like, Mr. Rowan,' he said cheerfully.

'Thanks, Dennis. We'll walk.'

He saluted as he pulled away and I looked at Deborah. 'Now what am I going to do with you?'

'I don't know.'

'Aren't you tired of this? Do you *like* being rushed around by people who don't speak to you for an hour at a time?'

'Yes.'

246

'My God. Do you want a drink? Do you want to go and hear some music? How do you feel?'

I was only half kidding. Really a little puzzled.

'I feel fine. I want you to come home with me.'

'What for?'

'I'm still interested in you.'

'As a curiosity?'

'Yes.'

I laughed. 'Where do you live?'

'In the Village.'

We got a cab at the corner and went down Sixth Avenue in silence.

'Why don't you stop being insincere with me?' she said coolly. 'You're sincere with everyone else.'

'There's a speech,' I said. 'Now look, Deborah—Brandon. I don't dig you, as the boys say. Even your name, if you'll forgive me, gets me down a little. I don't know whether you're infantile, or kidding, or a spook or what. I don't believe your story either. You're probably a reporter from *PM*.'

She shook her head. 'What do you feel about power?'

'Electric power?'

'Personal power. Your job. Running the city.'

'So. I'm the Mayor now. Well, I didn't want the job but I was flattered when they picked me. I like to figure out how to make things work and then try them out. I'm pleased when they do work. To a certain extent, you might say I've been irresponsible. A little too casual, at least. I'm serious but I'm also having fun. A job with plenty of variety is always fun.'

'For your temperament.'

'Yes, for my temperament. When it's finished, I'll go back to my old job. If I'm lucky.'

'Aren't you afraid of having power?'

'Nope. I know just about what I'm worth and it doesn't bother me. Power isn't dangerous except to people who feel inferior.'

'Isn't it?'

'Maybe. I don't know. Sometimes lately I've thought I might be having a little too much fun. But that could be the fever.' I sat up and snorted. 'My God! What solemn idiocy. Power!'

'You despise abstractions, don't you?'

Sherlock Holmes's hardest case.

'I despise abstractions,' I said, 'including you. What do people really call you?'

'My husband used to call me Checker.'

'Why?'

'Because I asked questions.'

I really laughed at that.

'Will I meet him?'

'No. We're divorced.'

'Oh,' I said seriously. 'Was it bad?'

'Yes. Pretty bad.'

'I suppose it would be. I never thought about it.'

'It's like changing your country,' she said. 'About four months ago. I think I'm a little off base even yet.'

That funny self-possession.

'This is it, lady,' the driver said.

I paid him and he took the money.

One of the back streets in the Village. A narrow but well-proportioned brick house, painted black with a lighter trim. Two stories and dormer windows. A stoop, a fanlight, and a wrought-iron handrail twisted like ribbon. One of the pleasant and smart little houses of the 1820's.

She let us in. A good heavy Federal mirror, with its rampant gilt eagle, in the hall. The small white stairway, just faintly curved, led past a stair niche. A Delft bowl with pennywort and blue straw-flowers in it.

The living room was in the front of the house on the second floor. Very nice. Not too large and everything jelled. The walls done in a frosty raspberry tempera. A Chippendale highboy. Big chairs. The fire was laid. She borrowed a match from me and lighted it.

248

'Take your coat off,' she said. 'I'll get you a robe.'

Dark-blue silk. I looked at it.

'Did this belong to——'

She nodded.

I laid it down on another chair. 'I know what's the matter now.'

She stood looking at the fire. 'Yes. Nobody ever refused it before. I think it's what's called a compulsion neurosis. I hang up his coat'—she made the motion—'and bring out his robe. Then I make a drink and lay his pajamas out. It's always the same. If I don't do everything just right it won't be any good. But it isn't any good. I know it's insane but I can't help it.'

'No chance at all?'

She shook her head. 'He has a new wife.'

'Hasn't anybody seen what was——'

She shrugged. 'Why should they? I haven't had anybody as nice as you.'

'Or as tired,' I said. 'Even so, *I'll* make the drinks. Any food in the house?'

She laughed sadly. 'He never ate anything at night.'

'Well, I do.'

'So do I.'

We carved thick slices of duck for sandwiches. Crabmeat stirred up with Durkee's mayonnaise. An orange layer cake.

'Keep talking,' I said lightly. 'I'll go home when I've eaten what you've got. Meantime I promise to listen.'

She touched my hand and smiled. 'No. Don't go home.' She was buttering bread.

'You're interested in me?'

'Isn't that dreadful?' she said, giggling. 'I keep saying that. It's all I can think of.'

'With your face you can say anything. No. I take that back. The face is fine but that's the wrong remark. Oh. And that awful thing you said in the car. About feeling you over. My God, woman.'

She giggled so hard she dropped the knife.

249

'I don't know *why* I said that. It just popped out. I must be getting tough.'

She sat down and laughed with the tears coming between her fingers. A little hysterical.

'Come on,' I said. 'Pour the milk. I'm hungry. How's that?'

I'd made a double-decker out of crabmeat and duck.

'See if you can get your face around it.'

She opened her mouth wide, bit into it, and the mayonnaise ran down her chin. I dabbed it off. She rubbed her cheek against mine.

'Don't do that,' I said, half seriously. 'Maybe I ought to go home now.'

She held my arm and shook her head vigorously, chewing away.

'Um-*huh*,' she said earnestly.

We sat down in front of the fire.

'I don't know. It's a perfect setup for blackmail. You know I've got a wife. You think I'm the Mayor. A mysterious house in the quiet purlieus of the Village. What are purlieus? Very nice inside. Everything first cabin. Men seen going in there late at night. The woman is always well dressed but has no visible means of support. The neighbors say she talked vaguely about a neurosis.'

'Wait a minute,' I said softly, eying her. 'Maybe it *isn't* blackmail. Are the men ever seen coming *out*?'

She looked at me with her eyes bugged and blew a mouthful of sandwich into the fireplace. She was gasping.

She came over and put her arm around my neck. 'You're *insane*. I take back what I said before. You're the most awful man I ever met.'

'Please. Not around the neck. I'm a little nervous.'

She sat down on the footstool and pointed her finger at me.

'But you're wrong. I *have* got visible means of support. Visible on Madison Avenue. I'm a decorator. I'm the silent partner in Haley and Chadbourne. So there.'

I sat working away on the sandwich, considering it.

'Well?' She joggled my knee.

I took a slow pull at the milk. 'All right,' I said. 'Tentatively all right. But my mind isn't settled yet.'

I pretended to study her. Wavy black hair and the delicate hollows in the cheeks. Gray eyes and a good mouth, set rather primly now. She watched me like an expectant child.

'You're about as handsome an ax murderer as I ever saw,' I said.

She whimpered with vexation and joggled my knee. 'I thought you said you were tired. It's after four. Go to bed.'

'I'm tired all right. But I don't know. I'm normally a fellow that likes to go home and mind his own business. But this week, would you believe it, I've been a little male spider. Dozens and dozens of times I just got away before I was eaten. And if you've been having all these boys up——'

She made a face. 'I was exaggerating.'

'Oh, indeed. And tell me. Is there anything special about this bed of yours?'

'Me,' she said, pointing primly.

'Yes, I know. Very nice too. But I mean—any special devices? A little guillotine in the canopy, for example?'

She snatched my half-finished plate of cake. 'Take it back.'

'Okeh. I take it back.'

The phone buzzed. 'Oh, hello,' she said, and in a lower tone: 'No. I'm afraid not. My mother is here.'

I looked at her when she came back. 'He got away?'

'But I've still got you,' she said.

'Nonsense,' I said. 'I'm your mother.'

It was warm in bed in the peach room. Very snug and female. Net skirts and bowknots on the dressing table.

I sighed. 'Who'd have thought it? Old Jim Rowan from Indiana right here in the middle of——'

She joggled me. 'Are you from Indiana?' she said excitedly. 'Where?'

'Over near Merom.'

'I'm from Illinois,' she said. 'From Lawrenceville. Why, that's right across the river.'

SIX

1 WHEN I got home they had a robin in the house. He swerved past my head, twittering, as I came in, and Rachel doubled over and laughed silently and uncontrollably at the way I ducked. The robin lighted on the end of the mantelpiece, very chesty, looking at me with black bright eyes. Then he sang.

'Where did *he* come from?'

Rachel took a minute to get her breath. 'Ain't he sweet, though? He come in last night and Mr. Cornbill shut the window on him and give him something to eat. I was just going to feed him again.'

She put a newspaper down, scattered a few bread crumbs on it, and stood back. The robin watched us. He hopped down in a swirl, picked up a crumb, and was back in watching position before you could even think of saying Jack Robinson.

'Mr. Cornbill is in the guest room,' Rachel said, 'and Miss Flattery's in your bed.'

The robin took another crumb.

'Sleeping at this hour?' I said righteously.

I went in and took Eunice's hand.

'Oh, leave me alone,' she said and opened her eyes.

'Jim!' she said, and sat up.

In the other room, Bill was grumbling to himself. I asked Rachel to see about breakfast in my room and Bill called: 'What has he been doing, Eunice? See if he's got a new perfume.'

Eunice beckoned me. 'Come here. Lemme smell.'

253

She pulled me down, kissed me, then again.

'Yep, he has, Bill,' Eunice called. 'Cheap too. Mais Oui, I think.'

'That reminds me,' Bill called back. 'Wee-wee.'

He fumbled into the bathroom.

Eunice looked at me sullenly. 'Yes, and he's better than you are, too.'

I called to Bill. He stuck his head out the door in a minute and yelled: 'What?'

'Bill, Eunice says you're better than I am. I told her of course you were.'

'My goodness gracious, no,' Bill said in horror. He came in in my pajama pants and flopped on Niobe's bed. 'I'm very poor. I've been thinking of going to a doctor and having him strap some of that hormone stuff on my thigh.'

Eunice looked from me to Bill and said something very tough about our male solidarity.

'Why, Eunice,' Bill said mildly. 'Don't you ever read anything but sidewalks?'

Rachel brought a tray for Eunice and one for Bill. She set up breakfast for me on the bedside table between them. Hot cereal, and ham and eggs, and guava jelly with the toast.

'Umm-mh,' Eunice said. 'Am I hungry.'

'Didn't you find anything last night?'

She shook her head.

Bill said: 'Well, you know. The boss's house.' He added thoughtfully: 'We found the Scotch.'

I told them about Dick, and as I talked I could still see him there with his head up on the low pillow in the odd austerity of death.

Dennis came in and there was another mouth to feed. I looked at Rachel.

'I don't know,' she said in a high soft voice. 'I'll see.'

Dennis got his ham and eggs all right and ate them at the radio. The early-morning weather report. The cold still traveling our way. Nothing drastic happening on the short wave.

He'd brought the Sunday papers, skinny as cats. The Joint Congressional Subcommittee to Investigate Conditions in New York City was on the move. Senator Rowley of Arkansas, chairman, announced that his agents were already at work in New York.

The Governor had called out the National Guard upstate and confirmed the deadline: six P.M. Monday. 'This situation must not be allowed to continue to threaten the health of the rest of the country,' he said. 'My responsibility is plain. Public order must be restored.' The old grandstand play. But things were really closing in.

'Wait a minute,' Bill said softly. 'Take a look at this.'

He handed me the *Herald Tribune* news section. Lester J. Long, city Treasurer, had denounced the emergency setup as inadequate, wasteful, and against the best interests of the city. 'If strong measures had been taken at once,' Long's statement said, 'much of our present difficulty might have been averted. Now we are in a bad way, but strong measures can still be taken. The property and health of the city must be rescued from the irresolute weaklings who now control it.'

Eunice was reading over my shoulder. John Kane had answered him. Mr. Long, he said, is himself a member of the committee he has set out to impugn. He has been present at every meeting. He represents a small minority of venal power seekers in that committee, a minority which has been outvoted on every issue by the public-spirited majority. Many of these, unlike Mr. Long, are elected officials of the city government. He has a right to speak his piece. 'If he has a bill of particulars against his fellow members,' John said, 'he should give it to the people. If he hasn't, he should resign. I promise not to kiss him good-by.'

We smiled at each other but it was sad too. The first open break.

'Here's another good one,' Bill said, and read from the *Times*: 'A committee was formed yesterday, headed by Martin T. Handley, a lawyer with offices at 50 Broad Street, to further the choice of John B. Kane, Acting Mayor, President of the City Council and Chairman of the Committee for the Public, as coalition candidate for Mayor in the city elections in November.' Handley said that Kane's 'prompt and effective action in the present emergency,' etc., etc. John couldn't have been in on that, but of course he must have known about it. The *Times* didn't have much on Handley. Probably an amateur beating the gun.

Eunice and Bill looked at me wryly.

'Good for John,' I said.

Eunice shrugged. 'Now if you gentlemen will get out of here——'

We did. I tried to call Carson at the Weather Bureau and the operator had to route me through a Brooklyn exchange. Something wrong downtown. Carson wasn't there but another man gave me the dope.

Yes, we could expect a cold wave soon all right. Probably snow. Perhaps tomorrow or the next day. Temperature down six degrees to forty-nine in New York. Large falls of snow at Pittsburgh. Down thirty degrees in one day, to fourteen, in Chicago. He said the wind would probably haul round to the northwest when the high came in.

Then I called Pete and prodded him about the Health Department job.

'Well, I talked to the superintendent and the President of the Board of Governors at the hospital,' he said. 'Told them it was tentative, of course. They seemed to feel pretty much as I did. Nobody would get any credit out of it but it had to be done. I told them I felt I could go in now and bow out when the thing was over and you people got a chance to pick somebody else. How's that?'

'Sounds fine.'

'Oh. And I don't like to boast,' Pete said, 'but we've got it.'

'Got——'

'The vaccine.'

'My God!'

'Yep, the ferrets came through. Not to mention the patients. Twenty-one immune reactions out of twenty-four.'

256

I asked him how long it would take to get it in quantity.

'Might be six months for the amounts you'd need.'

'Lovely,' I said. 'But that's nothing against the job you did. Congratulations, Doctor.'

'But we have a new mixture in that ascorbic-acid-plus combination.' He sounded amused. 'Maybe you'd like to hear about that. Nineteen recoveries overnight, out of twenty patients we gave it to. The twentieth is almost normal. That interest you?'

'What's the catch? How soon can we get that in quantities?'

'As soon as the chemists can make it up.'

'How soon is that?'

'Oh, a day or so, I imagine. It's fairly simple.'

I whooped. 'Mister, we're in. You're a wiz, Pete. We'll put up statues of you in all the parks. You'll be as famous as—as Orestes A. Brownson. I'll call you back.'

I spread the news to Bill in the bathroom and Eunice, who was dressing. She came to the door in her slip.

'I don't know that I'm so happy about it,' she said, and turned away without saying anything else.

Bill came out with lather on his face. The robin flew around his head with loud cheeps.

'He knows,' Bill said.

We opened the window.

'Liberty,' Bill said to the robin. 'Liberty and justice for all.'

The robin hopped up on the sill, looked round at us with his bright eyes, and spun away.

2

I LOANED Bill a coat and took my light one. We made a great play of wrapping Eunice up in the car and snuggling her close between us until we could get over to her place for a warm coat. But she held our hands under the robe. A girl never knew, she said. Actually it wasn't much colder than the day before. We were just whistling for weather.

I went up to the office with them and asked Eunice to order a flower piece for Dick. Then I walked over to City Hall. The wind seemed to have died down a little. The commissioners' meeting was early, eleven o'clock, in the Board of Estimate room.

One of our little curses is that we don't think of a city hall as a place where anything good can happen, and God knows some pretty bad things had happened in this one. Some pretty good ones, too.

But it was a place all right. As soon as you got inside, that wonderful delicate unexpected staircase slapped you in the eye. And upstairs, in the Board of Estimate room, the white pickets framed off the long mahogany curve of the board table like a stage.

A half dome above, decorated with a course of laurel leaves and a fretted cornice. Nice clean Ionic columns and a crystal chandelier with globes on it and a lacy white cornice dome over the main window behind the chairman's seat. A gathered valance, brocade, and the modest gilt eagle topping it. A little thronish, maybe, but easy and clean and comfortable and urbanely balanced. Damned good, in fact.

The voices echoed a little as I came in. The boys were lined up behind the big table and down below at the clerks' tables. I thought I saw Lester Long in a mask. Most of the boys were wearing them. John Kane had saved a seat for me.

A stranger in a mask on the other side of him. He motioned us together. 'Jim, this is Mr. George Hartsell, an investigator from the Congressional subcommittee. Commissioner Rowan.'

We shook hands, looking each other over. A thickset silent man in a brown suit. The transcript was open to him, of course, but he took notes all through the meeting. Didn't trust us, probably.

I started things off and before I got my mouth shut Lester Long was on his feet.

'Mr. Chairman. I want to protest the public conduct of a member of this committee.'

258

John looked down at the table.

'You're out of order, Lester, but go ahead,' I said.

Long said in his sharp driving voice: 'This morning the newspapers carried a report that a downtown lawyer was starting out to nominate John Kane for Mayor. Would he do that on his own hook? Without authorization? I don't believe it. This was a put-up job by the temporary Mayor of this city, who is trying to make political capital out of the emergency—an emergency that threatens the health and the lives of his fellow citizens. Can you answer that?' he shouted up to John.

John got up slowly. 'That wasn't the *only* thing in the papers this morning, Lester,' he said mildly, and people laughed. 'For that matter, I guess I agree with you. Up to a point. I want to read you the carbon of a letter I wrote three days ago. It's addressed to Mr. Martin T. Handley.'

He took a flimsy out of his pocket and read it: 'Dear Martin: As you know, I am grateful for your support and always will be, but I do *not* feel'—he emphasized the *not*—'that this is the time for a political announcement. We have a job on our hands that must be licked first. Besides, I haven't made up my mind yet. When I do, you'll be the first to know it. Cordially,' etc.

They laughed and cheered and clapped ironically, looking at Lester.

'It *could* be a stall,' John said ruefully. 'You'll have to take my word for it that it wasn't. I tried to stop him but he was sure this was the right time. I'm a damn fool all right, but I'm not *that* much of a damn fool.'

They clapped him as he sat down. Somebody called: 'Later, John! Later!' and they clapped a little harder that time. John shrugged.

Long had to have the last word. 'I've got just one thing more to say. John Kane has called on me publicly to resign. My answer to that is: I'll resign when he does and not before.'

They cheered him raucously and we got down to business. Dr. Barry had sent over a report from the Health Department. The estimate of cases in New York up nearly 400,000, to 1,960,000. Slackening off a little, at least. Despite the quarantine, a few cases were spilling over into the Long Island and Westchester towns. The U. S. Public Health Service announced that all Chicago cases had recovered in the cold weather over the Lakes country.

Justin said quarantine-running was getting to be a kind of sport in the outskirts of the city. Mostly young bloods determined to get in or out of town to see their girls. Some of them used bicycles or hid in food trucks. Others put hoods over their heads and crawled through the trees at night.

Then he said: 'I have a report on the South Brother incident last night from the officer in charge of the harbor squad boat.'

Arnie got up and shouted: 'Wait a minute. Before you try to pin anything on me, I was at a midnight movie with my wife. Want to hear about the picture?'

The others laughed and Arnie grinned and flopped his hand as he sat down.

Justin read the report. A crowd of Queens men had beached a ferry on South Brother about ten o'clock and taken possession of the island. The ferry was the one George Romanelli hadn't been able to find. The harbor-squad boys rounded them up, put them ashore in Astoria, and brought the ferry back to the dock in the Bronx. They dismantled the engines so that it couldn't be used.

Justin said he had a fairly complete list of names for the people who had taken part in both expeditions. I looked at him but he shook his head. Niobe wasn't among them. At least not under her right name.

Regan hadn't said a word.

Harold Brownell, the Corporation Counsel, was wigwagging earnestly. 'I've got a confession,' he said. 'You know we were asked for a ruling on South Brother Island. In all this fuss, nobody got round to it till yesterday. We don't know yet which borough, if any, is entitled to claim it. But we do know this: it belongs to the estate of Jake Ruppert.' He looked at Regan and Genovese. 'If you boys want to buy it, you'd better see the heirs.'

The whole crowd roared at that.

Justin held up a paper. An application for a parade permit, from the Society for the Preservation of Happiness.

'Here's the rest of it,' he said and rolled a heavy cylinder of paper down to me. Names. About 15,000 of them, signed to the petition. I noticed three or four bandleaders' names: Duke Ellington, Benny Goodman, Louis Armstrong, Henry Seaborn, Muggsy Spanier, Bob Crosby. Might get something out of Henry.

Justin said soberly that a thing like that could turn into the wildest riot the city had ever known. Just not enough cops free to control it.

'What about the volunteers?' Satin called.

Justin shook his head. 'We couldn't trust them with this. One wrong move and it might blow the town sky-high. Ever hear about the Seventh Regiment and the Orangemen's parade?'

I said it sounded to me as if we'd have to issue the permit. Worse if we didn't. They could always raise the civil-liberties issue too.

'Who's running the show?' Young asked.

Nobody knew. Some of the names were fake and the real ones weren't talking. The list was headed by a woman no one had ever heard of—Bessie T. Peyton.

We decided to replace most of the cops in the quarantine lines with volunteers and pull as many as we could spare out of the control stations. Jones said most of them were on the 'two-platoon— or one-platoon system' now.

I talked about the weather, a very lively subject. The Weather Bureau was holding out some strong hopes.

Then I said: 'I suppose you all know what happened to Dick Wirth' and told them how he died. We voted the fine words you vote for a dead colleague, who can't hear them.

'John has a list of honorary pallbearers here,' I said, and read the names. 'You'd better see him about arrangements after the meeting. The funeral is at Temple Emanu-El, ten-thirty A.M. Monday.'

John and I buzzed each other a minute about the new commissioner. We were pretty well agreed that Barry didn't have enough of a reputation and that we'd have to get somebody whose record was more impressive. Leeson had turned the idea down.

John got up and outlined the situation. 'Maybe I'm crazy,' he said, 'but I'll waive the appointive power—it's doubtful anyhow in this situation—and put in the man you elect. After we've investigated a little, of course. And if we can get him.'

'Do you want that to go in the record, John?' Onderdonck called.

'Why not?'

We had a list of names and pedigrees the medical advisory group had made up for us. We talked them over and got three or four nominations.

'Any more?'

No more.

'Okeh. I'm probably out of order now,' I said. 'But there's a man named Dr. Seneca B. Jenkins. Director of the Cass-Jordan virus clinic at Kip's Bay Medical Center. He's been doing a large-scale study of the fever. I've spent an hour a day up there since we organized on it and I feel that he probably knows as much about it as anybody except Dick did. That's a layman's opinion and it may not be worth a damn. But I think he's the man for the job. I've sounded him and he's willing to help us out until the emergency is over and we can get somebody else. I wish somebody'd nominate him for me.'

Mason Emery did and Romanelli seconded.

'Did you say this was irregular?' Lester Long said. 'It's damned irregular. What right has John Kane got to delegate his appointive power to us? What gives us the right to circumvent the charter?'

'I think we can justify that,' Brownell said mildly. 'The——'

Long kept right on talking. 'Now Rowan wants us to elect some friend of his we don't know anything about.'

I said: 'Well, it is a little irregular, and it's true Pete Jenkins isn't very well known. Modesty is a sort of occupational disease

262

with doctors. It's true he is a friend of mine. That's no fault of his. He just got into bad company.'

They smiled.

'There's one point I haven't mentioned. It ought to go into the record before we vote. I think Pete's entitled to this job. He doesn't want it, but he'll take it, and I think we should give it to him, because he's the man who found out how to stop the fever.'

They were all yelling at once. I waited laughing until they calmed down.

'Give me a chance. He's got two things. One is a vaccine. A preventive. Used as a nasal spray. We'd need about six months to get enough of it but it does mean we probably won't have to go through this again.

'The other is a fairly simple mixture of chemicals and stuff. We can get all we need in a day or two. Just a pill you take with a glass of water. That one does cure the fever.'

They cheered.

'Wait a minute,' Justin said. 'Are you sure, Jim?'

'I wouldn't say sure. Call it a ten-to-one shot. I've been watching the experiments as they went along. Jenkins isn't the kind of man who'd tell you he's got something if he hasn't. I haven't seen the people he cured. But he's holding them for observation. I guess you could go up and have a look.'

Somebody yelled: 'Vote! Vote!' and Pete was elected almost unanimously. John promised to look into it and make the appointment right away if everything was clear. We elected Mason Emery to take charge of procuring and distributing the stuff.

'What about the Governor?' Maurice Satin called. 'How are we going to hold him off?'

'We can't,' Al Elias said. 'He can't back down on that deadline now.'

'I'll get him on the phone,' John said. 'If I can't talk him out of it, we'll just have to beat him to the punch.'

'And what about this kibitzer?' Arnie Genovese said, jerking his thumb at the Congressional investigator.

Hartsell cleared his throat. 'You'll hear from me later,' he said solemnly as we broke up.

John squeezed my arm as we were going out. 'Thought you said you weren't a politician, Jim?'

I laughed and shook my head. 'Not smart enough, John.'

'Hoho! After the way you held out that news about the cure and slipped it in where it'd do the most good? Better run for something.'

I laughed. The newspapermen were waiting. They crowded around him.

3

WHEN I got back up to the office Eunice said the florist couldn't promise deliveries. No help.

'We'll pick it up.'

'And—a Miss Brandon called you.'

She looked at me.

'Oh.'

'Uh-huh,' Eunice said. 'Last night,' and slapped my face hard just as Bill came in.

'Gracious,' said Bill.

I grabbed her arm and twisted it behind her, not hard.

'Say uncle.'

'I won't say anything to you—you, you wolf!'

'All right. Say aunt.'

'Mamma!' she hollered, and I let go.

I hadn't hurt her but she was crying. Bill put his arm around her.

'The big stiff,' Bill said. 'Want me to hit him and lose my job?'

Eunice was wiping her eyes. 'We'll smash all his records.'

I sighed. 'I suppose this means I have to buy dinner at the Algonquin or someplace.'

'Oh no,' Bill said. 'You can't get away with that. This little lady's feelings have been hurt. Hurt *bad*. Slip your coat on, dear.' He helped her, very solicitously. 'We'll see what the nice lawyer will say.'

'The Gotham,' I said.

'Oh no,' said Bill. 'Come along, dear.'

'The Plaza.'

'Did you hear what the man said, honey lamb?'

Eunice sulked, her right foot turning in and out.

'Okeh,' I said. 'The Ritz, Pierre, the Colony. Anything.'

'Now you can talk to him, dear,' Bill said. 'Ask him if he's trooly-ooly sorry.'

We looked at him in horror.

On the way uptown with Dennis I said: 'Where do you want to go?'

'How about Sardi's?' Bill suggested. 'Just in case.'

Eunice said: 'Yep, Sardi's is good.'

That was nice of her. I kissed her cheek.

At Herald Square a red-white-and-blue sound truck lettered SOCIETY FOR THE PRESERVATION OF HAPPINESS was blasting away. A good crowd. I got out and talked to the driver. He shrugged. Said he worked for a trucking firm. He didn't know anything about it. The man inside was just an actor hired to read a script. I got the name of the trucking firm and passed that barren information on to headquarters.

Renee wasn't in the cloakroom at Sardi's. She might have heard something about Niobe. As we sat down I noticed Mallett at the bar and went over to him. He was austerely melancholy. He handed me a card postmarked in the Bronx the day before: 'Don't worry, Chris. I'll be back. Love.' Unsigned, but I knew the backhand scrawl.

'Don't worry, don't worry,' he said distantly, gazing into his Martini.

Eunice and Bill and Dennis and I had dinner together **very** pleasantly.

Bill ate a forkful of roast duck and sighed. 'Life *can* be good in Rowan's Corners,' he said thoughtfully, and waved his hand. 'If only the little inequalities, the little irritations, the little contre-temps—contretempses?—could be smoothed away and——'

'You talk too much,' Eunice said.

'Do I?'

'Now you're doing it *again*,' she said.

Some of the girls had their masks pushed daintily up on their noses while they ate. Various people in show business, people who knew me as Niobe's husband, came over and put their hands on my shoulder and told me how sorry they were.

One of the women didn't seem to be too sorry to twinkle at me and say: 'But you're looking frightfully fit, Jim.'

I was afraid Eunice would kick her in the shins.

4

BILL was on his way down to headquarters and Eunice decided to go with him.

I called Pete Jenkins and told him we'd been deliberating on his case.

'I suspected that,' he said slowly. 'They had a man up here from the Health Department an hour ago. He looked at the patients and went through the records. My record too. Miss Adams called me from downstairs about it. Said he was very nosy about my administrative record. Is that your normal routine?'

I laughed. 'They probably sent a man from the Safe and Loft Squad by mistake.'

'Your friend Emery was here too. Very nice guy. Wanted the ascorbic-acid-plus formula. I loaned him our head biochemist. They're working on the drug houses now—Schering, Squibb, Parke-Davis, Ciba, and the others. He didn't mention the—appointment.'

266

'That reminds me,' I said solemnly. 'Congratulations, Commissioner. They'll probably notify you this afternoon.'

'Oh, God,' he said gently. 'Think it'll be all right, Jim?'

'The best Commissioner of Health New York ever had. Bar none.'

I thought of calling Deborah to find out what she wanted but decided not to.

Dennis drove me to the florist's. They had the spray made up. It looked very nice. The man wouldn't take any money but I insisted. Almost superstitious about paying for what I was getting for Dick. I thought afterwards it might have been a little guilty feeling. If I'd only tried harder to persuade him to take a few days off——

The man shrugged and said: 'A quarter.'

Dick's apartment was crowded. People from downtown, and the hospitals, and the Wirths' friends. Dennis, very big and red and curly blond, stood beside the coffin with me, cap in hand. He crossed himself.

'A good man, sir,' he whispered and nodded.

I saw how sadly worn Dick looked. Nothing but bones and the scant brown hair. For a moment I had the pride of service we all felt at times. The pride in being used, even used up, for the city. Nice happy thought for a politician. But I wasn't one, really.

Someone squeezed my arm. Emma. I murmured something to her.

'Poor Jim,' she whispered and kissed my cheek.

She nodded over her shoulder, looking at me. 'The Mayor's in there.'

'John?'

'No, Oliver. He came in through the quarantine. He said he had to get to Dick's funeral.'

'Good for Ollie. I'll go talk to him.'

I kept saying hello to people. There was a crush in the other room—Hickey, Satin, Porter, Romanelli, and some of the others. Bodine was talking to Onderdonck in a corner.

'Hello, Jim,' he said and shook hands.

I saw that he was uneasy, that he'd come only because he was fond of Dick. Or perhaps he felt a little responsible too. I hinted to him about coming back but he shook his head.

'I'm a railroad man now, Jim,' he said, half as a joke, half sadly. But he was staying in town.

I said good-by to Emma on the way out.

5

As WE started uptown the radio said: 'Car 1. Car 1.'

'Yes. Over, please.'

'Commissioner Emery wants to talk to you, Mr. Rowan.'

Em said: 'Just a progress report, Jim. Jenkins loaned us his biochemist. Chase. He's a shark. We've got nearly eight hundred pounds of the drug promised for noon tomorrow. Half of it by tomorrow morning.'

'Very, very good,' I said. 'How much do you need for a dose, Em?'

'Oh, very little, Jenkins says. A few grains. The pharmaceutical houses will put up as much as they can in tablet form. Jenkins is getting up some instructions to the health stations and hospitals.'

'Working for us already?'

'Yes indeed,' Em said. 'John Kane talked to him about half an hour ago. What are you doing?'

I told him.

'Good luck.'

Dennis turned through the park and went up Seventh Avenue. Harlem. All the faces were colored now and people in Sunday clothes were cutting up and laughing on the street. But I knew better. I knew every last statistic. This was our failure. This was the thing that canceled out all the other things we tried to do. This was the place where babies weren't allowed to live.

I kept thinking of plans as we went uptown and turned off in the hundred-and-forties. Dennis stopped in front of a concrete-block apartment house, fairly new. A center court. The fire escapes —they were stairways too—webbed up through the court. I ducked under one of them and rang a bell on the ground floor. Three kids stopped playing and watched me.

I could hear Henry Seaborn's collie pup making a row inside.

Grace opened the door and her eyes rolled up. 'Why, Jim,' she said. 'What're you doing here? Come in.'

'Only for a minute, Grace. Where's Henry?'

'He went down to the Hollywood. They're having a little session over to Charlie Briscom's later. He left his drums over there last night. He wanted me to go but I wasn't feelin' so good.'

'What's the matter?'

'Oh, I don't know. Just tired, I guess. How is Niobe?'

I watched her as she said it. She didn't even flicker. Handsome and gentle and self-possessed. She talked easily and seriously. But we'd known Grace and Henry a long time. Her accomplished and mischievous and intelligent wit. Waiting just under the surface, ready to catch me in whatever my latest folly might be.

'I don't know,' I said. 'She's gone.'

'Gone?' Grace's eyebrows went up slowly. 'You mean she left you?'

I told her about it. The pup, with a jingle of collar metal, put his forepaws up on my knee and licked the back of my hand slowly.

'Now, Stomp!' Grace clapped her hands. 'You get down from there.'

'He's all right,' I said.

Stomp went on licking.

As I talked, Grace's eyes got wider and wider. She began to giggle gently. Then she laughed outright, laughed and laughed. I looked at her and got laughing too.

'If she isn't the *cutest* woman,' Grace said. 'She'll do anything, won't she?'

Still I couldn't tell whether she was kidding me or not.

I got up and sighed. 'That's what I wanted to talk to Henry about. I saw his name on the parade petition. I suppose it's no use asking you. Once you sharp girls get together on something——'

'Why, Jim. You know I wouldn't——' She rolled her eyes at me, just able to keep from laughing.

'Why don't you come over with me and meet Henry? Surprise him. You should see the car I've got,' I said ruefully. 'Maybe you'd respect me more.'

'Just wait till I get a coat.' She called from inside the house: 'I don't feel up to going with you, Jim, but I got to see that car.'

She noticed Dennis and was very sedate. 'Well!' she said softly. 'Is it really yours?'

'The Mayor's car.'

She murmured: 'You better get it back before they find out.' She touched my arm and laughed gently. 'And tell that woman to call me when she comes home. Will you?' She waved.

We drove over to the Hollywood. I'd been there before, though it wasn't a place the Peckerwoods went to. A big Sunday crowd. The walls done in careful cubist angles. Positive orange and blue.

Henry saw me come in. He had a kidding way of laughing silently with his shoulders loose.

'Well, if it ain't the Perfessor,' he said softly, accenting all three syllables.

I smiled. 'Mr. Henry Seaborn.'

'Whatcha say, man?' Henry said, and shook hands. His drummer's hand was like an old suède glove.

He led me over to the bar. 'You know Sidney de Paris, man. And Mr. J. C. Higginbotham. And James P. And Pops.'

I did know everybody except Pops. I grinned and shook hands all round. 'I'd buy a drink but I'm afraid you boys might object.'

'No, go ahead, man,' James P. said, very seriously.

'Daniel,' Henry said to the bartender, nodding in time to the words and speaking with tremendous soft pomp. 'The gentleman mentioned a desire to discuss a drink.'

'Comin' right up,' Daniel said.

We smiled and raised the glasses at each other. I told Henry I'd been over to his place and seen Grace. He wanted me to come to the session.

'Okeh. But I can't stay very long. Drive around with me first, will you? I want to ask you something.'

He glanced at me quickly, nodded, and finished his drink. 'Me and Fess is going along,' he said. 'We'll see you over to the place.'

They nodded. Henry put his fine hand on the car and looked at me. I laughed.

Dennis drove uptown. I told Henry I'd seen his name on the parade list. We wanted to stop it if we could. Afraid we couldn't handle things. People might get hurt. The only way to stop it was to find out who was running it.

'I don't know, Fess,' Henry said soberly. 'They asked me if I wouldn't put the band in the parade. Said Duke was, and Louis, and the rest of the cats. I told 'em yes. That's all.'

'Who asked you?'

'I don't know,' Henry said. 'Somebody from the committee. They called me on the telephone.'

'Man or woman?'

He was troubled. 'I can't tell you, Fess. I promised I wouldn't. I didn't tell Grace.'

I touched his shoulder. 'Okeh, Henry. I know how it is. But I wish she'd come home. What's the society's address? Did you get that?'

'I don't know,' Henry said. 'They just asked us to bring our instruments, be at Washington Square twelve-thirty sharp tomorrow afternoon. Said they'll have a wagon for us.' He put his hand gently on my knee. 'I'm sorry, man.'

'It's all right, Henry. I'm a damn fool to worry about her.'

We were somewhere over east of Coogan's Bluff. Dennis started downtown again. Charlie Briscom's place on the top floor of a house on 140th Street, a block up from Strivers' Row. Good big apartment. Charlie was an arranger for name bands. I suggested to Dennis that he could get himself a couple of drinks and come back in an hour.

A sizable crowd upstairs. I knew some of them—musicians, fans, reporters from *Metronome* and the other papers, people in the trade, and their girls and wives. I got a chair down front.

Chatter going on. The boys in the band were waiting for Wellman Braud, the bass player. They went through the usual interminable business of getting settled, like a dog bedding down. I remembered how I used to be myself. Fiddling with the reed and trying it out. Little runs. Dragging the chair over closer to the trumpet. Ribbing a minute, heads close together. Braud ambled in with his big fiddle under his arm. Through the window behind them I could see the level roofs of Harlem, the maze of chimney pots and aerials below St. Nicholas Park. A dun Sunday.

Two beats, the horns hit solidly together, and they were into *Balling the Jack*. An old one. One of the ones Bunk taught Louis. The deep satisfaction in the pit of your stomach. Something you knew, something that was part of you, happening as it should happen. Growing with the variations. But not quite right yet. The band would take an hour or so to melt together.

Three numbers and a pause. People talked a little. The band was resting, just idling. That was part of it—knowing how to let go in between. Henry began his slow beat, waiting for it to take hold.

He nodded across to Jimmy Johnson at the piano and said softly: 'We will now discuss the blues.'

The piano began sadly. Just piano and drums. Henry looked at me and said: 'The Perfessor will sing 'em.'

I shook my head. Unless you were doing it every night, singing blues was like giving testimony at camp meeting. Only for the pure in heart, the saved, telling about the rain and the darkness. The righteous blues.

'Come on, Perfessor,' James P. said from the piano.

I nodded. A thousand verses and a thousand more to come. You could hardly tell whether you remembered them or made them up.

272

I been walkin in the water an I got my feet all wet
Yes walkin in the water I got my feet all wet
Won't you come back honey an see what you will get?

Most of the boys were from New Orleans. Always talking about their food. I'd eaten it with them.

Got some jambalaya got some gumbo with a bay leaf
Got some fat pink shrimps got some hot rice cakes got some
  bouilli beef
You want to come back home honey you know I just as lief

People laughed and some of the women shrieked a little as I mentioned each dish. I sang two more verses and stepped down and the band went into the last chorus, crowding together and intermingling in a wonderful tight stretto that unwound itself in the final bar.

6

DENNIS picked me up and I talked to Rich Jones on the way downtown. He said Em was doing very well. He'd already got hold of enough of the stuff to treat eight or ten thousand people.

'We had a burst water main up in Washington Heights,' Rich said. 'They hunted all over the place for Freddie Schepper. Know about him?'

I said no.

'He's a fellow works for the water department over in Brooklyn. Plugs the pipe with a whittled broomstick. A marvel at it. The hole isn't very big, usually. Most of the time just the tap blows. The connection. We found him in a bar in Brooklyn. He did the job all right. Don't have to use hydrophones with Schepper around.'

He said Reger had tracked down dozens of the parade permit names. Nothing. Most of them phonies. The others said they didn't know anything about it. Same answer from the sound-truck people. A woman named Peyton hired them. Paid in advance.

I picked Bill and Eunice up at the Commodore bar and we drove uptown to the Croydon for dinner. Big, quiet place on East Eighty-Sixth Street with cool gray-blue murals. We had a Boston-style shore dinner with steamed clams, a fine lobster chowder, and huckleberry slump.

We talked over plans for catching Niobe, in case she turned out to be the evangelist at the Garden.

'Why don't you let the poor girl alone?' Eunice said.

I grinned at her.

'No, I mean it. You'd think she was a criminal or something. She's having fun, isn't she? She's coming on, that's all—just like you.'

Bill said: 'Goodness!'

'Oh, it's not that. I like Niobe,' Eunice said. 'I always have, but now I'm—— With women it's——'

'Oh, well,' Bill said.

As we were leaving, someone touched my arm. A fat little dark man in a blue-serge suit, cranberry tie, and shaved light-gray astrakhan tarboosh. I'd noticed him looking at us.

He apologized and said he'd seen me eating hookleberry sloomp. Would I explain what it was, pliss? He'd asked the waiter but the waiter didn't seem to know. The four of us had a long and involved colloquy about what huckleberry slump was, what it tasted like, what it was made of and where it came from. None of us knew, really.

Absent-mindedly he got into the car with us. He had a genteel smell of musk. What could he be? Even the Turks didn't wear tarbooshes any more. Egyptian?

We listened to the dispatcher relaying an ambulance call to the Chelsea station. Then he said: 'Car 1. Car 1.'

'Yes? Over.'

'Commissioner Rowan, Commissioner McKeogh requests that

you meet him here as soon as you can. He will be waiting in his office.'

'I'll be right down.'

The little man had been listening. He asked Bill where we were going. Downtown, Bill said. He whispered that I was a looney, that I liked to talk to the short-wave radio, which wasn't equipped for outgoing calls.

'But very wealthy,' Eunice whispered.

The little man listened with his brows up. His eyes were gleaming. 'I like to come,' he said. 'Exciting. I have an appointment with a laydee. She will wait.'

Dennis pulled up at Police Headquarters and I went in. They told me afterwards that he saw me go in and watched the cops going in and out.

'Is he in throuble?' the little man asked gently.

Bill shook his head. 'He thinks he knows the Commissioner. Always giving him advice. The Commissioner humors him.'

Justin told me as gently as he could that they had a woman at the Bellevue morgue who might be Niobe. 'The resemblance is close, but not close enough for me. I wish you'd do it as a favor, Jim.' He put his hand on my arm. 'I don't want to worry about it afterwards.'

He got into his own car and we followed him to the Pathological Building at Bellevue. I talked to Justin for a minute and the others came in behind us.

A clean place. Concrete floors and a cat. Row on row of what looked like numbered and hasped meat-safe doors lining the walls. I was a little too preoccupied to notice but Bill told me afterwards that the little man followed us in with his hands behind his back, looking around as if he were in a museum.

McKeogh spoke to one of the attendants.

The man said: 'No. 230, Commissioner.'

The tarboosh stood on tiptoe, trying to look over Eunice's shoulder. The attendant opened No. 230 and slid the body out on

275

the steel shelf. He uncovered the head. A stranger. The dark-red shining bob and the young bones of the face that would never be touched by love again. By anybody, anytime, anywhere.

I shook my head and the man slid the body back in. 'What happened to her?'

'The window,' Justin said. 'She's all in pieces from the neck down.'

None of us had noticed the little man fold down into a heap behind us. I felt like joining him.

7

WE REVIVED the tarboosh, drove him up to his waiting laydee, and got to Madison Square Garden about nine. The cops had the side streets roped off but there weren't enough men to hold the lines. Eighth Avenue was milling.

We pushed through and found the inspector in charge. He said he hadn't been able to spare any of the people from his detail to hunt for Mrs. Rowan but he'd arranged to pick her up quietly after she left the platform. His men at the entrances and the few private Garden police still on the job had her description. They'd been on the lookout for her since seven o'clock. I found out later that she'd slipped in about five. Had dinner sent in to the Rangers' dressing room.

We did a squirming lock step up the ramp inside, Eunice hanging onto the tail of my coat. She nudged me in the small of the back. Paulsen, the NYU man, was grinning at me over the heads of the crowd. He edged up behind us and I introduced him to Eunice.

'Miss Flattery,' he said, in a tone that meant: 'Nice Miss Flattery.'

Maybe somebody else will get kicked in the shins now, I thought.

The auditorium opened out into a vast crowd murmur. It would take about 19,000 people. Most of them there. Somebody talking on the loudspeakers. The smoky trusses high up under the roof and the long pitch of the seething galleries. We nudged down on to the floor. I passed the word ahead to Bill and Dennis, and back to Eunice. Break up. Grab what singles we could find. Meet afterwards when the crowd got out.

Eunice slid into a place and I got a seat down toward the middle. The long smoking ribbons of light angled down into a brilliant circle on the platform. The man talking. I didn't catch much of it. I was trying to get the feel of the crowd. Nothing ugly or potentially violent. High and happy. The individual euphoria of the fever screwed up a notch or two by the excitement of sharing it.

The loudspeakers began to rumble out the *Happiness Anthem* and everybody got up and sang from the song sheets. Nothing the boys over on Fiftieth Street had cooked up. This had Greenland's icy mountains in it. The old American Protestant yearning in a march hymn. We have wandered in the valley and we wait the rosy sun. We are banded here together and the many march as one.

We bawled it out and I took a look at the faces around me. Not a special audience. A little of everybody. A few tailcoats. Broadway sharpies and the Village look. Men and women and kids from Amsterdam Avenue and East Broadway and Lenox Avenue and Rockaway and Roosevelt Avenue and Kingsbridge Road. Hoping for something, and trying to get together on it. It scared me for a minute. This could turn into anything. What the hell was happiness?

Almost before we got hunkered down in the chairs again, the man at the microphone shouted: 'Miss Sanderson!' and put out his arm, and she was there, from nowhere I could see, with the crowd roaring.

Niobe all right. A tall young woman in a getup that made her look like a female pasha. Long white fitted crepe, swathed across the waist. The feeling of a Bengalese sari about it. A row of cloth buttons down the side. Pale-blue elbow gloves. A floor-length loose cape, gauzy and silvery, and a white turban that covered her hair. A sort of marabou pompom over the brow. Made her look nine feet tall. Perfect for what she was doing.

All this against a tremendous pale-blue silk banner with the word HAPPINESS in white across it. She stood there for an instant, unmoving, like a mother hen gathering in her chicks. Tremendous.

She said in a voice that curled like a whip inside you: 'What do you want?'

'Happiness!' they shouted. The galleries rolled with it.

'Do you want to take it away from somebody else?'

'No!'

'Do you want to beat down somebody else to get it?'

'No!'

'Is it free?'

'Yes!'

'Is it free as the sky for everybody?'

'Yes! Yes!'

'Is it free for the white man and the yellow man and the colored man?'

'Yes! Yes! For everybody!'

'Will you make it free for everybody?'

'Yes! Yes!'

'Did the good Lord put us on this earth to be unhappy?'

'No, Lord!'

'Didn't he give us our eyes and ears and mouths to look at this world and smell it and touch it and eat it and find it good?'

'Yes, Lord!'

'Didn't he say: "Be merciful! Be tender! Help the afflicted and the weak and the lost! Be kind to the children who wander in darkness!"?'

'Yes! Yes!'

'Didn't he say to us: "Man, you are walking on this earth in a little light between one darkness and another darkness!"?'

'Yes, Lord!'

'And didn't he say to us: "Little man! Poor little man! You worry and fret yourself right into your grave when all I want you to do is to go and be happy the best way you can. *I didn't want you to kill yourself with grieving! I wanted you to be happy!*"?'

'Happy! Yes, Lord!'

'Lord says: "But you can't be happy unless your neighbor's happy! You run to him right now and tell him: Neighbor, you say, we got a long road but the sun's out, man, the sun's shining and the Lord says to be happy! Be happy with all your heart!"'

'Happy! Happy! Happy! Yes, Lord!'

It rolled out in a tremendous chorus. People were crying and kissing each other. Some of them hysterical. I sat there stupefied. She meant it, by God. Niobe.

She took them down hard. 'Now go home to bed,' she called. 'March in the parade tomorrow. The world is yours for the asking.'

She bowed twice to the roaring sound and waved them out. People began to move into the aisles. I stood on the seat to watch the platform. I could see Bill, two or three rows back on the other side, doing the same thing. Niobe was still there, at the center mike, talking to the man who had introduced her.

Then I saw the cops. Strolling in on her from three sides. I almost shouted at them. The God-damn fools. They had their orders to pick her up after she left the platform. If they took her now, and people caught on, we'd have the worst riot since the Civil War. Ten thousand men in that audience feeling like tough Galahads about her. Could I get up the aisle? Not a chance. Over the seats? Too far. I glanced back at Bill. He shook his head.

I groaned as she leaped off the platform and dived under the crowd. The star forward of the girls' basketball team, Indiana University, Class of '29. The nearest cop made a dash, the announcer went down on one knee like a blocking back, and the cop sailed over him in a long sprawl. People stirred for a moment where she'd gone in. Then the word went down the line, they straightened up and it was just an orderly crowd moving out.

The cleverest thing possible, if you were agile enough. But the cops at the exits would get her. They had the dressing rooms blocked off too. She wouldn't try that. Bill watching, and Eunice off to the left, and Dennis behind me, near Paulsen. Eunice's mouth formed words at me: 'I hope she gets away.' We watched for a sudden stir in the crowd and tried to keep an eye on the rows of chairs. She could stoop between them.

The galleries were clear now. I asked the others to keep watching and went through the last of the crowd. I found the inspector at Exit G.

'What the hell did those boys on the platform think they were doing?'

He shook his head. 'They figured they couldn't take a chance. One of them noticed a trapdoor right near where Mrs. Rowan was standing. They use it to rig the mikes.'

'Anything from the exits?'

'Nothing yet.'

I went back in. Dennis had found the white dress and turban trampled gray in a side aisle. We spent the next half-hour searching. The inspector sent a sergeant in. The place was cleared now. Everybody out, so far as they knew. None of the cops had seen anyone who looked like Mrs. Rowan. They were going through the ramps and corridors.

Paulsen, nosing around up on the platform, found a slip of paper tucked into the grille of one of the microphones. He called to me. It was folded once. I opened it: 'Dear Jim: Love. Niobe.'

SEVEN

1 I WOKE up alone in my own bed. Eight-thirty. A sharp blue morning, but already beginning to cloud over. Still only half awake, I seemed to be marching to music, some brilliant music I knew. I got a cigarette lighted, humming, and realized in a minute that the music was *Shim-Me-Sha-Wabble*. Spencer Williams's great New Orleans jazz tune. Niobe's favorite.

I got up and found the record Zutty Singleton had made of it. Red Allen and Benny Morton on trumpet and trombone. Lil Armstrong on piano, Ed Hall playing clarinet, Addison on guitar, and Pops Foster on bass. Every tub on his own bottom and the devil take the hindmost. I let it play over and over while I shaved and dressed.

Dennis and a Western Union boy came in together. The telegram from Jerry in Washington: YOU WIN EAST SIDE SITE AGREED ON. Then it went on for a dozen more lines, as government telegrams sometimes did. Dennis put the short wave on and listened quietly until I asked him to breakfast.

We ate in the dining room. Rachel stood to the left of my chair and said: 'Mr. Rowan, can I bother you for a little private talk?'

'Sure, Rachel. Sit down.'

She sat. Wanted to know when she could leave. She'd got the appointment to a post-office job and she had a few things she wanted to do in between.

'Why didn't you tell me?' I said. 'Congratulations. Look. Why

281

don't you and Elizabeth take the day off and come back tonight? If we have any luck, Mrs. Rowan may be home by that time and you can fix it up with her.'

Dennis was eating his grapefruit and minding his own business. Rachel's eyes got big.

'Okeh?'

She nodded and went to get the coffee. I asked her to bring a cup for herself. We sat there quietly, each musing on his little problems. I went through the *Times*. Good old *Times*. Still getting out a city edition by seven in the morning.

The Governor had made final preparations for taking over the city. General Whittaker would move over the city line from Westchester precisely at six P.M. Make his headquarters at City Hall. That was that.

I called the Weather Bureau before we left. New York temperatures down four more degrees. Hanging just over the freezing mark, Carson said. Pretty sure to have snow out of the northwest before the day was over. Much colder tomorrow, probably the rest of the week.

He paused and murmured in the same civil-service tone: 'That's the story. We've done all we can for you. You're on your own now.'

'Thanks, mister. I guess we can handle it.'

2 THEN we were walking out beside Dick, out behind the tremendous rose window at Temple Emanu-El. Arnie's mouth tight because he was damn near crying, Hanauer heavy and dark, Rich Jones with his glasses clouded, and Justin's Irish hangman's face chopped out of a block of wood. The corps spirit, closing up. Dick was our man, and we bore him out on our figurative shoulders into the city he had tried to save.

282

People loitered on Fifth Avenue, watching. Oliver was there. John Kane and Romanelli and Maurice Satin and Al Elias and the others. Hannah Miegs with her face all stiff and Emma crying gently into a muslin handkerchief. We stood around her. I took her hand for a moment and kissed her and saw Arnie's mouth tighten. The air was raw. People getting into the cars: Dick's and Emma's relatives and friends and the honorary pallbearers.

The rest of us started downtown. Pete Jenkins and Em got in with me. Stiff assignment, Pete said, trying to get the whole town dosed with ascorbic acid-plus before six P.M.—even if we could get enough of it. Would the Governor——

Not a chance, I said. Especially in an election year. But martial law, coming on top of the fever, would knock the town flat on its back.

'Then we've got to get it distributed,' Em said.

'How much can we round up today?'

Em thought about 800 pounds, with all the pharmaceutical houses in the East working on it. Some of it could be flown in. We might get a bit more from the Middle Western people, but probably not in time.

'Would that much do it?' I asked Pete.

'Oh yes. If we can distribute it.'

I shrugged my overcoat together. Chill air, and the mottled clouds coming over the sky.

'There's always the weather,' Em said.

I had a sudden qualm. 'Wait a minute. What about that idea that freezing weather makes the bugs quiescent? Isn't there something missing there? It may numb the free ones. We may not have any new cases. But people's body temperatures—the people already infected, I mean, like us—won't go down to freezing. How——'

Pete sighed. 'I know,' he said. 'It's silly. It's humorous. It's the wildest kind of loose analogy. But we tried it and it worked. All the animals and patients we tried it on got well.'

'How?'

'We don't know yet. Probably something about the oxygenation temperature. We asked two patients in the cold chamber to breathe rapidly. They recovered a little faster than the others.'

'How long did it take?' I asked.

'Oh, less than a half-hour. About twenty-four minutes, on the average.'

'Seems almost impossible,' Em murmured.

'It does. But it happened.'

'And when they came out of the cold chamber——' I said.

'They were all right. Seemed perfectly normal. We've kept a daily check on them since. No sign of reinfection or relapse.'

3

WE GOT together again about eleven-thirty in Hickey's long room. The man from the Congressional subcommittee, looking smug. A dozen or so empty chairs. Dick's pallbearers missing. Justin working on the parade arrangements. John Kane on the wire to Albany for some last-ditch stalling. Pretty grim. Nobody ate much and the waiters had orders to keep things moving.

I glanced at the stack of reports. No time for that now.

'We'll have to get through this in a hurry,' I said. 'The weather may help but our main problem is to get those ascorbic-acid-plus tablets distributed in time. How can we do it? Any suggestions?'

Maurice Satin thought we might commandeer all private automobiles and make a house-to-house canvass.

Feuerman shook his head. 'People are living in the streets, Maurice. Some of them haven't been home for days.'

'We've got to take advantage of some *habit* pattern,' Leslie Wahler said. 'That's our only chance. Something people do every day as automatically as they brush their teeth.'

'Milk!' Satin called.

Hickey grinned at him. 'Too late for today.'

'Horses! Policy!' Arnie said.

We laughed.

Haggstrom, the Borough President of Brooklyn, put his hand up. 'Why not newspapers?' he said doubtfully.

I looked at him. 'That's it. Put the tablets in envelopes and stick 'em on the front page. Print the instructions.'

They nodded down the table.

Hanauer said: 'We'd better move fast. The home editions are late but they'll be on the street in a few minutes.'

'Okeh,' I said quickly. 'We get in touch with the papers. Foreign language, *Daily Racing Form*, everything. Ask 'em to hold editions. Have the mailing-room crews stick the envelopes on. Give them extra help. Pete Jenkins will check the medical end and Emery cover distribution. Ready to vote?'

It was carried. Em jumped for a phone with Pete just behind him.

'Okeh. We've made arrangements with John Kane to handle things in case the troops take over. Whether they do or not, we'll meet here tomorrow. If we break the fever before the deadline, somebody's got to convince Albany.'

Onderdonck looked down at his plate. 'I'd like that job. The Governor and I are both members of old New York families.' Quiet irony. 'One of his ancestors was Cornelius van Tienhoven, who got his fingers into the city till. One of my ancestors was a *schepen* who raised Old Nick about it. I'll remind the Governor, if necessary.'

We elected him to work with John Kane.

Hickey said: 'We've got to get out of here, Jim. That parade starts in thirty-five minutes.'

'Okeh,' I said. 'Anything else?'

Nothing else. We adjourned. I slumped for a moment, looking at the dark sky through the window, the flag at City Hall limp on its staff. It flapped a little, rippled slowly, then stood straight out, whipping hard to the southeast.

The storm. I saw it for an instant without seeing it. 'The flag,' I said, and went over to the window.

They crowded in behind me, still tense.

'What the hell's this?' Arnie Genovese muttered.

I pointed. 'The flag. Over at City Hall. I've been watching it for a week.'

'You like flags?' Arnie said. 'He likes flags. Blue-and-orange flags he likes. Yah. Nice.'

'Can't you see it's shifted?'

'So it's shifted,' Arnie said. 'So what are we doing?' He raised his eyebrows.

'It means the weather's changed, Arnie. I'm a farm boy. I can tell. Cold. Snow. Brrrrr! Catch on?'

'Ohhh,' Arnie said, nodding. 'I get it. He means the pardon came. Yahoo!' he yelled suddenly.

He wasn't the only one. We were acting like a lot of kids, milling around, laughing and yelling.

'School's out,' Arnie said, pushing his way through. 'I'm going to the parade.'

4 I WAITED for Bill and Eunice in the car and we started uptown, looking at newsstands on the way. Most of them were empty. One dealer said he couldn't find out why the trucks weren't making deliveries, so we told him.

We got out at a stand near Houston Street on Broadway. I picked up a World-Telegram. Big headline: CITY FACES MARTIAL LAW. Over the head an ordinary business envelope stuck on with gummed tape. To the left, a printer's fist pointing toward the envelope, and an ear that read: 'The tablets in this envelope will cure your fever if you have it and may protect you if you haven't.

Take one in a glass of water. It can't hurt you. Help save your city. Dr. S. B. Jenkins, Commissioner of Health.'

We took a couple of papers and lined up at the soda fountain inside. The proprietor, a thickset Jewish man, said he guessed he'd join us. He fetched a paper, gave one of the tablets to his smiling wife, and we raised our glasses.

'Happiness,' he said.

The tablet tasted like sharp orange candy.

As far down as Bleecker Street, the crowd was so thick that Dennis had to detour over east. People swarming from every direction toward Washington Square.

At Astor Place I got out and talked to a police captain. 'Look at them,' he said, with a nod at the hurrying, laughing people. 'Everybody in the city will be here in an hour.'

Swamped. The reports he had showed that the thing was already pretty well out of control, though there hadn't been any serious trouble.

We could hear a band over west. A trumpet high and clear.

'They got started fifteen minutes ago. A woman leading off. A drum major. Got pianos on the wagons. Bull fiddles. Everything.'

He looked like a man whose nightmare had come true.

Dennis circled south and west out of the area, then north. Stuff coming in on the car radio. Double and triple the expected crowd at point after point. Still moving in. Police lines washed out. Car and bus traffic dead. The Long Island bridges dense with westward-moving people. The police air patrols found enormous crowds as far north as Mount Morris Park.

We left the car over near Eighth Avenue and got through to the Empire State Building. I wanted binoculars. They hunted around and found me a pair and we went up to the observation deck on the eighty-sixth floor.

As we came out, the wind was biting, the sky a heavy gray. I had a sense of tremendous and joyous excitement. Good time coming. Yes, Lord. Eunice wrapped up and shivering. But her shining eyes.

She leaned over and kissed me. 'Merry Christmas, Jim.'

'Merry Christmas, darling.'

Bill had his arm around her. They kissed gently.

The people along the parapet made room for us. I turned the glasses down Fifth Avenue. Worked the screw slowly. Almost at the same moment I felt not so much sick as not very well. Head aching a little. Tired. Tired and strained. My eyes stung. Thinking of the tooth I'd been promising to have fixed and the piles of work stretched ahead of me. A lumber yard of work. Like falling out of love. An ordinary woman, a little sad now, saying good-by. I realized what had happened all right. The fever was almost gone.

Shivering now, I watched the parade come up the avenue. A disorderly march, filling the street from curb to curb. Recruits pouring in from every cross street. Men, women, and children of all the colors and nationalities under heaven. The banners, some of them the blue-and-white HAPPINESS flag I'd seen at the Garden. Bunting-clad wagons for the bands and the black horses with cockades in their crowpieces.

For the first time I was a little terrified. This wasn't a parade. It was a folk movement, a vast human migration—men, women, children, and animals. Gentle and resistless, marching with banners. Horns and banners. Where to, for God's sake? Where?

Three mounted cops trying to clear the roadway ahead. They were almost up to Thirty-First Street now. Twenty yards behind them, ahead of the first bandwagon, a girl drum major, all in white except for the black shako three feet high. She was marching backwards. The silvery baton flickered in her hand.

I could feel my heart thumping as I tried to focus on her. My teeth chattering. Eunice had gone inside with Dennis, and Bill was leaning on my shoulder. She faced front, head up. A red curl under the strap of the bearskin and her wonderful legs going up and down in the school-horse prance.

As I watched, the lens seemed to be misting over. The first dry snow on my bare head. In a few moments it was driving hard. A curtain over the glass. The parade blurred under us and the noise of the bands and shouts was muffled. Bill and I looked at each other, feeling the moist silence and the darkness of mortality on us again.

We went inside. No coffee. We had a Ballantine's and went downstairs. The lobby packed. We tried to move toward Fifth Avenue but the crowd was solid. Somebody told Dennis the police had blocked the street with a double row of cars.

We turned west. Like walking up to your neck against a mountain stream. Dennis, firm and tactful, made openings for us. Eunice was hanging onto my hand. We got to the car and went over to Tenth Avenue before we were clear, then uptown. We might get through on foot at Rockefeller Center. If not, the park.

We left the car again, edging slowly through Fiftieth Street toward Fifth. I was sick and shaking. All I wanted now was to get Niobe out of it. Get home. People looked sober now. Some of them a little frightened. But they couldn't stop.

The mass crushed forward. A low murmur, here and there a shout. The silent buildings and the snow. A gray veil. Dennis's shoulder nudged deeper and deeper into the crowd. His tact and the uniform got us through. Out to the edge of the street. The small bare trees.

A lone cop trying to keep people out of the avenue. They moved past him in the crisp driving white. On tiptoe, I could see the head of the parade, almost at Forty-Ninth Street. No bands playing now. Only the voice of the crowd, hushed by the wind and snow.

The mounted cops came on, their horses prancing forward a few inches at each step, bridling, prancing, sidling with their flanks and forequarters. The cops' voices: 'Come on now. Move back.' 'Can't see the parade if you don't let 'em pass.' 'That's right. Back to the sidewalk.' 'Plenty of room on the sidewalk.'

There wasn't, of course. A window crashed in Saks Fifth Avenue. Good-naturedly the crowd folded back. Ribbing the cops. I understood suddenly that it was all over. Nothing like the people at the Garden the night before. This was the normal New York crowd. Easygoing, critical, indulgent. No feeling about the parade now. Just curious. Spectators.

They melted back under the bare snowy trees at the curb. A few of them, pushed out into East Fiftieth Street, turned away. The avenue was almost clear now, the cops past. I got my first close look at the girl drum major in white. Niobe.

The fine body and the delicate bones of her face. But the feeling of the thing was gone. She looked cold and bewildered. Trembling. Nothing but nerve now, and all at once it was shabby and pathetic. People in the crowd laughed. Snow on her satin shoulders, on the dark bearskin. Henry Seaborn's band huddled in the wagon behind her. A tarpaulin over the drums. Ed Hall nursing the clarinet under his overcoat.

I felt again the silly searing futile passion to protect her somehow, anyhow, against the whole weight of mortality. But she turned, took three steps backward, and lifted the baton. The crash of the band filled the street. Their own music in the Northern snow, greatest of the New Orleans marches. *High Society.* For a moment it was triumph again.

Niobe was past me now, in front of the dark cathedral. She faced forward, tossed the baton. It slipped through her wet fingers. As if she had suddenly come to herself, she stopped and put her hand to her face. The driver pulled up behind her. She yanked the shako off, tossed her head, and ran toward East Fifty-First Street. The crowd made way for her, as a crowd will for anyone in costume.

I shook my head at Bill, ducked behind the wagon, saw Henry's concerned face for an instant above me, then edged into the parting she'd made in the crowd. She squeezed into a cab marooned in the middle of the street and I got in the other door.

She didn't notice me at first. People were yammering for souvenirs. The most ungodly of human passions. They wanted a piece of her blouse, the strap of her shako, the cloth of her shorts. An excited youth tried to climb in the door beside her. I pushed him out gently by the face and closed the door.

She saw me then and crouched back into the corner, big-eyed, like a high-school girl caught robbing a locker.

That broke me up. I put my hands over my face and tried to hang onto myself but it was no use.

She slid over and around me whispering: 'Jim, Jim.'

'You fool,' I said thickly. 'You God-damn fool.'

As if it were her fault.

She said something to the driver and we began to edge forward. Rushing the motor. The crowd parted slowly. I took my overcoat off and buttoned it around her with the collar up. She lay back trembling, her dark russet hair against the seat. Even her mouth was cold.

'Have you missed me?'

'You idiot. I've been missing you at every corner for the last week. And well you know it.'

She smiled faintly. 'What did you think when you found out I'd gone?'

'Just what you wanted me to think.'

'What?'

'That I'd go after you and get you.'

'Yes,' she said, satisfied. 'Did you—amuse yourself while you were looking for me?'

'Never mind. Did you?'

'Never mind.'

We looked at each other and laughed. A little sadly. But we laughed. She touched my face.

'Jim the wolf,' she said.

It took us about five years to get over to Lexington Avenue and another two or three to make Sixty-Eighth Street.

I stretched her out on the couch, got a blanket and the rubbing alcohol, and stripped off her clothes. She was white and exhausted but she was also a little amused at my businesslike solicitude.

'Ow. You tickle.'

'I didn't mean it that time. Sometime I'll mean it.'

The doorbell rang. I folded the blanket over her and went to answer it. I opened the door and a thin man in a whipcord raincoat put his foot in. I kicked it out.

'Play nice,' I said.

He looked down. 'I'm sorry. Uh, Commissioner Rowan?'

'Yes?'

He slipped a paper out of his breast pocket, put it in my hand, mumbled something, and walked away. A subpoena from the Joint Congressional Subcommittee to Investigate Conditions in New York City.

I showed it to Niobe. 'This time I *will* bring you a Senator.'

'A big one?' she said.

ABOUT THE AUTHOR

VINCENT McHUGH, novelist and poet, was born in Providence, Rhode Island, in 1904 and died in 1983 in Sacramento, California. Among his published works, McHugh authored five novels: *Touch Me Not* (1930); *Sing Before Breakfast* (1933); *Caleb Catlum's America* (1936); *I Am Thinking of My Darling* (1943); and *The Victory* (1947). Of his writing it was said that he "has known and written of the traumas of war, depression, and political chicanery; he has known and written of the exhilaration of visual beauty, of restorative compassion, and of corrective action." McHugh was also a serious poet and wrote two books of poetry—*The Blue Hen's Chickens* and *Alpha: The Mutabilities*—and, with C. H. Kwôck, translated a collection of poetry from Mandarin Chinese entitled *Old Friend From Far Away* (1980). In addition, McHugh served as the editor-in-chief of the New York City office of the Federal Writers' Project, was a staff writer for *The New Yorker*, and was a writer and film director for the Office of War Information. After leaving New York for California he did brief stints as a filmwriter for Paramount Studios and lived in San Francisco from 1952–1965. Throughout his career he held teaching positions at New York University, University of Denver, University of Missouri, University of Colorado, and San Francisco State College. In 1949 Vincent McHugh received the Award for Literature from the American Academy and Institute of Arts and Letters.

BOOKS FROM YARROW PRESS

FICTION

McHugh, Vincent. *I Am Thinking of My Darling.*
Introduction by Mark Singer. pbk: $9.95

Powell, Dawn. *The Locusts Have No King.*
Introduction by John Guare. pbk: $9.95

Powell, Dawn. *A Time to Be Born.* pbk: $9.95

ART

Carlin, John. *How to Invest in Your First Works of Art:
A Guide for the New Collector.*
Illustrations by Patrick McDonnell. pbk: $11.95

Schwartz, Sanford. *Artists and Writers.* cloth: $24.95;
pbk. $14.95

CHILDREN'S BOOKS

Fern, Eugene. *Pepito's Story.* Hardcover, $14.95

Yarrow Press books are available at your local bookstore or send
check or money order to Yarrow Press, 225 Lafayette Street, No.
312, New York, N.Y. 10012. Include $2.50 for postage and
handling for the first book and 50 cents for each additional book.
New York residents please add applicable New York State sales tax.